A SOUTHERN HARVEST

A
SOUTHERN
HARVEST

SHORT STORIES BY SOUTHERN WRITERS
EDITED BY ROBERT PENN WARREN

Cherokee Publishing Company
Atlanta, Georgia

Library of Congress Cataloging in Publication Data

Warren, Robert Penn, 1905-   ed.
    A Southern harvest.

    Reprint of the 1972 ed. published by N. S. Berg,
Dunwoody, Ga.
    1. Short stories, American--Southern States.
I. Title.
PZ1.W28So 1978 [PS551]   813'.01   78-23168
ISBN 0-89783-008-3

Manufactured in the United States of America

ISBN: 978-0-87797-328-7 Hardcover
ISBN: 978-0-87797-329-4 Paper

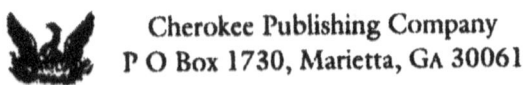

Cherokee Publishing Company
P O Box 1730, Marietta, GA 30061

TO
JOHN CROWE RANSOM

ACKNOWLEDGMENTS

GRATEFUL acknowledgment is made to the authors and publishers for their courteous permission to use the following stories:

Woman in the House, by Jesse Stuart
> Taken from *Head O'w-Hollow*, by Jesse Stuart, published and copyrighted by E. P. Dutton & Co., Inc., New York.

Kneel to the Rising Sun, by Erskine Caldwell
> From *Kneel to the Rising Sun*, by Erskine Caldwell. Copyright, 1935. Published by The Viking Press, Inc., New York.

Record at Oak Hill, by Elizabeth Madox Roberts
> From *The Haunted Mirror*, by Elizabeth Madox Roberts. Copyright, 1932. Published by The Viking Press, Inc., New York.

A Tempered Fellow, by Paul Green
> From *Wide Fields*, by Paul Green, published by Robert M. McBride & Company, 1928.

That Evening Sun, by William Faulkner
> Reprinted from *These Thirteen*, by William Faulkner, with the special permission of the copyright owners, Random House, Inc.

The Immortal Woman, by Allen Tate
> Reprinted with the kind permission of the editors of *The Hound and Horn* and of the author.

Jesus Knew, by E. P. O'Donnell
> Reprinted with the kind permission of Maxim Lieber and of the author.

The Gay Dangerfields, by Lyle Saxon
> From *Old Louisiana*, by Lyle Saxon, published and copyrighted by D. Appleton-Century Company, Inc., New York.

He, by Katherine Anne Porter
> From *Flowering Judas*, by Katherine Anne Porter, published and copyrighted by Harcourt, Brace and Company, Inc., New York.

If Only, by John Peale Bishop
> From *Many Thousands Gone*, by John Peale Bishop, published and copyrighted by Charles Scribner's Sons, New York.

ACKNOWLEDGMENTS

The House of the Far and Lost, by Thomas Wolfe

From *Of Time and the River*, by Thomas Wolfe, published and copyrighted by Charles Scribner's Sons, New York.

Old Red, by Caroline Gordon

Reprinted from *Scribner's Magazine* with the permission of Charles Scribner's Sons.

Benny and the Bird-Dogs, by Marjorie Kinnan Rawlings

Reprinted from *Scribner's Magazine* with the permission of Charles Scribner's Sons.

Shadows on Terrebonne, by Stark Young

From *Feliciana*, by Stark Young, published and copyrighted by Charles Scribner's Sons, New York.

Jericho, Jericho, Jericho, by Andrew Lytle

Reprinted from *The Southern Review* with the kind permission of the author.

A Proudful Fellow, by Julia Peterkin

Reprinted from *The Century Magazine* with the kind permission of the author.

Sairy and the Young 'Uns, by Beulah Roberts Childers

Reprinted from *Story* with the kind permission of the author.

The Horn that Called Bambine, by Elma Godchaux

Reprinted from *The Southern Review* with the kind permission of the author.

Good-Bye to Cap'm John, by S. S. Field

Reprinted from *The Southern Review* with the kind permission of the author.

Cold Death, by Roark Bradford

Reprinted from *Let the Band Play Dixie*, with the kind permission of the author.

The Ginsing Gatherers, by Howell Vines

Reprinted from *The Southern Review* with the kind permission of the author.

The Guy in the Blue Overcoat, by Edward Anderson

Reprinted from *Story* with the kind permission of the author.

CONTENTS

INTRODUCTION

I

THIS book is a collection of short stories by Southern writers. And that involves two questions which more than once had to be considered in the making of this book. What is a Southern writer? And what is a short story?

What is a Southern writer? Or rather, what is the South — where does it leave off as the traveler moves northward or westward? The answer is not so simple as one once given in a very fine poem: 'Of the Ohio the bank sinister, of the Mississippi the bank sinister.' For there is, after all, Arkansas and most of Louisiana. And there is Texas to be considered, or at least part of Texas, the part where blood and temperament and old political affiliations and Confederate monuments all point back, sometimes incongruously, to Alabama or Tennessee or the slopes at Gettysburg.

Nor can the roster of the late Confederate States of America provide an answer quite simply, for there remain Kentucky and West Virginia, which here are represented by Elizabeth Madox Roberts, Caroline Gordon, Jesse Stuart, Allen Tate, and John Peale Bishop. Although the Confederacy lost Kentucky to Miss Roberts's fellow Kentuckian, Abraham Lincoln, it does not follow that an anthologist of Southern stories should deny himself the keen pleasure of including such a story as 'Record at Oak Hill.' As for the case of West Virginia and Mr. Bishop, it is only necessary for one to come down from Chambersburg, in Pennsylvania, to Charlestown, in West Virginia, and to read the fiction which Mr. Bishop has written concerning that region, to decide that, despite the special circumstances of the founding of West Virginia, Mr. Bishop's credentials are in order. By printing the work of Mr. Stuart in this volume, however, the anthologist must take issue with another anthologist who, several years ago in *The New Republic*, included a poem by Mr. Stuart in a regional group for the Middle West. Since Mr. Stuart is a native of Eastern Kentucky, and writes only about the people of that section, it may be that the anthologist of *The New Republic* derived his definition of a literary Middle West from terms somewhat more mystical than those rather mystical ones supplied by history, geography, and sociology. Even though the arguments supplied by history, geography, and sociology may flutter and fail for breath in the atmosphere of the sphere inhabited by the anthologist who printed Mr. Stuart's poem, it still may be proper to take into account Mr. Stuart's own feeling in the matter. And Mr. Stuart has kindly given permission for one of his stories to be printed in *A Southern Harvest*.

There is no rough-and-ready answer to the general question: What is a Southern writer? But the particular question about a particular writer rarely causes confusion, for we can leap to our conclusion without bothering about definition. The work will usually tell us all we have to know. The fiction by Mr. Bishop, for instance, has its center of gravity in a way of life that no one could mistake. And the stories by Mr. Stuart seem to belong properly to mountains with ranges running only southward, across Kentucky and Tennessee, not northward. And the work by Mr. Wolfe — even those reports about Harvard or Paris or the rhapsodies about America — is constantly conditioned by the mythical city of Altamont and by the epic figure of old Gant. We know what subjects have engaged the minds and energies of these writers; and the question is answered for us. But there are other writers concerning whom the question is, except for statistical purposes, irrelevant. For instance, Conrad Aiken, the author of some penetrating and finely moulded stories. But those stories have no readily discernible affiliations with any life which we can feel as specifically Southern. The fact that he was born in Savannah, Georgia, is as irrelevant as the fact that Robert Frost was born in California and was named after General Robert E. Lee, C.S.A. After all, in one sense, the question is irrelevant in reference to all of these writers, for their fiction springs, without much concern for social or geographical definition, from the life which they have known best and have felt most deeply; that life has happened, simply, to be of the South. The question, however, remains for the anthologist; each story in this book is part of the answer.

And there is the other question: What is a short story? Here the answer is indeed rough-and-ready. A short story is a story that is not too long.

II

Southern writers of fiction have, in recent years, been highly advertised, and there has been some talk of a Southern renaissance. We do not know how the Southern renaissance will seem to us forty years from now, or thirty years, or twenty. Many of the writers included in this volume, for example, are very young and are writers of a fine promise rather than a positive achievement. And the promise of some will not be fulfilled. But meanwhile, if we are simply concerned with no more in time than our present and no more in space than America, we can grant that the advertising has not been entirely unwarranted.

There is, in fact, a kind of literary ferment in the South. It is not entirely new, though of recent years the range and vigor of its activity have rapidly increased. It is not new, for we can trace it back to the years immediately after the World War. And, more significantly, it is not an isolated thing; it is part of a general cultural ferment in the section. Since the War the general process of change in the South has been enormously accelerated and has become enormously complicated. It is not easy in the South now to define issues. In the days before the World War, after the bitter confusions of Reconstruction, the issues seemed, on the whole, simple; or now, as we look back, they seem to have seemed simple in that time of Grady and Page and Harris. On the one hand there was the cantankerous band of die-hards, easy enough to define in their hatred and their piety; on the other, there were those men who, from a variety of motives, wanted to take their fellow Southerners up to the high places and show them certain wonders situated north of the Potomac; and in between, as always, there were a great many people wrapped exclusively and unreflectively in their daily concerns. But the process of change was slow; and the issues simple.

In the last twenty years the process has not been slow; nor the

INTRODUCTION

issues simple. The collisions of interests and patterns of living and principles are constant now. It is a time of dramatic choices and of re-definitions. The South has been engaged in a process of self-scrutiny and self-definition. Its history has been re-written within the last twenty years and the sociologists and economists have devotedly applied their methods of analysis to the nature and structure of Southern life. And that life has involved bankers and politicians and share-croppers and labor organizers and Negroes — and, even, as we may sometimes be inclined to forget, the happy couple of 'The Ginsing Gatherers' and the old lady of 'Jericho, Jericho, Jericho.' There is little harmony among the voices raised to describe this life, or to prescribe for it. And all the choices have not yet been made.

The new literature of the South is, then, but a part of this general ferment, a part of the process of self-scrutiny and self-definition. Perhaps it is stimulated by the same collisions, the same underlying situation that has provoked the more general development. This is not to say that the writers of stories and novels are making little allegories to support the conclusions of social scientists (although, as a matter of fact, some of them have done precisely that). This is, rather, to say that the writers have been trying to explore in the human terms of their art the same materials which have engaged, in other terms, the historian, the politician, the labor organizer, the banker, and the sociologist: and to say that the writers have in their best work rebuked, perhaps unwittingly, the ledger, the table of statistics, the slogan, and the blind prejudice.

Much of this new literature, fiction and poetry, displays a strong historical bias. It has been said that the Southerner is incurably and incorrigibly historical-minded; and this seems to be true. It has also been said that many Southern writers take refuge in an idealized past, accustoming their vision to the comforting and comfortable afterglow of vanished glories that — and the rest of the sentence follows with brisk automatism on the tongue — never existed. This is true of certain writers, in the South, and, one may add, elsewhere. It is a human impulse, as old as the race, to seek in the safe past the form of the myth; and when the myth is achieved, it is a repository of values, but of values made immediately comprehensible in human action. But we are told this kind of writing is sentimental. Sometimes it is. It is sentimental when it fails, and fails by the criterion which the writer himself proposes: he proposes that we as human beings, not as Liberals or Conservatives, Baptists or Catholics, Democrats or Republicans, be convinced of the 'life' of his work. And by that rigorous standard not only work that exhibits the historical bias, but also work that is vindictively contemporary, may sometimes turn out to be sentimental. No one, we may guess, can write unsentimentally of the past unless he has a lively sense of his present; but, conversely, no one can write unsentimentally of the present who is contemptuous of the past. Meanwhile, it can probably be maintained safely enough that 'Old Red,' by Miss Gordon, or 'The Ginsing Gatherers,' by Mr. Vines, is no more, and possibly less, vulnerable to the charge of sentimentality than is 'Kneel to the Rising Sun,' by Mr. Caldwell. And, further, it might be hazarded that the stories by Miss Gordon and Mr. Vines are as 'important' — to borrow the word which, among reviewers, is used to divert attention from the inspection of the work in question to the latest newspaper headlines — as the excellent story by Mr. Caldwell. Accepting that particular category of the 'important,' the category of contemporary social relevance, one can maintain such an opinion, unless it can be proved that Miss Gordon, or Mr. Vines, has put a libel on human nature. But if their stories do, however modestly, quicken our comprehension of general human nature and of a particular heritage, then they have fulfilled their 'social' function for all possible readers except the fanatic; for if any adjustment is to be reached among the various issues at conflict in Southern life, it will scarcely be reached in disregard of those factors.

These stories, however, are in this book not because of their value as social documents. They are here because they seem to be fairly representative of the work being done in that form by contemporary Southern writers; and because, it is hoped, they are good stories.

If they are good stories, each is good in its own terms and not because of some special quality shared with all the others. But such a quality may exist as a common feature, not only of these stories, but of most contemporary Southern novels as well. Most Southern writers of fiction have abjured the straight realistic approach, the reportorial temper. Many of them have reported the Southern scene, and scrupulously; but the reporting has been absorbed, usually, into a context that subordinates the purely realistic element. There is a pervasive poetic quality to be found in most contemporary Southern fiction, a quality shared by writers as diverse as Miss Porter, Mr. Caldwell, Mr. Faulkner, Miss Roberts, Miss Gordon, Mr. Bradford, Mr. Lytle, and Mr. Field. The grotesque and the humorous effects in the work of Mr. Caldwell and Mr. Faulkner spring from the same basic impulse that produces the most delicate lyrical perceptions in the work of Miss Roberts. Miss Reba in *Sanctuary*, old Gant in *Look Homeward, Angel*, Uncle Bascom in *Of Time and the River*, the old fisherman in *Alec Maury*, the girl in *The Time of Man*, the captain in 'Good-bye to Cap'm John,' and Jeeter in *Tobacco Road* all represent deviations from the ordinary fictional norm of reported actuality. In other words, these writers, with varying degrees of excellence in the finished product, have attempted to assume the responsibility of creating characters from the inside out; they have not been content with the routine process of penetrating the surface of reported actuality merely far enough to establish simple 'motivation' in accordance with a preconceived pattern of interpretation. And the effect of this attitude on the approach to the question of style can be readily observed if a reader will put a few pages by Mr. Faulkner over against a few pages by Mr. Lewis. This quality does not, of course, belong exclusively to the fiction of Southern writers; nor does it always manifest itself happily in their work. But it does seem to belong to the work of the majority of those writers who have appeared in recent years; and it does seem to be a basic quality of their best work and to define the special nature of its excellence.

ROBERT PENN WARREN

OLD RED

CAROLINE GORDON

I

WHEN the door had closed behind his daughter, Mister Maury went to the window and stood a few moments looking out. The roses that had grown in a riot all along that side of the fence had died or been cleared away, but the sun lay across the garden in the same level lances of light that he remembered. He turned back into the room. The shadows had gathered until it was nearly all in gloom. The top of his minnow bucket just emerging from the duffel-bag glinted in the last rays of the sun. He stood looking down at his traps all gathered neatly in a heap at the foot of the bed. He would leave them like that. Even if they came in here sweeping and cleaning up — it was only in hotels that a man was master of his own room — even if they came in here cleaning up, he would tell them to leave all his things exactly as they were. It was reassuring to see them all there together, ready to be taken up in the hand, to be carried down and put into a car, to be driven off to some railroad station at a moment's notice.

As he moved toward the door, he spoke aloud, a habit that was growing on him:

'Anyhow, I won't stay but a week. . . . I ain't going to stay but a week, no matter what they say. . . .'

Downstairs in the dining room they were already gathered at the supper table, his white-haired, shrunken mother-in-law, his tall sister-in-law who had the proud carriage of the head, the aquiline nose, but not the spirit of his dead wife, his lean, blond new son-in-law, his black-eyed daughter who, but that she was thin, looked so much like him, all of them gathered there waiting for him, Alexander Maury. It occurred to him that this was the first time he had sat down in the bosom of the family for some years.

1

They were always writing saying that he must make a visit this summer or certainly next fall. '... all had a happy Christmas together but missed you....' They had even made the pretext that he ought to come up to inspect his new son-in-law. As if he hadn't always known exactly the kind of young man Sarah would marry! What was the boy's name? Stephen, yes, Stephen. He must be sure and remember that.

He sat down, and shaking out his napkin spread it over his capacious paunch and tucked it well up under his chin in the way his wife had never allowed him to do. He let his eyes rove over the table and released a long sigh.

'Hot batter bread,' he said, 'and ham. Merry Point ham. I sure am glad to taste them one more time before I die.'

The old lady was sending the little Negro girl scurrying back to the kitchen for a hot plate of batter bread. He pushed aside the cold plate and waited. She had bridled when he spoke of the batter bread and a faint flush had dawned on her withered cheeks. Vain she had always been as a peacock, of her housekeeping, her children, the animals on her place, anything that belonged to her. And she went on, even at her advanced age, making her batter bread, smoking her hams according to that old recipe she was so proud of; but who came here now to this old house to eat or to praise?

He helped himself to a generous slice of batter bread, buttered it, took the first mouthful and chewed it slowly. He shook his head.

'There ain't anything like it,' he said. 'There ain't anything else like it in this world.'

His dark eye roving the table fell on his son-in-law. 'You like batter bread?' he inquired.

Stephen nodded, smiling. Mister Maury, still masticating slowly, regarded his face, measured the space between the eyes — his favorite test for man, horse, or dog. Yes, there was room enough for sense between the eyes. But how young the boy looked! And infected already with the fatal germ, the *cacoëthes scribendi*. Well, their children would probably escape. It was like certain diseases of the eye, skipped every other generation. His own father had had it badly all his life. He could see him now sitting at the head of the table spouting his own poetry — or

2

Shakespeare's — while the children watched the preserve dish to see if it was going around. He, Aleck Maury, had been lucky to be born in the generation he had. He had escaped that at least. A few translations from Heine in his courting days, a few fragments from the Greek, but no, he had kept clear of that on the whole. . . .

The eyes of his sister-in-law were fixed on him. She was smiling faintly. 'You don't look much like dying, Aleck. Florida must agree with you.'

The old lady spoke from the head of the table. 'I can't see what you do with yourself all winter long. Doesn't time hang heavy on your hands?'

Time, he thought, time! They were always mouthing the word and what did they know about it? Nothing in God's world! He saw time suddenly, a dull, leaden-colored fabric depending from the old lady's hands, from the hands of all of them, a blanket that they pulled about, now this way, now that, trying to cover up their nakedness. Or they would cast it on the ground and creep in among the folds, finding one day a little more tightly rolled than another, but all of it everywhere the same dull gray substance. But time was a banner that whipped before him always in the wind. He stood on tip-toe to catch at the bright folds, to strain them to his bosom. They were bright and glittering. But they whipped by so fast and were whipping always ever faster. The tears came into his eyes. Where, for instance, had this year gone? He could swear he had not wasted a minute of it, for no man living, he thought, knew better how to make each day a pleasure to him. Not a minute wasted and yet here it was already May! If he lived to the Biblical three score and ten, which was all he ever allowed himself in his calculations, he had before him only nine more Mays. Only nine more Mays out of all eternity, and they wanted him to waste one of them sitting on the front porch at Merry Point!

The butter plate which had seemed to swim in a glittering mist was coming solidly to rest upon the white tablecloth. He winked his eyes rapidly and laying down his knife and fork squared himself about in his chair to address his mother-in-law:

'Well, ma'am, you know I'm a man that always likes to be learning something. Now this year I learned how to smell out fish.' He

3

glanced around the table, holding his head high and allowing his well-cut nostrils to flutter slightly with his indrawn breaths. 'Yes, sir,' he said, 'I'm probably the only white man in this country knows how to smell out feesh.'

There was a discreet smile on the faces of the others. Sarah was laughing outright. 'Did you have to learn how or did it just come to you?' she asked.

'I learned it from an old nigger woman,' her father said. He shook his head reminiscently. 'It's wonderful how much you can learn from niggers. But you have to know how to handle them. I was half the winter wooing that old Fanny. . . .'

He waited until their laughter had died down. 'We used to start off every morning from the same little cove and we'd drift in there together at night. I noticed how she always brought in a good string, so I says to her, "Fanny, you just lemme go 'long with you." But she wouldn't have nothing to do with me. I saw she was going to be a hard nut to crack, but I kept right on. Finally I began giving her presents. . . .'

Laura was regarding him fixedly, a queer look on her face.

'What sort of presents did you give her, Aleck?'

He made his tones hearty in answer. 'I give her a fine string of fish one day and I give her fifty cents. And finally I made her a present of a Barlow knife. That was when she broke down. She took me with her that morning. . . .'

'Could she really smell fish?' the old lady asked curiously.

'You ought to 'a' seen her,' Mister Maury said. 'She'd sail over that lake like a hound on the scent. She'd row right along and then all of a sudden she'd stop rowing.' He bent over, wrinkling his nose and peering into the depths of imaginary water. ' "Thar they are, White Folks, thar they are. Cain't you smell 'em?" '

Stephen was leaning forward, eyeing his father-in-law intently. 'Could you?' he asked.

'I got so I could smell feesh,' Mister Maury told him. 'I could smell out the feesh, but I couldn't tell which kind they were. Now Fanny could row over a bed and tell just by the smell whether it was bass or bream. But she'd been at it all her life.' He paused, sighing. 'You can't just pick these things up. You have to give

4

yourself to them. Who was it said "Genius is an infinite capacity for taking pains"?'

Sarah was rising briskly. Her eyes sought her husband's across the table. She was still laughing. 'Sir Izaak Walton,' she said, 'we'd better go in the other room. Mandy wants to clear the table.'

The two older ladies remained in the dining room. Mister Maury walked across the hall to the sitting room, accompanied by Steve and Sarah. He lowered himself cautiously into the most solid-looking of the rocking-chairs that were drawn up around the fire. Steve was standing on the hearthrug, back to the fire, gazing abstractedly off across the room.

Mister Maury glanced up at him curiously. 'What you thinking about, feller?' he asked.

Steve looked down. He smiled, but his gaze was still contemplative. 'I was thinking about the sonnet,' he said, 'in the form in which it first came to England.'

Mister Maury shook his head. 'Wyatt and Surrey,' he said. 'Hey, nonny, nonny. . . . You'll have hardening of the liver long before you're my age.' He looked past Steve's shoulder at the picture that hung over the mantel shelf: Cupid and Psyche holding between them a fluttering veil and running along a rocky path toward the beholder. 'Old Merry Point,' he said; 'it don't change much, does it?'

He settled himself more solidly in his chair. His mind veered from the old house to his own wanderings in brighter places. He regarded his daughter and son-in-law affably.

'Yes, sir,' he said, 'this winter in Florida was valuable to me just for the acquaintances I made. Take my friend, Jim Barbee. Just to live in the same hotel with that man is an education.' He paused, smiling reminiscently into the fire. 'I'll never forget the first time I saw him. He came up to me there in the lobby of the hotel. "Professor Maury!" he says. "You been hearin' about me for twenty years and I been hearin' about you for twenty years. And now we've done met!"'

Sarah had sat down in the little rocking-chair by the fire. She leaned toward him now, laughing. 'They ought to have put down a cloth of gold for the meeting,' she said.

Mister Maury shook his head. 'Nature does that in Florida,' he said. 'I knew right off the reel it was him. There were half a dozen men standing around. I made 'em witness. "Jim Barbee," I says, "Jim Barbee of Maysville or I'll eat my hat!" '

'Why is he so famous?' Sarah asked.

Mister Maury took out his knife and cut a slice from a plug of tobacco. When he had offered a slice to his son-in-law and it had been refused, he put the plug back in his pocket. 'He's a man of imagination,' he said slowly. 'There ain't many in this world.'

He took a small tin box out of his pocket and set it on the little table that held the lamp. Removing the top he tilted the box so that they could see its contents: an artificial lure, a bug with a dark body and a red, bulbous head, a hook protruding from what might be considered its vitals.

'Look at her,' he said, 'ain't she a killer?'

Sarah leaned forward to look and Steve, still standing on the hearthrug, bent above them. The three heads ringed the light.

Mister Maury disregarded Sarah and addressed himself to Steve. 'She takes nine strips of rind,' he said, 'nine strips just thick enough.' He marked off the width of the strips with his two fingers on the table, then picking up the lure and cupping it in his palm he moved it back and forth quickly so that the painted eyes caught the light.

'Look at her,' he said, 'look at the wicked way she sets forward.'

Sarah was poking at the lure with the tip of her finger.

'Wanton,' she said, 'simply wanton. What does he call her?'

'This is his Devil Bug,' Mister Maury said. 'He's the only man in this country makes it. I myself had the idea thirty years ago and let it slip by me the way I do with so many of my ideas.' He sighed, then elevating his tremendous bulk slightly above the table level and continuing to hold Steve with his gaze he produced from his coat pocket the oilskin book that held his flies. He spread it open on the table and began to turn the pages. His eyes sought his son-in-law's as his hand paused before a gray, rather draggled-looking lure.

'Old Speck,' he said. 'I've had that fly for twenty years. I reckon she's taken five hundred pounds of fish in her day. . . .'

6

The fire burned lower. A fiery coal rolled from the grate and fell onto the hearthrug. Sarah scooped it up with a shovel and threw it among the ashes. In the circle of the lamplight the two men still bent over the table looking at the flies. Steve was absorbed in them but he spoke seldom. It was her father's voice that rising and falling filled the room. He talked a great deal, but he had a beautiful speaking voice. He was telling Steve now about Little West Fork, the first stream ever he put a fly in. 'My first love,' he kept calling it. It sounded rather pretty, she thought, in his mellow voice. 'My first love . . .'

II

When Mister Maury came downstairs the next morning the dining room was empty except for his daughter, Sarah, who sat dawdling over a cup of coffee and a cigarette. Mister Maury sat down opposite her. To the little Negro girl who presented herself at his elbow he outlined his wants briefly: 'A cup of coffee and some hot batter bread just like we had last night.' He turned to his daughter. 'Where's Steve?'

'He's working,' she said, 'he was up at eight and he's been working ever since.'

Mister Maury accepted the cup of coffee from the little girl, poured half of it into his saucer, set it aside to cool. 'Ain't it wonderful,' he said, 'the way a man can sit down and work day after day? When I think of all the work I've done in my time . . . Can he work *every* morning?'

'He sits down at his desk every morning,' she said, 'but of course he gets more done some mornings than others.'

Mister Maury picked up his saucer, found the coffee cool enough for his taste. He sipped it slowly, looking out of the window. His mind was already busy with his day's program. No water — no running water — nearer than West Fork three miles away. He couldn't drive a car and Steve was going to be busy writing all morning. There was nothing for it but a pond. The Willow Sink. It was not much but it was better than nothing. He pushed his chair back and rose.

7

'Well,' he said, 'I'd better be starting.'

When he came downstairs with his rod a few minutes later the hall was still full of the sound of measured typing. Sarah sat in the dining room in the same position in which he had left her, smoking. Mister Maury paused in the doorway while he slung his canvas bag over his shoulders. 'How you ever going to get anything done if you don't take advantage of the morning hours?' he asked. He glanced at the door opposite as if it had been the entrance to a sick chamber.

'What's he writing about?' he inquired in a whisper.

'It's an essay on John Skelton.'

Mister Maury looked out at the new green leaves framed in the doorway. 'John Skelton,' he said. 'God Almighty!'

He went through the hall and stepped down off the porch onto the ground that was still moist with spring rains. As he crossed the lower yard he looked up into the branches of the maples. Yes, the leaves were full grown already even on the late trees. The year, how swiftly, how steadily it advanced! He had come to the far corner of the yard. Grown up it was in pokeberry shoots and honeysuckle, but there was a place to get through. The top strand of wire had been pulled down and fastened to the others with a ragged piece of rope. He rested his weight on his good leg and swung himself over onto the game one. It gave him a good, sharp twinge when he came down on it. It was getting worse all the time, that leg, but on the other hand he was learning better all the time how to handle it. His mind flew back to a dark, startled moment, that day when the cramp first came on him. He had been sitting still in the boat all day long and that evening when he had stood up to get out his leg had failed him utterly. He had pitched forward among the reeds, had lain there a second, face downwards, before it came to him what had happened. With the realization came a sharp picture of his faraway youth: Uncle Quent lowering himself ponderously out of the saddle after a hard day's hunting had fallen forward in exactly the same way, into a knot of yowling little Negroes. He had got up and cursed them all out of the lot. It had scared the old boy to death, coming down like that. The black dog he had had on his shoulder all that fall. But he himself

8

had never lost one day's fishing on account of his leg. He had known from the start how to handle it. It meant simply that he was slowed down that much. It hadn't really made much difference in fishing. He didn't do as much wading but he got around just about as well on the whole. Hunting, of course, had had to go. You couldn't walk all day shooting birds, dragging a game leg. He had just given it up right off the reel, though it was a shame when a man was as good a shot as he was. That day he was out with Tom Kensington last November, the only day he got out during the season. Nine shots he'd had and he'd bagged nine birds. Yes, it was a shame. But a man couldn't do everything. He had to limit himself. . . .

He was up over the little rise now. The field slanted straight down before him to where the pond lay, silver in the morning sun. A Negro cabin was perched halfway up the opposite slope. A woman was hanging out washing on a line stretched between two trees. From the open doorway little Negroes spilled down the path toward the pond. Mister Maury surveyed the scene, spoke aloud:

'Ain't it funny now? Niggers always live in the good places.'

He stopped under a wild cherry tree to light his pipe. It had been hot crossing the field, but the sunlight here was agreeably tempered by the branches. And that pond down there was fringed with willows. His eyes sought the bright disk of the water, then rose to where the smoke from the cabin chimney lay in a soft plume along the crest of the hill.

When he stooped to pick up his rod again it was with a feeling of sudden, keen elation. An image had risen in his memory, an image that was familiar but came to him infrequently of late and that only in moments of elation: the wide field in front of his uncle's old house in Albemarle, on one side the dark line of undergrowth that marked the Rivanna River, on the other the blue of Peters' Mountain. They would be waiting there in that broad plain when they had the first sight of the fox. On that little rise by the river, loping steadily, not yet alarmed. The sun would glint on his bright coat, on his quick-turning head as he dove into the dark of the woods. There would be hullabaloo after that and

9

shouting and riding. Sometimes there was the tailing of the fox —
that time old Whiskey was brought home on a mattress! All of
that to come afterward, but none of it ever like that first sight of
the fox there on the broad plain between the river and the mountain.

There was one fox, they grew to know him in time, to call him
affectionately by name. Old Red it was who showed himself
always like that there on the crest of the hill. 'There he goes, the
damn' impudent scoundrel!' . . . Uncle Quent would shout and
slap his thigh and yell himself hoarse at Whiskey and Mag and the
pups, but they would have already settled to their work. They
knew his course, every turn of it by heart. Through the woods and
then down across the fields again to the river. Their hope was
always to cut him off before he could circle back to the mountain.
If he got in there among those old field pines it was all up. But he
always made it. Lost 'em every time and then dodged through to
his hole in Pinnacle Rock. . . . A smart fox, Old Red. . . .

He descended the slope and paused in the shade of a clump of
willows. The little Negroes who squatted, dabbling in the water,
watched him out of round eyes as he unslung his canvas bag and
laid it on a stump. He looked down at them gravely.

'D'you ever see a white man that could conjure?' he asked.

The oldest boy laid the brick he was fashioning out of mud down
on a plank. He ran the tip of his tongue over his lower lip to
moisten it before he spoke. 'Naw suh.'

'I'm the man,' Mister Maury told him. 'You chillun better quit
that playin' and dig me some worms.'

He drew his rod out of the case, jointed it up and laid it down
on a stump. Taking out his book of flies he turned the pages, considering. 'Silver Spinner,' he said aloud. 'They ought to take
that . . . in May. Naw, I'll just give Old Speck a chance. It's a
long time now since we had her out.'

The little Negroes had risen and were stepping quietly off along
the path toward the cabin, the two little boys hand in hand, the
little girl following, the baby astride her hip. They were pausing
now before a dilapidated building that might long ago have been a
henhouse. Mister Maury shouted at them. 'Look under them old

10

boards. That's the place for worms.' The biggest boy was turning around. His treble 'Yassuh' quavered over the water. Then their voices died away. There was no sound except the light turning of the willow boughs in the wind.

Mister Maury walked along the bank, rod in hand, humming: 'Bangum's gone to the wild boar's den . . . *Bangum's* gone to the wild boar's den . . .' He stopped where a white, peeled log protruded six or seven feet into the water. The pond made a little turn here. Two lines of willows curving in framed the whole surface of the water. He stepped out squarely upon the log, still humming. The line rose smoothly, soared against the blue and curved sweetly back upon the still water. His quick ear caught the little whish that the fly made when it clove the surface, his eye followed the tiny ripples of its flight. He cast again, leaning a little backward as he did sometimes when the mood was on him. Again and again his line soared out over the water. His eye rested now and then on his wrist. He noted with detachment the expert play of the muscles, admired each time the accuracy of his aim. It occurred to him that it was four days now since he had wet a line. Four days. One whole day packing up, parts of two days on the train and yesterday wasted sitting there on that front porch with the family. But the abstinence had done him good. He had never cast better than he was casting this morning.

There was a rustling along the bank, a glimpse of blue through the trees. Mister Maury leaned forward and peered around the clump of willows. A hundred yards away Steve, hatless, in an old blue shirt and khaki pants, stood jointing up a rod.

Mister Maury backed off his log and advanced along the path. He called out cheerfully, 'Well, feller, do any good?'

Steve looked up. His face had lightened for a moment, but the abstracted expression stole over it again when he spoke. 'Oh, I fiddled with it,' he said, 'all morning, but I didn't do much good.'

Mister Maury nodded sympathetically. '*Minerva invita erat,*' he said, 'you can do nothing unless Minerva perches on the roof tree. Why, I been castin' here all morning and not a strike. But there's a boat tied up over on the other side. What say we get in it and just drift around?' He paused, looked at the rod Steve had

11

finished jointing up. 'I brought another rod along,' he said. 'You want to use it?'

Steve shook his head. 'I'm used to this one.'

An expression of relief came over Mister Maury's face. 'That's right,' he said, 'a man always does better with his own rod.'

The boat was only a quarter full of water. They heaved her over and dumped it out, then dragged her down to the bank. The little Negroes had come up, bringing a can of worms. Mister Maury threw them each a nickel and set the can in the bottom of the boat. 'I always like to have a few worms handy,' he told Steve, 'ever since I was a boy.' He lowered himself ponderously into the bow and Steve pushed off and dropped down behind him.

The little Negroes still stood on the bank staring. When the boat was a little distance out on the water the boldest of them spoke: 'You reckon 'at ole jawnboat going to hold you up, Cap'm?'

Mister Maury turned his head to call over his shoulder. 'Go 'way, boy, ain't I done tole you I's a conjure?'

The boat dipped ominously. Steve changed his position a little and she settled to the water. Sitting well forward Mister Maury made graceful casts, now to this side, now to that. Steve, in the stern, made occasional casts, but he laid his rod down every now and then to paddle, though there was really no use in it. The boat drifted well enough with the wind. At the end of half an hour seven sizable bass lay on the bottom of the boat. Mister Maury had caught five of them. He reflected that perhaps he really ought to change places with the fish. 'But no,' he thought, 'it don't make any difference. He don't hardly know where he is now.'

He stole a glance over his shoulder at the young man's serious, abstracted face. It was like that of a person submerged. Steve seemed to float up to the surface every now and then, his expression would lighten, he would make some observation that showed he knew where he was, then he would sink again. If you asked him a question he answered punctiliously, two minutes later. Poor boy, dead to the world and would probably be that way the rest of his life! A pang of pity shot through Mister Maury, and on the heels of it a gust of that black fear that occasionally shook him. It was he, not Steve, that was the queer one! The world was full

12

of people like this boy, all of them walking around with their heads so full of this and that they hardly knew where they were going. There was hardly anybody — there was *nobody* really in the whole world like him. . . .

Steve, coming out of his abstraction, spoke politely. He had heard that Mister Maury was a fine shot. Did he like to fish better than hunt?

Mister Maury reflected. 'Well,' he said, 'they's something about a covey of birds rising up in front of you . . . they's something. And a good dog. Now they ain't anything in this world that I like better than a good bird dog.' He stopped and sighed. 'A man has got to come to himself early in life if he's going to amount to anything. Now I was smart, even as a boy. I could look around me and see all the men of my family, Uncle Jeems, Uncle Quent, my father, every one of 'em weighed two hundred by the time he was fifty. You get as heavy on your feet as all that and you can't do any good shooting. But a man can fish as long as he lives. . . . Why, one place I stayed last summer there was an old man ninety years old had himself carried down to the river every morning. . . . Yes, sir, a man can fish as long as he can get down to the water's edge. . . .'

There was a little plop to the right. He turned just in time to see the fish flash out of the water. He watched Steve take it off the hook and drop it on top of the pile in the bottom of the boat. Eight bass that made and two bream. The old lady would be pleased. 'Aleck always catches me fish,' she'd say.

The boat glided on over the still water. There was no wind at all now. The willows that fringed the bank might have been cut out of paper. The plume of smoke hung perfectly horizontal over the roof of the Negro cabin. Mister Maury watched it stream out in little eddies and disappear into the bright blue.

He spoke softly: 'Ain't it wonderful . . . ain't it wonderful now that a man of my gifts can content himself a whole morning on this here little old pond?'

13

III

Mister Maury woke with a start. He realized that he had been sleeping on his left side again. A bad idea. It always gave him palpitations of the heart. It must be that that had waked him up. He had gone to sleep almost immediately after his head hit the pillow. He rolled over, cautiously, as he always did since that bed in Leesburg had given down with him, and lying flat on his back stared at the opposite wall.

The moon rose late. It must be at its height now. That patch of light was so brilliant he could almost discern the pattern of the wall paper. It hung there, wavering, bitten by the shadows into a semblance of a human figure, a man striding with bent head and swinging arms. All the shadows in the room seemed to be moving toward him. The protruding corner of the washstand was an arrow aimed at his heart, the clumsy old-fashioned dresser was a giant towering above him.

They had put him to sleep in this same room the night after his wife died. In the summer it had been, too, in June, and there must have been a full moon, for the same giant shadows had struggled there with the same towering monsters. It would be like that here on this wall every full moon, for the pieces of furniture would never change their position, had never been changed, probably, since the house was built.

He turned back on his side. The wall before him was dark, but he knew every flower in the pattern of the wall paper, interlacing pink roses with thrusting up between every third cluster the enormous, spreading fronds of ferns. The wall paper in the room across the hall was like that too. The old lady slept there, and in the room next to his own, Laura, his sister-in-law, and in the east bedroom downstairs the young couple. He and Mary had slept there when they were first married, when they were the young couple in the house.

He tried to remember Mary as she must have looked the day he first saw her, the day he arrived from Virginia to open his school in the old office that used to stand there in the corner of the yard. He could see Mister Allard plainly, sitting there under the sugar tree with his chair tilted back, could discern the old lady — young

14

she had been then! — hospitably poised in the doorway, could hear her voice: 'Well, here are two of your pupils to start with. . . .' He remembered Laura, a shy child of nine hiding her face in her mother's skirts, but Mary was only a shadow in the dark hall. He could not even remember how her voice had sounded. 'Professor Maury,' she would have said and her mother would have corrected her with 'Cousin Aleck. . . .'

That day a year later when she was getting off her horse at the stile blocks. . . . She had turned as she walked across the lawn to look back at him. Her white sunbonnet had fallen back on her shoulders, her eyes meeting his had been wide and startled. He had gone on and had hitched both the horses before he leaped over the stile to join her. But he had known in that moment that she was the woman he was going to have. He could not remember all the rest of it, only that moment stood out. He had won her. She had become his wife, but the woman he had won was not the woman he had sought. It was as if he had had her only in that moment there on the lawn. As if she had paused there only for that one moment, and was ever after retreating before him down a devious, a dark way that he would never have chosen.

The death of the first baby had been the start of it, of course. It had been a relief when she took so definitely to religion. Before that there had been those sudden, unaccountable forays out of some dark lurking place that she had. Guerrilla warfare and trying to the nerves, but that had been only at the first. For many years they had been two enemies contending in the open. . . . Toward the last she had taken mightily to prayer. He would wake often to find her kneeling by the side of the bed in the dark. It had gone on for years. She had never given up hope. . . .

Ah, a stout-hearted one, Mary! She had never given up hope of changing him, of making him over into the man she thought he ought to be. Time and again she almost had him. And there were long periods, of course, during which he had been worn down by the conflict, one spring when he himself said, when she had told all the neighbors that he was too old now to go fishing any more. . . . But he had made a comeback. She had had to resort to stratagem. His lips curved in a smile, remembering the trick.

15

It had come over him suddenly, a general lassitude, an odd faintness in the mornings, the time when his spirits ordinarily were always at their highest. He had sat there looking out of the window at the woods glistening with spring rain; he had not even taken his gun down to shoot a squirrel.

Remembering Uncle Quent's last days he had been alarmed, had decided finally that he must tell her so that they might begin preparations for the future — he had shuddered at the thought of eventual confinement, perhaps in some institution. She had looked up from her sewing, unable to repress a smile.

'You think it's your mind, Aleck. . . . It's coffee. . . . I've been giving you a coffee substitute every morning. . . .'

They had laughed together over her cleverness. He had not gone back to coffee, but the lassitude had worn off. She had gone back to the attack with redoubled vigor. In the afternoons she would stand on the porch calling after him as he slipped down to the creek, 'Now, don't stay long enough to get that cramp. You remember how you suffered last time. . . .' He would have forgotten all about the cramp until that moment, but it would hang over him then through the whole afternoon's sport, and it would descend upon him inevitably when he left the river and started for the house.

Yes, he thought with pride. She was wearing him down — he didn't believe there was a man living who could withstand her a lifetime! — she was wearing him down and would have had him in another few months, another year certainly. But she had been struck down just as victory was in her grasp. The paralysis had come on her in the night. It was as if a curtain had descended, dividing their life sharply into two parts. In the bewildered year and a half that followed he had found himself forlornly trying to reconstruct the Mary he had known. The pressure she had so constantly exerted upon him had become for him a part of her personality. This new, calm Mary was not the woman he had loved all these years. She had lain there — heroically they all said — waiting for death. And lying there, waiting, all her faculties engaged now in defensive warfare, she had raised as it were her lifelong siege; she had lost interest in his comings and goings, had once even encouraged him to go out for an afternoon's sport. He

16

felt a rush of warm pity. Poor Mary! She must have realized toward the last that she had wasted herself in conflict; she had spent her arms and her strength against an inglorious foe when all the time the real, the invincible adversary waited. . . .

He turned over on his back again. The moonlight was waning, the contending shadows paler now and retreating toward the door. From across the hall came the sound of long, sibilant breaths, ending each one on a little upward groan. The old lady . . . she would maintain till her dying day that she did not snore. He fancied that he could hear from the next room Laura's light, regular breathing, and downstairs were the young couple asleep in each other's arms. . . .

All of them quiet and relaxed now, but they had been lively enough at dinner time! It had started with the talk about Aunt Sally Crenfew's funeral Tuesday. Living as he had for some years away from women of his family he had forgotten the need to be cautious. He had spoken up before he thought:

'But that's the day Steve and I were going to Barker's Mill. . . .'

Sarah had cried out at the idea. 'Barker's Mill!' she had said, 'right on the Crenfew land . . . well, if not on the very farm in the very next field.' It would be a scandal if he, Professor Maury, known by everybody to be in the neighborhood, could not spare one afternoon, one insignificant summer afternoon from his fishing long enough to attend the funeral of his cousin, the cousin of all of them, the oldest lady in the whole family connection. . . .

She had got him rattled; he had fallen back upon technicalities:

'I'm not a Crenfew. I'm a Maury. Aunt Sally Crenfew is no more kin to me than a catfish. . . .'

An unlucky crack, that about the catfish. Glancing around the table he had caught the same look in every eye. He had felt a gust of the same fright that had shaken him there on the pond. That look! Sooner or later you met it in every human eye. The thing was to be up and ready, ready to run for your life at a moment's notice. Yes, it had always been like that. It always would be. His fear of them was shot through suddenly with contempt. It was as if Mary were there laughing at them with him.

17

She knew that none of them could have survived what he had survived, could have paid the price for freedom that he had paid. . . .

Sarah had come to a full stop. He had to say something. He shook his head:

'You think we just go fishing to have a good time. The boy and I hold high converse on that pond. . . . I'm starved for intellectual companionship, I tell you. In Florida I never see anybody but niggers. . . .'

They had all laughed out at that. 'As if you didn't *prefer* the society of niggers,' Sarah said scornfully.

The old lady had been moved to anecdote:

'I remember when Aleck first came out here from Virginia, Cousin Sophy said: "Professor Maury is so well educated. Now Cousin Cave Maynor is dead, who is there in this neighborhood for him to associate with?" "Well," I said, "I don't know about that. He seems perfectly satisfied now with Ben Hooser. They're off to the creek together every evening soon as school is out."'

Ben Hooser. . . . He could see now the wrinkled face, overlaid with that ashy pallor of the aged Negro, the shrewd, smiling eyes, the pendulous lower lip that dropping away showed always some of the rotten teeth. A fine nigger, Ben, and on to a lot of tricks, the only man really that he'd ever cared to take fishing with him. . . .

But the first real friend of his bosom had been old Uncle Teague, back in Virginia. Once a week, or more likely every ten days, he fed the hounds on the carcass of a calf that had had time to get pretty high. They would drive the spring wagon out into the lot, he, a boy of ten, beside Uncle Teague on the driver's seat. The hounds would come in a great rush and rear their slobbering jowls against the wagon wheels. Uncle Teague would wield his whip, chuckling while he threw the first hunk of meat to Old Mag, his favorite.

'Dey goin' run on dis,' he'd say, 'dey goin' run like a shadow. . . .'

He shifted his position again, cautiously. People, he thought . . . people . . . so bone ignorant, all of them. Not one person in a thousand realized that a fox hound remains at heart a wild beast and must kill and gorge, and then when he is ravenous kill and gorge

18

again. . . . Or that the channel cat is a night feeder. . . . Or . . . His daughter had told him once that he ought to set all his knowledges down in a book. 'Why?' he had asked. 'So everybody else can know as much as I do?'

If he allowed his mind to get active, really active, he would never get any sleep. He was fighting an inclination now to get up and find a cigarette. He relaxed again upon his pillows, deliberately summoned pictures up before his mind's eye. Landscapes — and streams. He observed their outlines, watched one flow into another. The Black River into West Fork, that in turn into Spring Creek and Spring Creek into the Withlicoochee. Then they were all flowing together, merging into one broad plain. He watched it take form slowly: the wide field in front of Hawkwood, the Rivanna River on one side, on the other Peters' Mountain. They would be waiting there till the fox showed himself on that little rise by the river. The young men would hold back till Uncle Quent had wheeled Old Filly, then they would all be off pell-mell across the plain. He himself would be mounted on Jonesboro. Blind as a bat, but she would take anything you put her at. That first thicket on the edge of the woods. They would break there, one half of them going around, the other half streaking it through the woods. He was always of those going around to try to cut the fox off on the other side. No, he was down off his horse. He was coursing with the fox. He could hear the sharp, pointed feet padding on the dead leaves, see the quick head turned now and then over the shoulder.

The trees kept flashing by, one black trunk after another. And now it was a ragged mountain field and the sage grass running before them in waves to where a narrow stream curved in between the ridges. The fox's feet were light in the water. He ran steadily, head down. The hounds' baying was louder now. Old Mag knew the trick. She had stopped to give tongue by the big rock, and now they had all leaped the gulch and were scrambling up through the pines. But the fox's feet were already hard on the mountain path. He ran slowly now, past the big boulder, past the blasted pine to where the shadow of the Pinnacle Rock was black across the path. He ran on and the shadow rose and swayed to meet him. Its cool

19

touch was on his hot tongue, his heaving flanks. He had slipped in under it. He was sinking down, panting, in black dark, on moist earth while the hounds' baying filled the bowl of the valley and reverberated from the mountainside.

HE

KATHERINE ANNE PORTER

LIFE was very hard for the Whipples. It was hard to feed all the hungry mouths, it was hard to keep the children in flannels during the winter, short as it was: 'God knows what would become of us if we lived North,' they would say: keeping them decently clean was hard. 'It looks like our luck won't never let up on us,' said Mr. Whipple, but Mrs. Whipple was all for taking what was sent and calling it good, anyhow when the neighbors were in earshot. 'Don't ever let a soul hear us complain,' she kept saying to her husband. She couldn't stand to be pitied. 'No, not if it comes to it that we have to live in a wagon and pick cotton around the country,' she said, 'nobody's going to get a chance to look down on us.'

Mrs. Whipple loved her second son, the simple-minded one, better than she loved the other two children put together. She was forever saying so, and when she talked with certain of her neighbors she would even throw in her husband and her mother for good measure.

'You needn't keep on saying it around,' said Mr. Whipple; 'you'll make people think nobody else has any feelings about Him but you.'

'It's natural for a mother,' Mrs. Whipple would remind him. 'You know yourself it's more natural for a mother to be that way. People don't expect so much of fathers, some way.'

This didn't keep the neighbors from talking plainly among themselves. 'A Lord's pure mercy if He should die,' they said. 'It's the sins of the fathers,' they agreed among themselves. 'There's bad blood and bad doings somewhere, you can bet on that.' This behind the Whipples' backs. To their faces everybody said, 'He's not so bad off. He'll be all right yet. Look how He grows!'

Mrs. Whipple hated to talk about it, she tried to keep her mind off it, but every time anybody set foot in the house, the subject

21

always came up, and she had to talk about Him first, before she could get on to anything else. It seemed to ease her mind. 'I wouldn't have anything happen to Him for all the world, but it just looks like I can't keep Him out of mischief. He's so strong and active, He's always into everything; He was like that since He could walk. It's actually funny sometimes, the way He can do anything; it's laughable to see Him up to His tricks. Emly has more accidents; I'm forever tying up her bruises, and Adna can't fall a foot without cracking a bone. But He can do anything and not get a scratch. The preacher said such a nice thing once when he was here. He said, and I'll remember it to my dying day, "The innocent walk with God — that's why He don't get hurt."' Whenever Mrs. Whipple repeated these words, she always felt a warm pool spread in her breast, and the tears would fill her eyes, and then she could talk about something else.

He did grow and He never got hurt. A plank blew off the chicken house and struck Him on the head and He never seemed to know it. He had learned a few words, and after this He forgot them. He didn't whine for food as the other children did, but waited until it was given Him; He ate squatting in the corner, smacking and mumbling. Rolls of fat covered Him like an overcoat, and He could carry twice as much wood and water as Adna. Emly had a cold in the head most of the time — 'she takes that after me,' said Mrs. Whipple — so in bad weather they gave her the extra blanket off His cot. He never seemed to mind the cold.

Just the same, Mrs. Whipple's life was a torment for fear something might happen to Him. He climbed the peach trees much better than Adna and went skittering along the branches like a monkey, just a regular monkey. 'Oh, Mrs. Whipple, you hadn't ought to let Him do that. He'll lose His balance sometime. He can't rightly know what He's doing.'

Mrs. Whipple almost screamed out at the neighbor. 'He *does* know what He's doing! He's as able as any other child! Come down out of there, you!' When He finally reached the ground she could hardly keep her hands off Him for acting like that before people, a grin all over His face and her worried sick about Him all the time.

'It's the neighbors,' said Mrs. Whipple to her husband. 'Oh, I do mortally wish they would keep out of our business. I can't afford to let Him do anything for fear they'll come nosing around about it. Look at the bees, now. Adna can't handle them, they sting him up so; I haven't got time to do everything, and now I don't dare let Him. But if He gets a sting He don't really mind.'

'It's just because He ain't got sense enough to be scared of anything,' said Mr. Whipple.

'You ought to be ashamed of yourself,' said Mrs. Whipple, 'talking that way about your own child. Who's to take up for Him if we don't, I'd like to know? He sees a lot that goes on, He listens to things all the time. And anything I tell Him to do He does it. Don't never let anybody hear you say such things. They'd think you favored the other children over Him.'

'Well, now, I don't, and you know it, and what's the use of getting all worked up about it? You always think the worst of everything. Just let Him alone, He'll get along somehow. He gets plenty to eat and wear, don't He?' Mr. Whipple suddenly felt tired out. 'Anyhow, it can't be helped now.'

Mrs. Whipple felt tired too, she complained in a tired voice. 'What's done can't never be undone, I know that good as anybody; but He's my child, and I'm not going to have people say anything. I get sick of people coming around saying things all the time.'

In the early fall Mrs. Whipple got a letter from her brother saying he and his wife and two children were coming over for a little visit next Sunday week. 'Put the big pot in the little one,' he wrote at the end. Mrs. Whipple read this part out loud twice, she was so pleased. Her brother was a great one for saying funny things. 'We'll just show him that's no joke,' she said; 'we'll just butcher one of the sucking pigs.'

'It's a waste, and I don't hold with waste the way we are now,' said Mr. Whipple. 'That pig'll be worth money by Christmas.'

'It's a shame and a pity we can't have a decent meal's vittles once in a while when my own family comes to see us,' said Mrs. Whipple. 'I'd hate for his wife to go back and say there wasn't a thing in the house to eat. My God, it's better than buying up a

23

great chance of meat in town. There's where you'd spend the money!'

'All right, do it yourself then,' said Mr. Whipple. 'Christamighty, no wonder we can't get ahead!'

The question was how to get the little pig away from his ma, a great fighter, worse than a Jersey cow. Adna wouldn't try it: 'That sow'd rip my insides out all over the pen.' 'All right, old fraidy,' said Mrs. Whipple, '*He's* not scared. Watch *Him* do it.' And she laughed as though it was all a good joke and gave Him a little push towards the pen. He sneaked up and snatched the pig right away from the teat and galloped back and was over the fence with the sow raging at His heels. The little black squirming thing was screeching like a baby in a tantrum, stiffening its back and stretching its mouth to the ears. Mrs. Whipple took the pig with her face stiff and sliced its throat with one stroke. When He saw the blood He gave a great jolting breath and ran away. 'But He'll forget and eat plenty, just the same,' thought Mrs. Whipple. Whenever she was thinking, her lips moved making words. 'He'd eat it all if I didn't stop Him. He'd eat up every mouthful from the other two if I'd let Him.'

She felt badly about it. He was ten years old now and a third again as large as Adna, who was going on fourteen. 'It's a shame, a shame,' she kept saying under her breath, 'and Adna with so much brains!'

She kept on feeling badly about all sorts of things. In the first place it was the man's work to butcher; the sight of the pig scraped pink and naked made her sick. He was too fat and soft and pitiful-looking. It was simply a shame the way things had to happen. By the time she had finished it up, she almost wished her brother would stay at home.

Early Sunday morning Mrs. Whipple dropped everything to get Him all cleaned up. In an hour He was dirty again, with crawling under fences after a possum, and straddling along the rafters of the barn looking for eggs in the hayloft. 'My Lord, look at you now after all my trying! And here's Adna and Emly staying so quiet. I get tired trying to keep you decent. Get off that shirt and put on another, people will say I don't half dress you!' And she boxed

Him on the ears, hard. He blinked and blinked and rubbed His head, and His face hurt Mrs. Whipple's feelings. Her knees began to tremble, she had to sit down while she buttoned His shirt. 'I'm just all gone before the day starts.'

The brother came with his plump healthy wife and two great roaring hungry boys. They had a grand dinner, with the pig roasted to a crackling in the middle of the table, full of dressing, a pickled peach in his mouth and plenty of gravy for the sweet potatoes.

'This looks like prosperity all right,' said the brother; 'you're going to have to roll me home like I was a barrel when I'm done.'

Everybody laughed out loud; it was fine to hear them laughing all at once around the table. Mrs. Whipple felt warm and good about it. 'Oh, we've got six more of these; I say it's as little as we can do when you come to see us so seldom.'

He wouldn't come into the dining room, and Mrs. Whipple passed it off very well. 'He's timider than my other two,' she said, 'He'll just have to get used to you. There isn't everybody He'll make up with; you know how it is with some children, even cousins.' Nobody said anything out of the way.

'Just like my Alfy here,' said the brother's wife. 'I sometimes got to lick him to make him shake hands with his own grand-mammy.'

So that was over, and Mrs. Whipple loaded up a big plate for Him first, before everybody. 'I always say He ain't to be slighted, no matter who else goes without,' she said, and carried it to Him herself.

'He can chin Himself on the top of the door,' said Emly, helping along.

'That's fine, He's getting along fine,' said the brother.

They went away after supper. Mrs. Whipple rounded up the dishes, and sent the children to bed and sat down and unlaced her shoes. 'You see?' she said to Mr. Whipple. 'That's the way my whole family is. Nice and considerate about everything. No out-of-the-way remarks — they *have* got refinement. I get awfully sick of people's remarks. Wasn't that pig good?'

Mr. Whipple said, 'Yes, we're out three hundred pounds of pork, that's all. It's easy to be polite when you come to eat. Who knows what they had in their minds all along?'

'Yes, that's like you,' said Mrs. Whipple. 'I don't expect anything else from you. You'll be telling me next that my own brother will be saying around that we made Him eat in the kitchen! Oh, my God!' She rocked her head in her hands, a hard pain started in the very middle of her forehead. 'Now it's all spoiled, and everything was so nice and easy. All right, you don't like them and you never did — all right, they'll not come here again soon, never you mind! But they *can't* say He wasn't dressed every lick as good as Adna — oh, honest, sometimes I wish I was dead!'

'I wish you'd let up,' said Mr. Whipple. 'It's bad enough as it is.'

It was a hard winter. It seemed to Mrs. Whipple that they hadn't ever known anything but hard times, and now to cap it all a winter like this. The crops were about half of what they had a right to expect; after the cotton was in it didn't do much more than cover the grocery bill. They swapped off one of the plow horses, and got cheated, for the new one died of the heaves. Mrs. Whipple kept thinking all the time it was terrible to have a man you couldn't depend on not to get cheated. They cut down on everything, but Mrs. Whipple kept saying there are things you can't cut down on, and they cost money. It took a lot of warm clothes for Adna and Emly, who walked four miles to school during the three-months session. 'He sets around the fire a lot, He won't need so much,' said Mr. Whipple. 'That's so,' said Mrs. Whipple, 'and when He does the outdoor chores He can wear your tarpaullion coat. I can't do no better, that's all.'

In February He was taken sick, and lay curled up under His blanket looking very blue in the face and acting as if He would choke. Mr. and Mrs. Whipple did everything they could for Him for two days, and then they were scared and sent for the doctor. The doctor told them they must keep Him warm and give Him plenty of milk and eggs. 'He isn't as stout as He looks, I'm afraid,' said the doctor. 'You've got to watch them when they're like that. You must put more cover onto Him, too.'

'I just took off His big blanket to wash,' said Mrs. Whipple, ashamed. 'I can't stand dirt.'

'Well, you'd better put it back on the minute it's dry,' said the doctor, 'or He'll have pneumonia.'

Mr. and Mrs. Whipple took a blanket off their own bed and put His cot in by the fire. 'They can't say we didn't do everything for Him,' she said, 'even to sleeping cold ourselves on His account.'

When the winter broke He seemed to be well again, but He walked as if His feet hurt Him. He was able to run a cotton planter during the season.

'I got it all fixed up with Jim Ferguson about breeding the cow next time,' said Mr. Whipple. 'I'll pasture the bull this summer and give Jim some fodder in the fall. That's better than paying out money when you haven't got it.'

'I hope you didn't say such a thing before Jim Ferguson,' said Mrs. Whipple. 'You oughtn't to let him know we're so down as all that.'

'Godamighty, that ain't saying we're down. A man is got to look ahead sometimes. *He* can lead the bull over today. I need Adna on the place.'

At first Mrs. Whipple felt easy in her mind about sending Him for the bull. Adna was too jumpy and couldn't be trusted. You've got to be steady around animals. After He was gone she started thinking, and after a while she could hardly bear it any longer. She stood in the lane and watched for Him. It was nearly three miles to go and a hot day, but He oughtn't to be so long about it. She shaded her eyes and stared until colored bubbles floated in her eyeballs. It was just like everything else in life, she must always worry and never know a moment's peace about anything. After a long time she saw Him turn into the side lane, limping. He came on very slowly, leading the big hulk of an animal by a ring in the nose, twirling a little stick in His hand, never looking back or sideways, but coming on like a sleepwalker with His eyes half shut.

Mrs. Whipple was scared sick of bulls; she had heard awful stories about how they followed on quietly enough, and then suddenly pitched on with a bellow and pawed and gored a body to pieces. Any second now that black monster would come down on Him; my God, He'd never have sense enough to run.

She mustn't make a sound nor a move; she mustn't get the bull started. The bull heaved his head aside and horned the air at a fly. Her voice burst out of her in a shriek, and she screamed at Him to come on, for God's sake. He didn't seem to hear her clamor, but kept on twirling His switch and limping on, and the bull lumbered along behind him as gently as a calf. Mrs. Whipple stopped calling and ran towards the house, praying under her breath: 'Lord, don't let anything happen to Him. Lord, you *know* people will say we oughtn't to have sent Him. You *know* they'll say we didn't take care of Him. Oh, get Him home, safe home, safe home, and I'll look out for Him better! Amen.'

She watched from the window while He led the beast in, and tied him up in the barn. It was no use trying to keep up, Mrs. Whipple couldn't bear another thing. She sat down and rocked and cried with her apron over her head.

From year to year the Whipples were growing poorer. The place just seemed to run down of itself, no matter how hard they worked. 'We're losing our hold,' said Mrs. Whipple. 'Why can't we do like other people and watch for our best chances? They'll be calling us poor white trash next.'

'When I get to be sixteen I'm going to leave,' said Adna. 'I'm going to get a job in Powell's grocery store. There's money in that. No more farm for me.'

'I'm going to be a school-teacher,' said Emly. 'But I've got to finish the eighth grade, anyhow. Then I can live in town. I don't see any chances here.'

'Emly takes after my family,' said Mrs. Whipple. 'Ambitious every last one of them, and they don't take second place for anybody.'

When fall came Emly got a chance to wait on table in the railroad eating-house in the town near-by, and it seemed such a shame not to take it when the wages were good and she could get her food too, that Mrs. Whipple decided to let her take it, and not bother with school until the next session. 'You've got plenty of time,' she said. 'You're young and smart as a whip.'

28

With Adna gone too, Mr. Whipple tried to run the farm with just Him to help. He seemed to get along fine, doing His work and part of Adna's without noticing it. They did well enough until Christmas time, when one morning He slipped on the ice coming up from the barn. Instead of getting up He thrashed round and round, and when Mr. Whipple got to Him, He was having some sort of fit.

They brought Him inside and tried to make Him sit up, but He blubbered and rolled, so they put Him to bed and Mr. Whipple rode to town for the doctor. All the way there and back he worried about where the money was to come from: it sure did look like he had about all the troubles he could carry.

From then on He stayed in bed. His legs swelled up double their size, and the fits kept coming back. After four months, the doctor said, 'It's no use, I think you'd better put Him in the County Home for treatment right away. I'll see about it for you. He'll have good care there and be off your hands.'

'We don't begrudge Him any care, and I won't let Him out of my sight,' said Mrs. Whipple. 'I won't have it said I sent my sick child off among strangers.'

'I know how you feel,' said the doctor. 'You can't tell me anything about that, Mrs. Whipple. I've got a boy of my own. But you'd better listen to me. I can't do anything more for Him, that's the truth.'

Mr. and Mrs. Whipple talked it over a long time that night after they went to bed. 'It's just charity,' said Mrs. Whipple, 'that's what we've come to, charity! I certainly never looked for this.'

'We pay taxes to help support the place just like everybody else,' said Mr. Whipple, 'and I don't call that taking charity. I think it would be fine to have Him where He'd get the best of everything . . . and besides, I can't keep up with these doctor bills any longer.'

'Maybe that's why the doctor wants us to send Him — he's scared he won't get his money,' said Mrs. Whipple.

'Don't talk like that,' said Mr. Whipple, feeling pretty sick, 'or we won't be able to send Him.'

'Oh, but we won't keep Him there long,' said Mrs. Whipple. 'Soon's He's better, we'll bring Him right back home.'

'The doctor has told you and told you time and again He can't ever get better, and you might as well stop talking,' said Mr. Whipple.

'Doctors don't know everything,' said Mrs. Whipple, feeling almost happy. 'But anyhow, in the summer Emly can come home for a vacation, and Adna can get down for Sundays: we'll all work together and get on our feet again, and the children will feel they've got a place to come to.'

All at once she saw it full summer again, with the garden going fine, and new white roller shades up all over the house, and Adna and Emly home, so full of life, all of them happy together. Oh, it could happen, things would ease up on them.

They didn't talk before Him much, but they never knew just how much He understood. Finally the doctor set the day, and a neighbor who owned a double-seated carryall offered to drive them over. The hospital would have sent an ambulance, but Mrs. Whipple couldn't stand to see Him going away looking so sick as all that. They wrapped Him in blankets, and the neighbor and Mr. Whipple lifted Him into the back seat of the carryall beside Mrs. Whipple, who had on her black shirtwaist. She couldn't stand to go looking like charity.

'You'll be all right, I guess I'll stay behind,' said Mr. Whipple. 'It don't look like everybody ought to leave the place at once.'

'Besides, it ain't as if He was going to stay forever,' said Mrs. Whipple to the neighbor. 'This is only for a little while.'

They started away, Mrs. Whipple holding to the edges of the blankets to keep Him from sagging sideways. He sat there blinking and blinking. He worked His hands out and began rubbing His nose with His knuckles, and then with the end of the blanket. Mrs. Whipple couldn't believe what she saw; He was scrubbing away big tears that rolled out of the corners of His eyes. He sniveled and made a gulping noise. Mrs. Whipple kept saying, 'Oh, honey, you don't feel so bad, do you? You don't feel so bad, do you?' for He seemed to be accusing her of something. Maybe He remembered that time she boxed His ears, maybe He had been scared that day with the bull, maybe He had slept cold and couldn't tell her about it; maybe He knew they were sending Him away for good and all because they were too poor to keep Him. Whatever it was, Mrs. Whipple couldn't bear to think of it. She began to cry, frightfully, and wrapped her arms tight around Him. His head rolled on her shoulder: she had loved Him as much as she possibly could, there were Adna and Emly who had to be thought of too, there was nothing she could do to make up to Him for His life. Oh, what a mortal pity He was ever born.

They came in sight of the hospital, with the neighbor driving very fast, not daring to look behind him.

KNEEL TO THE RISING SUN

ERSKINE CALDWELL

I

A SHIVER went through Lonnie. He drew his hand away from his sharp chin, remembering what Clem had said. It made him feel now as if he were committing a crime by standing in Arch Gunnard's presence and allowing his face to be seen.

He and Clem had been walking up the road together that afternoon on their way to the filling station when he told Clem how much he needed rations. Clem stopped a moment to kick a rock out of the road, and said that if you worked for Arch Gunnard long enough, your face would be sharp enough to split the boards for your own coffin.

As Lonnie turned away to sit down on an empty box beside the gasoline pump, he could not help wishing that he could be as unafraid of Arch Gunnard as Clem was. Even if Clem was a Negro, he never hesitated to ask for rations when he needed something to eat; and when he and his family did not get enough, Clem came right out and told Arch so. Arch stood for that, but he swore that he was going to run Clem out of the country the first chance he got.

Lonnie knew without turning around that Clem was standing at the corner of the filling station with two or three other Negroes and looking at him, but for some reason he was unable to meet Clem's eyes.

Arch Gunnard was sitting in the sun, honing his jack-knife blade on his boot top. He glanced once or twice at Lonnie's hound, Nancy, who was lying in the middle of the road waiting for Lonnie to go home.

'That your dog, Lonnie?'

Jumping with fear, Lonnie's hand went to his chin to hide the lean face that would accuse Arch of short-rationing.

32

Arch snapped his fingers and the hound stood up, wagging her tail. She waited to be called.

'Mr. Arch, I ——'

Arch called the dog. She began crawling toward them on her belly, wagging her tail a little faster each time Arch's fingers snapped. When she was several feet away, she turned over on her back and lay on the ground with her four paws in the air.

Dudley Smith and Jim Weaver, who were lounging around the filling station, laughed. They had been leaning against the side of the building, but they straightened up to see what Arch was up to.

Arch spat some more tobacco juice on his boot top and whetted the jack-knife blade some more.

'What kind of a hound dog is that, anyway, Lonnie?' Arch said. 'Looks like to me it might be a ketch hound.'

Lonnie could feel Clem Henry's eyes boring into the back of his head. He wondered what Clem would do if it had been his dog Arch Gunnard was snapping his fingers at and calling like that.

'His tail's way too long for a coon hound or a bird dog, ain't it, Arch?' somebody behind Lonnie said, laughing out loud.

Everybody laughed then, including Arch. They looked at Lonnie, waiting to hear what he was going to say to Arch.

'Is he a ketch hound, Lonnie?' Arch said, snapping his fingers again.

'Mr. Arch, I ——'

'Don't be ashamed of him, Lonnie, if he don't show signs of turning out to be a bird dog or a fox hound. Everybody needs a hound around the house that can go out and catch pigs and rabbits when you are in a hurry for them. A ketch hound is a mighty respectable animal. I've known the time when I was mighty proud to own one.'

Everybody laughed.

Arch Gunnard was getting ready to grab Nancy by the tail. Lonnie sat up, twisting his neck until he caught a glimpse of Clem Henry at the other corner of the filling station. Clem was staring at him with unmistakable meaning, with the same look in his eyes he had had that afternoon when he said that nobody who worked for Arch Gunnard ought to stand for short-rationing. Lonnie lowered his eyes. He could not figure out how a Negro could be braver than he was. There were a lot of times like that when he would have given anything he had to be able to jump into Clem's shoes and change places with him.

'The trouble with this hound of yours, Lonnie, is that he's too heavy on his feet. Don't you reckon it would be a pretty slick little trick to lighten the load some, being as how he's a ketch hound to begin with?'

Lonnie remembered then what Clem Henry had said he would do if Arch Gunnard ever tried to cut off his dog's tail. Lonnie knew, and Clem knew, and everybody else knew, that that would give Arch the chance he was waiting for. All Arch asked, he had said, was for Clem Henry to overstep his place just one little half-inch, or to talk back to him with just one little short word, and he would do the rest. Everybody knew what Arch meant by that, especially if Clem did not turn and run. And Clem had not been known to run from anybody, after fifteen years in the country.

Arch reached down and grabbed Nancy's tail while Lonnie was wondering about Clem. Nancy acted as if she thought Arch were playing some kind of a game with her. She turned her head around until she could reach Arch's hand to lick it. He cracked her on the bridge of the nose with the end of the jack-knife.

'He's a mighty playful dog, Lonnie,' Arch said, catching up a shorter grip on the tail, 'but his wagpole is way too long for a dog his size, especially when he wants to be a ketch hound.'

Lonnie swallowed hard.

'Mr. Arch, she's a mighty fine rabbit tracker. I ——'

'Shucks, Lonnie,' Arch said, whetting the knife blade on the dog's tail, 'I ain't never seen a hound in all my life that needed a tail that long to hunt rabbits with. It's way too long for just a common, ordinary, everyday ketch hound.'

Lonnie looked up hopefully at Dudley Smith and the others. None of them offered any help. It was useless for him to try to stop Arch, because Arch Gunnard would let nothing stand in his way when once he had set his head on what he wished to do. Lonnie knew that if he should let himself show any anger or resentment, Arch would drive him off the farm before sundown that night. Clem Henry was the only person there who would help him, but Clem . . .

The white men and the Negroes at both corners of the filling station waited to see what Lonnie was going to do about it. All of them hoped he would put up a fight for his hound. If anyone ever had the nerve to stop Arch Gunnard from cutting off a dog's tail, it might put an end to it. It was plain, though, that Lonnie, who was one of Arch's share-croppers, was afraid to speak up. Clem Henry might; Clem was the only one who might try to stop Arch, even if it meant trouble. And all of them knew that Arch would insist on running Clem out of the country, or filling him full of lead.

'I reckon it's all right with you, ain't it, Lonnie?' Arch said. 'I don't seem to hear no objections.'

Clem Henry stepped forward several paces, and stopped.

Arch laughed, watching Lonnie's face, and jerked Nancy to her feet. The hound cried out in pain and surprise, but Arch made her be quiet by kicking her in the belly.

Lonnie winced. He could hardly bear to see anybody kick his dog like that.

'Mr. Arch, I . . .'

A contraction in his throat almost choked him for several moments, and he had to open his mouth wide and fight for breath. The other white men around him were silent. Nobody liked to see a dog kicked in the belly like that.

Lonnie could see the other end of the filling station from the corner of his eye. He saw a couple of Negroes go up behind Clem and grasp his overalls. Clem spat on the ground, between outspread feet, but he did not try to break away from them.

'Being as how I don't hear no objections, I reckon it's all right to go ahead and cut it off,' Arch said, spitting.

Lonnie's head went forward and all he could see of Nancy was her hind feet. He had come to ask for a slab of sowbelly and some molasses, or something. Now he did not know if he could ever bring himself to ask for rations, no matter how much hungrier they became at home.

'I always make it a habit of asking a man first,' Arch said. 'I wouldn't want to go ahead and cut off a tail if a man had any objections. That wouldn't be right. No, sir, it just wouldn't be fair and square.'

Arch caught a shorter grip on the hound's tail and placed the knife blade on it two or three inches from the rump. It looked to those who were watching as if his mouth were watering, because tobacco juice began to trickle down the corners of his lips. He brought up the back of his hand and wiped his mouth.

A noisy automobile came plowing down the road through the deep red dust. Everyone looked up as it passed in order to see who was in it.

Lonnie glanced at it, but he could not keep his eyes raised. His head fell downward once more until he could feel his sharp chin cutting into his chest. He wondered then if Arch had noticed how lean his face was.

'I keep two or three ketch hounds around my place,' Arch said, honing the blade on the tail of the dog as if it were a razor strop until his actions brought smiles to the faces of the men grouped around him, 'but I never could see the sense of a ketch hound having a long tail. It only gets in their way when I send them out to catch a pig or a rabbit for my supper.'

Pulling with his left hand and pushing with his right, Arch Gunnard docked the hound's tail as quickly and as easily as if he were cutting a willow switch in the pasture to drive the cows home with. The dog sprang forward with the release of her tail until she was far beyond Arch's reach, and began howling so loud she could be heard half a mile away. Nancy stopped once and looked back at Arch, and then she sprang to the middle of the road and began leaping and twisting in circles. All that time she was yelping and biting at the bleeding stub of her tail.

Arch leaned backward and twirled the severed tail in one hand while he wiped the jack-knife blade on his boot sole. He watched Lonnie's dog chasing herself around in circles in the red dust.

Nobody had anything to say then. Lonnie tried not to watch his dog's agony, and he forced himself to keep from looking at Clem Henry. Then, with his eyes shut, he wondered why he had remained on Arch Gunnard's plantation all those past years, sharecropping for a mere living on short rations, and becoming leaner

36

and leaner all the time. He knew then how true it was what Clem had said about Arch's share-croppers' faces becoming sharp enough to hew their own coffins. His hands went to his chin before he knew what he was doing. His hand dropped when he had felt the bones of jaw and the exposed tendons of his cheeks.

As hungry as he was, he knew that even if Arch did give him some rations then, there would not be nearly enough for them to eat for the following week. Hatty, his wife, was already broken down from hunger and work in the fields, and his father, Mark Newsome, stone-deaf for the past twenty years, was always asking him why there was never enough food in the house for them to have a solid meal. Lonnie's head fell forward a little more, and he could feel his eyes becoming damp.

The pressure of his sharp chin against his chest made him so uncomfortable that he had to raise his head at last in order to ease the pain of it.

The first thing he saw when he looked up was Arch Gunnard twirling Nancy's tail in his left hand. Arch Gunnard had a trunk full of dogs' tails at home. He had been cutting off tails ever since anyone could remember, and during all those years he had accumulated a collection of which he was so proud that he kept the trunk locked and the key tied around his neck on a string. On Sunday afternoons when the preacher came to visit, or when a crowd was there to loll on the front porch and swap stories, Arch showed them off, naming each tail from memory just as well as if he had a tag on it.

Clem Henry had left the filling station and was walking alone down the road towards the plantation. Clem Henry's house was in a cluster of Negro cabins below Arch's big house, and he had to pass Lonnie's house to get there. Lonnie was on the verge of getting up and leaving when he saw Arch looking at him. He did not know whether Arch was looking at his lean face, or whether he was watching to see if he were going to get up and go down the road with Clem.

The thought of leaving reminded him of his reason for being there. He had to have some rations before supper time that night, no matter how short they were.

'Mr. Arch, I . . .'

Arch stared at him for a moment, appearing as if he had turned to listen to some strange sound unheard of before that moment.

Lonnie bit his lips, wondering if Arch was going to say anything about how lean and hungry he looked. But Arch was thinking about something else. He slapped his hand on his leg and laughed out loud.

'I sometimes wish niggers had tails,' Arch said, coiling Nancy's tail into a ball and putting it into his pocket. 'I'd a heap rather cut off nigger tails than dog tails. There'd be more to cut, for one thing.'

Dudley Smith and somebody else behind them laughed for a brief moment. The laughter died out almost as suddenly as it had risen.

The Negroes who had heard Arch shuffled their feet in the dust and moved backwards. It was only a few minutes until not one was left at the filling station. They went up the road behind the red wooded building until they were out of sight.

Arch got up and stretched. The sun was getting low, and it was no longer comfortable in the October air. 'Well, I reckon I'll be getting on home to get me some supper,' he said.

He walked slowly to the middle of the road and stopped to look at Nancy retreating along the ditch.

'Nobody going my way?' he asked. 'What's wrong with you, Lonnie? Going home to supper, ain't you?'

'Mr. Arch, I . . .'

Lonnie found himself jumping to his feet. His first thought was to ask for the sowbelly and molasses, and maybe some corn meal; but when he opened his mouth, the words refused to come out. He took several steps forward and shook his head. He did not know what Arch might say or do if he said 'no.'

'Hatty'll be looking for you,' Arch said, turning his back and walking off.

He reached into his hip pocket and took out Nancy's tail. He began twirling it as he walked down the road towards the big house in the distance.

Dudley Smith went inside the filling station, and the others walked away.

After Arch had gone several hundred yards, Lonnie sat down heavily on the box beside the gas pump from which he had got up when Arch spoke to him. He sat down heavily, his shoulders drooping, his arms falling between his outspread legs.

Lonnie did not know how long his eyes had been closed, but when he opened them, he saw Nancy lying between his feet, licking the docked tail. While he watched her, he felt the sharp point of his chin cutting into his chest again. Presently the door behind him was slammed shut, and a minute later he could hear Dudley Smith walking away from the filling station on his way home.

II

Lonnie had been sleeping fitfully for several hours when he suddenly found himself wide awake. Hatty shook him again. He raised himself on his elbow and tried to see into the darkness of the room. Without knowing what time it was, he was able to determine that it was nearly two hours until sunrise.

'Lonnie,' Hatty said again, trembling in the cold night air, 'Lonnie, your pa ain't in the house.'

Lonnie sat upright in bed.

'How do you know he ain't?' he said.

'I've been lying here wide awake ever since I got in bed, and I heard him when he went out. He's been gone all that time.'

'Maybe he just stepped out for a while,' Lonnie said, turning and trying to see through the bedroom window.

'I know what I'm saying, Lonnie,' Hatty insisted. 'Your pa's been gone a heap too long.'

Both of them sat without a sound for several minutes while they listened for Mark Newsome.

Lonnie got up and lit a lamp. He shivered while he was putting on his shirt, overalls, and shoes. He tied his shoelaces in hard knots because he couldn't see in the faint light. Outside the window it was almost pitch-dark, and Lonnie could feel the damp October air blowing against his face.

'I'll go help look,' Hatty said, throwing the covers off and starting to get up.

39

Lonnie went to the bed and drew the covers back over her and pushed her back into place.

'You try to get some sleep, Hatty,' he said; 'you can't stay awake the whole night. I'll go bring Pa back.'

He left Hatty, blowing out the lamp, and stumbled through the dark hall, feeling his way to the front porch by touching the wall with his hands. When he got to the porch, he could still hardly see any distance ahead, but his eyes were becoming more accustomed to the darkness. He waited a minute, listening.

Feeling his way down the steps into the yard, he walked around the corner of the house and stopped to listen again before calling his father.

'Oh, Pa!' he said loudly. 'Oh, Pa!'

He stopped under the bedroom window when he realized what he had been doing.

'Now that's a fool thing for me to be out here doing,' he said, scolding himself. 'Pa couldn't hear it thunder.'

He heard a rustling of the bed.

'He's been gone long enough to get clear to the crossroads, or more,' Hatty said, calling through the window.

'Now you lay down and try to get a little sleep, Hatty,' Lonnie told her. 'I'll bring him back in no time.'

He could hear Nancy scratching fleas under the house, but he knew she was in no condition to help look for Mark. It would be several days before she recovered from the shock of losing her tail.

'He's been gone a long time,' Hatty said, unable to keep still.

'That don't make no difference,' Lonnie said. 'I'll find him sooner or later. Now you go on to sleep like I told you, Hatty.'

Lonnie walked towards the barn, listening for some sound. Over at the big house he could hear the hogs grunting and squealing, and he wished they would be quiet so he could hear other sounds. Arch Gunnard's dogs were howling occasionally, but they were not making any more noise than they usually did at night, and he was accustomed to their howling.

Lonnie went to the barn, looking inside and out. After walking around the barn, he went into the field as far as the cotton shed.

40

He knew it was useless, but he could not keep from calling his father time after time.

'Oh, Pa!' he said, trying to penetrate the darkness. He went farther into the field.

'Now, what in the world could have become of Pa?' he said, stopping and wondering where to look next.

After he had gone back to the front yard, he began to feel uneasy for the first time. Mark had not acted any more strangely during the past week than he ordinarily did, but Lonnie knew he was upset over the way Arch Gunnard was giving out short rations. Mark had even said that, at the rate they were being fed, all of them would starve to death inside another three months.

Lonnie left the yard and went down the road towards the Negro cabins. When he got to Clem's house, he turned in and walked up the path to the door. He knocked several times and waited. There was no answer, and he rapped louder.

'Who's that?' he heard Clem say from bed.

'It's me,' Lonnie said. 'I've got to see you a minute, Clem. I'm out in the front yard.'

He sat down and waited for Clem to dress and come outside. While he waited, he strained his ears to catch any sound that might be in the air. Over the fields towards the big house he could hear the fattening hogs grunt and squeal.

Clem came out and shut the door. He stood on the doorsill a moment speaking to his wife in bed, telling her he would be back and not to worry.

'Who's that?' Clem said, coming down into the yard.

Lonnie got up and met Clem halfway.

'What's the trouble?' Clem asked then, buttoning up his overall jumper.

'Pa's not in his bed,' Lonnie said, 'and Hatty says he's been gone from the house most all night. I went out in the field, and all around the barn, but I couldn't find a trace of him anywhere.'

Clem then finished buttoning his jumper and began rolling a cigarette. He walked slowly down the path to the road. It was still dark, and it would be at least an hour before dawn made it lighter.

41

'Maybe he was too hungry to stay in the bed any longer,' Clem said. 'When I saw him yesterday, he said he was so shrunk up and weak he didn't know if he could last much longer. He looked like his skin and bones couldn't shrivel much more.'

'I asked Arch last night after supper time for some rations — just a little piece of sowbelly and some molasses. He said he'd get around to letting me have some the first thing this morning.'

'Why don't you tell him to give you full rations or none?' Clem said. 'If you knew you wasn't going to get none at all, you could move away and find a better man to share-crop for, couldn't you?'

'I've been loyal to Arch Gunnard for a long time now,' Lonnie said. 'I'd hate to haul off and leave him like that.'

Clem looked at Lonnie, but he did not say anything more just then. They turned up the road towards the driveway that led up to the big house. The fattening hogs were still grunting and squealing in the pen, and one of Arch's hounds came down a cotton row beside the driveway to smell their shoes.

'Them fattening hogs always get enough to eat,' Clem said. 'There's not a one of them that don't weigh seven hundred pounds right now, and they're getting bigger every day. Besides taking all that's thrown to them, they make a lot of meals off the chickens that get in there to peck around.'

Lonnie listened to the grunting of the hogs as they walked up the driveway towards the big house.

'Reckon we'd better get Arch up to help look for Pa?' Lonnie said. 'I'd hate to wake him up, but I'm scared Pa might stray off into the swamp and get lost for good. He couldn't hear it thunder, even. I never could find him back there in all that tangle if he got into it.'

Clem said something under his breath and went on towards the barn and hog pen. He reached the pen before Lonnie got there.

'You'd better come here quick,' Clem said, turning around to see where Lonnie was.

Lonnie ran to the hog pen. He stopped and climbed halfway up the wooden-and-wire sides of the fence. At first he could see nothing, but gradually he was able to see the moving mass of black

42

fattening hogs on the other side of the pen. They were biting and snarling at each other like a pack of hungry hounds turned loose on a dead rabbit.

Lonnie scrambled to the top of the fence, but Clem caught him and pulled him back.

'Don't go in that hog pen that way,' he said. 'Them hogs will tear you to pieces, they're that wild. They're fighting over something.'

Both of them ran around the corner of the pen and got to the side where the hogs were. Down under their feet on the ground Lonnie caught a glimpse of a dark mass splotched with white. He was able to see it for a moment only, because one of the hogs trampled over it.

Clem opened and closed his mouth several times before he was able to say anything at all. He clutched at Lonnie's arm, shaking him.

'That looks like it might be your pa,' he said. 'I swear before goodness, Lonnie, it does look like it.'

Lonnie still could not believe it. He climbed to the top of the fence and began kicking his feet at the hogs, trying to drive them away. They paid no attention to him.

While Lonnie was perched there, Clem had gone to the wagon shed, and he ran back with two singletrees he had somehow managed to find there in the dark. He handed one to Lonnie, poking it at him until Lonnie's attention was drawn from the hogs long enough to take it.

Clem leaped over the fence and began swinging the singletree at the hogs. Lonnie slid down beside him, yelling at them. One hog turned on Lonnie and snapped at him, and Clem struck it over the back of the neck with enough force to drive it off momentarily.

By then Lonnie was able to realize what had happened. He ran to the mass of hogs, kicking them with his heavy stiff shoes and striking them on their heads with the iron-tipped singletree. Once he felt a stinging sensation, and looked down to see one of the hogs biting the calf of his leg. He had just enough time to hit the hog and drive it away before his leg was torn. He knew most of his overall leg had been ripped away, because he could feel the night air on his bare wet calf.

43

Clem had gone ahead and had driven the hogs back. There was no other way to do anything. They were in a snarling circle around them, and both of them had to keep the singletrees swinging back and forth all the time to keep the hogs off. Finally Lonnie reached down and got a grip on Mark's leg. With Clem helping, Lonnie carried his father to the fence and lifted him over to the other side.

They were too much out of breath for a while to say anything, or to do anything else. The snarling, fattening hogs were at the fence, biting the wood and wire, and making more noise than ever.

While Lonnie was searching in his pockets for a match, Clem struck one. He held the flame close to Mark Newsome's head.

They both stared unbelieving, and then Clem blew out the match. There was nothing said as they stared at each other in the darkness.

Clem walked several steps away, and turned and came back beside Lonnie.

'It's him, though,' Clem said, sitting down on the ground. 'It's him, all right.'

'I reckon so,' Lonnie said. He could think of nothing else to say then.

They sat on the ground, one on each side of Mark, looking at the body. There had been no sign of life in the body beside them since they had first touched it. The face, throat, and stomach had been completely devoured.

'You'd better go wake up Arch Gunnard,' Clem said after a while.

'What for?' Lonnie said. 'He can't help none now. It's too late for help.'

'Makes no difference,' Clem insisted. 'You'd better go wake him up and let him see what there is to see. If you wait till morning, he might take it into his head to say the hogs didn't do it. Right now is the time to get him up so he can see what his hogs did.'

Clem turned around and looked at the big house. The dark outline against the dark sky made him hesitate.

'A man who short-rations tenants ought to have to sit and look at that till it's buried.'

Lonnie looked at Clem fearfully. He knew Clem was right, but

44

he was scared to hear a Negro say anything like that about a white man.

'You oughtn't talk like that about Arch,' Lonnie said. 'He's in bed asleep. He didn't have a thing to do with it. He didn't have no more to do with it than I did.'

Clem laughed a little, and threw the singletree on the ground between his feet. After letting it lie there a little while, he picked it up and began beating the ground with it.

Lonnie got to his feet slowly. He had never seen Clem act like that before, and he did not know what to think about it. He left without saying anything and walked stiffly to the house in the darkness to wake up Arch Gunnard.

III

Arch was hard to wake up. And even after he was awake, he was in no hurry to get up. Lonnie was standing outside the bedroom window, and Arch was lying in bed six or eight feet away. Lonnie could hear him toss and grumble.

'Who told you to come and wake me up in the middle of the night?' Arch said.

'Well, Clem Henry's out here, and he said maybe you'd like to know about it.'

Arch tossed around on the bed, flailing the pillow with his fists.

'You tell Clem Henry I said that one of these days he's going to find himself turned inside out, like a coat-sleeve.'

Lonnie waited doggedly. He knew Clem was right in insisting that Arch ought to wake up and come out there to see what had happened. Lonnie was afraid to go back to the barnyard and tell Clem that Arch was not coming. He did not know, but he had a feeling that Clem might go into the bedroom and drag Arch out of bed. He did not like to think of anything like that taking place.

'Are you still out there, Lonnie?' Arch shouted.

'I'm right here, Mr. Arch. I ——'

'If I wasn't so sleepy, I'd come out there and take a stick and — I don't know what I wouldn't do!'

Lonnie met Arch at the back step. On the way out to the hog

45

pen Arch did not speak to him. Arch walked heavily ahead, not even waiting to see if Lonnie was coming. The lantern that Arch was carrying cast long flat beams of yellow light over the ground; and when they got to where Clem was waiting beside Mark's body, the Negro's face shone in the night like a highly polished plowshare.

'What was Mark doing in my hog pen at night, anyway?' Arch said, shouting at them both.

Neither Clem nor Lonnie replied. Arch glared at them for not answering. But no matter how many times he looked at them, his eyes returned each time to stare at the torn body of Mark Newsome on the ground at his feet.

'There's nothing to be done now,' Arch said finally. 'We'll just have to wait till daylight and send for the undertaker.' He walked a few steps away. 'Looks like you could have waited till morning in the first place. There wasn't no sense in getting me up.'

He turned his back and looked sideways at Clem. Clem stood up and looked him straight in the eyes.

'What do you want, Clem Henry?' he said. 'Who told you to be coming around my house in the middle of the night? I don't want niggers coming here except when I send for them.'

'I couldn't stand to see anybody eaten up by the hogs, and not do anything about it,' Clem said.

'You mind your own business,' Arch told him. 'And when you talk to me, take off your hat, or you'll be sorry for it. It wouldn't take much to make me do you up the way you belong.'

Lonnie backed away. There was a feeling of uneasiness around them. That was how trouble between Clem and Arch always began. He had seen it start that way dozens of times before. As long as Clem turned and went away, nothing happened, but sometimes he stayed right where he was and talked up to Arch just as if he had been a white man, too.

Lonnie hoped it would not happen this time. Arch was already mad enough about being waked up in the middle of the night, and Lonnie knew there was no limit to what Arch would do when he got good and mad at a Negro. Nobody had ever seen him kill a Negro, but he had said he had, and he told people that he was not scared to do it again.

46

'I reckon you know how he came to get eaten up by the hogs like that,' Clem said, looking straight at Arch.

Arch whirled around.

'Are you talking to me . . . ?'

'I asked you that,' Clem stated.

'God damn you, yellow-blooded . . .' Arch yelled.

He swung the lantern at Clem's head. Clem dodged, but the bottom of it hit his shoulder, and it was smashed to pieces. The oil splattered on the ground, igniting in the air from the flaming wick. Clem was lucky not to have it splash on his face and overalls.

'Now, look here . . .' Clem said.

'You yellow-blooded nigger,' Arch said, rushing at him. 'I'll teach you to talk back to me. You've got too big for your place for the last time. I've been taking too much from you, but I ain't doing it no more.'

'Mr. Arch, I . . .' Lonnie said stepping forward partly between them. No one heard him.

Arch stood back and watched the kerosene flicker out on the ground.

'You know good and well why he got eaten up by the fattening hogs,' Clem said, standing his ground. 'He was so hungry he had to get up out of bed in the middle of the night and come up here in the dark trying to find something to eat. Maybe he was trying to find the smokehouse. It makes no difference, either way. He's been on short rations like everybody else working on your place, and he was so old he didn't know where else to look for food except in your smokehouse. You know good and well that's how he got lost up here in the dark and fell in the hog pen.'

The kerosene had died out completely. In the last faint flare, Arch had reached down and grabbed up the singletree that had been lying on the ground where Lonnie had dropped it.

Arch raised the singletree over his head and struck with all his might at Clem. Clem dodged, but Arch drew back again quickly and landed a blow on his arm just above the elbow before Clem could dodge it. Clem's arm dropped to his side, dangling lifelessly.

'You Goddamn yellow-blooded nigger!' Arch shouted. 'Now's your time, you black bastard. I've been waiting for the chance to

47

teach you your lesson. And this's going to be one you won't never forget.'

Clem felt the ground with his feet until he had located the other singletree. He stooped down and got it. Raising it, he did not try to hit Arch, but held it in front of him so he could ward off Arch's blows at his head. He continued to stand his ground, not giving Arch an inch.

'Drop that singletree,' Arch said.

'I won't stand here and let you beat me like that,' Clem protested.

'By God, that's all I want to hear,' Arch said, his mouth curling. 'Nigger, your time has come, by God!'

He swung once more at Clem, but Clem turned and ran towards the barn. Arch went after him a few steps and stopped. He threw aside the singletree and turned and ran back to the house.

Lonnie went to the fence and tried to think what was best for him to do. He knew he could not take sides with a Negro, in the open, even if Clem had helped him, and especially after Clem had talked to Arch in the way he wished he could himself. He was a white man, and to save his life he could not stand to think of turning against Arch, no matter what happened.

Presently a light burst through one of the windows of the house, and he heard Arch shouting at his wife to wake her up.

When he saw Arch's wife go to the telephone, Lonnie realized what was going to happen. She was calling up the neighbors and Arch's friends. They would not mind getting up in the night when they found out what was going to take place.

Out behind the barn he could hear Clem calling him. Leaving the yard, Lonnie felt his way out there in the dark.

'What's the trouble, Clem?' he said.

'I reckon my time has come,' Clem said. 'Arch Gunnard talks that way when he's good and mad. He talked just like he did that time he carried Jim Moffin off to the swamp — and Jim never came back.'

'Arch wouldn't do anything like that to you, Clem,' Lonnie said excitedly, but he knew better.

Clem said nothing.

'Maybe you'd better strike out for the swamps till he changes his mind and cools off some,' Lonnie said. 'You might be right, Clem.'

Lonnie could feel Clem's eyes burning into him.

'Wouldn't be no sense in that, if you'd help me,' Clem said. 'Wouldn't you stand by me?'

Lonnie trembled as the meaning of Clem's suggestion became clear to him. His back was to the side of the barn, and he leaned against it while sheets of black and white passed before his eyes.

'Wouldn't you stand by me?' Clem asked again.

'I don't know what Arch would say to that,' Lonnie told him haltingly.

Clem walked away several paces. He stood with his back to Lonnie while he looked across the field towards the quarter where his home was.

'I could go in that little patch of woods out there and stay till they get tired of looking for me,' Clem said, turning around to see Lonnie.

'You'd better go somewhere,' Lonnie said uneasily. 'I know Arch Gunnard. He's hard to handle when he makes up his mind to do something he wants to do. I couldn't stop him an inch. Maybe you'd better get clear out of the country, Clem.'

'I couldn't do that, and leave my family down there across the field,' Clem said.

'He's going to get you if you don't.'

'If you'd only sort of help me out a little, he wouldn't. I would only have to go and hide out in that little patch of woods over there awhile. Looks like you could do that for me, being as how I helped you find your pa when he was in the hog pen.'

Lonnie nodded, listening for sounds from the big house. He continued to nod at Clem while Clem was waiting to be assured.

'If you're going to stand up for me,' Clem said, 'I can just go over there in the woods and wait till they get it off their minds. You won't be telling them where I'm at, and you could say I struck out for the swamp. They wouldn't ever find me without bloodhounds.'

'That's right,' Lonnie said, listening for sounds of Arch's coming

49

out of the house. He did not wish to be found back there behind the barn where Arch could accuse him of talking to Clem.

The moment Lonnie replied, Clem turned and ran off into the night. Lonnie went after him a few steps, as if he had suddenly changed his mind about helping him, but Clem was lost in the darkness by then.

Lonnie waited for a few minutes, listening to Clem crashing through the underbrush in the patch of woods a quarter of a mile away. When he could hear Clem no longer, he went around the barn to meet Arch.

Arch came out of the house carrying his double-barreled shotgun and the lantern he had picked up in the house. His pockets were bulging with shells.

'Where is that damn nigger, Lonnie?' Arch asked him. 'Where'd he go to?'

Lonnie opened his mouth, but no words came out.

'You know which way he went, don't you?'

Lonnie again tried to say something, but there were no sounds. He jumped when he found himself nodding his head to Arch.

'Mr. Arch, I ——'

'That's all right, then,' Arch said. 'That's all I need to know now. Dudley Smith and Tom Hawkins and Frank and Dave Howard and the rest will be here in a minute, and you can stay right here so you can show us where he's hiding out.'

Frantically Lonnie tried to say something. Then he reached for Arch's sleeve to stop him, but Arch had gone.

Arch ran around the house to the front yard. Soon a car came racing down the road, its headlights lighting up the whole place, hog pen and all. Lonnie knew it was probably Dudley Smith, because his was the first house in that direction, only a half a mile away. While he was turning into the driveway, several other automobiles came into sight, both up the road and down it.

Lonnie trembled. He was afraid Arch was going to tell him to point out where Clem had gone to hide. Then he knew Arch would tell him. He had promised Clem he would not do that. But try as he might, he could not make himself believe that Arch Gunnard would do anything more than whip Clem.

50

Clem had not done anything that called for lynching. He had not raped a white woman, he had not shot at a white man; he had only talked back to Arch, with his hat on. But Arch was mad enough to do anything; he was mad enough at Clem not to stop at anything short of lynching.

The whole crowd of men was swarming around him before he realized it. And there was Arch clutching his arm and shouting into his face.

'Mr. Arch, I . . .'

Lonnie recognized every man in the feeble dawn. They were excited, and they looked like men on the last lap of an all-night fox-hunting party. Their shotguns and pistols were held at their waist, ready for the kill.

'What's the matter with you, Lonnie?' Arch said, shouting into his ear. 'Wake up and say where Clem Henry went to hide out. We're ready to go get him.'

Lonnie remembered looking up and seeing Frank Howard dropping yellow twelve-gauge shells into the breech of his gun. Frank bent forward so he could hear Lonnie tell Arch where Clem was hiding.

'You ain't going to kill Clem this time, are you, Mr. Arch?' Lonnie asked.

'Kill him?' Dudley Smith repeated. 'What do you reckon I've been waiting all this time for if it wasn't for a chance to get Clem. That nigger has had it coming to him ever since he came to this county. He's a bad nigger, and it's coming to him.'

'It wasn't exactly Clem's fault,' Lonnie said. 'If Pa hadn't come up here and fell in the hog pen, Clem wouldn't have had a thing to do with it. He was helping me, that's all.'

'Shut up, Lonnie,' somebody shouted at him. 'You're so excited you don't know what you're saying. You're taking up for a nigger when you talk like that.'

People were crowding around him so tightly he felt as if he were being squeezed to death. He had to get some air, get his breath, get out of the crowd.

'That's right,' Lonnie said.

He heard himself speak, but he did not know what he was saying.

51

'But Clem helped me find Pa when he got lost looking around for something to eat.'

'Shut up, Lonnie,' somebody said again. 'You damn fool, shut up!'

Arch grabbed his shoulder and shook him until his teeth rattled. Then Lonnie realized what he had been saying.

'Now, look here, Lonnie,' Arch shouted. 'You must be out of your head, because you know good and well you wouldn't talk like a nigger-lover in your right mind.'

'That's right,' Lonnie said, trembling all over. 'I sure wouldn't want to talk like that.'

He could still feel the grip on his shoulder where Arch's strong fingers had hurt him.

'Did Clem go to the swamp, Lonnie?' Dudley Smith said. 'Is that right, Lonnie?'

Lonnie tried to shake his head; he tried to nod his head. Then Arch's fingers squeezed his thin neck. Lonnie looked at the men wild-eyed.

'Where's Clem hiding, Lonnie?' Arch demanded, squeezing.

Lonnie went three or four steps towards the barn. When he stopped, the men behind him pushed forward again. He found himself being rushed behind the barn and beyond it.

'All right, Lonnie,' Arch said. 'Now which way?'

Lonnie pointed towards the patch of woods where the creek was. The swamp was in the other direction.

'He said he was going to hide out in that little patch of woods along the creek over there, Mr. Arch,' Lonnie said. 'I reckon he's over there now.'

Lonnie felt himself being swept forward, and he stumbled over the rough ground trying to keep from being knocked down and trampled upon. Nobody was talking, and everyone seemed to be walking on tiptoes. The gray light of early dawn was increasing enough both to hide them and to show the way ahead.

Just before they reached the fringe of the woods, the men separated, and Lonnie found himself a part of the circle that was closing in on Clem.

Lonnie was alone, and there was nobody to stop him, but he

was unable to move forward or backward. It began to be clear to him what he had done.

Clem was probably up a tree somewhere in the woods ahead, but by that time he had been surrounded on all sides. If he should attempt to break and run, he would be shot down like a rabbit.

Lonnie sat down on a log and tried to think what to do. The sun would be up in a few more minutes, and as soon as it came up, the men would close in on the creek and Clem. He would have no chance at all among all those shotguns and pistols.

Once or twice he saw the flare of a match through the underbrush where some of the men were lying in wait. A whiff of cigarette smoke struck his nostrils, and he found himself wondering if Clem could smell it wherever he was in the woods.

There was still no sound anywhere around him, and he knew that Arch Gunnard and the rest of the men were waiting for the sun, which would in a few minutes come up behind him in the east.

It was light enough by that time to see plainly the rough ground and the tangled underbrush and the curling bark on the pine trees.

The men had already begun to creep forward, guns raised as if stalking a deer. The woods were not large, and the circle of men would be able to cover it in a few minutes at the rate they were going forward. There was still a chance that Clem had slipped through the circle before dawn broke, but Lonnie felt that he was still there. He began to feel then that Clem was there because he himself had placed him there for the men to find more easily.

Lonnie found himself moving forward, drawn into the narrowing circle. Presently he could see the men all around him in dim outline. Their eyes were searching the heavy green pine tops as they went forward from tree to tree.

'Oh, Pa!' he said in a hoarse whisper. 'Oh, Pa!'

He went forward a few steps, looking into the bushes and up into the tree-tops. When he saw the other men again, he realized that it was not Mark Newsome being sought. He did not know what had made him forget like that.

The creeping forward began to work into the movement of Lonnie's body. He found himself springing forward on his toes, and his body was leaning in that direction. It was like creeping up on a rabbit when you did not have a gun to hunt with.

He forgot again what he was doing there. The springing motion in his legs seemed to be growing stronger with each step. He bent forward so far he could almost touch the ground with his fingertips. He could not stop now. He was keeping up with the circle of men.

The fifteen men were drawing closer and closer together. The dawn had broken enough to show the time on the face of a watch. The sun was beginning to color the sky above.

Lonnie was far in advance of anyone else by then. He could not hold himself back. The strength in his legs was more than he could hold in check.

He had for so long been unable to buy shells for his gun that he had forgotten how much he liked to hunt.

The sound of the men's steady creeping had become a rhythm in his ears.

'Here's the bastard!' somebody shouted, and there was a concerted crashing through the dry underbrush. Lonny dashed forward, reaching the tree almost as quickly as anyone else.

He could see everybody with guns raised, and far into the sky above the sharply outlined face of Clem Henry gleamed in the rising sun. His body was hugging the slender top of the pine.

Lonnie did not know who was the first to fire, but the rest of the men did not hesitate. There was a deafening roar as the shotguns and revolvers flared and smoked around the trunk of the tree.

He closed his eyes; he was afraid to look again at the face above. The firing continued without break. Clem hugged the tree with all his might, and then, with the far-away sound of splintering wood, the top of the tree and Clem came crashing through the lower limbs to the ground. The body, sprawling and torn, landed on the ground with a thud that stopped Lonnie's heart for a moment.

He turned, clutching for the support of a tree, as the firing began once more. The crumpled body was tossed time after time, like a sackful of kittens being killed with an automatic shotgun, as charges of lead were fired into it from all sides. A cloud of dust rose from the ground and drifted overhead with the choking odor of burned powder.

Lonnie did not remember how long the shooting lasted. He found himself running from tree to tree, clutching at the rough pine bark, stumbling wildly towards the cleared ground. The sky had turned from gray to red when he emerged in the open, and as he ran, falling over the hard clods in the plowed field, he tried to keep his eyes on the house ahead.

Once he fell and found it almost impossible to rise again to his feet. He struggled to his knees, facing the round red sun. The warmth gave him the strength to rise to his feet, and he muttered unintelligibly to himself. He tried to say things he had never thought to say before.

When he got home, Hatty was waiting for him in the yard. She had heard the shots in the woods, and she had seen him stumbling over the hard clods in the field, and she had seen him kneeling there looking straight into the face of the sun. Hatty was trembling as she ran to Lonnie to find out what the matter was.

Once in his own yard, Lonnie turned and looked for a second over his shoulder. He saw the men climbing over the fence at Arch Gunnard's. Arch's wife was standing on the back porch, and she was speaking to them.

'Where's your pa, Lonnie?' Hatty said. 'And what in the world was all that shooting in the woods for?'

Lonnie stumbled forward until he had reached the front porch. He fell upon the steps.

'Lonnie, Lonnie!' Hatty was saying. 'Wake up and tell me what in the world is the matter. I've never seen the like of all that's going on.'

'Nothing,' Lonnie said. 'Nothing.'

'Well, if there's nothing the matter, can't you go up to the big house and ask for a little piece of streak-of-lean? We ain't got a thing to cook for breakfast. Your pa's going to be hungrier than ever after being up walking around all night.'

'What?' Lonnie said, his voice rising to a shout as he jumped to his feet.

'Why, I only said go up to the big house and get a little piece of streak-of-lean, Lonnie. That's all I said.'

He grabbed his wife about the shoulders.

55

'Meat?' he yelled, shaking her roughly.

'Yes,' she said, pulling away from him in surprise. 'Couldn't you go ask Arch Gunnard for a little bit of streak-of-lean?'

Lonnie slumped down again on the steps, his hands falling between his outspread legs and his chin falling on his chest.

'No,' he said almost inaudibly. 'No. I ain't hungry.'

SHADOWS ON TERREBONNE

STARK YOUNG

THE road from the highway to the Raymond house winds for two miles through cotton fields, sometimes with hedges alongside of Cherokee roses and honeysuckle; then comes the peach orchard, then at last the carriage-gate, of brick and iron, standing amid tall grass and palmettos that block the way. You drive nowadays through a side entrance near the old stable lot. To the right lies a pond, with willows, where once the swans floated above their white shadows but now only the frogs would be, no more swans these days and no more peach brandy. And then suddenly, after an avenue of water oaks, you make a turn and come on the house.

It is a rambling old house, though the front is rather correct and unexpected, with a small portico and white columns. The long central hall begins with glass and ends with glass. If you look from the front through the back door, you see, shimmering and far away, the dark mass of azalea bushes. In the hall and scattered through the rooms is the furniture that Joseph Carrière Raymond brought over from France when he built the house. There are books, pictures, damasks, and vases, and a bust of Napoleon, who was then the rage; you get the impression that this Joseph Raymond on his wedding trip was an extravagant young man. The ceilings are high, with stucco ornaments, the walls all white.

But the interior of the house is soon forgotten, once you pass through the hall door at the back and on to the terrace outside. Everything suddenly becomes quieter, the eye and the ear wait and listen. The birds that flutter in the garden hedges are fewer here; for instead of bushes and boughs, there is a stone terrace spreading out sixty or seventy feet. Old ivy beds, loose and vague as shades themselves, border this terrace, and from it spreads a greensward that slopes towards the water. The level bayou flows

57

past, and from it comes the name of the house, Shadows on Terrebonne.

They said that Joseph Raymond built his house here rather than at his other places, Mantua Plantation, Silence Plantation, and Picayune Plantation, which his father had left him, because of the soft water flowing in Terrebonne Bayou. Joseph liked to see water keep its place, his sister, Mrs. Percy, said; by which her sharp tongue meant that brandy was highly esteemed by her brother. Wild fowl came, and the long moss hung down from the trees along the stream's edge. It was a bayou large enough for the smaller steamboats to travel up and down, stopping at the various plantations, each with its landing. The truth was a single steamboat, the *Lorient*, coming and going once a week, served their needs well enough. Slowly the bosom of the stream spread its ripples here and there where a reed or a bed of water-hyacinths stood up through the surface. Or now and then a small snake or water-bug streaked the smooth stretch of it, or a bird's wing, tipped slantwise, grazed the clear water. It was all like time itself, the shadows, the wings, the passing ripples, against the steady, still stream.

At one end of the garden, against this stillness and the stream with its reflections under the open sky, two columns stand. They are white marble with leafy capitals, in the Corinthian manner, more or less, but more extravagant in their design. They rise from a kind of terrace, or rather flight of steps; for there are three marble steps descending toward the bayou.

One end breaks off abruptly as if there had been more columns to be added. In places time and the rain through the moss in the branches above have stained the marble to a pale rose color. The columns are ten feet high perhaps; the years have softened both their fluted lines and the rich leafage of the capitals.

Joseph Raymond married Julie Thérèse Deslonde, one of a New Orleans family known for the beauty of both its men and women. To them at Shadows on Terrebonne were born a son and a daughter, Alfred Deslonde and Hélène. Alfred was seven years older than his sister. He was a proud, noble little boy, with a smile so sweet and eyes so straight and clear that everyone loved him. His Aunt Percy, coming down from Parish Assumption to visit at The

Shadows and seeing this engaging manner and how easily it won everybody's favor and indulgence, thought that discipline would be wise, lest the boy be spoiled. 'Don't let any child grow up thinkin' the world belongs to him,' she said.

'Eh?' said his mother, thinking of the time she bent over to kiss him good night, lying in his small bed, and he said, 'I thought I heard a roseleaf popping.' It was only a game you played in the garden — you doubled up a rose petal and popped it against your lips — but how sweetly and gracefully whispered!

'Eh?' his mother said, politely, of course, but as if Aunt Percy could just answer that or stew in her own juice.

'I said my say.'

'When I see signs that Alfred is spoiled, then will be time enough. But have you ever seen a more generous child? Now tell me. Or eyes more eager? Why should I try to break his little will?'

'I reckon there's something in that.'

'It's true he hates to be stopped, but he brings the drawing to you as soon as it's completed; he'd give you his head.'

'I'm thinking of what life may do to Alfred some day. And I'm no fool, either.'

'He's the soul of honor, an honorable boy if one ever was, a lie's not in him. My father used to say that that was about all you have, honor was about all you can confront life with. Father had an old sword of his father's with an inscription in Spanish that said, Do not draw me without reason, do not·sheathe me without honor. So you see.'

'I remember how that plagued sword rattled in the scabbard,' said the old lady, screwing up her eyes.

When Alfred was eleven they engaged a gentleman from Boston for his tutor. Long as he was with the family, there remained some mystery about this man; they gradually learned that he had been at one time an actor but before that, when he had money, he had been a great traveller. He never gave any distinct account of himself. He was a good Latin scholar and knew Greek and French, in which language he sang many songs as well as in English and recited poetry with exquisite power. When he declaimed such lines as 'The mountains look on Marathon, and Marathon looks on the sea,' he would be so filled with it that he rose from his seat and held out his arms as if rapt. He slept in the same room with his pupil, so that the process of education was continually going on.

Then Monsieur Dumaine came for a while to stay at The Shadows, giving lessons in drawing to the two children, and to the children on the neighboring plantations, because Monsieur Dumaine wanted to earn money to go and study with David in Paris. Already Alfred, in place of study, had drawn pictures up and down the margins of his books, so that he became at once the artist's star pupil. This was not, of course, with the idea of becoming a painter, just say that and Alfred's father would have stopped the lessons! It was merely a way of acquiring an agreeable accomplishment — that was how they put it. A few years later found this boy at The Shadows growing into a youth very handsome, very much admired by his friends. His impetuous, high nature was eased and made charming by his sweet temper and natural talents. He was generous, he was given to trusting everyone, partly because of his bringing up. 'My father used to say,' Joseph Raymond said to him, 'never suspect people. It's better to be deceived or mistaken, which is only human after all, than to be suspicious, which is common, like trash.'

So the years went on, and the garden at The Shadows, which Joseph had planted at the time of his marriage, filled up with green and flowering plants. The quiet there seemed quieter for those rich green walls. The tall bamboo and the long moss threw farther shadows than even the name of the place implied, over the smooth bayou. The herons and other wild fowl came in their season; and when the day dawned for it, flew away, nobody knew where. Even the plantation bells that called the field hands to and from work seemed to have grown mellow. The boy heard them softly along toward sundown; he would stand sometimes and hear the bell fading away among the rustling leaves.

In the spring of 1816 his sister Hélène, at fifteen, became engaged to a young man in Parish Avoyelles. And in that same season, Alfred, who was twenty-two, taking along with him a great deal more money than he could spend, made the voyage to France. The Deslondes, his mother's people, had a cousin there, an old marquis, who had written Latin verses and knew all the scholars in Paris. There was also in Paris a lady. Aunt Percy's husband's sister, whom the royal family favored because once the exiled Bourbon princes, travelling in Louisiana, had been guests of her father's. One of them, the Duc d'Orléans, was to become a long time afterward the king of France. At any rate, Alfred would know these cousins and would also see the world. He had spoken French from his infancy.

From Paris Alfred wrote letters home, about the concerts, the French nation and Europe, how kind people were to him, how he went to balls, evening parties, *fêtes champêtres*. In May a letter came that said he was going off on some Mediterranean ship. He would visit Greece and perhaps go farther, at least the Ægean Islands. In June, from Greece, he wrote that he had taken up his drawing again, he had made a sketch of the Corinth temples. Then he wrote that he was going to travel across some territory east of the Mediterranean; he would write more of this shortly. But the letters broke off, it was three months at The Shadows, far into the summer, in fact, they had heard nothing.

That was one of the yellow fever years, and when Alfred's packet of letters was brought to him at Marseilles, on his return to France, there was added to the pile Father Barbier's letter telling him of the death of his father and mother. The letter said that such calamities were not unique among stricken families, that it was God's will, and that the sooner Alfred returned the better. Picayune Plantation, which was the farthest distant as well as the largest had gone to Hélène, whose husband would take charge of it; but there were The Shadows, Silence, and Mantua to be managed.

Alfred came home that autumn burnt from the sun, handsomer than ever, bringing with him his Paris clothes and gifts that he had bought before his news reached him. He also brought a portfolio of drawings. Three of four of his kin who lived nearest had come to The Shadows and waited, so that they might be with Alfred when he first arrived. Of that homecoming to the family that loved him, of the romance of his travels and the glamor of his adventure and the surprise of it, which he had meant to tell them all, his mother especially, what was there to say? where was it gone? All through the empty parlors and the long hall the candles were lighted, and through the open doors at the back the soft wind from across the bayou brought in the garden fragrance; but there seemed nothing. In the midst of supper Father Barbier arrived.

It was a strange scene in the parlor an hour later that night, with the young master of the plantation come home from abroad, his guests out of the kindness of their hearts entreating him to tell of his journey, and the portfolio of his drawings lying open on the table. The light of the tall candelabra fell on the sheets of paper as Alfred turned over one drawing after another. In a wide, unbroken desert, columns rose, a whole line of them, their flutings intact, the great leaves and garlands of their capitals still preserved. Or on another sheet were drawn the arches of an aqueduct going off into the distance, high arches, solitary, strong. Or here there was a single column on a great base, the capital gone and the shaft broken at the top and, in the ground beneath, long blocks of the entablature with its riotous ornament, under the black shadows of an Asiatic sun. In one of the drawings there was a whole temple shown, or at least a side of it; beyond the columns the wall of the shrine was still standing. It was drawn as if it were in moonlight, the sky pale and vague with a few stars, the earth lying rapt, but the temple shining out from its shadows, all as if there had been no years, no ruin, no ancient oblivion.

And so one by one the drawings appeared and seemed to make an agreeable entertainment for everyone. There were gasps of admiration, faint cries, polite questions. Father Barbier took the ruins for Greek and spoke of the glory that was Greece.

Certainly if these ancient monuments were Greek, Alfred had drawn them very badly; but he did not correct the gentle old priest who meant so well. Instead he began to explain to Father Barbier and his other guests that the drawings were not imaginary views, as they seemed to take them. They must not mistake these drawings for sheer embroideries or classical models.

Doubtless all men want to travel, Alfred said, and to have various seas and far roads bring them home again — *diverse maria et viae reportant,* as his old tutor had taught him from Catullus. Perhaps, also, his old tutor had filled him with the idea of Greece. However that was, he had gone there as a mere traveller along with travellers. And then one night in Athens he walked out past the city and down to the Piraeus harbor.

There was a café — a sort of arbor — by the waterside, where he sat down. It happened that beside him sat an Arab gentleman and, as people do, they fell to talking. In the course of it the Arab told Alfred of cities and temples in his country, across desert stretches or on the plains. Though they cared little about them, all his people knew of these things. But, so far as he had heard, nobody in Europe had ever reported them.

The Arab gentleman had a ring with a cornelian in it, scratched with Roman letters which his brother had picked up in a temple porch; he kept turning the ring on his finger. Next day Alfred sailed on the Levantine ship, arrived at the eastern end of the Mediterranean and journeying inland with his new acquaintance to the latter's town, hired escorts, dragomen with nothing to do otherwise, and set out, now along with some caravan, now along with his own party.

Everybody in the parlor listened to what Alfred said about the desert sands, the nights, the caravans, the sudden view of some ruined ancient city or temple columns; but they did not reopen the portfolio. It was clear that the drawings meant no more to them than chromos; in an upstairs hall at The Shadows was there not the Lions of Luxor? His cousins' faces were full of goodness and affection. It never occurred to Alfred, at the time, that there could be anything prophetic in the way his kin and friends took his drawings.

It was during that winter that Alfred set up the two columns at the garden end, by the water. From the stone platform, graded into steps, a row of columns was to rise. Through them the green vistas would be seen, the sheen of gardenia and camellia and oleander leaves, and Bayou Terrebonne. There was a young Italian in Thibodaux who knew how to work in marble and stone.

Sometimes in the evening Alfred would take out the drawings and divert himself by adding a few touches or making corrections in line and shading. As he looked at the drawings, there would

63

come suddenly back the memory of his enthusiasm. He would see again the stone, the marbles, their antique beauty, in a forgotten land, under the vast skies. A breathless night, a great boon, the sky fretted with stars, and the solitary marbles standing.

He would sail for France, when the plantation's affairs were settled, by the end of April!

In those days you had to depend for your knowledge of distant lands on the reports of travellers. All you could know was what some traveller said or had drawn or painted. The rest could be only rumor. And thus his drawings would show people in the great world of learning and art things they had never seen, never even heard of.

The upshot of Paris was that Alfred took the drawings to his cousin, the old marquis, with the nose that was yellow from snuff, who sent him to the famous De Vaux in the Palais Royal, who, scenting a rich colonial, charged double, but in the end turned out plates that hit the drawings to a T. He was four months at it. The plates were bound into portfolios and Alfred sent them to the scholars recommended by his cousin and to some of the great ladies who had salons. A copy went, on the recommendations of Miss Percy, to the Duchess d'Angoulême, sister of the lost Dauphin and daughter of Louis XVI and Marie Antoinette. Thus, before many weeks, the drawings were seen by the best people, both in the learned circles and in society. What happened was that everybody saw the drawings of the temples, strange walls and columns, but nobody believed these things existed.

Monsieur the marquis had executed another affair beside De Vaux's engraving the plates, he had planned a marriage for his young cousin. As representative, so to speak, of the Louisiana branch of the family, he proposed to his old friend, the Vicomte Fernay (Victor Ernest Antoine Fernay), a great classical scholar but far from wealthy, an alliance between his rich young cousin and the vicomte's daughter, Artémise, about whom many people took sides, as to whether she had more beauty than brains or more brains than beauty. To a young man brought up on classical poetry the name itself was enough to go to one's head.

With romance the marquis' counsels proved even more successful than with engraving. His young cousin fell deeply in love with the girl and she with him. The two young people, properly chaperoned, spent many hours together during those four months while De Vaux chose to work on the engravings.

The vicomte, despite the entreaties of the more practical man (a good marriage in cold fact not being an everyday matter), turned out to be one of the worst critics of the drawings.

'In the first place,' the vicomte said to Alfred, 'if you saw these things you must have drawn them badly. Roman architecture is not so coarse, not those crude, bold carvings, cut so deep, not that heavy style.'

'With all due respect,' said the young man, 'I drew them as they are.'

'An affront to classic tradition,' the vicomte said. It was clear to Alfred that he had talked the whole thing over with other scholars.

'But, sir, these things are what I saw.'

'If they look as you depict them, these remains are degenerate architecture, that's all,' said the vicomte, the veins swelling on his forehead.

'I've never said they were important. Though, if you saw them as I did — how beautiful! All I say is that nobody has described them to us before.'

'Not important, certainly. But remarkably complete as you draw them. To survive thus extensively, one naturally asks what proof is there?'

'Proof, sir?' said Alfred, red in the face.

'It is generally known that the Roman Empire flourished in these countries you appear to have seen. And the ancient world, it seems — I know it only by report — is likely to be dotted with fallen shafts and broken marbles. But if there existed ruins so extensive as these you show, we'd know of them.'

'Tut, tut,' cried the little marquis, who had just come in and whose hand Artémise had hastened to take. 'All this over a cracked architrave! Let me remind you what Epictetus said, the grammarians, he said, who would set the very letters of the alphabet quarrelling together. And why should not a young man dream?

65

Lord Byron wandered over classic lands, giving us their romance; but, of course, Byron couldn't draw. Why should not a young man, rapturous in the deserted ancient landscape, dream of Paris fame?'

'Nonsense!' Alfred shouted, losing control of himself. 'Doubtless they too say the same, the noble ladies, the princess ——' But seeing the distress on his cousin's vague old face, he stopped abruptly. 'I bid you all good day.' As he walked to the door he caught sight of Artémise, saw her eyes. The vicomte did not even glance at him.

Next day he received a formal note from Artémise's father breaking off the engagement. He wrote her every day for five days, and then the five notes were returned by the vicomte's servant. They were unopened.

'You will not see Artémise again,' said the marquis; 'this is Europe.'

So Paris would not believe his drawings! Alfred said to himself. They were too stupid, or too narrow, or too doubting in men's honor to give him even the benefit of the doubt. He made farewell visits to his cousins, the marquis and Miss Percy, and without adieus to anyone else, he boarded the *Liberté* at Boulogne and sailed for home. He had been absent almost a year.

Bad news, they say, travels fast. Word had already gone round New Orleans, at the parties and balls and among the gentlemen who met at the gambling-houses in Royal Street, or at the fencing academies in Exchange Alley, that Joseph Raymond and Thérèse Deslonde's son, Alfred, had published his classical drawings only to be smiled at by the Parisian scholars, who refused to believe the tale he told. A few older men like the bishop, the Chevalier Le Moyne, the tutor, Mr. Edmonds, from Yale, or Mr. Henry Perrault, the bookseller, who were academically minded and wanted the logic of fact upheld, talked gravely to people about the matter. They too said that if any such classic remains existed, the scholars in Paris would have known it.

Otherwise, but for the brief gossip — this classical matter, and the vicomte's breaking off his daughter's engagement — nobody cared two straws, only Alfred himself. He had too much character to take on a profession of melancholy, too much pride to pity himself, and too much taste to go on with the argument for which no proof was likely. But he was hurt at the centre somewhere. They had broken something that sprang from a generous and honorable nature. In the cabinet room at The Shadows hung portraits of his father and mother. He had some of his drawings framed and hung in this room.

Years passed, and middle age came on Alfred Raymond. He was in his late fifties when his sister died and left to him her daughter Ellen — Nellie. The child was Hélène's youngest, born to her after forty; her other children had died, killed, so their cousin Thankful Percy said, by the nurses while Hélène was waltzing at Mardi Gras.

Ellen's father had been a man of fashion in his time and had gambled away most of his possessions. And his widow had not done very much to better what estate was left her, a part of which, Picayune Plantation, had long since gone to pay the mortgages; she liked a fine carriage-horse and she collected laces. So that, in the end, Ellen turned out to be by no means an heiress. The horses were sold, of course; the laces were in a box along with the velvet case of a parure of diamonds that would serve very well some day at a wedding, an event inevitable.

The little girl of ten came to live at Shadows on Terrebonne, bringing there her black mammy, Cydalise, whom her mother had willed to her along with the laces. She was given the chamber with the dressing-room, over the parlor, and here she and her mammy lived, and Ellen slept in the Empire bed whose rosewood frame would have held a dozen of her, lengthwise and crosswise. In fact, old Cydalise used to put two or three of the little cousins in with Ellen sometimes, when they came visiting; to watch over them all in one bed was easier.

Alfred saw the bed one night with three in it. 'Might as well get in yourself, Mammy,' he said, smiling at the old woman.

'Nah, suh, I ain' go be sleepin' wid no wildcats.'

'Considering how many beds there are in this house, the blue room, and Father's room, the room Aunt Percy always has ——'

'Marse Alfred, I ain' lak de Bible proverb says. I puts all my eggs in one basket.'

'Mammy puts all her eggs in one basket,' Ellen cried, laughing and whirling over between the sheets.

'*Oui, mam'selle*, and you ain' washed the face. When your cher papa was a lil' boy at Grosse Tête he washed the face every night. I don' mean no cat lickin' either. I mean scrub.'

'Cher papa!' Ellen cried. 'But, Tante Cydalise, in the morning. Please!'

'Very well, for this once.'

Sometimes after supper, when the weather was mild, Ellen walked up and down on the terrace with her uncle. When he talked to her of those youthful scenes that he had known, the ancient walls, the sculptured images, the marble columns, they were tinged, it seemed to him, with the light that rose in Terrebonne from the moon and the dreaming clouds and water. Sometimes he thought it was her listening that made this so.

'Are they as tall as the columns in the garden, uncle?' said the little voice.

'Yes, Nellie.'

Meantime, if her uncle had been troubled as to whether or no Ellen would inherit the Deslonde beauty, a few years more served only to show how uselessly he had worried. The brown eyes were open and soft, luminous like a deer's, shadowed with passionate emphasis, strong with some loyalty of feeling, but shy and waiting.

By the time Ellen was seventeen it was clear that plenty of young men from the plantations around would have come oftener to The Shadows if she had so much as dropped a handkerchief. So far that seemed unlikely enough. Then in June, when her cousins came out to their plantation in Iberia, not far away from Terrebonne Parish, Ellen met a young man visiting there and fell in love. His name was Stewart Robard, and he lived at Randolph Gate in Parish Vermilion. His mother had been to school with her mother, and so it was the kind of love affair that pleased everyone. This young man, whose eyes were so gay, who sat his horse so well, who could shoot glass balls thrown in the air when there was a riding tournament, who was so often hunting in the pine woods or fishing in the Blanche Côte bays, would have come every day to The Shadows if he had lived near enough and if Ellen had let him. As it was, he came often those summer months, driving his claybank Arabians, and Nellie saw him also in New Orleans, at the D'Estrées'. But somehow nothing came of it.

She watched her uncle and Stewart together. They conversed like gentlemen, about the racing season, the hunting, the new roads in Parish St. Mary. But it seemed to her that neither of them said much that he cared to say.

'Do you think there are many people, Uncle Al,' she asked him one day, 'who say things to one that one likes? I mean that one likes to hear.'

'Sometimes,' he said, 'I think the point is not so much that we should like what people say to us. The point is that we should like what we say to them.'

Her sweet, perplexed heart whispered to her that this saying was like Uncle Alfred. How intelligent it was, it was something to think over!

She saw her uncle sometimes walking late in the evening up and down the terrace, saw the columns shining against the dusk, and beyond them the pale sheen of the bayou water.

'Darling Uncle Al,' she said to herself as she gazed at him from the curtains of the window, 'why do we not die? Why don't we fly south as the birds do? Uncle, I will stay by you, I'll never leave you.'

She would see him stop in his pacing and stand there with his arms folded, looking back at the house that his father had built and then at the two columns with their classic line against the dim fields beyond.

'I'll never leave you,' she thought.

She considered this in herself to be loyal and deep. 'Dear Uncle Alfred, what have they done to you? I won't leave you.'

The thought came to her, seeing the birds fly up from the bayou, of birds drifting in the sky above the ancient marbles. At the same moment, she thought of Stewart Robard; and at the thought the lines of a ballad they had taught her long ago came back —

> Oh, gentle wind that bloweth south,
> Where my true love repaireth,
> Convey a kiss to his dear mouth,
> And tell me how he fareth.

'Y'all could sing, Miss Nell, ef you jes try,' Mammy said.

By virtue of her youth and her lovely heart's imagination, the story at Shadows on Terrebonne now turns toward Ellen. It belongs to her rather than to an old man grown tired now even of ironic peace, weary of all things, even of hope.

By June their beloved cousin Thankful Percy was saying that Ellen would be an old maid before she knew it. She was going on eighteen now, and her mother when she married was little better than sixteen. Could anybody imagine a girl kicking every man that courted her? But some way or other it was all Ellen's uncle's fault, trust a man! And truly it was as plain as your nose on your face that Stewart Robard had graduated at the new State University in Mississippi and gone straight on home without stopping by The Shadows. Not even a mere pop call, Cousin Tank said.

The full summer came on in the Louisiana country. In the garden at Shadows on Terrebonne, rather neglected of late years and touched with extravagant growth, the roses had passed their prime, their fragrance mingled with the small grand duke jasmine and honeysuckle, and, when the sun was hot, with the sweet betsies. The lemon lilies were very sweet and the heliotrope. The red amaryllises, spread long ago beyond their beds, swung in heavy clusters; the water-hyacinths, pale as lilacs, crowded the edge of the bayou. At night the constellations shone close in the open sky; the stars spread out; and from the grass, the trees, the water, you heard the sounds of the small life there.

Sometimes the girl would begin a mimicry of these sounds: the cicadas; the bird across the bayou that was like a short flute-note, half finished; and the shrill tree frogs. Then pausing, she would listen to them all again as if they were her echoes.

Sometimes her uncle, seeing her crossing the green lawn to the bayou, thought of the saying that 'all heavenly things run on light feet.' Once when he repeated this to himself, it was autumn. All heavenly things run on light feet, he thought; and then he could hear the hush of falling leaves in such a silence as had not been before.

So the year 1859 passed into August; and in the orchard near the house Alfred Raymond, as he lay awake at night, heard the heavy fruit dropping to the ground. There came to him from the old orchard by that wing of the house the sound of fruit falling. 'Ripeness is all.' Did not Shakespeare say that? The apricots and pears, now and then, in the light wind, dropping to the ground. Ripeness is all — falling in the ripeness of summer. Another season would soon end, then another year.

A man thinks these things. But on the second Tuesday in the month, the *Lorient*, as she passed up the bayou, brought a visitor. Cydalise, whom nothing short of calamity could have prevented from watching for the boat every week, brought him into the hall where Ellen sat. The young man, still under thirty, was tall, with a high forehead and good, frank eyes. He made his apologies for not having written, but his time had been short. He had come because he had been on a journey, well, a sort of expedition, as it were, through the same country that her uncle had visited, so long ago, but now there was the camera to take along. He knew well her uncle's drawings, people had been too ignorant to believe them. He wanted to pay his respects and to present her uncle with an album of photographs.

He ran through the pages for her to see, while Cydalise went upstairs to announce the visitor.

'If it just won't smother me to death!' Ellen thought, as she felt her heart beating. She was in her own room now, and standing at the open window; but her heart beat like that.

There would be the photographs lying open on the table, her uncle and the young man gazing down on them up at the drawings on the walls. Here the camera had shown a scene, and here it appeared in her uncle's drawing. The line of columns, fluted, their capitals all graceful garlands and leaves, appeared in both. On the wall and in the album it was the same aqueduct, with the high arches going off into the distance, ruined but splendid. There was the same temple with the black shadows.

And so science, which everybody talked so much about these days, had supplied the proof.

What happens to our souls when nothing mocks them any more? Are they not free? And are not those who love us free then also?

She saw from the window the two columns at that end of the

71

garden near the bayou. How long it was since her uncle had put them there, but had never finished his plan!

On the wall downstairs and on a page of the young man's photograph album would be the picture of the single column on a great base, she said to herself. But the shaft was broken, the long stone blocks of the magnificent entablature had fallen.

Outside it was past noon, and under the noon sky the garden lawn and the fields of the air were shadowless. The bayou was still as a mirror.

And yet ——

She got up for the black writing-desk with mother-of-pearl flowers; and sitting down again, opened it on her knees.

'I do hope and believe' — she began, not writing the loved name just yet — 'that you will forgive whatever — whatever I have not seemed to return in your true love. For there are other things, too, that are so strong. But now that life here is changed ——' Then she said to herself that you would get the letter more like what you wanted if you waited. You could first just write his address on the envelope.

She began again, bending over the desk on her knees, and not letting her hand tremble — 'Randolph Gate Plantation, Parish Vermilion.'

A TEMPERED FELLOW

PAUL GREEN

ALL day long he hoed among his cotton. Row by row, and round by round he travelled, the rhythmic hanh, hanh, of his hoe keeping time to the turmoil of hurt and anger within him. It was near night, with the sun hanging low in the tops of the pines by Little Bethel Church. When he reached the fence he stopped and surveyed his handiwork behind him.

'Aih!' he said with grim exultation, 'three acres chopped and a hour to go yit.'

Turning sharply, he spat upon his hands and fell to thinning another row.

Ah, but he was a worker. Let it be rolling logs, splitting rails, or cutting with a cradle, he stood above them all. And many a hot August day, when 'the monkey was riding' old man Mc-Laughlin's hands in the bottom, Eddie's loud halloo could be heard among them, urging them on to their fodder-pulling. — But he had a bad temper. — Three hundred bundles a day was easy for him. Yea, he could pull five stacks in a week; had done it all right. And today he had set a new mark. Three acres of grassy cotton chopped out by one man was a record. He thought about it. Who could equal it? But on this day he was mad, mad to the bottom. Mad and hurt. And his hurt and anger drove him, beat on him like a flail. He had quarrelled with Ola. Aih, worse than that, he had slapped her. A little slap, not much — he glanced at his heavy hands.

But he had stood enough to make any man mad. What had got into her nohow? Here he was with the grass eating his cotton up and he hoeing his liver out trying to save it. So much rainy weather. And she. — Lying up in the house down there in the field, doing nothing — ready to spend every cent she could get, buying lace and jewelry from the peddlers who passed in the lane. 'Says

73

she's done working in the fields, she does,' he muttered wrathfully. 'Yea, but I'll see!' And his hoe flew over the ground. He had had no dinner, his stomach was empty. Evening was coming on. Everything looked gray, lonesome, it shore did. And now he'd have to go on home. The mule and cow had to be fed and there were the shoats too. 'Dang, I didn't never plan on things like this!'

He loved Ola, always had. — Temper it was. Too much temper. His mother used to say it would bring him trouble. He'd ought to be patient. Still, she had tried him — worried him nigh to death it seemed. And now he remembered that in their courting days old man McLaughlin had warned him of Ola's dressing and finery. Her pappy and mammy couldn't satisfy her. They were too poor. Take a bank to hold her, he had said. That's right, she didn't treat him decent, and he slaving day in and day out to get ready and buy a piece of land of their own. They were both the children of tenant farmers, the grandchildren of tenant farmers, the great-grandchildren, and on back. But he'd change it for himself. He'd pay taxes on his own land before he died, he would. Aih, she knew it when she married him and seemed glad. He stamped and spat upon the ground.

He tore through a dozen more rows before the dusk came down. And when the moon had begun to shine up in the middle of the sky, he laid his hoe down and stood gazing over the wide rich fields. He would make big cotton here, a bale and a half to the acre and more maybe. And over there towards the hollow was his corn, popping with strength and as green as poison. He was a farmer and this was his, the earth was his. It was fine, aye, it was, bless God. This level forty acres would be his in a year or two. McLaughlin had promised it as soon as he could pay a thousand down. Money. Ola would have to quit spending his money. Not another cent to waste, not another damn red. It was foolish. It was foolish for her always to be looking through Sears-Roebuck's catalogue, picking out lace curtains and tablecloths and window shades. He'd told her a thousand times. And then this morning — yes, God! — With a muttered oath, he turned and went off through the darkness home.

74

He fed the mule and cow and the clamorous pigs. As he came up the walk to the house where Ola had wasted a lot of good guano planting a border of cannas, he saw her sitting on the porch in a cool white dress. His heart softened towards her and he could have taken her in his arms. She was sweet. She was always clean and cool and sweet. He stopped before the steps embarrassed, trying to think of something to say. The lamp was lighted on the table in the room, and he saw the waiting supper spread out on a new white tablecloth. Aih, that was it — finery! She would ruin him yet. His heart hardened again.

'Supper's ready,' she said. 'I got tired of waiting and had mine.'

He went on into the kitchen, soused his face and arms in a pan of water and dried them hurriedly on a fresh towel, then seated himself to his meal.

'Don't you want nothing more, Ola?' he called.

'I've et,' she answered.

He leaned over the table eating in huge mouthfuls. He fed his hunger with beans, side-meat, corn-bread, preserves, and a few pieces of fried chicken, washing it all down with great gulps of black coffee. His sweaty arms made streaks on the new cloth, but what did he care, consumed as he was by hunger and the thoughts within?

When he had finished, he sat picking bits of meat from his teeth with his finger-nails. Now and then he could hear Ola stirring in her chair on the porch. He was tired and sleepy, and if all was right he might go happily to bed against the next day's labor. But now —— No, he was too worried to sleep. She was out there thinking things. He would go out and talk to her.

Sitting down on the steps, he took off his shoes and stretched his feet in the soft sand of the walk. He waited, hoping she would say something, for he could find no words. But she held her peace. Time went by and drowsiness began to steal over him. Like a dream he heard the frogs creaking down near the mill-pond, and an owl screaming farther in the swamp beyond.

'You're sweaty. The tub's by the well there.' Her words startled him. He fumbled with his shoes and made no answer. Presently

75

she went into the house and brought him some soap and a rag. As she came near him the odor of sweet cologne entered his nostrils. She was sweet enough to eat — sweet ——

'Peddler been by today?' he asked quietly, choking down his anger.

'No,' she answered coldly, 'no.'

'Looks like a new tablecloth. Thought maybe you'd been a-buying.'

'Your money didn't buy it. It was brung to me.' She turned sharply and sat again in her chair.

'Who brung it?'

'Ella and her friend from Raleigh. They et dinner here.'

'A high-collared dude, riding round this busy time of the year. He'd better stay away from here. I could take him in my two hands and break him like a dead dog-fennel.' Ola laughed softly. 'Now what do you mean by that?'

'I'm going to Raleigh tomorrow with him to visit Ella awhile.'

'And the grass eating up our crop!' he cried incredulously.

'Yes.'

'By God, you won't!' he roared wrathfully as he got up and began walking back and forth in the yard.

'I'm going, I tell you,' and her voice quavered. 'I'm gonna get a rest from your slaving and sweating and your dirt and all.'

'Well, for God's sakes, listen at her!'

'I won't be run to death. Pa didn't run me to death.'

'And look at him. He's gonna die in the pore-house. And I ain't, I tell you.' He slumped down on the steps, hugging his knees in anger.

'And this morning you hit me. If Pa knowed it, he'd come over here with his gun and shoot you down like a dog.' Now she began sobbing.

'Dry up, dry up, I tell you. — Hanh!' He snorted scornfully. 'I'd grab him up and bust his brains out ag'in the ground.' He got to his feet and slammed his way into the house. 'All right,' he called back. 'Go on if you wish. You'll be back in a week.' And he went to bed.

All night she sat on the porch, listening to his heavy snores coming from the little back room. When the dawn broke beyond the old mill and chickens flew out of the china tree with a clatter, she got up and started breakfast. While the biscuits were baking, she went out and milked the cow for the last time.

Ed rose and ate his meal in silence. When he'd filed his hoe and started into the fields, he stopped and called. 'Going, are you?'

'I am,' she said.

'Well, go and be damned!' he shouted, and off he went up the path, kicking the dust before him.

Again a second day he hoed from morn till evening. The fiery sun burned down upon his back, drying up the sweat and leaving splotches of salt upon his shirt. When night came he had another three acres hoed clean and standing up for the siding plow. Again he went home under the moon, devoured by hunger and thoughts within.

The house was closed and there was no light. He found a note stuck in the door. 'I am gone. Don't look for me till you see me coming,' it said. He could read the clear letters in the moonlight. Tearing the paper into bits, he made his way to the lot to feed. When he had cooked his supper, he gorged himself and lay down in his clothes on the bed. Soon again his snores echoed through the house.

The next morning he awoke and called her. And then he remembered that she had left him. It seemed as if his head flew all to pieces, for he began cursing in loud oaths, cursing her trimmings, and he even seized one of her flower-pots and hurled it into the yard. The calendars and magazine covers shook on the wall with the violence of his voice. He cooked his breakfast in the same unwashed pans and ate out of the same dirty plate of the night before. Why should he clean up now? Let the house rot down. Let the maggots work in the dishes. God knows, he didn't care.

All that week he did mountains of work. He hoed and ploughed and ploughed and hoed, driving his mule up and down the windy fields like one possessed. Old McLaughlin came and tried to commiserate with him, but grief and anger were eating in his heart like lye. He said, 'Please let me alone.' The loneliness of the

house, aih, that harried him to death. He became restless and
unable to sleep at night. And on Sunday morning when he had
shaved himself and sat alone on the porch staring across the wide
burning fields, he gave in. Fishing out a stub of a pencil, he wrote;
'Deer Ola,' he said, 'Won't you come back? i speck i done you
wrong. Ill do better, honest i will. the crop is in good shape. and
there ain't so much to do. there ain't nobody to churn and theys
a pile of eggs i caint eat. Im well and hope the same. — Ed.' He
set off up the road, dropped it in the mail-box and waited.

The next week he worked, worked and waited. The grass was
killed, the cotton sided, and all looked fine. Then came a note
from Ola saying: 'I am having a good time. Please look in the
top bureau drawer and send me my white slippers. — Ola.' He
was stupefied with rage. All that afternoon he sat on the porch
unmindful of his crops and the world about him. Near night he
rushed into the house and began putting on his store-bought suit.
'I'll go get her! I'll go get her!' he kept shouting to himself.
Hurrying to the barn, he hitched the mule to the buggy and went
driving away in a cloud of dust to the north.

Late that night he drove up the shining main street of the
capital city. The bright lights astonished, even frightened him.
But he held his way. Turning to the right near the middle of the
town, he went several blocks eastward and stopped before a small
frame house. There was a stir inside and a light came on as he
hammered on the door.

'Who's that, who's that?' Ella's sleepy voice called.

'It's me,' he cried, pushing his way into the hall. 'And I want
Ola.'

A door opened in the hall and Ola came out.

'Ola, Ola,' he said, 'come home.'

'Maybe next year,' she said, and gave a little laugh.

Ella went away and left them alone.

'Git your things, I tell you,' he almost whispered.

'I ain't going. Good night. You're crazy as a fool, Ed.'

— Temper, temper, that was it. For he couldn't keep his hands
off her — hands that could lift a bale of cotton. — She couldn't
make a whisper, not a sound.

Then he stumbled down the walk to his buggy. He'd done it all right. He'd killed her all right. He knew all the time, every long mile to Raleigh, that's the way it'd be. He'd choke her to death. — Temper, temper. With a clatter of blows, he urged his mule towards the south. A big star was shining above the road he travelled. It caught his eye as he drove, and he rocked his head in grief. 'I wisht I was where that star is, clean away. Oh, I do! — ' And he sobbed as he passed the moonlit hedges.

When the sheriff came for him in his little house, he was quiet and dignified. Poor fool, he was sitting on the porch dressed in his Sunday best with his head bent over in his hands. The dishes were washed, the floor swept, the flowers watered, and all in order. He went away like a child and stayed so till the last day.

THE HORN THAT CALLED BAMBINE

ELMA GODCHAUX

When I was a child, I used to hear Shoolie blow his horn. I used to feel sorry for Shoolie. When I grew to be a woman, I could still hear that horn sounding, and felt the same old sadness filling me up and choking me. It was always at sunset time that I heard the horn, when I was coming home from the field, dead-tired, feeling my heavy head and arms and the straight line of pain at the back of my neck as I dragged along. I heard Shoolie's horn and raised my head and looked over the cotton field and a green patch of cane, hunting for Shoolie, though I knew he wasn't there; I knew his horn was blowing in my head. I sighed, thinking of the things Shoolie had saved me from and the things he had brought me. Shoolie always liked me. But I never did nothing for Shoolie. I kept on down the road, thinking, and took the rise, thinking and hearing Shoolie's horn. The Lowell-sack full of cotton was awful heavy on my shoulder. I pulled it along and coughed, trying to get the dry cotton dust out of my throat. I felt my skirt sticking to my legs when I bent my knees, working up the rise. I couldn'tnever get used to the hill between my house and the cotton field, though I didn't know how many times I had climbed it from the field. Dan didn't think nothing of my climbing it. Dan didn't think much. He never thought why I couldn't get used to working in the field and lugging an old Lowell-sack. Mamma and Papa never believed in sending their girls to the fields. They said field work wasn't for white girls; if you were a nigger, it was different. Oh God, I thought, nobody couldn't tell what he might come to. Mamma and Papa would turn over in their graves, seeing me dragging the cotton. I kept on going, thinking if it hadn't been for Shoolie, maybe I wouldn't be harnessed to a Lowell-sack like a nigger. I heard his horn. But the blasts didn't sound full no more,

80

though, as if he was moving off or getting tired blowing. He used to get awful tired. He used to say he got tired enough to drop dead and his mouth hurt him. I used to wish he would stop, because I knew there wasn't no use in his blowing like that. But he wouldn't listen.

The blasts I heard were faint, faint. Then one of Fred Turner's fat white roosters hopped on the fence rail and crowed and killed Shoolie's horn; it was blotted out as if it had never been. Everything was quiet. Fred Turner's house looked bare and lonesome. It was a two-story house stuck on top of the hill. The whole world was beneath it. Far below it, the Turner pear trees and some bamboo made a blurry darkness; nothing grew near it. I could make out Mrs. Turner sitting on the gallery in one of the two rocking-chairs, rocking. I lowered my head and hurried on and got into the darkness of the big black oak and let out my breath. She was perched up there like she was sitting in a tower. She was rocking and rocking, nervous. I could hear her heels clicking. I coughed. Seemed to me, I could see her red eyes from where I was. They were always as red as blood. I wished I didn't have to see her or Fred or the house of theirs neither. I wondered were Mrs. Turner's eyes red from crying or because she ate morphine. She measured out her morphine on her long black fingernails. Everybody knew how she did it as good as if they seen her do it. Me and Dan often talked about her. He'd talk and talk until I got up and went about my business because I couldn't stand so much talk. He'd talk about Shoolie too. Talk about Miss Maime and Fred always led to talk about Shoolie. I wished I could forget them. But some things nobody forgot, things that marked lives the way trees and bushes marked roads and made them different from other roads. Shoolie and Fred had marked my life. I wondered if all the folks I knew had markers in their lives that I couldn't see. I stole another glance at Miss Maime. My sweat felt cold. None of us could see Miss Maime without a tremble. Miss Maime, we all called her since as far back as I could remember. She was some older than Fred Turner and looked a lot older. She had it easy too. But I didn't want it like she had it. I didn't want to be her.

81

My Lowell bumped against the tree roots and jogged over the ruts and hustled me along. The road was dropping down the hill and narrowing into the lane, following the bayou. Dead Bayou had been choked for a long time by matted hyacinths. I never did see any water in it. It looked under its flowers like the covered coffin I saw once in an old newspaper, an enormous long coffin lying there between the trees. Every summer and long into the fall, it was purple with flowers. That summer me and Dan got married, I used to pick big bunches of the hyacinths. But they died in no time and we stopped picking them. We never picked the black-eyed Susans that came later to the edges of the bayou. We soon found out we didn't have the time for flowers. The big coffin under the blanket of hyacinths stretched past my gate. Night was closing on it, sucking it in. I turned away and pushed on the gate. Dan never remembered to oil the hinges. I told myself I had to remind him again. I got tired reminding him about things. The iron pot I boiled my wash in swelled up, enormous, almost blocking the path to the house. We had put it in the shade of the sycamore tree, so I could work without the sun hitting me. I liked the pot. Dan said I was foolish, liking an old pot. But it used to belong to Mamma and stood in her yard. It reminded me of when I was a child. It made me think how rested and strong I felt when I was a child. A couple of days after Mamma died, me and Dan borrowed Turner's team and went over and fetched the pot and some of Mamma's other things. I didn't like Dan asking young Fred Turner for the team; but there was nothing else we could have done. I wanted the pot. I always remembered Mamma when I saw it and Bambine too, Bambine stirring the clothes with a wooden stick. When all of us children were small, Bambine used to come over on Mondays and help Mamma with the wash. Papa never minded Mamma getting help. He didn't expect us girls to wash heavy clothes no more than Mamma did. We had it easy. The boys had it hard, but not us girls. After I was married to Dan, I could see how easy I'd had it.

We helped Mamma in the house some and had to keep ourselves clean; and in the fall of the year we went to Turner's sugar mill after syrup. Sometimes old man Turner used to let us ride the mule that turned the crusher. I could ride the mule round and round longer than anybody else could. I could ride until old man Turner's nigger had to change the mule, because the mule got dizzy. Young Fred Turner used to watch me. Sometimes he laughed and called something to me. 'You can't stand no more than a mule.' Or something like that. I knew he was joking me. His words'd be all but smothered by giggles. When I got off the mule, I wouldn't be able to stand up and him and me would laugh together. Sometimes he'd follow me home; but most often he wouldn't; he'd have business to do at the mill; to have heard him talk, anybody would have thought he was running the mill instead of his old man. He'd stand and watch me. I'd feel his eyes on me as I climbed the stile and turned up the road. I passed my hand over the back of my dress to see if my skirt was down all right. I knew I looked ugly with the heavy bucket dragging one side of me down. Old man Turner gave me a big bucket for a nickel. Bees used to follow me home. Sometimes they bumped against the hand that toted the bucket; but they didn't sting me. When I got home, Bambine maybe would be in the yard, washing, and maybe Shoolie would be hanging over the fence, staring at her. They wouldn't be talking. Shoolie'd be staring at her like he couldn't see her enough, or hadn't ever seen her before and didn't live with her day in and day out in the cabin up Snake Lane. She would keep stirring the clothes, her heavy lips hanging down, still, like lips cut out of wood, and her breasts moving the least bit as she moved the stick; her breasts weren't loose like Mamma's; they looked hard, but full and heavy. I didn't blame Shoolie for hanging round looking at her. A silky flag of steam rose and floated over her head. She didn't pay any mind to Shoolie or little Toog playing near her or the clothes foaming over the top of the pot; she stirred and stirred like she was wound up to stir. I got to the gate and Shoolie jumped off it and held it open and looked at me. Then he leaned close to me and blurted out, 'Don't you tell your Mamma I is here,' talking fast and holding his breath. 'Don't you tell her nothing. You hear, Miss Florie? Please, Miss Florie.' Mamma didn't like him hanging round, staring at Bambine like he was crazy. But I knew Shoolie didn't mean no harm. And he never

83

kept Bambine from working. She raised her head and looked at me. Her hair stuck out. Her black face was shining with sweat, so was her neck; she looked polished all over like the fine piano the Turners had in their house. She stretched her flat nose. 'Florie,' talking, slow, in a deep voice, 'give me a lick of your syrup.' I held the bucket for her and she dug the handle of her stick into the syrup and lifted it out, dripping. Toog cried out and she leaned down and fed him. When she stood up again, her full height looked awful tall. She licked her hand and the stick.

It seemed to me now as I walked up the path round the fat pot that I could see Bambine standing up stirring, her heavy lips hanging, gleaming, painted with syrup. I could see Toog with his shift hardly covering his belly and Shoolie staring, green eyes clear as glass; I never saw a clear-eyed nigger until I saw Shoolie. I thought I could hear Mamma's chickens scuttling out of my path; she used to keep a lot of chickens; and the pigs raising themselves out of the mire and the old cow, Bottle, coming after me, nuzzling the bucket. Dan and me never had enough chickens to make a noise scuttling and we never bothered with pigs; we could buy pork at the store when we had money. And we could drive the cow out of the yard to live on the woods. We didn't milk her more than every other day in cotton-picking time. It was a good thing her feed was poor, I thought, or she'd have suffered not being milked. I knew I wasn't walking to Mamma's door, but my own. My baby came running to meet me. She was whimpering. I wiped her nose with my hand. Toog was stuffing some sticks into the stove.

'Toog,' I fussed, 'why you ain't started the fire before now? What you been doing? The baby's hongry. Why you didn't give her a cold sweet potato?'

Toog didn't answer. He went on shoving in the sticks. He never spoke much, like his mamma, and his lips hung down like hers. But his eyes were like Shoolie's, strange, light, not nigger eyes. The baby leaned against me, munching the potato. I took her in my arms.

'Toog,' sitting down and talking to his back, 'keep stirring the grits so it ain't going to be lumpy.' I was too tired to move. 'God,

I wish I could learn you.' The baby smelled hot. I held her close
to me. She was awful hungry. I kept fussing at Toog, 'Dish out
the food. Make haste. I don't know how come you let the baby get
so hongry.' He piled the food on the plate and set it on the table and
didn't talk back to me. He wasn't a sassy nigger. He was a lot
like Shoolie. I coughed. 'Dish out your supper, Toog,' I said.
'I reckon you're hongry enough to eat.'

He took his plate to the shed room and sat down on the bench
under the low roof. His back looked like a pencil line scratched on
the darkness, awful thin. I kept watching the little thin line that
was him. He helped me a lot and I always let my sharp temper
lash out at him. But I knew Toog didn't mind as long as I kept
him and fed him, and I was going to keep him as long as I kept
myself, the same as if he was my own. Darkness was covering the
yard and reaching into the room where I sat. I couldn't see
hardly anything but the sycamore tree raising its white trunk
high into the darkness. The locusts were singing. Dan ought to've
been coming home. I always had to worry about Dan. The baby
nestled down in my lap. But I wanted her to eat some more. I
wanted her to grow up fine. 'Come on,' I begged. 'Eat some more.
I want you to grow up fine. I don't want you picking cotton. I
don't want you having it hard. You ain't going to neither, not if me
and Dan can help it.' I knew I was a fool sitting up talking to the
baby and her sleeping. I went on talking like a fool, 'God, I'm
glad you're a girl.' I sniffled and coughed and hugged her and she
was sleeping and the darkness made me feel bad. It made me feel
like I wanted to see my boys. They were the same as dead. Night
was like death, I thought, foolish, as black and secret. Dan was
hard on the boys. He was too hard. But I knew he didn't mean no
harm to them. But he beat them awful. The boys ran away because they hated him. He beat them so awful. Oh God, thanks for
making my baby a girl. Girls didn't get beat and girls didn't leave
home. Bambine had left. But she was a nigger. Folks said she
went clear to New Orleans. After that, Shoolie took to blowing his
horn every day at sunset.

We children used to go down the lane to watch him. He'd step
out of his cabin and turn right up the lane and puff his cheeks,

blowing hard on the cow horn a good number of times; then he'd turn left and blow. I'd call to him when I couldn't stand to watch him no more, 'Shoolie.' And he'd lower the horn. He was always a polite nigger. 'Bambine's in New Orleans,' I'd say. 'She ain't going to hear you no matter how hard you blow.' He'd answer, stubborn, 'She going to hear. Listen. Don't you hear that sound traveling away?' Nobody could tell that nigger nothing about blowing for Bambine. But he was a good nigger. I kept at him, 'You oughtn't to wear yourself out blowing like that. Bambine's having a good time in New Orleans. Folks say that yellow nigger that took her has got some money.' He panted, 'Just let me tell her I'm waiting.' Little Toog stood in back of his papa, watching. Shoolie went on, 'She coming back. You going to see.' Then he leaned forward and whispered, breathless, 'You better be watching out for yourself, Miss Florie. Something tells me maybe I'm going to be blowing for you some day like I'm blowing for Bambine now. You better be watching out some yellow man don't tote you off. He ain't no nigger, but he's yellow as some niggers. You better watch out, Miss Florie. You is too pretty for your own good.' I laughed and pretended I didn't know what he was talking about. I said, 'Shoolie. Don't talk crazy.' Everybody laughed because they all thought he wasn't all there. He didn't pay any mind to them. 'I'm telling you for your own good,' he whispered. 'Mind out for yourself.' I stopped laughing. His face looked awful sad; I couldn't laugh; and his eyes kept watching me as though his eyes were going to tell me things his mouth couldn't. I knew he liked me. Maybe because I never told Mamma when I caught him hanging on the fence behind Bambine.

I thought a lot about Shoolie, mostly at sunset time. He made me feel all choked up and bad. I hoped he knew I was keeping Toog. I could hear one of my scrawny hens that was too hungry to roost pecking round Toog's feet. Toog dropped her some sweet potato. Toog was always good to dumb beasts. I knew he was good to the baby too.

I called out, 'Toog. Don't you give that old hen all your sweet potato.'

Then I heard Dan in the yard. I knew it was him by the way

his feet dragged. I got up and lit the lamp and put his food on to heat. His body made a black smear in the doorway. I looked at him. He looked strange, so black and heavy.

He came close to me and stooped over the baby. 'What she's doing, asleep already?' he fussed. 'Ain't she asleep early?' He put his hand over her face.

'Don't you wake her up,' I cried. 'She's all wore out and she just ate.'

He kept looking at her and blurted all of a sudden, 'They got a new school-teacher over at Cotton Port. Old Babe Landry just told me. I bet this kid is going to be smart, smarter than the boys.' He stopped and wet his lips. He sat down at the table, quick, and I put his food in front of him. I didn't know what had come over him because we never talked about the boys.

'Eat your supper,' I said, trying to cover up his words. I sat facing him. 'Did you get the wagon loaded?' I asked, natural.

'Sho'. It's loaded.' And dropped his fork.

'Well, why you don't eat?' I asked.

'I been studying about Fred Turner's crop,' he said, slow, like he was choosing his words. 'He's got a nice crop on the land he works with the niggers, plenty nicer than ours. I reckon you know what that means.'

'No,' I said, biting my lip. 'No. What it means?'

'Well, maybe he ain't going to let us go halves with him next year. He ain't the one to let us go halves if we don't make much. He's got to keep Miss Maime in morphine, don't he?' He kind of laughed.

'Don't start that talk,' I cried. 'For God sake. What we going to do if he don't let us go halves?'

'Don't ask me. How do I know?'

My lip hurt. 'He'll let us go halves,' I cried. 'You see if he don't. It ain't so much work for him. We have all the worry,' I hurried on, 'and he gets half our crop no matter what.'

'We ain't going to make eight bales this year,' Dan said, pushing my words aside. 'We ain't going to make five.'

'This is a bad year for everybody,' I reminded him. 'We ain't had no rain in the growing time.'

87

'Turner did good on the land he worked himself,' he said again. 'It held the wet good. He worked it a lot.'

'Well, eat your supper,' I said, tired. I knew there wasn't no use trying to tell Dan something. 'It's seven o'clock right now,' I went on. 'We got to get to bed. We got to be up at three if you got the wagon loaded. It's loaded, ain't it, Dan?' keeping at him. 'It's ready to drive to the gin? Ain't it? Ain't it?'

The baby moved and fussed.

'Stop yelling,' Dan cried. 'You're waking up the baby yourself.'

'Hush, hush, dearie. She ain't awake,' I whispered. 'You got it loaded? Ain't you? It's loaded?' It wasn't that he was lazy. But I had to keep after him.

'I said it was,' he growled. 'I reckon you heard me.'

'Well, make haste now,' I said, 'and come to bed.'

I went to the next room and put the baby on the bed. I didn't wash her because she was sleeping.

I called out, 'Dan. Come on to bed.' I didn't want him sitting fretting.

For once, he got right up and came into the dark room. I could make him out, standing near me, fiddling with his clothes. I began working with mine. My body felt heavy and big. Dan unbuttoned his clothes, slow. I could smell the sweat on him and me. I went to the shed and washed. But Dan was too tired.

I climbed into bed after him and pulled down the baby's night-gown. Dan touched her once and turned away from her and me. I could hear the locusts singing and singing. I couldn't sleep. It was hot in the bed. I smelled cotton.

Me and Dan left the baby sleeping on the bed.

Outside, everything was still. No wind moved the leaves. Only a white mist was moving, rising from the bayou. I could hear the horse thudding in the deep dust. Dan was leading him by a loose rein. I wasn't thinking a thing about Fred Turner. I was just walking along, and there he was. He was coming down the hill, a couple of niggers with him. The sight of him knocked out my breath. It always did, no matter how often I saw him. I wasn't scared of him exactly. I just didn't like seeing him. I prayed God he wasn't going to stop us. He came, walking a little ahead of the

88

niggers, big, his hip-pocket bulging with the gun he always toted, his chest sticking out, tearing through the mist. Fred Turner was always like that, always seemed to be tackling something with all his strength. I couldn't catch my breath. He was just across the bayou from me, right close, looking at me. His eyes were two points. I waited like a fool instead of walking on.

He shouted at me, 'You all sho' you got enough cotton to tote to the gin?' and laughed. 'You all are some farmers,' laughing.

His laughs prickled up my back like icy fingers. Me and Dan didn't say nothing. Fred Turner's eyes were gone; all of a sudden as if they had been rubbed out. I heard Dan and the old horse thudding on. I knew I had to move.

I could see our wagon-load of cotton by the side of the road. It needed packing down. I got my shoes off, quick, and climbed on the load and stamped. I stamped, fierce. I wished I was stamping Turner. Then I felt like I was stamping him. My face burned. I was mashing him out of my life. I wasn't talking to him. I was just mashing him. He wasn't going to be a marker no more. I was paying him for what he did to Shoolie.

Dan called to me, 'For God sakes, that's enough. What you reckon you packing down?'

I stopped and looked at Dan and jumped off the wagon. I watched it rumble into the darkness and get swallowed.

The milky mist was moving off over the fields, slow. It made them look sad and kind of scary. I walked on down the road through the stillness, stretching my legs wide. They were strong as a man's legs. My heart was big and strong too. I could feel it beating. I ought to have talked up to Turner, I thought, mad with myself. He wasn't no better than me and Dan. I ought to have talked right back to him. I stood still, hearing wagon-chains rattling, knowing they were Turner's. I waited and saw him coming, riding above the mist. I made myself stand there and look straight at him. I had bold eyes and I made them hold Turner. They seemed to drag his wagon to a stop. He looked down at me. His eyes got under my clothes. Fred Turner's eyes always did that.

He laughed that laugh of his as if he wasn't having any fun.

'Well, if it ain't Miss Florie again. Hello, Florie.' His hard voice smashed the silence. I looked down at my feet. So did the nigger beside him look down. 'You ain't lost your tongue, have you?' he yelled 'You can say good morning, I reckon, without dying from it.'

I worked my tongue. But I didn't make a sound. I nodded, and that seemed to satisfy him. I was sweating. My body felt awful hot.

He took his eyes off me at last and looked over the field. 'I might get that white nigger down the road named Lamson to go halves with me,' he said and spit over the side of the wagon. 'This is good land. I'm going to make a good crop off it. Now what you going to say to that? What you going to say?' he kept on. 'You better speak up.'

I coughed and swallowed. 'There ain't been no rain,' I panted. 'You can't do nothing without rain.'

'You can work the ground good,' he threw back. 'The fellow you married is too lazy.' He never had no use for Dan. 'You work the ground good,' he went on, 'and the crop'll be good. I ain't going to have no scraggly cotton with no bolls, throwing away the land. I ain't going to have it. Damn it.'

I didn't move and neither did the nigger. Turner took his eyes off me and put them on the nigger and on me again. He was watching how dead-quiet he made me and the nigger.

He raised his whip and touched me with it, squirming it over my shoulder, and I didn't flinch so much as an eyelash. 'Yes ma'am,' he whined, 'you all better watch out. You might find yourselves chased off here and that nigger, Lamson, going halves.' He watched me a long minute and I didn't move. One of his horses blew some air through its nose and that roused him and he gave the horse a lick with the whip. I knew he wanted to make the beast as quiet as he did us humans, me and the nigger. 'Gid-dap,' he cried, giving the horse another lick. The wagon rattled. The nigger jolted by me like a rag doll, so still and spineless.

I stood there. Oh God, I thought, I was a fool; I couldn't open my mouth to Turner. I was a fool believing I could mash him out of my life. He wasn't no dead marker neither. He was a cat with

90

busy claws. He had caught me and Dan and the baby too. We were the mice. 1 couldn't do nothing. I wished Dan was the man to stand up to Turner. But I knew there wasn't no use wishing. Dan couldn't do nothing, no more than Shoolie could. I raised my heavy feet and moved. I was tired trying to do something against Fred Turner. I was tired thinking too. Poor Shoolie. His horn was still now.

Fred had been dead-set against his blowing. Everybody felt sorry for Shoolie; but not Fred Turner, he didn't feel sorry. He said Shoolie didn't have no right blowing and sending the sound out over the Turners' field. Fred always made it a point to make the nigger stop blowing. No matter where Fred was when he heard the horn, he would quit what he was doing and go off down Shoolie's lane and stop before Shoolie and holler and, if Shoolie didn't stop quick enough, he'd grab the nigger's arm. I saw him many a time. The nigger would turn his scared eyes to Fred and lower the horn. Fred'd laugh and spit. 'The nigger's crazy,' he'd say to me after he finished spitting. 'I ain't going to have that horn blowing in my ears. He ain't going to make me crazy or deaf neither.' And Shoolie looked at me. He never looked long at Fred. 'I hate good-for-nothing niggers like Shoolie,' Fred went on.

I walked, slow, lugging my heavy thoughts. The mist was gone. The hyacinths looked faded and old. The sky was red; it made a wall in front of me. The air was heavy. I couldn't hardly breathe. Miss Maime was sitting on the gallery. I watched her rocking and the sound she made rode across the bayou to me. She had a white shawl round her head. She looked like a ghost. Her heels kept clicking, sharp, rocking and never stopping. Seemed like her heels were following me.

I half ran down the hill, thanking God I wasn't her. I kept thinking I wasn't her and thanking God for it and for Dan and my baby who was a girl. Dan wasn't quick and smart like Fred Turner was or nothing like that and I knew it. But I didn't care. I wouldn't have been Miss Maime married to Fred Turner for nothing on earth. I wiped my face.

I shoved open my gate, and my baby was sitting on the ground. I grabbed her, quick, and hugged her. She squirmed. She didn't

91

like to be grabbed and hugged like that. I sat her down and laughed; but I didn't feel like laughing. Toog had a fire going on the bricks under the wash pot. He was limping round the yard, hunting sticks. I watched him and all of a sudden I was wondering if he remembered me when I was a kid stopping in his daddy's cabin. If I went to the woods in back of the cabin to pick black-berries, I always stopped to see Shoolie. I'd always give Shoolie a big helping out of my bucket. I never asked Toog if he remembered something, and he never said.

Toog and me used to watch Shoolie stuff the berries down his throat. Shoolie'd laugh. 'You all are having as much fun as if you all was eating,' he'd say. Then he'd stand up and wipe his hands on his pants and say, 'Me and Toog is much obliged for the berries. Since Bambine is gone, we ain't got no time for picking.' He'd break off and open his eyes and go on in a changed voice, 'I swear to God, Miss Florie, you sho' is pretty, too pretty for your own good. You is like Bambine, I always said it, too fine for your own self.' I didn't laugh. I kept staring back at him. I knew he hated Fred. All the niggers hated Fred Turner. They were scared of him. I used to feel kind of proud of the way the niggers all hated Fred and were scared of him. I used to look at Fred's cold gray eyes and his heavy hands and his strong neck and the way it sat in the middle of his square shoulders and I used to think Fred Turner couldn't help being fine and strong and making folks scared of him. And he wasn't scared of nothing.

Me and Fred used to go walk at the end of the long summer days. Mamma and Papa never cared, because Fred was a Big Dog and I was doing good for myself getting Fred Turner. We always went to the Scary Woods. The path there was hidden and dark and me and Fred could press close together. The cypress trees and oaks and sycamores, reaching above us, looked like tall haunts. Fred would squeeze my arm and I'd feel his touch run through me. 'You ain't scared?' he'd whisper. I giggled, 'I am and I ain't.' And wouldn't know if it was fear or love that made my skin creep. He twisted my arm close to him, and I didn't cry out; I didn't mind being hurt; I knew his strong love made him hurt me. I didn't want to leave the woods. I wanted to be hidden with Fred.

We walked along, slow, squeezing each other and stopping sometimes and following the path that was like a hole through the trees
and coming out at last into the open where the pale light of dusk
was lying. 'You wasn't scared?' Fred asked. His eyes made my
face hot. 'You don't have to be scared of nothing when you're
with me,' he went on, spitting the way he did when he said something he meant real hard. 'I got a gun,' he explained. 'Look here.
Nobody can't afford to go nowheres without a gun.' I said, 'Put
it up. For goodness sake.' And grinned. 'I didn't know a gun was
good for haunts.' His rough voice pushed against my face. You
knew the kind of man Fred was the minute he opened his mouth.
'I don't give that for a man that don't tote a gun,' snapping his
fingers. I said again, 'Put it up.' Shoolie's horn swallowed my
words. He was blowing it, hard. Fred's face got fiery and there
was a white line round his mouth. He cried out, 'There's that fool
nigger. I'm going to make him stop that blowing if it's the last
thing I do. He's got his nerve blowing like he owned the world.'
I was scared, I didn't know why, of something in Fred's red and
white face. I argued, 'He ain't hurting you. Why you don't let
him alone?' He turned on me, yelling, 'I don't like that blowing.
I ain't never liked it. If you like a nigger making a racket, I don't.
And I been telling Shoolie.' He grabbed my wrist and started down
Shoolie's lane. The blowing swelled out and sounded awful mournful. I tried to pull away, crying, 'I don't want to go yonder. I
ain't going.' His voice was hard, strong, like iron. 'Come on,' he
cried. 'And look here,' turning me to face him, 'when we're
married, you ain't going to be saying what you going to do and what
you ain't.' He gave me a funny look like he was seeing me for the
first time. And pulled me on. His grip on my arm felt like an iron
grip. The horn sound was opening like a funnel and we were walking into the middle of it. Shoolie was standing in the lane with
Toog near; little Toog was pouting and picking his nose. Fred
yelled out, 'Stop that blowing.' Shoolie took the horn out of his
mouth. The sound broke off like it was stepped on. Shoolie began
begging, 'I got to be blowing. Excuse me, Mr. Fred. It's time.'
Fred hollered, 'You quit.' But the nigger raised the horn and
blew. Fred grabbed the nigger's arm and yelled, 'You god-damn

93

sassy nigger.' Shoolie pulled away. I never knew what got into Shoolie that day. He yanked his arm away from Fred. He was little and thin; but he was strong. He was panting, 'It ain't nothing to you, white man. I'm got to blow. Bambine might be waiting. I got to blow for her to come home.' He blew, stubborn. Fred yelled, 'Quit. Quit, you black son of a ——' The blowing was going off over Fred's head when his shot smashed it. The awful loud shot knocked the horn out of Shoolie's mouth, broke against the trees. A thin ribbon of smoke moved away. Shoolie screamed. He was holding his stomach and screaming. Blood slid between his fingers. He looked at it. Then looked at Fred and babbled out, 'You killed me. You killed me.' He said it over and over. 'You killed me. For nothing. I wasn't doing you nothing. I was blowing for Bambine. She was listening for me to blow. You killed me.' He rocked and turned his eyes to me; they were clear as clear mirrors. 'Miss Florie,' he cried and toppled down, slow, and hit the ground and his eyes kept hold of me and didn't change as though they didn't feel the fall. 'Miss Florie, you seen him,' he went on, 'you seen him. I didn't do him nothing. He did it for nothing. You seen him. You better go on away from him. You better go on,' in a new strong voice, 'go on. Run.' He rolled a little like a log finding a place on a pile. His mouth was open. One big blood bubble ballooned between his fingers. I screamed and ran. My throat felt tight. Fred called me. I couldn't hardly breathe. He kept yelling. But he wasn't chasing me. I ran past my house. I knew Dan would be at the store, wishing I had let him come over home.

There was a lot of men on the store gallery. They were talking and yawning and chewing and spitting like always. I didn't hardly see them. I ran to Dan and threw my arms around his neck and hugged him and cried. Dan's arms covered me and I felt safe. But that day was a long time ago. I never felt that safe again.

I wiped my face, wishing Shoolie was back again. I stirred the clothes in the pot, slow, like I used to see Bambine stir them, wishing the old days were back with Bambine in Mamma's yard and Shoolie hanging over the gate. I blew my nose on my apron and stirred and stirred. Steam kept blowing up from the pot and covering me. I stirred. I didn't stop when I heard Dan fumbling with the gate. He came on in the yard, touching the baby's head when he passed her.

I called to him, 'Dan. How much'd the load make?'

'A bale,' he said, 'four hundred and eighty pounds.'

'That ain't much.'

'It ain't bad,' he gave back, pulling off the horse's bridle.

'Well,' I said, and stopped stirring. I could feel my heart hanging in me, heavy. 'You saw Turner?'

'Sho'. He was yonder. Getting ginned.' I waited. And Dan saw me wait. 'He didn't say much,' Dan said. 'But we're going halves another year. He let that out.' I didn't move. Dan watched me. 'Well,' he asked me, 'ain't you satisfied?'

'Sho',' I said and stirred. The smell and the mist from the steaming clothes rose up between me and Dan. The gray mist was as good as walls around me. I was in the world alone; but only for a minute and Shoolie's horn was sounding and breaking down my walls. I never had heard his horn before in the broad daylight. The sound was close to me, covering me and moaning, moaning words about me and Dan. Me and Dan, we were mice in the same cat's paws, the paws that had killed Shoolie. We couldn't do nothing. Me and Dan kept staring at each other. And Shoolie was tired. The blowing faded. It spread out, thin, over the fields and dropped down into the hollow where the bayou was. I pulled my eyes away from Dan's and lowered my head and stirred; he moved across the yard; and I kept stirring.

THE GINSING GATHERERS

HOWELL VINES

I

THE elderly man and the youngish woman pulled off their shoes and waded the Glaze Shoals in the Little River and came out on the other side not far above the mouth of Glaze Creek. They had left their home across the river on the tip end of the bluff that overlooked the whole Glaze Bend with its rich bottom farm and dense cane brakes. The four o'clocks were open over there in the yard, and two powerful and smart dogs were at home to protect the fowls from small varmints and keep the wolves and panthers scared away at night so that the sheep and calves would not be molested in their stables. And in daylight the purple martins or the jaybirds, or both, would keep the hawks scared away from the fowls. The married son would turn out the sheep and calves the next morning and put them up at night.

The 'ginsing' season of the year had come and the muscadines were also ripe, and the man and woman were off on a little journey up the length of Glaze Creek and a little beyond to gather ginsing and eat muscadines. The wild fruit and herb hunt would end with a sojourn over the week-end at a neighbor's house about four miles away and near the famous Indian spring where Glaze Creek started. But as for the muscadines, they would eat them just to be doing and for enjoyment, as they could hardly work in the fields, or fish, or walk in the fowl range along the river and below the bluff and hillside without being under a river-muscadine arbor. They were really after ginsing and meant to turn it into gold. Glaze was the man's name and he had given his name to the creek, the bend, and the shoals. Daniel was his given name and Sookie was the woman's given name. Daniel found a girl strange to the country on the bank of the river one day and took her home with him; and that night they started living together as man and wife and had been doing it ever since. She said her name was Sookie and that was all she told him, or so he always said. Daniel was a little stocky, and dark in mien; and Sookie was dark as dusk, and as deep, and built, one could tell, around tendons of great strength and passion.

They were simply out for mutual enjoyment in the woods as had been their custom together for some ten or twelve years. She was a young girl when he got her, for shortly after he had buried his Cherokee wife — the mother of his children — on the bank of the river, Daniel found Sookie and they took up together. Making their something to eat and wear, and spend — on yearly wagon trips to the little capital town of Tuscaloosa about seventy-five miles away — was an easy matter, considering that all this grew in the rich bottom land and in the woods, and in the river, for them while they slept. They followed the creek's course and stopped to fill their sacks whenever they came to the black soil against the coves and foothills where the beeches grew. Wherever Daniel could find beeches standing and dropping mast from which he tolled his mast-fattened hogs, there he was almost certain to find ginsing growing. Eating muscadines wherever they found them was only incidental to these pauses for the ginsing roots, as was fondling each other, and it was no great trouble to fill two sacks in the tuber patches splotched up and down the mazy banks of the tiny creek.

And this year they meant sure enough to find a Chinaman somewhere, if possible, and turn these ginsing roots into gold. They might not be able to do it in Tuscaloosa but they ought to in Mobile. If necessary, Daniel would get up a flat-bottomed boat trip to Mobile and try to see a Chinaman. He had in his time helped engineer numerous boat trips to Mobile in the winter time and early spring, and he would get up another one if together they failed to see a Chinaman in Tuscaloosa. People said Chinamen had crossed the great water; and he sincerely hoped that at least one had been dribbled in to the new state of Alabama and found himself in the capital town. But failing in Tuscaloosa, there was the thought of Mobile. He could stop at Demopolis on the way down. And he could find out about Montevallo and Huntsville. One thing certain, he meant to get in touch with the first Chinaman to come to Alabama.

Once he could find some Chinamen, fabulous riches were growing in patches as big as his house all around him. And Sookie was with him, if not ahead of him, in all this. Ginsing was about as plentiful as the mast on which his hogs and the squirrels fattened or the beggar lice on which his cows fed. It was as bountiful as poke sallet which they themselves fed on every spring, or sassafras from the roots of which they made tea every winter. When Daniel or Sookie had indigestion, they could chew a ginsing root and get well; and they could trade it to the stores in Tuscaloosa for provisions, but that seemed a small matter when a Chinaman would give you a pound of gold for a pound of ginsing. Pound for pound: that's the way it was. And if they once located a Chinaman or two, the white-flowering ginsing in the spring would become their fallen stars and they would visit them just to look and admire against the time they could pull up the roots in late summer and early fall. Why, already they loved to see the flowers in spring and note how the seed pods increased each bed year by year even as they gathered. And if they would let the roots grow they would get bigger and heavier every year until they would be sights to look at. That new bend up the Little River he had bought back at the land sale, why, he would let the three-leaved and five-leaved herb take the top of all the black ground there. Already it was as thick as heartleaves there. Some of the tubers were as big as his arm, and they would get bigger and bigger in the ground as the catfish and turtles did in the river. Going after a sack of gold would be like going to the beech woods. That was the size of it. He had plenty as it was, but naturally he wanted to be rich. If enough Chinamen would come within reach before he died he would be as rich as doe's cream. That was the problem and all there was to it.

Daniel and Sookie stopped to rest and cool off a little, and compute their ginsing at the spring at the head of Glaze Creek. The little creek and the Cherokees had made the spring famous. The man and woman they were going to see had lived there a little while but had moved out to where they then lived to more cleared ground. Sookie was lying back against the green bank by the spring while Daniel fooled around picking up Indian arrowheads at the old shop place left by the blacksmith who had moved out from the rolling ridge to good open land. He saw a big coachwhip wrapped around a half-grown rabbit, and he teased it to get it to run him. He picked up a white flint rock and chunked at it and the coachwhip looked him over. He made a fuss at the snake and the snake licked out its tongue at him and complied with the worst fuss it could make. Then it uncoiled the rabbit and started for him, and ran him down the bank to the creek, which was called a branch that far up. One had to say, 'That's Glaze Creek,' or think the thought to recognize it as Glaze Creek there. When Daniel stopped to get something to kill it with, the snake balanced itself on a big embedded rock right over his head, opened its mouth, and made its scariest fuss. That was the climax and Daniel outran the snake to where Sookie sprawled back, looking at the daylight, and did not try to bother the snake any more. He laughed and shivered pleasantly and Sookie joined him.

It took no more than such as this to show Daniel and Sookie a good time and get up a pleasant conversation and a big laugh between them. Anything, just so it thicketed them together more. Daniel had learned to live the thickety life with the Cherokees as tutors and a Cherokee woman as helpmate and partner in daylight and in the dark to such a degree of perfection that he became one of their leaders and their spokesman to the whites. His own farm home and his summer home were filled with Indian utensils, relics, and trinkets such as 'tommy hawks,' bows and arrows, shawls and blankets. His neighbors could only guess at the Indian secrets he knew, for Daniel played shutmouth along that line. He wouldn't talk, the neighbors said. He had opened up to one person only, his son Daniel — the first white child born in the country — who was then married and raising a family of his own with a white girl, directly across the river from his father. In fact, Little Daniel had sons to whom he was beginning to open up Cherokee secrets. The two Daniel Glazes conversed in the Cherokee tongue as often as in English when off together. There were some important things Daniel had kept from Sookie so that she felt that she hardly knew him. But to compensate for this he never pressed her about her life before he found her, a newcomer in the river country.

Nevertheless, Sookie understood him pretty well and knew the way to his heart. She knew how to enjoy life with him so well that their neighbors said they were as happy as 'fee-larks' together. On this day their minds had traveled with them so that they had forgotten the four o'clocks in the yard at home, and the purple martins. When they tried, they could give themselves to the four o'clocks and hold back nothing and virtually be one of the martins; but when they were in the woods, they were in the woods. There their minds traveled like squirrels traveling in the timber, or the Indian hens through it, or the ground hogs under it. At times their minds sped through the timber like the red deer or to a branch like a mink or a weasel. They had seen so many of all the wild animals while out in the woods together that they could go to sleep of nights counting them up and seeing them again. People said that Daniel had buried himself in the woods. At first a Cherokee woman was buried with him. And some said that later he buried himself deeper with Sookie. Others said that he had buried a white girl with him just as the Cherokee girl had buried him with her. At any rate, Daniel and Sookie played and wallowed and rolled around at the head of the creek, lay down on their all-fours to drink from the spring, and then walked on out the wagon road to Jack Smith's and Alice's house. On the way, there wasn't a step but what they could touch some kind of a tree and keep walking in the road.

II

Alice Smith looked down the spring path and saw them coming. 'I see Daniel and Sookie coming,' she said. 'And they're out gatherin' ginsing of course. They've got their sacks full.'

'Yes, it's Daniel and Sookie — I might say Daniel and Ginsing,' Jack said. 'And I just as soon see the old devil and his wife coming as to see them strollops. They'll stay out their welcome. You can bet your bottom dollar on that.'

Some of the children and a visiting boy — one of the Waldrops — heard the conversation.

Jack Smith never had known anybody as well fixed as Daniel Glaze who wanted to strollop around so. Neither had Alice. Or anybody else for that matter. Not on the Warrior River or back on the Savannah River in Georgia — and across in South Carolina — where they had come from to the spank-fired new state. Daniel had learned it from the Cherokees and that Cherokee wife of his. They were all gadabouts. They didn't know anything else. That Sookie had made him worse in his old days. An old man had no business taking up with a girl even if he did discover her. That woman couldn't be still at the house like a decent woman was supposed to. They had followed the wild animals so that Daniel was just like one of them, let alone Sookie. That was the reason the Indians never had anything. They went forth and called on the spirits of spots, or places, and streams as Daniel said. That was their religion. It was a traveling sort of religion. Animals traveled, and so did Daniel and his mate. No other woman would be content to leave the martins and jaybirds in charge of the chickens and guineas and things. But since they bet on the martins that way, they did see to it that the martins stayed with them even after they had raised. Daniel raised a patch of what he called his martin-gourds every year and kept putting up more poles. Somehow or other he charmed them. They had up an understanding, it seemed. Daniel said birds could tell when you loved them to the bones. He said he loved the very hearts of the purple martins and made them know it. He made them appreciate him as their friend, he said, but he gave all the credit to the Cherokees. Whenever you saw a martin at your house you could safely say, 'There's one of Daniel's martins.'

Daniel and Sookie and deep dusk came to the Smith homestead at one and the same time. 'Light, hitch, and come in, as Uncle Cape used to say,' Jack said. Alice bade them come in and make themselves at home. It developed that they were all getting along the best kind.

Daniel gave Jack a going-over for not coming across the river and helping him drink rum. He had kept a jug named for Jack Smith from his friends Tommy Lisper and Tommy Prescott and was still looking to some good fellowship over the jug with Jack. He always tried to make it a point to get over a jug of likker with each good friend at least once a year. And Sookie gave them a going-over for not coming over the river and helping them eat watermelons. They had had the *most* of them. The only way to enjoy watermelons to the fullest was to have your friends visit you and help you eat them. Why, watermelons grew like 'punkins' for them on the river bank. It was fun to see how much they would grow overnight. Jack and Alice had just not had time to get over; but they would get over there one of these days. 'We'll come when you're not expecting us, Daniel,' Jack said.

The men folk went to the lot to see about feeding the things while the women folk remained in the kitchen preparing supper. It was a sumptuous meal fit to weight down the revolving table and fill the large family and visitors besides. One thing Daniel had schooled Sookie in to perfection. He had taught her to cook as his Cherokee wife cooked before her. Thus Sookie naturally told Alice again, as she had time before, how she cooked according to the Cherokees. So the two women actually enjoyed themselves telling each other how they cooked.

Sookie's cooking was more like a man's cooking out in the woods or on the river. Say camped out on a wild hog hunt or a midnight supper on a coon hunt at night, or a fish gigging where the fish are cooked on the spot. When she prepared 'rosenears' for the table, she roasted them in the shucks in coals. She not only fried fish in the skillet but baked it in a shuck in the coals as well. And she would bake fish on a hot rock. The best way to cook cornbread or flourbread was to bury it in the coals and have roasted hoe-cakes. Ash cake, she called it. Alice roasted her sweet potatoes in the coals and ashes and that was all. And Sookie had to tell her all about the stews and fixments and messes she made of herbs from the riverbank, fish and turtles from the river, and game from the woods. Daniel's house was noted for its dried fish and dried venison and beef, and Sookie talked a blue streak about that.

Alice in turn cooked everything in the old-time white woman's way by boiling, baking, or frying — and sometimes broiling over the log fireheap in the fireplace. The supper consisted of victuals from the garden and field, the bread barrel, and the smoke house prepared in this way, plus milk from the spring served in big goblets and butter served in a huge bowl with much milk still in it. It was a supper the Glazes enjoyed the best kind, and certainly appreciated as a change, but it would have been hard to have eaten a meal at their house without eating fresh eating from the mast or canebrakes, or fish from the river, or dried meat of some kind from the woods. They could not have lived and done well on so many vegetables and field crops all the time as they knew the Smiths mostly did. There was plenty of cured hog meat from the smoke house, or the Glazes would have been at a loss even while enjoying the sumptuous change of fare.

III

On the front porch Daniel was explaining how thunder killed turkeys in the egg. He was going into details and speaking from personal experiences. He said that was the reason turkeys do not raise more in the woods than they do. If every close clap of thunder that came did not kill them in the egg, they would raise so fast that they would be as plentiful in the woods as partridges or jorees. And that might not be a good thing, for that many turkeys would tear up the ground and take the country.

Daniel and the grown boys were talking of going down in Jack's branch field and catching a coon or two, when, all of a sudden, the wolves came in from the head of Black Creek or the mouth of Wolf Creek and tried to get to the sheep in the stable. This scared the children in bed and got up a general excitement, and a 'sicking' on of the dogs. Jack's cur and hound were joined by Bill Glaze's cur and hound who ran over to investigate, and the race was on toward the fork of the creeks. Bill Glaze was Daniel's cousin who had come into the Indian realm on the river with Daniel. It was a moonlight night and there were paths to follow, and Daniel fled after the dogs without looking to see who was going with him. Such as this excited him. He had to get out and follow the dogs regardless. Without saying a word, Sookie and the grown boys followed.

Jack and Alice sat on the porch, thinking about the Glazes and talking. They talked about Daniel and his two brothers and cousin who were the first whites to enter the country. They had respect for Bill Glaze, their near neighbor, who had waited for more whites to come in and married a good white girl. Indeed they had been glad for one of their girls to marry one of Bill's boys. He had helped replenish the new country in the good old Bible way just as they had seen it done back in Georgia and across the river in Carolina. Daniel and Bill were raising up two different races of dogs entirely. Each race had its own kind of sharpness. But the Smiths were all for Bill and his set and against the wild life of Daniel's set. They believed in education and training. People were like animals. They had to be trained. They had to be schooled, and not by peckerwoods and soft-shelled 'turtles' and wild hogs. This raising children up in the woods to be regular old ground hogs would not do. They spoke with great respect when mentioning Daniel's brother Tom, who traded around with him until he finally hung in at Tuscaloosa and became the first banker there. They knew very little about their brother Bill, who stayed on a while longer with Daniel and finally went to Tom in Tuscaloosa. They had heard that he followed the Indians into Mississippi.

Daniel was too wild a flower for them. They would not go that deep into the woods. They looked back to the garden flowers the Glaze boys had been back in Charleston. Daniel had thrown himself away and could have done better. He had buried himself in the woods first with a Cherokee woman and then with a strolloping, no 'count, low-down, ignorant white girl. A cultivated, well-educated South Carolinian of Charleston had turned ground hog. He was at first as well prepared for a political career as anybody in Charleston. Daniel had it in him to be somebody. And as long as he was legislator representing the Two-Warriors territory at Cahaba and Tuscaloosa it seemed that he had found himself. But the woods finally closed in on him forever, once the Indian questions had been settled. Now he would be a fit representative for the beavers and otters but not for human beings who believed in progress. He was a good example of what the woods would do to a man if he let himself go. He would go wild and mate with anything that came along just so it was a woman. He had forgotten his A B C's and she never had learned them. It was a sight to see the fine Charleston furniture and stuff Daniel had in his farm home and his summer home and think what he had come to. It was something to study about.

The dogs ran the wolves along Black Creek and on across Dividing Ridge, down Cymbling Branch and into the Short Creek country where Tommy Lisper and his boys lived. All this time Daniel and Sookie kicked around and found themselves in several beds of ginsing and heartleaves against the spots where the beeches grew; and the boys went to the branch field, where the coons had been eating the corn, to see how things looked. Tomorrow ginsing could be gathered there and maybe some roots shaped like a man could be found. If that could be done, it would help out when a Chinaman was found. People said it would make a Chinaman fall all over himself and mumble. Some of these stems had five leaves, too. That would bear investigation the next day. How much a wealthy Chinaman would give to be able to walk in the beech shades and kick around in ginsing and heartleaves! From the way the heartleaves smelled, Chinamen ought to be able to turn them into something valuable. People said these Chinamen believed ginsing would *cure* anything. And a root shaped like a man would *do* anything. If the Chinamen knew about this country they would come over here and settle if they could get permission.

While milling around in this way the Warrior River pair happened upon a doe and some slinks licking salt at a salt lick in a boggy place near a spring. Their hearts beat like bluebirds flitting about in a limb, and in the moonlight night the deer looked white as sheep. Daniel was glad that he had no weapon, not even one of his bows and arrows. It was a picture of heaven to the man and woman with the timber-traveling minds. It took Daniel back to many inspirations such as these encountered with his Cherokee mate out in the woods when their hearts burrowed the earth and drew them down wallowing. Back then they always went out —

day or night — and sought such benediction scenes when they wanted to be most intimate with one another. They believed that children should come from such times and that such a child bore a charmed life. Under such circumstances as these he had had the red deer follow him and his mate nearly home. Partly because of such incidents the idea got abroad that the red deer were not afraid of the Cherokees and would even follow them. Daniel told Sookie that the deer mostly followed the Cherokees west — that they had very few deer left compared to what they had when he came to the country. They were afraid of the whites for more reasons than their guns. The red deer were important in the timber-traveling religion Daniel was converted to when he mated with the Cherokee girl.

Following the benevolence of this scene, Daniel and Sookie entered into an intimacy such as Daniel used to enter with his Cherokee wife. Sookie had learned to expect her best times with Daniel upon such occasions and in such spots. He did not believe in the house for such intimacies and neither did Sookie. That's what Daniel liked about Sookie. She had a mind, and a heart, and a body for the woods; and that is what others did not know about her. Daniel had more passion than Jack Smith could appreciate and so did Sookie. No other girl in the country since the native girls had gone west could have matched Daniel even with old age coming upon him. He had wanted to live through such scenes as this with every beautiful grown girl he ever had seen and end up by being buried on the spot. But he considered the Cherokee girls best for such a life except an occasional white girl like Sookie. The Indian girls could best enter into the earthy religion of it all. Oftentimes he wished he could single out these grown girls with the earthy religion in their hearts and experience life with them one by one on the spots all over the river world, and die with them as people said some fish die after such action and be buried in a green bank in the same hole with them. His idea of heaven was to be a young god of the woods, forever living intensely enough to kill and being ever intense enough for an awakened life. That, however, he knew would make a man the equal of the Supreme Being and could not be. In his ordinary moments when he considered this mating business he thought that any man ought to be mighty glad to marry any woman. That was the plan of life. Almost any girl would answer and answer well so that she would be a blessing if taught right. Few if any normal women were at fault if they were not benedictions to their husbands. He believed that almost any normal woman could follow the greatest of men. There were great men and ordinary men and sorry men. But most all women could be great if given the right man.

IV

In the morning it was Saturday. Jack Smith usually spent sweet Saturdays in his blacksmith shop. No matter what the work through the week, he always reserved Saturday for his mendings and creations at the forge and anvil. He was known as a good horse master. All of his boys were talented smiths. People said that it ran in the Smith blood. They could make anything and do anything in a blacksmith shop. They could please themselves and thought they could please God best when in a shop using their heads to invent and their hands to fashion. A man was given a mind to guide the hand in its creations in the blacksmith shop, to farm, to read the Bible, the almanac, and pieces of paper. All of the Smiths believed in knowledge as such and in doing things. But that morning the man from across the river and his mate were there in the way. The Smiths, however, would not have been in the way of the Glazes if they had been across the river that morning. Perhaps the Glazes would have taken them into the woods to show them or tell them something, or down to the river. The Glazes believed in knowledge that carried feeling with it. Going about the comfortable Glaze home place would in itself have been like being in the woods, for Daniel and Sookie made their home place, which showed beautifully that human beings used there, seem like a part of the green thicket. But the Smith home place was another kind of using place which tallied not at all with the using places of the red deer. Nevertheless, the Glazes enjoyed the change of scene and the contact with other minds. Sookie enjoyed it primarily because Daniel did. They were both fond of

107

the growing Smith girls. Some of the children resented this and some did not. The boys simply enjoyed hearing Daniel talk and did not mind Sookie, for she was Daniel's dough-baker and bed-fellow.

Daniel hung around the shop and kept Jack in a bad humor. Sookie hung around the house and garden and worried Alice a little and interested her some, especially when telling about the Chinaman they hoped to find in town. Jack was a firm and fractious man. He had what was called the Smith fits. That is, he had mad spells, and Daniel brought on these mad spells that morning. Two or three times between watermelon cuttings in the shop and at the house Jack Smith threw his hammer against the shop walls and mildly blasphemed it, the unsatisfactory work he was doing, and all that. Daniel tried to tell him things about the work that made him wall his eyes and want to spit fire.

However, the men got to talking about the Bible and this was a godsend part of the time. Smith was a great Bible reader, although he was not such a terribly religious man. Daniel had read the Bible a good bit in his time but had quit as he had quit other books long before. Like a stroke from this talk on the Scriptures Smith said, 'I am just as glad that there's a devil and a hell as I am that there's a God and heaven.' He was known for this idea. The young people thought it was an infidelity or something bordering that but often decided he was right about it when they grew older and knew more about the earth life. Daniel knew enough about the earth life to appreciate the idea and said so. But his idea of hell was not Smith's idea, and he said it was not. The one thought hell was a place of fire and brimstone and the other thought it was a state of being lost and desolate in some place. Hell to Daniel was a place where there were no friendly spirits of spots and none of the earthiness that they congregate to. Smith adduced all this to Daniel's having buried himself in the woods, kept the thought to himself, and got mad at his hammer again.

But the men did agree on the Bible in many places. They agreed on it when it spoke on the man and woman business. Smith never thought of the women and girls as nymphs, and consequently never talked about them from that angle. But he had thought about them in many of the good old Bible ways and could lead any conversation along these lines. Daniel thought there was little difference in the end between the Bible on women and his own thickety ideas on women and he was right there with Smith when he said, 'You see, the man that made this world and his legal advisers made a blunder when they made a man without a woman. They seen it wouldn't work. They was experimenting. They seen their mistake when they seen all the man's blunders and mismanagements.' The two dark-featured and well-built pioneers got together on this and enjoyed themselves mutually. And Smith went on, 'You take me and let me get old and some sixteen or eighteen year old girl come along and I'll want her. If Alice was to be dead, I'd want to marry her. I'd take up with her somehow or other or bust a gut. And if I was to marry the girl, she could ride me a bug hunting to the bluff and make me jump off and think it was fun. A young woman can do to an old man any way under the sun. You take that beautiful young girl who warmed King David's bed. If he'd been left alone with her he'd a give her his kingdom and him a man after God's own heart. The Lord knows we're weak that way and He don't fall out with us for that weakness.' They agreed again and Daniel said that Sookie was like the women back in King Solomon's time. She was easy to get along with. Women honored the men folk back then. Solomon had seven hundred wives and three hundred concubines and cooks and housegirls. The women were good women, easy to please and not hard to satisfy. Sookie was like that. Well, Alice was, too.

And about dinner time Jack got to asking Daniel some questions about Charleston, the Cherokees, his Cherokee wife, his terms as a legislator in Tuscaloosa, and Sookie, which Daniel evaded or turned off. Jack did not mind telling all about how he came to the Warrior Rivers with Alice from the Savannah River in Georgia in one of Tommy Thompson's mule wagons in 1820 and first stopped at the great basin in the fork and was outbid on the basin at the land sales. But Daniel knew all about that anyhow. One man had no secrets and the other one had a whole flock of them.

109

V

Daniel and Sookie went off to the woods for ginsing that afternoon. Daniel, especially, was not out only for ginsing. He was out to strike Cherokee trails where in his day he had had some rolling times. In fact, anywhere he tolled his hogs from the beech mast or acorns, or followed his cattle through the beggar lice or the red deer over their drives to the canebrakes on the riverbank, or the black bear, he could strike these paths. When he went out and killed a wild turkey eating turkey peas, or cut down a tree for a coon, or caught a red horse in the river, he was apt to strike up with the spirits of spots, the ghosts of particular places, still in their old lodgings even with the Cherokees gone. Most of these presences, he thought, had followed the Cherokees west but some remained. Those who remained kept his religion alive. But there was a wistfulness and a sadness about these that remained not encountered among them in the good old rolling days. Nevertheless, the best that remained hovered over and along these old Indian paths.

That night at Jack Smith's house they had a fine mess of red horses for supper. Daniel and Sookie made the Smiths give way while they prepared the fish and the meal; and the Smiths could not help but enjoy it. They forgot that Daniel and his woman were strollops. While finishing supper Daniel got a fish bone lodged in his throat and couldn't get it out. He tried and tried and followed suggestions, but couldn't make it. The Smiths liked fish as well as the Glazes. Jack had as big a craving for fish in his mouth as Daniel had, but just couldn't take time off to get out and catch them. When he went fishing he had to take off from his work. But Daniel seemed to have no such sacrifices to make in order to get the fish. If Jack had lived right on the river as Daniel did it would have been the same way with him, he declared.

After supper Daniel and the boys were fixing to go to the branch field and catch a coon or two. The coons were eating up the corn. Daniel promised that he would come back over and show them how to catch the last one of them; but in the meantime they would catch one or two and scare the others for awhile. He was also coming back and help them build a wolf pen. Nobody else in the country, he said, knew as well how to catch coons or build wolf pens unless it was Tommy Lisper.

But as they were making preparations to start to the branch field they heard a panther squall. 'Listen at that painter,' more than one said. 'I heard it,' more than one replied. Others said, 'Yes, it's a painter.'

By this time the panther was considerably nearer; in fact, near the house. It was circling and hollering. 'It hollers like a woman,' Daniel said. Others agreed that it hollered just like a woman. It would jump on a woman if cornered, and it would carry off a child. Woe be unto anything it could seize. Also woe be unto anything it sprung upon. Would the dogs run it? Just then the cur gave his own answer that *he* would. Jack and the grown boys ran out to the stables and by then Bill Glaze's cur had joined Jack's cur and a race was on. Bill Glaze's hound had come over and it joined Jack's hound and together they made a great noise on the trail; but they were afraid and would not *run* it. The panther circled for the Glaze Creek woods and would perhaps go to the river directly across from Daniel's house. Daniel and Sookie halfway decided to get their ginsing and go home. They couldn't carry it all, could they? Yes, they thought so.

While Daniel was out listening and hollering with the boys, the Waldrop boy got a chance alone and told Daniel what Jack Smith said when he saw him coming. Daniel said well, that he was going home anyway and now he certainly would. He found Sookie at the ginsing which she had rounded up and told her that they were going home, that the painter was circling that way. Then he got a chance and asked Jack if he said it. Jack said, 'Well, I don't know whether I used exactly them words or not; but I said something like it.' Daniel was sorry that he felt that way about it and that was all he said. The ginsing gatherers shouldered their sacks, which bore them down considerably, and lit a shuck after the curs and the panther. All the while Daniel was trying to unlodge the fish bone and Sookie was talking to him about it. He told her what Jack Smith had said. Thank God they could live

111

at home. They didn't have to go see Jack Smith and Alice to get their something to eat.

The panther circled in the Glaze Creek woods a long time and finally struck out for the river at the point directly across from their house. They heard their own dogs join the two curs. They kept to the path, and in spite of a few stops to rest they reached the river as the dogs ran the panther up the river above the field. The dogs were hot in pursuit as they ran over the spot Daniel guessed to be the bank where his Cherokee wife and their child were buried. Daniel and Sookie reached the graves and lay down to rest, and listened to the dogs, wishing all the while that the dogs would tree or catch the panther. In the moonlight night the long blades of grass, the green moss, deer's tongue, ginsing, ferns, the heartleaves, the plantains, wild hyacinths, and the violet plants which covered the bank and its graves — always in the shade — could be told by shape, feel, and smell.

But the dogs did not tree the panther and could not catch it. Finally they quit the chase and came back by the graves where Daniel and Sookie were. There was one thing Daniel had never told a living soul except his son Daniel. Young Daniel later told it to his boys and they in turn told it to an outsider. When Daniel saw the Cherokee girl and wanted her he had to run her down to catch her. He had to run her all over the place on both sides of the river and at last caught her on the bank where she now lay buried. She was willing to be his and became his on that bank. When their child died, she wanted the family graveyard started there. There was where she wanted to be buried. As Daniel prospered, he came to own all the land on both sides of the river where he had to run down the Cherokee maiden. Across the river from where Daniel and Sookie were lying out Daniel had five good houses. In the bend way up the river which he had bought at the land sales was where he and his young wife spent their honeymoon the next day and night. Ever since that day and night up there with her and nothing to interfere but the hum of the great woods, the sounds of the creatures, and the ripples on the rocks, he had been attached to that particular bend. There was where he had so many untouched ginsing beds.

112

Daniel would be old before he knew it but was still a very strong man, so that he did not at the time mind meeting a black bear or a painter out in the woods. Except for Sookie, he would have been a broken man. As it was, much of the time he was a sad man notwithstanding his natural jovial spirits. But he kept it to himself for the most part. He could sit on his porch at home across the river where the four o'clocks were open and the martins asleep and see the clump of beeches and whiteoaks shading the bank where his Cherokee wife and their child lay. He knew that she died of a broken heart brought on when all her people were forced to go west. At least, he attributed it to that. His daughter and her husband and one of his boys had gone West to look for their mother's people and had found some of them. He had labored in Tuscaloosa and Cahaba for more than one term in the interest of the Cherokees. More and more he had become embittered in his heart by the thought of the garden variety of life the whites always tried to advance to as he had experienced it in Charleston. He pitied the whites for their religion. It had come to be almost pointless to him. But he hated the hard hearts among them. But some white men like Tommy Lisper had hearts in them and were good to be with. And best of all, Sookie was like the women back in King Solomon's time.

They lay out together all night enjoying the moonlight night and the river, and the bank, and each other's company, and Daniel thought serious thoughts. The fish bone in his throat bothered him some but less than it had, and they decided it would eventually work out without serious consequences. At the first crack of day they pulled off their shoes and waded the river with half of the ginsing. They would come back for the other later. On their way up the hill path to the house they heard the chickens and guineas fly down out of the cedar trees. Daniel complained about the fish bone in his throat as Sookie started a fire from coals still alive deep in the ashes.

When the fire was blazing hot Sookie said, 'Here, pull down your breeches and back up close to the fire.'

'Why?'

'It makes no difference why. Do like I tell you.'

Daniel obeyed.

Sookie got some tallow and warmed it and went to rubbing Daniel. 'If it don't do you no good, it won't do you no harm,' she said.

Daniel got to laughing and coughed up the fish bone.

And that day they spent a sweet Sunday together.

RECORD AT OAK HILL

ELIZABETH MADOX ROBERTS

THE house, built of bricks, was square in outline, was a pile of old bricks standing on a rise among the rolling plains. From the spaces under the trees about the house one looked toward the south and saw a faint undulation of small mountains, the Knobs, thirty miles away. The fields were spread, right and left, before and behind the old dwelling. The farm belonged to Morna Trigg, born a Laughlin, and one or another of her sons or her nephews had farmed for her through the years of her ownership. Richard Dorsey, the present incumbent, was her great-nephew. The rooms were sparely furnished with pieces that had been made before the old war. Almost weekly Morna turned away from the door those relic hunters, often ill-mannered, who had recently acquired a taste for ancient things, and the dealers who trafficked in the needs of these persons.

Behind the larger mass of the dwelling the log house which had once been the home of the pioneer Laughlins stood in a partially preserved state. When the better house had been built, it had been preserved as a kitchen and workroom, and later was used only for storage. Tall old beeches and oaks grew about the entire community of buildings. The walls were bare of vines and stood forth, partly shuttered and mellow, up on the wind and the sun.

Richard Dorsey came up from the field where his men were cutting the hay, his rough field shoes knocking on the paving flags behind the house. As he came he called the hunting dogs from their sleeping before the woodhouse door, gathering them with a cry so that they followed at his heels. The sundial his uncles had drawn long ago on the south front of the log house was marking a point near to the hour of noon. Inside the house his sister Ruth would be directing and helping the brown girl to bring dinner to readiness, and his great-aunt Morna would be sitting now beside a window to read from one of the old books.

A child's voice came now and then, shouting, like the cry of a shrill bird under the high trees. This would be his child Dick, playing with the hound pups before the front wall of the house. Down in the bushes beyond the garden some turkey hens were crying lightly to their young. Will Neal, his sister's husband, having no employment, had come with Ruth to stay at the farm. He would be helping with the hay, or walking back from the field when they came in together; he would be speaking.

'What's the matter with the world is . . . ' he would attack a new point in the circle of his troubled conjectures. His voice would be lifted in imaginary argument and real anger. He had lost his farm during Nineteen Thirty-One. 'From buying high-priced machinery and selling low-priced wheat and tobacco,' he had shouted once toward the rolling hills that were vaguely misty under the midday heat. All morning he had driven one of the mowers over the hayfield. Now the Negro men would be bringing the teams to the barn to give them their noon feedings and water. As a defeated man, Neal worked with fervor, giving himself entirely to each task, laboring endlessly, willing, put-upon by an ill system, having lost his home. He had made many journeys here and there to try to find employment. He would be muttering:

'Four-fifths of the value of a ham is hog. They can stick pretty labels on it all they please, and cart it about from place to place. They can dress it out with oil paper. . . . People don't eat labels. . . . Labels won't make life in a man. . . . '

He would tell of a poor man, one of his former neighbors, who had sold his tobacco crop in the open market. When all the expenses of production were met, the man had sixty cents for his year's work. 'Sixty cents and a gaunt living,' Neal said, beginning anew, telling of another case. They would be hunting young squirrels along the creek woods, walking slowly in the dusk. 'I'd like to thrust and cut,' Neal said. 'I'd like to get my grip ahold of some throat. Let it be something strong, any size you please. So I could get my hands ahold onto it. . . . ' Or stacking bundles of cut grain, making shocks, '"System" is what's the matter,

they say. What's "System"? "Conditions" are bad, they say.
I'd cut a hole clear through the damned heart of "Conditions."
. . . Who made conditions?'

He would be sullen and quiet for many days, or talkative again.
'What's the matter,' he would say, beginning calmly again, 'is,
there's too much city-mindedness.' He would be bending beside
the farm truck, greasing the wheels. Quiet again, walking with
bowed head all day, eating his food in humility. 'Fine paved
roads were no advantage to the poor. . . . Horses fall down on the
concrete. Can't get any grip on asphalt. . . . Forced him to buy
high-priced trucks. "Created a demand" is what they called it.
. . . God help us! . . . Wheat sells this week for fifty cents a
bushel. . . . Has the price of a machine decreased in proportion
with the decrease in wheat? in corn? Not on your life. . . .'

They would be talking together — reasons, prophecies, conjectures, helplessness, and at last dropping of all those things
which they could not foretell or control, beginning anew with
pride.

'Aunt Morna wouldn't borrow — years when she lived here on
milk and bread and knotty turnips, or a little knotty fruit the
worms left her in the orchard. She made the taxes somehow, and
didn't sell out neither. . . .

'What's the matter, really, is . . . the wealth of the country is
in the hands of one-third of one per cent of the population.'

'What's wealth?' They would be arguing. Agreeing again:

'The manufacturer's tariff . . . a culture founded on sharp prac-
tices. . . . The end of another age. . . . Eighteen, say, Sixty-Five
to Nineteen Thirty. It was long enough. Sixty-five years.'

These troubled reasons pervaded Richard's intentions for the
hounds and made less his pleasure in them, but he gathered them,
distastefully, having decided to house them for a day that they
might be the more keen on the hunt. Morna's voice came from
the west doorway. She was shouting and calling to Lem, the black
man who worked about the stables, calling: 'Lem, Lem, you, Lem,
there. Did you feed my jennets? I don't want you starvin' my
mules. You feed my jennets.'

Richard brought the hounds into the log cabin behind the

117

main dwelling and gave them small pones of bread. While the dogs undulated about over their food, leaping from pone to pone with eagerness that made their flanks quiver, he closed the windows, drawing the wooden shutters. The hounds were fine beasts. They seemed lank and swift as they bent over the food to snap it into their jaws and swallow it quickly. When the eating was done, they went hungrily about, looking for more. Richard took his coat from a peg beside the fireplace, where it had hung since early morning, preparing himself now for dinner. As he swept his finger along the wall to lift the coat, a sharp pricking caught at his skin and scratched a light wound across his fingers.

The dinner bell was ringing, sharp and swift, the wound leaping to him from the bell Ruth or the aunt, Morna, always rang when the meal was near at hand. He waited to look at the pointed edge that had caused his slight hurt, and he pried at the point with his fingers. It was sharp and fine, a blending of things, as if it might be the fine point of a nail or knife imbedded in the plaster that was chinked between the logs. Neal's feet knocked at the flags outside, going toward the house, heeding the bell. Richard pried at the plaster again and again, and he broke a little of it away from the fine point, which now seemed to belong to some tool of an undetermined length that reached back into the mass of the chinking. He broke a lump of the plaster, following the line of the tool which lay, sharply tapering, fine and clean-cut, exposed for three inches now and receding into the hard chinking of the wall.

It was a file or a dagger, he supposed. He pried at it, drawing at it with his fingers, but it was fixed and did not yield. The dinner bell rang again with a faint questioning in its quick tinkle, as if Morna would say: 'Why not come now?' and he laid the broken pieces of the chinking over the hole he had made and covered the exposed point of the tool. He drove the dogs back into the cabin when they tried to follow him out and went quickly toward the house. As he walked he thrust his arms into the sleeves of the jacket which he wore at the table. Walking toward the house in the noon sunlight, his shadow went crouching at his feet, the bulk of it crumpled and distorted from his lank body, which was tall by inheritance and hard and lean from much work. He went

118

along the flags, south and west, toward the west portico and entered the doorway, coming at once into the dining room.

Morna was sitting at the table, and Will Neal and Ruth were waiting beside the east door, the child Dick slipping into his chair. Morna was firm and graceful in her old age, past eighty, her face a sequence of fine masculine planes that had grown out of the feminine softness of her youth and middle age. She sat at the end of the board, opposite his own place, and she began to pour the coffee, swaying rhythmically from one cup to the next as the stream ceased to arc from the silver spout. Her body had hardened in lines of perpetual grace.

The Negro girl would come from the kitchen and pass slowly about the table, vaguely negligent unless she was directed by Morna's brief orders. The business of serving being done, Richard was about to speak of the hidden tool or weapon buried in the plaster of the cabin, but he came swiftly to a new mind regarding it. If he spoke of it, some other, one of the Negro hands, might, being curious of it, dig it out before he came to it. He decided to say nothing of it.

Morna sat erect above the cups and saucers, having poured the coffee. Her hair was but partly gray and her eyes were quick under a faint dimness that merely veiled their vigor. Although her hands were old and often tremulous, they were light at whatever they performed. '*Prometheus?*' he asked her, remembering the old book he had seen in her hand when he came indoors during the morning. The fading brown covers of the old frayed book had been dusted over with gray in the bright light of a window where the sun shone, the book held close to her eyes.

'*Prometheus*, this morning?'

'Agamemnon,' she said. Her smile was quick to run with the syllables, making them into a song.

His child, little Dick, felt the leaping pulse of the word and began to sing, patting the table: 'Agamemnon, Agamemnon . . .'

Richard bent to his coffee, thinking, 'Will she live forever? Will she live forever?' wanting her to take no new sign of coming departure, regretting and admiring in one confused emotion. She was still speaking:

119

'. . . Led from the land their armaments of a thousand ships of the Argives . . . screaming through passion of a great noise of war . . .' Mellowed learnings, old and well rehearsed, stood frequently about her. All the people that had stood between himself and her were dead; she was of the strong strain, of the Laughlins. The dogs in the cabin outside were of the strain Morna's father had bred, the breed enriched by frequent additions of new sires. It was thus with the Laughlins, by whatever name they might be called — Dorsey, Ennis, Froman, Trigg. Acting without design, following their taste, they had thus come down through two centuries, and farther back lay vague assurances of similar choices and habits, running back. Neal was quiet at the table, troubled and preoccupied. He sat opposite his wife who had placed herself near to Richard's child, caring for it. His ruddy face was pinched with distress and bitterness under its excellent vigor. His hands were strong above his plate, cutting the food heartily or resting on the cloth at the side. He leaned forward sometimes as if he were spent by a blow, but suddenly, at times, he would seem crouching, as if he were ready to spring forward. Oaths came easily to his lips now. His eyes were blue and mild. Richard knew that he would be quiet at the table, that he would not enter his troubled accounts and arguments. Leaning over his meat pie, Richard's thought leaped about among many objects, trailing among such old things about the house as were continually being found out of the past, hidden things that had never been concealed, that had merely been dropped away into forgotten corners and out-of-the-way places, to be found a long while afterward.

'Screaming through passion of a great noise of war,' Morna said, quoting again from the old translation. 'Did Lem feed my jennets, Richard? He's a trifler. I don't want my little mules starved.'

'I saw him go that way with corn in a basket.'

'I saw him with a fork of hay.'

Morna, having found the old book to read, had put a renewed dignity over the noon. The signs offered indicating that the young mules had been fed were accepted as sufficient. Neal sat quietly at the table, indifferent of the learning which he did not completely share, and Richard came again, by the way of the Greeks, to the sharp tool imbedded in the plaster of the cabin, it belonging to their past somehow. He knew that the living give to the trinkets of the dead an excess of meaning. Any thought of their past came presently to a high pitch in Tom Laughlin, Morna's father, his great-grandfather. Stories and sayings clustered around him. It was hard to make a real, fleshly man of all that he signified in fine ways and courageous opinions. Richard viewed with amusement the chance that any might make a mystery of the tool in the cabin. It was a gimlet or an awl, thrust at somebody's whim into the fresh plaster.

'Your father, old Tom Laughlin, what was he like?' he asked Morna. His tone was pleasantly mocking and affectionate. It made nothing of the generations that lapped, one over the other, through time. Sitting there together, himself, Morna, and the child Dick, were a line running back to Tom Laughlin and gathering with him into one being that was present, that was everywhere identical with the whole aggregate. Mockingly he asked her, the woman, his equal in affection and wit: 'What was old Tom? What was his style?'

'He was quiet,' Morna said. 'You'd think he was timid at a first encounter. But you'd get fooled if ever you thought that long. He was a tall man. It was always said I favored him in the way he looked. And he was a reverent man, religious even, but he had little to say about these things. Like all the balance in his time, gentlemen I mean, he was a hunter, out a many is the night with his dogs and his friends. Over toward the river bluffs. He'd forget his dinner if a hunt was on.'

The art of being a hunter was no new thing surely, Richard was thinking, since he himself could make a very good thing of it. Hunting foxes by moonlight, the pointed face of the fox, pointed eyes, looking out from among the pointed briars, and there were no women in it. The moon spreads down from the sky in a great wash of white and brown indents the hollow places of the fields and pushes into the leafless brush. There were fewer fields then, more forests. Two or three vassals, Negroes, helped make the sport, then as now, riding down the field to collect the dogs at the ford. Courte-

121

sies, 'Good evenin', Mr. Bell, good evenin', Mr. Goddard, good evenin', Mr. Laughlin.' Ruth was asking:

'Religious? What's religious? How do you mean he was religious?'

Morna continuing: 'And he was a breeder of fine horses.' A summary, and no new thing, here retold. 'He went often to see the horses race. In nobody's debt for long. A proud man. Quiet. Arrogant, maybe. Kind, too, kind to his poor neighbors always . . .'

'Was that his religion, maybe?'

'He went to church on Sunday and gave to the steward whenever a fund was wanted, but he wouldn't hold a church office. He sat far back, quiet about it. Religious, is what I said he was, but not fanatical. He died a clean death, in his own bed.'

He had often heard his aunt say of one: 'He died with his boots on,' meaning that the man had died in a brawl or in battle. Morna was making a vague picture, a man arising. He was bright in face, she said, a brightness more than was in his eyes. He was a wanderer perhaps, but not a wanderer in the flesh, for he stayed in his own region after he came back from the war. Men would listen when he talked, but they would shake their heads and walk away, puzzled and not quite willing. 'You ought to write that down in a book,' they would say. 'In a book it would make good matter to read.'

'A fine gentleman, he was, and no slouch,' Morna said, and with such vigor that Richard sat more straight and Ruth fumbled at her hair. 'He dyed his hair as long as our mother lived, but after she died he let himself get old. He carried a cane, a fine stick made of ebony, and the head was overlaid with gold.' She turned to little Dick and spoke as if she laid a precept before him: 'And when he went to cities he wore a silk hat.'

Morna was carried by her subject into newer fluency and a vaguely romantic cast of speech. She saw her subject in an entirety and she glossed it with a choice of fine points. The figure stepped lightly, afflicted with corns, well-booted in leather that was polished every morning. She closed her eyes a moment under the spell of the picture she had evoked, but she opened them suddenly and leaned forward.

'You want to know what he was? When he died, he said to me: "Come here, Morna ..." He was no fanatic, worried about his inner state. I'll tell you some time what he said when he died.'

'A pretty good old scout,' Richard said, ready now to leave the matter.

'A man of peace. He wouldn't fight unless he must. Order in the country was what he wanted.' She continued somewhat wearily, as if she would like to be done, as if she were already finished. But she began again, determined to have forth all of it. 'When he died, he said to me ...'

Richard moved uneasily. Nobody likes to hear these things. Pass it by, he was thinking. Ask for something else. Nobody cared what he mumbled. A rheumy old man, crumpled together, bent at the shoulders, feet dragging, his mind gone down the road to senility. But he turned about and came back, up the way, straightened his shoulders, and spat out the rheum. He stepped out freely and got himself red blood in his cheeks, a hearty laughter in his thin face. Thomas Laughlin, Eighteen Ninety, Eighteen Seventy and earlier. Morna was speaking, her head lifted, her body leaning forward.

'He called me to come to him, many times, in the last of his life. "I did what I did and I'm not afraid to face all heaven and hell," that's what he said.'

'A man of peace. Did he have any enemies?'

'Everybody had enemies.'

They knew what would follow. Everybody had enemies. The War of the Confederacy over but scarcely finished. Old sores were not healed. 'People counted up what they had suffered and trouble came in from the outside.'

'It's because the will won't break,' Neal said. 'It won't give up its pledges. It makes itself right ...'

'He was a man of peace.'

A man of peace, he had just come back from the war, his company of twenty-odd young men returning that had gone out above fifty in number. A young men's company; it was the young men who went south from Kentucky, the southern cause being the Junker cause here. They came back to settle to their homes, to live next to men who had never gone to war, older men who were not spent of their war lust. Richard had heard much of this story before, told in parts, now coming together. It was a war now to bring an end to war lust, a war to demobilize, mind and body, war in the parlor, in the market, in the barnlot. The right of *habeas corpus* had been taken away. Men lingered in prison without trial. Morna was beautiful, sitting back from the table, her thin body folded into a graceful robe she had devised.

'We wanted peace,' she said. 'Father wanted the arts of neighborly intercourse. Money was scarce and cash was gone. It was a time of barter. Men wanted offices, salaries, government prizes. Some were mad with victory and anger.'

She sank into a reverie, as if she had withdrawn the whole past from the present to defend it. Their questions seemed irrelevant now, for they asked in anger and high feeling, talking, several together.

'Who was his enemy?' Richard asked.

'You said there was an enemy. What enemy?'

'The threat was that state lines would be abolished.'

'The big had begun to destroy the little,' Neal called out. 'It was the beginning of what we have now.'

'State lines were abolished for awhile. Kentucky's lines.'

'They violated their pledges to her neutrality.'

'Camp Dick Robinson!'

'It was the beginning . . .'

'I always hated Grant, anyhow,' Ruth said.

'What's that got to do with it?'

'He made a triumphal journey around the world. To get the plaudits of the nations.'

Ruth was urging little Dick to finish his milk, urging him to take the last of it. She had helped the Negro maid all morning, making berry conserve, and her fingers were stained at their tips with the dark red juice of the fruit. She seemed scarcely of any weight beyond a man's need of her youth and her gift of making men comfortable. Being given to inattentive reveries and nervous changes of interest, she seemed to drop a matter before it was begun. But out of this self-centered beauty which seemed to fold

124

more inwardly even when she was giving pleasure, giving food, she made quick decisions and supported attitudes of thought from which she could not be moved by argument, for she had said her say and would say no more. Her small quick face was a diminished and altered replica of the older face, Morna's, brought her to youth and piquancy. She leaned now above the child and secured his interest in the milk. Morna remained quiet, and Richard prepared a pipe slowly and lit the tobacco. He pushed his chair back as if he would go to the fields, and Neal made ready to join him.

'Who was his enemy?' he asked.

Morna was quiet, answering quietly, as if she defended all the dead. Her replies were meager now.

'His name was Buchman.'

'What became of him?'

'What happened to him?'

'He is dead.'

The Negro girl had taken away the plates and the child had run away to play with the little dogs. Morna sat dreamily brooding, withdrawing all the past, withholding, as if she might at any moment make an end, might walk to the door and call out an order to Lem: 'Feed my little mules, you, Lem, there. Open the gate to the paddock. Let the colts in to the water . . .'

But she did not go. 'He was a strong man,' she said. 'I saw him three times. A dark man, a scowling face, a hard look when he saw me. Cruelty pinched his face about the mouth. Great bold eyes somewhat protruding. He was guilty of a hundred crimes, I reckon. He didn't go to the war. He stayed at home and managed, and got rich, but he went south at the end to be at hand for the looting. Dark and secret; I saw him three times. His name was Buchman. He had a part in the Great Hog Swindle of 1864. Burbridge was military commander in Kentucky. Burbridge and a man named Symonds led in the swindle. It was pretended that the Federal government had fixed the price of hogs. They paid the farmers one to two cents less than the market price. Forced the farmers to sell to the conspirators. Resold them to the government at the market price . . .'

125

He had begun as a stock trader — Buchman — buying cattle for the markets. Money from outside came into his hands. Morna continued, warmed now in the telling, roused out of her dream. Retaliations were required. Men in jail for no crime and without trial were taken out and shot or hanged. Six of their neighbors were killed to pay for the death of one who was killed by an outlaw. There was a fight about the jail door and a man named Webb was killed. One death brought on another. The war had come home from the war and fought now at any man's door.

'Some tried to be patient and tried to get the old law to work again. Law would come from the outside, Buchman said. Men said there was law enough here already, but he continually warped it. Buchman had mightily to do with the bad blood that was up in the neighborhood. Civil life could scarcely live where Buchman was. When he finally went, the worst of the trouble came to an end. Brother Horace had just come back from the army — Wheeler's Cavalry. It was the summer after the surrender. The Provost Marshal was in command in Louisville, military rule until the next fall when we got rid of it. Buchman kept the country in a ferment. The war was honorably over. Lee had surrendered. Brother Horace had come home. Buchman said he had no right to come there. Home Guards, they called the country police. They used to ride over the country, sixty men to a company, armed with muskets provided by the Federals, but they got out from under Federal control. Buchman used the Home Guards for his purposes. He said Brother Horace had no right to come back there. Horace said he'd be sure to kill three men if he stayed. He went away to Canada. What was I telling?'

'About his enemy.'

'Everybody had enemies. It was no new thing, no wonder.'

'About Horace. How he fled to Canada.'

'About Buchman. Tell about what became of him.'

'I'll tell about Brother Horace. It's all the same story. Buchman said he had no right to come home. Home Guards, they called these men. They rode hard over the country to spy out trouble and to make trouble. I remember fine jewelry the Buchman girls wore at boarding school, a different set of jewels every day or so,

126

loot they'd brought back from Mississippi. Buchman died with his boots on.'

She looked at them as if they were strangers.

'What is it now?' she asked, computing the years, finding that sixty-five had passed. She was vague of some of the recent events of their history. Vague years closed slowly about her as the covers of an old, slowly fading book inside of which was written the record of a life, of any life, of all the living. She looked at them in anger, accusing them. Morna was gone and some other seemed to sit in her place. Her eyes were bright and angry. She was speaking:

'Mankind is like that in war.'

She looked at them, these strangers, the living and the young. She held them off from her with her hard look that came from behind veiled eyes.

'You won't believe me. I'll never be believed. War is like that. Keep your peace. War never settles anything. The battles are fought after the war is over. You're no better than all I've got to say. Buchman was found dead in his own garden. It was never known who killed him.'

It was all a long while ago, she said, weary now from these recollections. Spent, less from the effort of telling than from the passions retold, she made as if she would leave the room and go to her afternoon rest. Another time perhaps she would tell the rest of it, she said. They had the same at hand, within themselves. These events were all a long time gone, the same continually happening. Why make a recital of what was always at hand? She shrank visibly, her shoulders drooping, her head seeming to sink into her breast. Looking toward some far scene, her eyes narrowed beneath shrunken lids, she was speaking again:

'I was a girl of seventeen, about to marry for the first time. All my wedding was in a manner marked by what went on in the country. When I stood at the altar I thought all the time, "Who killed Buchman?" as if the minister might at any time ask it. The ceremony cast a spell over me, and the music burst out suddenly. I thought all the time, "Who killed Buchman?" I forgot Mr. Froman, who stood beside me to be my husband.'

127

She wandered away from the incident by the altar and told of the dress, of the silk and crinoline. The wire hoops, the iron net of the inmost skirt, was a symbol, she said. She was amused, telling of the dress, which was, she said, a fortification reinforced with steel. There was an old rhyme:

> Forty-seven yards of yaller-packer gingham
> To cover up the hoop-te-doodle-doo.

'Why, they were as smart as we are,' Ruth called out.
'As what?'
'I mean they had as much fun. . . .'
'It was September,' Morna said, telling of her wedding. 'Horace had come back from Canada. Buchman was dead. He could come now without manslaughter.' His coming and the solemn words of the altar had cast a spell over her, she thought now, looking back. She would tell some time what happened at the altar. She was smiling, swaying lightly from the waist, remembering the old dress and the old demeanors. Sweetness and yielding gathered about her. Richard brought her back to the fine point of the tale, the point she had withheld, asking, 'What had happened at the altar?' She might as well finish it, he said. They were all standing now.

'The minister asked: "Do you, Morna Laughlin . . ." My ears heard clearly what was said, but my mind changed it to some other speech. My mind went blank on every other side. "Who killed Buchman?" was in my mind, spread over my whole consciousness, as if there was not any other question. . . . Then I said in a whisper, but the minister heard it: "He deserved his death, he deserved his death." The minister asked me twice before I said what was wanted.'

Ruth was asking an astonished question. Did such a thing ever happen to anybody else in the family? It was nothing, Morna said, making rational her mental lapse. It might happen to anybody under fatigue and excitement. Their voices were falling swiftly together and Morna was going from the room.

Richard had engaged a thresher to beat out the grain cut earlier in the summer. Now the great engine was set in the midst of the wheatfield, stretched out across a rise, and all hands were needed to haul the shocks up to the thresher and to take away the sacks of threshed grain. There was noise and heightened labor in the farm, the throb of the engine beating above the laughter of the men. The middle of August had come. Morna called Lem from the stables and set him to work in the kitchen garden, telling him to cut the weeds and to prepare ground for winter crops, crying from the door: 'You, Lem, there, make ground for the turnips! Make a clear space for the winter greens!'

When the grain was threshed and sacked and the thresher gone from the farm, the sheep were let eat in the stubble fields. There would be an interval before the cutting of the maize, and the quiet of the farm centered now about the dwelling, leisure deliberation following the week of work and clatter. Richard turned back to the tool he had partly disclosed, prying at it through a bright morning while the sun slanted in a hard white shaft through the opened shutter. Neal came to the cabin to watch what he did, and they took turns at prying away the plaster. When they had freed the weapon and had cleared it of the lime and sand, the blade, a dagger about twelve inches long, protruded from a handle which seemed now to be the handle of a walking stick. The steel was three-sided and sharp at the point, and it was inscribed with a minute script that was cut minutely into the blade.

Neal brought acid and scouring powder to the cabin. Working in the cool shelter, the dogs about their feet, he would be talking, analyzing, censuring:

'What we want is faith in what we already know. . . . The result is a down-trodden, despised peasantry, a put-upon, discriminated-against hayseed, a Rube, an old farmer, a dolt, a yokel, a country bumpkin. Six cents he gets this week for a dozen eggs. Let him eat the eggs, they say. I say: "Taxes, taxes, taxes!"'

They bent over the dagger, now one and now the other taking it in hand. Richard thought it was such a weapon as was carried concealed in a cane, a cane-sword, and he conjectured what manner of sheath or scabbard the cane might have been. They examined it minutely and they scoured it anew. The point was still sharp and the edge well turned; in the hand of a strong man it might even yet inflict a fatal wound.

'There it is,' Neal said, 'polished to a finish now.'

It passed back and forth between them.

'A farmer ought to be allowed to pay his taxes in produce,' he said, continuing, 'the value not dependent on the value of currency, but on productivity. That's the whole evil. Out of every hundred bushels raised, a bushel, or two, or five, whatever is required, to the governments. You can see what would happen . . .'

At the weapon again, polishing, wiping, scraping, searching. 'It was the tool of a man. . . .' Richard said, 'thought highly of himself — A man in danger. Lived in danger . . .' The handle was daintily carved, the straight cane-handle of a man of leisure, finely polished, not too large to become easily the hilt of the dagger. Richard brought a glass to the cabin and magnified the carving that was finely written into the blade. Blurred in the minute interstices with rust which the polish could not reach, the name was still clearly to be read or conjectured, 'Thomas Laughlin' cut in small square letters.

'You see what would happen,' Richard said, when he ceased to scrutinize the script on the steel. . . . 'I knew it would belong to the old man. His mark, his tool, his defense in danger. Back to what you say, it was true once. Men paid tax in tobacco. Money was scarce, but everybody had a living.'

'It's a screaming necessity,' Neal said. 'One year a man pays, for taxes, three hundred dollars, five hundred if you like, and it's a tenth of what he makes. Another year and three hundred is all he makes, every blasted cent. Let the government gather the tax produce in warehouses. Let these goods be sold for enough to cover the farmer's quota, no more. . . . You'd see what would become of profiteering. . . . Government takes no account of drought or flood or army worms or blight.'

Richard said that the crops were too varied for such a program. People would grow some other, not the tax crops, which might reasonably be corn, tobacco, cotton, rice, potatoes, wheat. He was amused. People, he said, would grow aspidistra and lespedeza.

'I'm in earnest,' Neal said. 'I know what I'm talking about. Let every kind be a tax crop. Let the speculators go squeal. Let them learn what work is. I'd like to get a sword into my own hand,

God knows I would. . . . I could strike a dagger into the heart of every glib-tongued, lying salesman with no thought inside his knotty head but to sell somebody. . . .'

They could not find the sheath that had concealed the weapon although they probed into all the altered plaster that chinked the cabin walls. It would be of such and such a kind, they said, conjecturing, a light walking stick, carried in the hand as a part of the costume. They tried the blade, thrusting at the air. The heft of it was easily accepted, but Richard said:

'It's hard to imagine anger when it's put by. Anger enough to drive the dagger into a living body.'

He claimed the intention of the weapon as his own and moved backward into the past, vindicating. Carried privately, the tool was nevertheless not secret, for the name was written on the blade. The owner might have hammered the steel shapeless at the smith's shop of the farm. It was curious that he had chosen to bury it in the plaster. They, those young men and their young fathers, lived in turmoil, trying to hold fast to the old representative republic, and seeing, not two causes sharply opposed, but many causes breaking apart the converging. They were put upon by politicians and bandits, military despots and brawls. They were about the house and about the farm again. They were walking slowly, together, conferring privately, sending secret warnings from farm to farm. Young men and young girls, about to be married, understanding each other, spoke together with their kind eyes. Neal was muttering:

'. . . Something to fight for, something set square against something else, is what I want. A line-up, sides, is what we need. I'd like to thrust and hack and stick something. . . . I'd like to get a sword into my hands and see a God-forsaken, blustering, smug, smooth profiteer, maker of high-priced machines . . . a tin rattle-trap that cost about sixty dollars to make and he sold it for six hundred. Show me a man made million dollars and I'll show you a villain. Old, look at 'im . . . whoever he is. . . . A scared, old face, features sharp. A little dried-up walnut meat for a brain . . .'

Richard had examined the dagger again with the glass, the wood of the hilt, the lines carved there. There was a cupboard in the cabin, a rude old cherry piece that had been made when the cabin was built. He unlocked a drawer and laid the weapon inside among dusty things, old garden seeds that had been abandoned to the weevil and a few small broken tools. The day had clouded over but no rain seemed about to fall, a day for hunting squirrels. He took from the drawer the loads for the rifles and locked it again, securing the dagger with his supply of hunting shells.

He took the squirrel rifles from the upper part of the cupboard and set them beside the door, an invitation, and Neal acquiesced in silence, crushed and sullen. They walked away from the house to the woodland beside the creek in the gray of the clouded midday, searching the trees for game. Above in the wheat stubble the sheep were quietly feeding, their small pointed faces bent to the grass, being satisfied with the sufficiency there, owning the field by the act of eating it.

Richard laid the dagger on the mantel shelf in the dining room, on the long middle reach of the high shelf between the clock and the brown jar into which Morna dropped bits of paper, memoranda, receipts from tax-gatherers and tradesmen. She continued to read the Greek plays, drooping toward the closely printed page and savoring each fateful phrase. A day later, when he came to the house at noon, he saw that she had discovered the weapon.

She was turning it about when he came upon her, but she put it back on the mantel and walked indifferently away to sink, at the window, into abstraction, looking without at some distant vista or horizon. She roused suddenly and went to the door, calling the black boy, bidding him put the brown colt in the pasture, crying: 'Lem, you, Lem, there. Put the brown filly in the big pasture.'

After an hour or two, when Richard came near, she asked: 'Where did you find the old relic?'

'What relic?'

'The dagger on the mantel.'

He told her where he had found it, and she asked a few questions. She stood, tall and unbent, beside the fireplace, turning it over and over, putting it by and returning to take it again.

'Did you ever see it before?' he asked her. He did not show her the name on the blade.

132

She waited, not answering. She sniffed lightly and pursed her thin lips, repelling the question. When Richard left she had not replied.

In the evening when Richard returned from courting Annie Singleton who would be his wife and the stepmother to Dick after a little, he saw that a light burned in Morna's room. She would be reading the last of the *Agamemnon*, he thought, or talking with Neal and Ruth. In the dining room he looked for the weapon, but it was gone from the mantel shelf. He walked through the faintly scented dark of the hall to the door from which fell the pungent mingled odors of lavender and peppermint and old age. Morna was sitting beside the table near the middle of the room. She was dressed in a long purple dressing gown that flowed like a cascade of dark blood beneath the lamplight.

A restless presence in the room, scarcely discovered at first, but felt rather, a shadow looming in the dark corner, a bulk gathering into the edge of the lamp-glow, Neal was wandering about the room looking restlessly at a photograph — one of Morna's children in infancy — or fingering a book on the shelf between the east windows. The dagger which had been uncovered in the plaster of the cabin lay on the table in the full light of the lamp. The book in Morna's hand, the lamp, and the dagger on the table, these three objects stood most clearly before the dark purple and red of the robe she wore. A clock on the high mantel shelf held slender hands before a mellowed ivory-tinted face and scarcely suggested an hour, not marking it.

Morna was answering his greeting:

'Was Annie pretty tonight?'

'As pretty as she should be, but no prettier.'

'Annie is a good girl,' she said.

A voice muttering back in the shadow, Neal continuing something he had been saying before Richard came. 'The growers ought to get together. Ought to act as one man. ... What I said in town Saturday on the courthouse steps. ... Big business is sick because little business has been squeezed dry. Everything goes out and nothing comes back. ... ' There was a faint jostling of things, as of books moved on a shelf or a chair pushed off the edge of the carpet, but the speaker kept in the shadow. 'Everything moved outward toward Mr. Big Myself, genius for finance, holding companies, overlords, parasites. . . . Got their big mouths fastened hard onto the orange. . . . ' A long shape bending to sit on a chair, but arising again at once, dimly defined against the long dark window hangings, the voice still muttering: 'He'll be surprised. The dry-sucked orange can rot and make a stench he won't relish. I've said so before. . . . '

Richard had not taken his thought from Morna, the muttering of the darkened corner of the room having arisen and sunk away. He stood above her, wanting to assert himself as the dominant person, the male of the strain. He thrust his hands into his pockets and stood erect, his head slightly to one side.

'What any man dare I durst,' he said, looking at her fine book, the Æschylus. She was to him the one conscious element in the line, the strain, in the unity of being in fluid time. He had meant his speech for humor, but his humor faded before the knowledge of her as the conscious element which neared departure and was aware. Defeated by this thought he still stood before her concealing his horror and pity. He turned his emphasis to another matter quickly, asking grimly:

'Did your father, my grandfather, did he in your memory own a dagger or a saber of any peculiar sort?'

She looked at the back of the brown book, thinking. 'What makes you ask that?' she said.

'I've asked now, haven't I?'

He loved her at the moment with a greater love, and his eyes followed the fine thin line of her nose and the crumpled muscles about her mouth where her beauty still quivered in and out with the bending of her lips in speech. She looked at the back of the brown book and at the stamped traceries that made indented formal designs there of unworldly flowers. Her first finger was inserted between the pages to keep her place, and her thumb, lightly moving the fine crape of the skin, quivered at the book's edge.

'How long has it been since Buchman was murdered?' he asked.

134

'Killed is a better word for it, taken off.'

'How long then? Taken off?'

'What is it now? Thirty-two. It's been sixty-five years.'

'Was he killed with a thin, fine blade, a third of an inch in thickness and three-cornered in shape? Twelve or fourteen inches long from the point to the hilt?'

'Is it written down somewhere, on some old paper?' she asked slowly, making then a long pause in which she stared at the book. 'In some old paper? Did you find something?'

'The blade that fitted secretly into a cane, a cane-sword?'

'I didn't know anything certainly. I took the common report as it came. Whoever thrust in the weapon took it out with his own hand. Nobody knew who killed him. It was the kind of blade you describe, though.'

He leaned over her to whisper, 'Do you remember such a cane in the house? The stick of a gentleman. Anywhere in the house?'

She began to speak in a trance, staring at the book and at the floor.

'I was a sly child. Little went on I didn't know. I was quiet and penetrating in the house. My mother and father hardly had a secret I didn't know, not one private or secret thing. I knew about the cane. It fitted, the two parts together, so snug you'd never suspect.'

'Then the time came when you never saw that cane any more?'

'No, I never did.'

'But he carried a cane to the end of his life, another sort.'

'Yes.'

'Then came your wedding, in a few weeks after. Sixteen, you were, or seventeen, was it? You were at the altar and all the people, your friends, were present. You were carrying a suspicion and a fear in your mind and you went blank except on that one side. Is that right?'

'If I hadn't been so young, it would never have happened,' she called out quickly, raising her voice slightly. 'It was a load for a girl to carry. It never happened again.'

'And if you hadn't been about to marry? Apathy induced by the approaching nuptials.'

'Yes.'

'You went blank on every side but one, and you called out: "He deserved his death. . . ."'

The voice was muttering with passion in the darkened quarter of the room. A dense shadow was cast by the lampshade that was tilted to light the book at the top of the table. Morna had arisen. Her hands on the book were still in the light and her face leaned near the upper beams that escaped from the shade above. She was beautiful thus, driven sixty-five years by furies, made beautiful by her denial of these driving fiends. Neal was speaking, his voice breaking into coherence and anger.

'He had better luck. Something firm to stick a sword into. What we want is a villain to thrust. I could name twenty in America. Something has got to be done, now or soon. Burn! I say, kill, thrust, scare his liver white, ride on a rail, find him out where he wallows in fat ease. . . . He punches the clock every day, they say, the same as his men do. Punch him, nevertheless. A decoy, the clock is, when he punches it. Let the clock have a holiday. What I want is a blade in my hand. What I want is something to kill. A sword to kill with and a plain point to strike, is what I want.' His voice fell away to muttering anger. 'Let the clock have a holiday. . . . What we want is life. . . . They're all against us. . . .'

Morna had taken the dagger into her hand slowly and she turned it once about, holding it as if it were any tool, as if it were a knitting needle or a knitting hook. She held it in her palm, grasping it at the middle. 'The blade is mine,' she said, absently, speaking quietly. 'Stand here. Here, give me something. Give me the scarf there. Nobody else has any claim on it. It's mine. Turn the light down a little, Richard, it's too high. Close the window about halfway, the night begins to be chilly.' She took a soft white silk scarf from the back of her chair and wrapped it about the sword, folding it lightly and swiftly over the steel without order, twisting it about. She passed then to a chest that stood in the shadow and, when she had opened the lid, she pushed the wrapped dagger deep among the things inside. Then she closed the lid and fastened the latch, turning the key. 'It's put away now,' she said. 'It's mine.'

136

THE IMMORTAL WOMAN

ALLEN TATE

WE NEVER knew why she came, but it was always in October when the warm days were few, and the fallen leaves under the thick shade stuck to the dampness on the walk that the sun could not dry. It was usually the last of October. We wondered how long she had been here, a round little old lady in black holding her head up on the left side and leaning on a heavy black cane. When I saw her I thought: she has already passed several times. Then I remembered that was last year or two years ago. It got so that when I saw her for the first time in the fall, I said: it is another year. My aunt says she came every fall for fifteen years but I know it was only in the last four or five that she took to walking with a cane. Stringy, lead-looking grey hair fringed the edge of the small black hat that she wore close to her temples, and her thick glasses gave her eyes a fixed stare. She walked steadily to the corner by the grey brick house, crossed the street to the green bench by the College gate, and sat down facing the house. Her clothes were always the same and it is hard to remember what she wore. She seemed to sink into the faded anonymity of the old street.

Only the leaves have renewed themselves here since I was a boy. On our side there are tall trees, sugar maples and sycamores, from the far corner, which is out of sight, down to the old square house where stands, heaving up the bricks in the walk, a giant oak; across the street runs the high wall of the old College. The same damp trickle has held to the wall the same patch of grey moss as long as I can remember. Early in the morning, and more distinctly in the fall, you can hear if you listen closely the clatter of the main street down by the Potomac, a low hum of noise that seems to bring with it the smell of the fishmarket. At noon there is a moment, filled always with surprise, when the sunlight falls quietly through the trees.

137

We see few people. Nothing happens. We never visit and no one comes to our house. I think that none of our neighbors ought to be living here. I suppose the trees know what was here, and what it was, but no one knows who planted the trees. They know something that we never hear and they contain years that we cannot see. On the third of every month Mr. Higgins comes to collect the rent. 'It's a fact now. Mark my word. It won't be five years till there's niggers in all these houses.'

There is the old brick house on the corner across from the College gate. I see first the wall running out of the side of the house down the side street. It encloses the garden, and midway along it opens, or opened once, an iron gate now a rusty green. I have never seen inside. The dull slate roof, cracked everywhere and littered over with twigs and leaves, slopes front and back; at each end, wide apart and perilously tall, two slender chimneys rise. Six windows stretch across the front of each of the three stories. In the exact center of the house stands the door; it opens into the second floor at the end of two curved flights of stone steps, one on each side. It is a double door, two plain panels with small tarnished brass knobs set in a carved but very simply carved frame that is arched over by a fan light of many small panes. Some of the panes are broken and the paint is peeling off the door. The house must have been built before this country was a nation, when there was no city east of the creek and Georgetown was a town in the Proprietary Colony of Maryland.

From my window I could just see the old lady where she sat on the green bench, day after day, and towards noon I got so that I began to look for the large white-haired man in blue serge, who came to take her away. A black derby high on his head gave him a little more than his real height, and although he must have been past seventy he was heavy and of powerful frame — the sort of man you would like to see on a big bay horse, cantering down a quiet street and, without changing pace or his own expression, gravely lifting his hat to the ladies as he passed. He never spoke to the old lady but with great simplicity removed his hat, holding it across his chest while she rose; then they started off, the old lady keeping an even distance in the rear. I am sure that in all these years he never uttered a word, but the old lady talked constantly, not to her husband but as if his presence made it easier for her to talk to herself. The large man — I am certain of this too — never once looked at the old house.

And not more than twice did he fail to come for her. The first time must have been five or six years ago, when a tall very old man, who looked tall at any rate because his knees were so long, drove up in a muddy Victoria. A doctor, I am certain; his white hair flowed over his shrunken shoulders; he wore a wrinkled Prince Albert and a shining stovepipe hat, and he held a gold-headed cane. As the carriage slowed down he moved as though he were about to get out; but he thought better of it and the old lady, old but many years younger than he, climbed slowly in. The Negro boy driver turned — I remember he had on a greasy linen duster and a colorless felt hat decorated with a rooster's tail — and, with a solemn face, distinctly said: 'Good mornin', Miss Jane.' She nodded. The old doctor leaned forward and kissed her and they began talking; I could hear nothing they said. Without raising his voice the old gentleman talked more and more vehemently, pointing and rubbing the side of his long white nose with the knob of his cane. At last she nodded, as if she had at last got a difficulty out of her mind — as if to say: Yes, that's it, I remember now. The old doctor spoke to the boy, who pulled up the reins and drove briskly down the street.

The old house has not been occupied for years. Aunt Charlotte says that people lived in it when we first came here. There were no children and I never looked much at the place. It is too elegant for poor people, and too large; too shabby, in too shabby a neighborhood, for the rich. Aunt Charlotte cannot distinctly remember the last tenants; they lived there less than a year. But the house looked shut up even then, and quite untouched, as if it were going its own way. Every year it seems to settle a little more into the ground. The windows look dimmer, defying the light to disturb the perfect shadows within.

Further than 'Miss Jane' we never knew the names of any of the people who came back to look at the house, though I must have seen the old lady and her husband, the vigorous Western man, thirty or forty times a year for ten years — the time I've been an invalid — and my aunt, sewing at her machine every morning in the other front room across the hall, watched them come and go a good five years longer. You have understood that Aunt Charlotte is a sempstress. She had been a clerk in the Patent Office — snapped rubber bands around papers and envelopes, whose purpose and destiny she did not know, from nine to five — until I came back from overseas, paralyzed. We are Pennsylvania people from a small town, Greencastle, who came here, my father and mother and Aunt Charlotte, her sister, to go into the Government service, when I was a child; my parents are dead. I went from the high-school to the war, but when I was eleven or twelve I spent my after-noons at the Smithsonian and wandered over to the Fisheries and the Army Medical Museum where they keep South American mummies and wax representations of diseases, and monsters in jars. We are the only members of our family left in Georgetown. We never hear from our relatives and we are poor.

I shall never forget how the old lady nodded to the doctor, as if but for a slight piece of information she knew all that the house contained; and how he nodded in return, affectionately but a little absently, not thinking very much about the house. He must have known all the people there long ago, but he had not lived there. It was that, I think, more than the old lady's coming and going that started me to thinking about her. I began to wonder where she lived, and where I myself should live since this town is not my home; and then too I ask Aunt Charlotte where the people are who ought to be living in the square house. I don't think she quite knows what I mean. She says the neighbors all came after they left, and they either forgot or never knew the name. My aunt is very busy, and lately she has got so much fashionable patronage that she seems a little giddy, as giddy as an anxious old maid could ever be.

But she does good work, and somehow the ladies who go to F Street have decided that a shabby street in Georgetown is the place to go. There is Mrs. Ritter, she comes in a Cadillac, I don't know where she is from; she talks about her parties, sometimes as if she and Aunt Charlotte were really together and the parties weren't hers; but one day she said, 'I just hate poor people.' But Aunt Charlotte is so innocent. The senator's daughters are pretty and they don't know what they want and they are afraid to let a sewing-woman tell them. I fall into these currents of life around me and I like to think how far away they run. When a car drives up or the knocker sounds I roll my chair to the window and look out. I roll over to the door, open it, get behind it and wait for the lady to begin talking.

There is old Mrs. Dulany and, come to think of it, it must have been old Mrs. Dulany who lives down near the Tenallytown Road who got all these people coming to our house.

'No, don't thank me. My dear, I don't know any of them. I just told Mrs. Roberts you did splendid plain sewing and I reckon she told someone else who told all the others.'

Every spring, every fall, Mrs. Dulany comes three or four times to have some old silk dresses made over or a new black voile. She says:

'My dear, I don't know them at all.'

Her right eye suddenly squints, and that side of her face twitches spasmodically until she holds it a moment with her hand. Then she talks on. Sometimes I go into the sewing-room when she is there. 'Mr. Hermann, you are looking better this spring.' Or 'this fall' — as it happens. She always says that, and you feel a great kindness. She gives Aunt Charlotte minute directions about a skirt. 'It don't make much difference how I look, I'm gettin' so old.'

When I wish to compose myself I close my eyes, and I can hear Mrs. Dulany's voice. It is a little cracked for she must be nearly eighty but the tone is at once sharp and fluent, and what she says is neither memorable nor foolish. She must have come in one day while I was dozing. I felt that she was there though she had not spoken, and I was startled at thinking that I knew what she was going to say.

'Well, Miss Charlotte, maybe you think this street has always been just like it is.'

As I looked across the hall Mrs. Dulany was bending a little forward, whether to see what Aunt Charlotte was doing or in

141

some inner excitement I could not tell. The mid-morning light fell on the heap of scraps, the odds and ends of muslin and silk, velvet and bits of thread, that covered the big table where Aunt Charlotte with her aimless patience was picking about here and there. Mrs. Dulany had spoken; my aunt looked up, her eyes blank, like a surprised beetle.

'Yes'm, only I tell John it ain't as bad as it might be if my work took me out.'

Thinking the talk would go on that way I wheeled my chair back to the window — and yet I felt illuminated and pleased. The sun was just over the College wall. It struck me full in the face. It was time to put up the window and let the warm air come in. This is my greatest pleasure. The light shakes the big sycamore leaves, and the sycamore balls in the sudden heat burst, and fall softly to the ground. It is wonderful to watch the rays of the sun lift the branch by my window at least a foot higher than it seems to be in the evening shade. There is a faint crackle in the air as the night mist from the river steams up out of the leaves. I knew that when I leaned over the sill I should see the old lady. She was coming slowly up the street, head and shoulders hidden by a tree, and it struck me for the first time how she walked — as if she were being propelled from the outside, by a force that she neither knew nor could control — like the dressmaker's form in the sewing-room, moving with an even glide — a slightly stooped form for old ladies' fittings. And with a start I thought how curious it was that she needed a cane. She put little weight upon it and at regular short intervals jabbed the rubber ferule noiselessly against the bricks as if indeed that were her way of testing her distance from the ground.

There are some things we know so little about; yet I suppose I looked at the old lady with new eyes because a tone or phrase in what Mrs. Dulany had said put something into my mind.... I reckon you think this street has always been just like it is.... I cannot remember what I thought she really meant, or whether I thought about it at that moment. There are times when my sight grows dim and my head whirls; I grip the wheels of my chair, move a few feet very rapidly; objects begin to reappear. I think I know things only in action; there are the surprising and intolerable crises that a trivial act of will dissipates as breath a soap bubble — those harassing swivets of the mind. I tell Aunt Charlotte that if one must be an invalid one must have a wheeled chair, not to go anywhere in but to give one something to do. I can only say that going over to the window and seeing the old lady float by was my way of understanding what Mrs. Dulany had said.

To understand even a little of what one sees one must at every moment understand more than there is to be understood, or looked at another way, a great deal less. I see, of course, very little. When I remember that the old lady stopped coming by at last, in a way that told me she would not come again, I thought how foolish it was to say that she had always looked this way or had done this or carried that. It takes years to understand the easy things: I recall the exhilaration I felt swarming over my face and eyes when I suddenly and definitely knew that no two days are alike, no person the same two days running. There was the beach down on the bay that I had been to as a child, where the shallow utmost reach of the surf deposited at each thrust a thin filament of sand, but never at the same place twice over.

I do know, of course, that the old lady held her head up a little to the left, as if she were about to sniff, that she wore black worsted mittens, and carried a black reticule that sagged under the weight of shapeless objects: the crazy stare through the thick rimless glasses and the apparently useless cane completed the miscellany of her appearance, one's sense of animated odds and ends. I thought she might fall apart, or go up in a wisp of smoke. She had merely been put together by all past generations, and she saw no need of doing anything about it; I mean that she could not have known that she had a self. The gliding ease of her step, the unshakable regularity of her habits, had all the perfection of an untested desire. I felt, as she passed that last time, though I did not know then it was the last, that she was as perfect as a cyclone, as terrible, with the same suffocation vortex inside.

I am trying, I suppose, to see what she really looked like. I cannot imagine a picture of her. Could she have sat every day for a photograph, for a whole year, always on the same plate, one image upon another, there would have appeared an outline indistinct as a distant shadow, or perhaps one should say that her picture would have been like a whisper in an empty room. Just nothing, in the sense that impalpable fear is nothing: precisely nothing at all. And then I suddenly knew that I had been hearing the voice all this time, the words from the sewing-room forming a single moment with the image in the street.

'. . . I knew them all of course, I knew them because old Cousin John Gibson, that was the father of the girls, and my own father were second cousins. And I knew Cousin Georgiana too, his wife. We used to go up there when I was a little girl and I knew them that way, but all the girls were young ladies, too old for me to be intimate with and too young to be married and have children my age. My mother said Cousin Georgiana paid a heavy price for not having any boys. That was why the family broke up. Of the four girls, only one, Mary Anne, made a good match, a Federal naval officer. Old Cousin John, their father, said a Yankee and a rebel looked about the same to him. I reckon he was right about it for that Yankee, such a handsome young gentleman, was the only good husband any of them got.'

'Yes'm, that's what papa said, the rebel soldiers that come to Greencastle was mighty well-behaved, didn't steal a thing. I'll just baste this hem so you won't have to try on the skirt again.'

'Yes, I don't like to stand on my feet. . . . That Yankee officer bought out the shares of the other sisters — that was after the war and their father was dead — in the land down in St. Mary's. It was the worst thing they could have done. There was Anna; she never married, I reckon I ought to go to see her, she's ninety at least, lived on charity for forty years, in the Home for Incurables ever since her mother died. Susan married my cousin on my mother's side, Captain Charles Sterrett. He warn't much force. Aunt Martha, the old Negro woman who nursed the girls, helped them, but Cousin Charlie always said: Hadn't the white folks supported her before the war? Just like he'd done it. Cousin Lottie I knew best; she married a clerk at Beckitt and Wylie's, a nice deserving young man, only we never knew where he came from — old Major Beckitt said it was all nonsense, folks had to

144

live, and the boy was well-mannered and industrious. But that boy took to drinking and Cousin Lottie supported her family with her needle. Mama said it wasn't right for old Cousin John to leave the land to the girls after they'd been raised in town. Once I heard Mama talking to somebody, that Cousin John had an awful temper, and hit Cousin Georgiana on the head with a tin cup. After that she was never the same. One time she got the old gentleman when he was very intoxicated, sewed him up in two stout linen sheets, and horsewhipped him till he was sober. She was never the same after that and he wasn't either. He never touched another drop. They never said much about that tin cup, but after he was dead and buried, and Cousin Georgiana and Anna were living alone in the old house towards the end of the war, Mama showed me the place where she'd whipped him at the top of the stairs. She had one sheet already spread out; he was so unsteady she tripped him with a poker. When he fell he went right to sleep, then the old lady started sewing the other sheet over him. Mama would whisper just as we came to the old lady's door, "Who would think she could have done it?" And Cousin John left the house to his sister, when he should have left it to the girls — his sister Anne, the one that married old Mr. Posey . . .'

When she had got to the corner she stood for an instant on the kerb; and looking at her, listening to the voice from the depths of the old house, I could see her incline her head from one side to the other and gaze, rather slyly, up and down the street. I saw her peering cautiously out of a door into a dark hall. With sudden speed she sailed across the street. I suppose she really looked like that at the moment. I see her in four or five distinct scenes, imperishable glimpses, but I know that each of these scenes is composed of many particles of memory, all of them striving day and night to come together and to take form. Before she had quite sat down on the bench she began to take odd pieces of string out of the reticule, laying them across her knees — she was too round to have a lap — and after a brief pause began tying the ends together and winding it into a ball. She rolled steadily and expertly, her hands on her knees; she raised the ball to the level of her eyes, winding all the time, back and forth from her eyes to her knees.

145

In a little while she rested. She looked around with jerks of her head but the head had a different focus from the eyes. Like a chicken pausing alertly between scratches. I suppose she was watching the house.

The sun always fell on her back, throwing the side of her face into a luminous shadow in the middle of which, from the temple to the chin, ran an almost straight line. It made her features thinner and younger. I had to look away. There was a firm and delicate line imbedded in the shapeless flesh. A group of students passed on their way to the College gate. A handsome boy in a bright green sweater looked back at her fumbling with her bits of string, and smiled.

I never wished to speak a word to that old lady. I try to think that after my first real awareness of her I never wanted to see her again. I could not help it — wheeling myself over to the window. I said to myself: it is to get the morning sun. It was to see the old lady. I have seen people as they ought not to be; I have seen whining monsters with only half a face and I myself am not as I ought to be. That is different. Something will hit you, the will of God, and you're no good for the rest of your life. The old lady was as good as she had ever been; she sagged a little, I think, in her whole being, but like the old house she was, all of her, there, in a kind of perfection that I had not known before. The house stood facing her, not a stick of it changed I am certain for a hundred and fifty years. I can imagine the windows every year getting smaller, sealing up the shadows until at last there will be one great impenetrable shadow within.

'. . . and when the war was over Cousin Anne and her husband moved up from Prince William and took possession of the house. Cousin Anne you see was much older than her brother who'd left her the place, and Mr. Posey was younger than she but still older than his brother-in-law. Their children were all grown up. Mama didn't go much to the house after they came, but I did. I was often in the old garden. On my way home from my music lesson at the Convent I had to pass the garden gate. Cousin Anne would lean out like she'd been waiting: "Come in, child, and have some cake."

She would take my hand and give me a sharp look. She was tall and thin and her nose tied her face up in a knot. I remember how the garden looked in the spring. We sat at a rickety little table under the back gallery. Cousin Anne poured half water and half sweet wine into tall glasses. She would say, "Honey, give your Cousin George some Sangaree." Cousin George was Mr. Posey. I took it to him where he sat at the other end of the porch. "Little Nellie, she shakes like jelly," he said, never taking the frown off his face, and that was his way of thanking me . . .'

I am now sure that I never wanted to see the inside of the house. I cannot help feeling for it a certain respect. It carries itself well. All effort is over and it is superior to anything its imagination might teach it to do. But it is, in its composure, a little menacing. Like the island of Sinbad the Sailor it is sudden and angry with an incalculable life of its own. I always take my 'walks' in the afternoon the year round; being down there with the old house, or with the old lady, myself with one of them, I should feel secure; I should have a single problem, and its simplicity would leave open the space between the street and my room. But to be there with them together, the old lady and the old house — that is to be entirely alone, with my watch ticking on my wrist, and arrested in time. I should have my own darkness inside, my own angry perfection, and I should no longer be able to say: the student going into the gate is returning from the movies to his room in Carroll Hall. There would be the student, the gate, and my watch ticking; then my watch ticking alone.

'. . . only I didn't shake because I was frail. That was all I ever heard him say. Old Mr. Posey sat in a big armchair with horse-hair upholstery, his knees wide apart and the black trousers tight on his heavy limbs. He wore a faded bottle-green coat with tails, and a loose black stock round his neck. There he sat frowning, picking his teeth with a gold toothpick that folded like a knife into a small carved ivory handle. I always wanted to touch it but I was afraid to ask him. Cousin Anne colored a tumbler of water with a little wine for me. We just sat there. She rocked vigorously in her chair, then abruptly stopped, as if she'd thought of something. At

147

the end of the garden by the stables was a big sycamore and along the wall by the street ran a high box hedge — it was dug up and sold years ago. On the other side round the kitchen and the quarters bushes of flowering quince grew in huge clusters. Only there was never any cake and at home we never called him Cousin George. He was Mr. Posey. They say he was in a rage all his life. That was peculiar and there was something else . . .'

I have never believed that anger has anything in it that one can touch and see; it is different from love which is always physical and so knows where to stop, at the end of familiar things. Aunt Charlotte I think never had any feeling about anything; she does not know one person from another; she had felt neither anger nor love. There is anxiety but that is kindness and kindness is not love. This is a neighborhood of strangers. Like me I suppose they have all felt that it is not innocent enough, a place that knows more than we can ever know, knows it all in a way that we cannot understand. It is absurd to say that an old house is angry. We get used to absurdity. To say that of the house seems to me as ordinary as saying that it is placed among unfamiliar things. We make it angry. It must have once loved familiar things. As I looked down at the old lady making her balls of twine I thought how furious she was, but then she could not know she was furious. With incredible fury she wound up the twine as if it were the last of familiar things; furiously she placed her forefinger against the side of her nose, taking in deep breaths; then she resumed her work with new fury.

'. . . and it was even more peculiar. There were Jane and Sarah Georgiana, or Sally George we called her, and it was Sally George who married Mr. Broadwater and went to the Southwest. They took Jane's meals up to her room; she never came out. There were Little George and Uncle Rozier, the two boys, and I expect Cousin Anne called her son uncle because Little George had a son; he had married one of old Major Beckitt's girls and gone out West. I never saw him in my life; he couldn't get along with his father so he went West. West was a word you heard all the time. Hundreds of people were going West. It seemed so far away. The land flowing with milk and honey, old Major Beckitt said sarcastically, but it did seem to flow because Little George made money out of that land he and Mr. Ben Tayloe had bought in the West before the war, and he sent money home. Then he sent his wife and child, a little girl, Little Jane we called her, named after her Aunt Jane, he sent them home to visit. After that visit Little George sent no more money back home, and before long they shut up the house, had to I reckon. Went up to Rockville and died there about the time I was grown. Later Uncle Rozier went West too. I saw him many times, it's right strange how you remember things. I can see him in the front hall coming down the wide white stairway in his carpet-slippers — I remember that because he was such a large man, six feet four they said, and he walked so quietly I noticed his feet. He was different from his father, had the sanguine temperament, but he swore every breath no matter who was present. I think it was this same day. He put his huge hand on my head and shook me. "By God, she's a pretty young un." Then he gave me a nickel. Old Aunt Martha, who sat in the back hall with a white cap and apron on — she was too old and fat to work so she answered the front doorbell that rang about twice a week — she whispered: "Don't you be scared, honey, they ain't no harm in Marse Rozier." She laughed and showed her big eyeteeth, all she had left, hanging down over her lower lip. The old hall was always dark. I could never see the faces in the frames on the wall opposite the stairs. They were Gibsons. You know the first Gibson was a dwarf. I think of those times, how I'm the only one of their kin left here. Jane died while Little George's wife and daughter were here on that visit. Doctor Lacy Beckitt, one of the major's boys, waited on her till she died. They said she just died, but don't crazy people live just as long as other people? Longer. Nobody saw her laid out. She was foolish about her little niece Jane, I reckon because she was her namesake. All morning she sat alone in her room and after dinner she peeped out into the dim hall, and called Little Jane. Little Jane went upstairs for her daily present. Jane cut up old newspapers into strips like ribbons all day long, and laid them in rows and piles. "Here's your present for today, child" — handing her some paper strips. She never spoke above a whisper; no one saw her smile; she was very gentle.

149

When she got a new dress she cut it right up into scraps — "They might come in handy," she'd say. She tied strings round empty boxes, they found hundreds of them in her wardrobe after she died. She saved the tinfoil and bits of thread, and made balls of twine. Sometimes I think the old house is waiting to be taken away too, and nobody will ever look inside again who knew what happened there. Not, my dear, that anything really happened . . .'

'That's what I tell my nephew, folks work so hard but don't never get anything out of it. Like carrying water uphill in a leaky bucket.'

When Aunt Charlotte broke the silence I knew that I had heard everything that Mrs. Dulany had said: I was brought up sharply against the innocence of my poor aunt, who had heard not a word of it, I mean really heard it. And yet I was convinced that Mrs. Dulany herself, could the question have entered her mind, would have seen nothing that was not perfectly plain. I knew, however, that as Aunt Charlotte spoke Mrs. Dulany was squinting her eye, and her face was twitching. These mysteries are understood in our bodies, not in the mind. I thought I understood that too: when the umbrella mender cries out in the street I feel restless, even a little exposed, and thinking suddenly that my bureau needs tidying up I wheel myself over to it and find myself brushing my hair.

That, too, must be a kind of anger. I looked out of the window. The old lady was tying up the ends of her strings to start a new ball. The air was still and warm and I knew it was almost noon. A coal truck pounded by on the cobblestones, leaving the noonday suspense deeper than before. I had seen into the old house, and there was the old lady, that cavernous bird of passage, across the street. Damnation had read itself out to me. I remembered the elderly gentleman who had come for her in the spattered carriage, and I wanted him to come again today. I found myself saying, Little Jane. There was the solemn Negro boy. Good mornin', Miss Jane. I suddenly thought: Doctor Beckitt, who knew the room in which the crazy woman had died. The old doctor whose carriage might have become his grave. I suppose I wanted Miss Jane to die, but I found myself wishing for her a distant grave, or perhaps — and I think this was it — a moving grave that would bring her back to the old grey house in Indian summer after the morning light of autumn had begun shaking the leaves. Though I knew it was impossible I could not bear to think of her dying in the old house. I saw her consumed by the rage of the invisible fire within. I kept thinking, foolishly enough, that she might be saved. But she had no place to die. She could neither die nor live.

The young man was coming rapidly down the street. He looked like a tower of new brick. He was all of six feet; his head, arms, legs moved all together. His clothes seemed carefully impersonal and subdued. He must have stepped out of a fashionable hotel. He wore thick glasses and looked occasionally up, then down, to satisfy himself that there was no obstacle in his way. He wore one glove; the other he carried in his bare hand. He walked quickly and deliberately and he scarcely touched the ground.

He was leaning over the old lady, kissing her, his arms at his side. She put both arms round his neck, and kissed him again and again. He withdrew at last. He sat down beside her. Neither spoke. The old lady fumbled with her bag and relaxed with a sigh. He rose, and standing with his legs slightly apart, the backs of his hands on his hips, he looked up at the house.

Still looking up, and I thought gradually tenser and more alert, he rocked on the balls of his feet. He stood suddenly still. He rubbed his bare fist slowly in the palm of his gloved hand. He turned abruptly, as if everything were quite clear, took her by the arm, tenderly, pulling her to her feet. The sun from over the wall lit up her face. I could see that she was in tears. He took her cane, a little awkwardly. She leaned heavily on his arm; they started slowly up the street. He hesitated as if he were about to speak, but thought better of it, smiled, and led the old lady on her way. I never saw her again.

THE HOUSE OF THE FAR
AND LOST

THOMAS WOLFE

IN THE fall of that year I lived out about a mile from town in a house set back from the Ventnor Road. The house was called a 'farm'— Hill-Top Farm, or Far-End Farm, or some such name as that — but it was really no farm at all. It was a magnificent house of the weathered gray stone they have in that country, as if in the very quality of the wet heavy air there is the soft thick gray of time itself, sternly yet beautifully soaking down forever on you — and enriching everything it touches — grass, foliage, brick, ivy, the fresh moist color of the people's faces, and the old gray stone with the incomparable weathering of time.

The house was set back off the road at a distance of several hundred yards, possibly a quarter of a mile, and one reached it by means of a road bordered by rows of tall trees which arched above the road, and which made me think of home at night when the stormy wind howled in their tossed branches. On each side of the road were the rugby fields of two of the colleges, and in the afternoon I could look out and down and see the fresh moist green of the playing fields, and watch young college fellows, dressed in their shorts and jerseys, and with their bare knees scurfed with grass and turf as they twisted, struggled, swayed, and scrambled for a moment in the scrimmage-circle, and then broke free, running, dodging, passing the ball as they were tackled, filling the moist air with their sharp cries of sport. They did not have the desperate, the grimly determined, the almost professional earnestness that the college teams at home have; their scurfed and muddy knees, their swaying scrambling scrimmages, their swift breaking away and running, their panting breath and crisp clear voices gave them the appearance of grown-up boys.

Once when I had come up the road in the afternoon while they were playing, the ball got away from them and came bounding out into the road before me, and I ran after it to retrieve it as we used to do when passing a field where boys were playing baseball. One of the players came over to the edge of the field and stood there waiting with his hands upon his hips while I got the ball: he was panting hard, his face was flushed, and his blond hair tousled, but when I threw the ball to him, he said 'Thanks very much!' crisply and courteously — getting the same sound into the word '*very*' that they got in '*A*meri*can*,' a sound that always repelled me a little because it seemed to have some scornful aloofness and patronage in it.

For a moment I watched him as he trotted briskly away onto the field again: the players stood there waiting, panting, casual, their hands upon their hips; he passed the ball into the scrimmage, the pattern swayed, rocked, scrambled, and broke sharply out into open play again, and everything looked incredibly strange, near, and familiar.

I felt that I had always known it, that it had always been mine, and that it was as familiar to me as everything I had seen or known in my childhood. Even the texture of the earth looked familiar, and felt moist and firm and springy when I stepped on it, and the stormy howling of the wind in that avenue of great trees at night, was wild and desolate and demented as it had been when I was eight years old and could lie in my bed at night and hear the great oaks howling on the hill above my father's house.

The name of the people in the house was Coulson: I made arrangements with the woman at once to come and live there: she was a tall, weathered-looking woman of middle age, we talked together in the hall. The hall was made of marble flags and went directly out onto a gravelled walk.

The woman was crisp, cheerful, and worldly looking. She was still quite handsome. She wore a well-cut skirt of woolen plaid, and a silk blouse: when she talked she kept her arms folded because the air in the hall was chilly, and she held a cigarette in the fingers of one hand. A shaggy brown dog came out and nosed upward toward her hand as she was talking and she put her hand upon its head and

153

scratched it gently. When I told her I wanted to move in the next day, she said briskly and cheerfully:

'Right you are! You'll find everything ready when you get here!' Then she asked if I was at the university. I said no, and added, with a feeling of difficulty and naked desolation, that I was a 'writer,' and was coming there to work. I was twenty-four years old.

'Then I am sure that what you do will be *very, very* good!' she said cheerfully and decisively. 'We have had several Americans in the house before and all of them were very clever! All the Americans we have had here were very clever people,' said the woman. 'I'm sure that you will like it.' Then she walked to the door with me to say good-bye. As we stood there, there was the sound of a small motor-car coming to a halt and in a moment a girl came swiftly across the gravel space outside and entered the hall. She was tall, slender, very lovely, but she had the same bright hard look in her eye the woman had, the same faint, hard smile around the edges of her mouth.

'Edith,' the woman said in her crisp, curiously incisive tone, 'this young man is an American — he is coming here tomorrow.' The girl looked at me for a moment with her hard bright glance, thrust out a small gloved hand, and shook hands briefly, a swift firm greeting.

'Oh! How d'ye do!' she said. 'I hope you will like it here.' Then she went on down the hall, entered a room on the left, and closed the door behind her.

Her voice had been crisp and certain like her mother's, but it was also cool, young, and sweet, with music in it, and later as I went down the road, I could still hear it.

That was a wonderful house, and the people there were wonderful people. Later, I could not forget them. I seemed to have known them all my life, and to know all about their lives. They seemed as familiar to me as my own blood, and I knew them with a knowledge that went deep below the roots of thought or memory. We did not talk together often, or tell any of our lives to one another. It will be very hard to tell about it — the way we felt and lived together in that house — because it was one of those

154

simple and profound experiences of life which people seem always to have known when it happens to them, but for which there is no language.

And yet, like a child's half-captured vision of some magic country he has known, and which haunts his days with strangeness and the sense of imminent, glorious rediscovery, the word that would unlock it all seems constantly to be almost on our lips, waiting just outside the gateway of our memory, just a shape, a phrase, a sound, away the moment that we choose to utter it — but when we try to say the thing, something fades within our mind like fading light, and something melts within our grasp like painted smoke, and something goes on forever when we try to touch it.

The nearest I could come to it was this: In that house I sometimes felt the greatest peace and solitude that I had ever known. But I always knew the other people in the house were there. I could sit in my sitting-room at night and hear nothing but the stormy moaning of the wind outside in the great trees, the small gaseous flare and jet from time to time of the coal fire burning in the grate — and silence, strong living lonely silence that moved and waited in the house at night — and I would always know that they were there.

I did not have to hear them enter or go past my door, nor did I have to hear doors close or open in the house, or listen to their voices: if I had never seen them, heard them, spoken to them, it would have been the same — I should have known they were there.

It was something I had always known, and had known it would happen to me, and now it was there with all the strangeness and dark mystery of an awaited thing. I knew them, felt them, lived among them with a familiarity that had no need of sight or word or speech. And the memory of that house and of my silent fellow-ship with all the people there was somehow mixed with an image of dark time. It was one of those sorrowful and unchanging images which, among all the blazing stream of images that passed constantly their stream of fire across my mind, was somehow fixed, detached, and everlasting, full of a sorrow, certitude, and mystery that I could not fathom, but that wore forever on it the old sad light of waning day — a light from which all the heat, the violence, and the substance of furious dusty day had vanished, and was itself like time, unearthly-of-the-earth, remote, detached, and everlasting.

And that fixed and changeless image of dark time was this: In an old house of time I lived alone, and yet had other people all around me, and they never spoke to me, or I to them. They came and went like silence in the house, but I always knew that they were there. I would be sitting by a window in a room and I would know then they were moving in the house, and darkness, sorrow, and strong silence dwelt within us, and our eyes were quiet, full of sorrow, peace, and knowledge, and our faces dark, our tongues silent, and we never spoke. I could not remember how their faces looked, but they were all familiar to me as my father's face, and we had known one another forever, and we lived together in the ancient house of time, dark time, and silence, sorrow, certitude, and peace were in us. Such was the image of dark time that was to haunt my life thereafter, and into which, somehow, my life among the people in that house had passed.

In the house that year there lived, besides myself and Morison, the Coulsons, the father and mother and their daughter, and three men who had taken rooms together, and who were employed in a factory where motor-cars were made, two miles from town.

I think the reason that I could never forget these people later and seemed to know them all so well was that there was in all of them something ruined, lost or broken — some precious and irretrievable quality which had gone out of them and which they could never get back again. Perhaps that was the reason that I liked them all so much, because with ruined people it is either love or hate: there is no middle way. The ruined people that we like are those who desperately have died, and lost their lives because they loved life dearly, and had that grandeur that makes such people spend prodigally the thing they love the best, and risk and lose their lives because it is so precious to them, and die at length because the seeds of life were in them. It is only the people who love life in this way who die — and these are the ruined people that we like.

The people in the house were people who had lost their lives because they loved the earth too well, and somehow had been slain by their hunger. And for this reason I liked them all, and could not forget them later: there seemed to have been some magic which had drawn them all together to the house, as if the house itself was a magnetic centre for lost people.

Certainly, the three men who worked at the motor-car factory had been drawn together for this reason. Two were still young men in their early twenties. The third man was much older. He was a man past forty, his name was Nicholl, he had served in the army during the war and had attained the rank of captain.

He had the spare, alert, and jaunty figure that one often finds in army men, an almost professional military quality that somehow seemed to set his figure upon a horse as if he had grown there, or had spent a lifetime in the cavalry. His face also had the same lean, bitten, professional military quality: his speech, although good-natured and very friendly, was clipped, incisive, jerky, and sporadic, his lean weather-beaten face was deeply, sharply scarred and sunken in the flanks, and he wore a small cropped mustache, and displayed long frontal teeth when he smiled — a spare, gaunt, toothy, yet attractive smile.

His left arm was withered, shrunken, almost useless, part of his hand and two of the fingers had been torn away by the blast or explosion which had destroyed his arm, but it was not this mutilation of the flesh that gave one the sense of a life that had been ruined, lost and broken irretrievably. In fact, one quickly forgot his physical injury: his figure looked so spare, lean, jaunty, well-conditioned in its energetic fitness that one never thought of him as a cripple, nor pitied him for any disability. No: the ruin that one felt in him was never of the flesh, but of the spirit. Something seemed to have been exploded from his life — it was not the nerve-centres of his arm, but of his soul, that had been destroyed. There was in the man somewhere a terrible dead vacancy and emptiness, and that spare, lean figure that he carried so well seemed only to surround this vacancy like a kind of shell.

He was always smartly dressed in well-cut clothes that set well on his trim spruce figure. He was always in good spirits, immensely friendly in his clipped spare way, and he laughed frequently — a rather metallic cackle which came suddenly and ended as swiftly as it had begun. He seemed, somehow, to have locked the door upon dark care and worry, and to have flung the key away — to have lost, at the same time that he lost more precious things, all the fretful doubts and perturbations of the conscience most men know.

Now, in fact, he seemed to have only one serious project in his life. This was to keep himself amused, to keep himself constantly amused, to get from his life somehow the last atom of entertainment it could possibly yield, and in this project the two young men who lived with him joined in with an energy and earnestness which suggested that their employment in the motor-car factory was just a necessary evil which must be borne patiently because it yielded them the means with which to carry on a more important business, the only one in which their lives were interested — the pursuit of pleasure.

And in the way in which they conducted this pursuit, there was an element of deliberate calculation, concentrated earnestness, and focal intensity of purpose that was astounding, grotesque, and unbelievable, and that left in the mind of one who saw it a formidable and disquieting memory because there was in it almost the madness of desperation, the deliberate intent of men to cover up or seek oblivion at any cost of effort from some hideous emptiness of the soul.

Captain Nicholl and his two young companions had a little motor-car so small that it scuttled up the road, shot around, and stopped in the gravel by the door with the abruptness of a wound-up toy. It was astonishing that three men could wedge themselves into the midget of a car, but wedge themselves they did, and used it to the end of its capacity, scuttling away to work in it in the morning, and scuttling back again when work was done, and scuttling away to London every Saturday, as if they were determined to wrest from this small motor, too, the last ounce of pleasure to be got from it.

Finally, Captain Nicholl and his two companions had made up an orchestra among them, and this they played in every night when

158

they got home. One of the young men, who was a tall fellow with blond hair which went back in even corrugated waves across his head as if it had been marcelled, played the piano; the other, who was slight and dark, and had black hair, performed upon a saxophone, and Captain Nicholl himself took turns at thrumming furiously on a banjo, or rattling a tattoo upon the complex arrangement of trap drums, bass drums, and clashing cymbals that surrounded him.

They played nothing but American jazz music or sobbing crooners' rhapsodies or nigger blues. Their performance was astonishing. Although it was contrived solely for their own amusement, they hurled themselves into it with all the industrious earnestness of professional musicians employed by a night-club or a dance-hall to furnish dance music for the patrons. The little dark fellow who played the saxophone would bend and weave prayerfully with his grotesque instrument, as the fat gloating notes came from its unctuous throat, and from time to time he would sway in a half circle, or get up and prance forward and back in rhythm to the music as the saxophone players in dance orchestras sometimes do.

Meanwhile the tall blond fellow at the piano would sway and bend above the keys, glancing around from time to time with little nods and smiles as if he were encouraging an orchestra of forty pieces or beaming happily and in an encouraging fashion at a dance floor crowded with paying customers.

While this was going on, Captain Nicholl would be thrumming madly on the strings of a banjo. He kept the instrument gripped somehow below his withered arm, fingering the end strings with his two good fingers, knocking the tune out with his good right hand, and keeping time with a beating foot. Then with a sudden violent movement he would put the banjo down, snatch up the sticks of the trap drum, and begin to rattle out a furious accompaniment, beating the bass drum with his foot meanwhile, and reaching over to smash cymbals, chimes, and metal rings from time to time. He played with a kind of desperate fury, his mouth fixed in a strange set grin, his bright eyes burning with a sharp wild glint of madness.

They sang as they played, bursting suddenly into the refrain of some popular song with the same calculated spontaneity and spurious enthusiasm of the professional orchestra, mouthing the words of Negro blues and jazz with obvious satisfaction, with an accent which was remarkably good, and yet which had something foreign and inept in it, which made the familiar phrases of American music sound almost as strange in their mouths as if an orchestra of skilful patient Japanese were singing them.

They sang:

> 'Yes, sir! That's my baby
> Yes, sir! Don't mean maybe
> Yes, sir! That's my baby now!'

or:

> 'Oh, it ain't gonna rain no more, no more
> It ain't gonna rain no more'

or:

> 'I got dose blu-u-ues'—

the young fellow at the piano rolling his eyes around in a ridiculous fashion, and mouthing out the word 'blues' extravagantly as he sang it, the little dark fellow bending forward in an unctuous sweep as the notes came gloating fatly from the horn, and Captain Nicholl swaying sideways in his chair as he strummed upon the banjo strings, and improvising a mournful accompaniment of his own, somewhat as follows: 'I got dose blu-u-ues! Yes, suh! Oh! I got dose blues! Yes, suh! I sure have got 'em — dose blu-u-ues — blu-u-ues — blu-u-ues!' — his mouth never relaxing from its strange fixed grin, nor his eyes from their bright set stare of madness as he swayed and strummed and sang the words that came so strangely from his lips.

It was a weird scene, an incredible performance, and somehow it pierced the heart with a wild nameless pity, an infinite sorrow and regret.

Something precious, irrecoverable had gone out of them, and they knew it. They fought the emptiness in them with this deliberate, formidable, and mad intensity of a calculated gaiety, a terrifying mimicry of mirth, and the storm wind howled around us in dark trees, and I felt that I had known them forever, and had no words to say to them — and no door.

There were four in the Coulson family: the father, a man of fifty years, the mother, somewhere in the middle forties, a son, and a daughter, Edith, a girl of twenty-two who lived in the house with her parents. I never met the son: he had completed his course at Oxford a year or two before, and had gone down to London where he was now employed. During the time I lived there the son did not come home.

They were a ruined family. How that ruin had fallen on them, what it was, I never knew, for no one ever spoke to me about them. But the sense of their disgrace, of a shameful inexpiable dishonor, for which there was no pardon, from which there could never be redemption, was overwhelming. In the most astonishing way I found out about it right away, and yet I did not know what they had done, and no one ever spoke a word against them.

Rather, the mention of their name brought silence, and in that silence there was something merciless and final, something that belonged to the temper of the country, and that was far more terrible than any open word of scorn, contempt, or bitter judgment could have been, more savage than a million strident, whispering, or abusive tongues could be, because the silence was unarguable, irrevocable, complete, as if a great door had been shut against their lives forever.

Everywhere I went in town, the people knew about them, and said nothing — saying everything — when I spoke their name. I found this final, closed, relentless silence everywhere — in tobacco, wine, and tailor shops, in book stores, food stores, haberdashery stores — wherever I bought anything and gave the clerk the address to which it was to be delivered, they responded instantly with this shut finality of silence, writing the name down gravely, sometimes saying briefly, 'Oh! Coulson's!' when I gave them the address, but more often saying nothing.

But whether they spoke or simply wrote the name down without a word, there was always this quality of instant recognition, this obdurate, contemptuous finality of silence, as if a door had been shut — a door that could never again be opened. Somehow I disliked them more for this silence than if they had spoken evilly: there was in it something ugly, sly, knowing, and triumphant that

161

was far more evil than any slyly whispering confidence of slander, or any open vituperation of abuse, could be. It seemed somehow to come from all the evil and uncountable small maggotry of the earth, the cautious little hatreds of a million nameless ciphers, each puny, pallid, trivial in himself, but formidable because he added his tiny beetle's ball of dung to the mountainous accumulation of ten million others of his breed.

It was uncanny how these clerk-like faces grave and quiet, that never spoke a word, or gave a sign, or altered their expression by a jot, when I gave them the address, could suddenly be alive with something secret, foul, and sly, could be more closed and secret than a door, and yet instantly reveal the naked, shameful, and iniquitous filth that welled up from some depthless source. I could not phrase it, give a name to it, or even see a certain sign that it was there, no more than I could put my hand upon a wisp of fading smoke, but I always knew when it was there, and somehow when I saw it my heart went hard and cold against the people who revealed it, and turned with warmth and strong affection toward the Coulson family.

There was, finally, among these grave clerk-like faces one face that I could never forget thereafter, a face that seemed to resume into its sly suave surfaces all of the nameless abomination of evil in the world for which I had no name, for which there was no handle I could grasp, no familiar places or edges I could get my hand upon, which slid phantasmally, oilily, and smokily away whenever I tried to get my hands upon it. But it was to haunt my life for years in dreams of hatred, madness, and despair that found no frontal wall for their attack, no word for their vituperation, no door for the shoulder of my hate — an evil world of phantoms, shapes, and whispers that was yet as real as death, as ever-present as man's treachery, but that slid away from me like smoke whenever I tried to meet, or curse, or strangle it.

This face was the face of a man in a tailor shop, a fitter there, and I could have battered that foul face into a bloody pulp, distilled the filthy refuse of his ugly life out of his fat swelling neck and through the murderous grip of my fingers if I could only have found a cause, a logic, and an act for doing it. And yet I never saw the

162

man but twice, and briefly, and there had been nothing in his suave, sly careful speech to give offense.

Edith Coulson had sent me to the tailor's shop: I needed a suit and when I asked her where to go to have it made, she sent me to this place because her brother had his suits made there and liked it. The fitter was a heavy shambling man in his late thirties: he had receding hair, which he brushed back flat in a thick pompadour, yellowish, somewhat bulging eyes, a coarse heavy face, loose-featured, red, and sensual, a sloping meaty jaw, and large discolored buck-teeth which showed unpleasantly in a mouth that was always half open. It was, in fact, the mouth that gave his face its sensual, sly, and ugly look, for a loose and vulgar smile seemed constantly to hover about its thick coarse edges, to be deliberately, slyly restrained, but about to burst at any moment in an evil, foully sensual laugh. There was always this ugly suggestion of a loose, corrupt, and evilly jubilant mirth about his mouth, and yet he never laughed or smiled.

The man's speech had this same quality. It was suave and courteous, but even in its most urbane assurances, there was something non-committal, sly, and jeering, something that slid away from you, and was never to be grasped, a quality that was faithless, tricky, and unwholesome. When I came for the final fitting it was obvious that he had done as cheap and shoddy a job as he could do; the suit was vilely botched and skimped, sufficient cloth had not been put into it, and now it was too late to remedy the defect.

Yet, the fitter gravely pulled the vest down till it met the trousers, tugged at the coat, and pulled the thing together where it stayed until I took a breath or moved a muscle, when it would all come apart again, the collar bulging outward from the shoulder, the skimpy coat and vest crawling backward from the trousers, leaving a hiatus of shirt and belly that could not be remedied now by any means.

Then, gravely he would pull the thing together again, and in his suave, yet oily, sly, and non-committal phrases, say:

'Um! Seems to fit you very well.'

I was choking with exasperation, and knew that I had been done, because I had foolishly paid them half the bill already, and now knew no way out of it except to lose what I had paid, and get nothing for it, or take the thing, and pay the balance. I was caught in a trap, but even as I jerked at the coat and vest speechlessly, seized my shirt, and thrust the gaping collar in his face, the man said smoothly:

'Um! Yes! The collar. Should think all that will be all right. Still needs a little alteration.' He made some chalk marks on me. 'Should think you'll find it fits you very well when the tailor makes the alterations.'

'When will the suit be ready?'

'Um. Should think you ought to have it by next Tuesday. Yes. I think you'll find it ready by Tuesday.'

The sly words slid away from me like oil: there was nothing to pin him to or grasp him by, the yellowed eyes looked casually away and would not look at me, the sensual face was suavely grave, the discolored buck-teeth shone obscenely through the coarse loose mouth, and the suggestion of the foul loose smile was so pronounced now that it seemed that at any moment he would have to turn away with heavy trembling shoulders, and stifle the evil jeering laugh that was welling up in him. But he remained suavely grave and non-committal to the end, and when I asked him if I should come again to try it on, he said, in the same oily tone, never looking at me:

'Um. Shouldn't think that would be necessary. Could have it delivered to you when it's ready. What is your address?'

'The Far-End Farm — it's on Ventnor Road.'

'Oh! Coulson's!' He never altered his expression, but the suggestion of the obscene smile was so pronounced that now it seemed he had to out with it. Instead, he only said:

'Um. Yes. Should think it could be delivered to you there on Tuesday. If you'll just wait a moment I'll ask the tailor.'

Gravely, suavely, he took the coat from me and walked back toward the tailor's room with the coat across his arm. In a moment, I heard sly voices whispering, laughing slyly, then the tailor saying:

'Where does he live?'

'Coulson's!' said the fitter chokingly, and now the foul awaited laugh did come — high, wet, slimy, it came out of that loose mouth, and choked and whispered wordlessly, and choked again, and mingled then with the tailor's voice in sly, choking, whispering intimacy, and then gasped faintly, and was silent. When he came out again his coarse face was red and swollen with foul secret merriment, his heavy shoulders trembled slightly, he took out his handkerchief and wiped it once across his loose half-opened mouth, and with that gesture wiped the slime of laughter from his lips. Then he came toward me suave, grave, and courteous, evilly composed, as he said smoothly:

'Should think we'll have that for you by next Tuesday, sir.'

'Can the tailor fix it so it's going to fit?'

'Um. Should think you'll find that everything's all right. You ought to have it Tuesday afternoon.'

He was not looking at me: the yellowish bulging eyes were staring casually, indefinitely, away, and his words again had slid away from me like oil. He could not be touched, approached, or handled: there was nothing to hold him by, he had the impregnability of smoke or a ball of mercury.

As I went out the door, he began to speak to another man in the shop, I heard low words and whispered voices, then, gasping, the word 'Coulson's!' and the slimy, choking, smothered laughter as the street door closed behind me. I never saw him again. I never forgot his face.

That was a fine house: the people in it were exiled, lost, and ruined people, and I liked them all. Later, I never knew why I felt so close to them, or remembered them with such warmth and strong affection.

I did not see the Coulsons often and rarely talked to them. Yet I felt as familiar and friendly with them all as if I had known them all my life. The house was wonderful as no other house I had ever known because we all seemed to be living in it together with this strange speechless knowledge, warmth, and familiarity, and yet each was as private, secret, and secure in his own room as if he occupied the house alone.

Coulson himself I saw least of all: we sometimes passed each other going in or out the door, or in the hall: he would grunt 'Morn-

165

ing,' or 'Good Day,' in a curt blunt manner, and go on, and yet he always left me with a curious sense of warmth and friendliness. He was a stocky well-set man with iron-gray hair, bushy eyebrows, and a red weathered face which wore the open color of the country on it, but also had the hard dull flush of the steady heavy drinker.

I never saw him drunk, and yet I think that he was never sober: he was one of those men who have drunk themselves past any hope of drunkenness, who are tanned, weathered in it so completely that it could never be distilled out of their blood again. Yet, even in this terrible excess one felt a kind of grim control — the control of a man who is enslaved by the very thing that he controls, the control of the opium eater who cannot leave his drug but measures out his dose with a cold calculation, and finds the limit of his capacity, and stops there, day by day.

But somehow this very sense of control, this blunt ruddy style of the country gentleman which distinguished his speech, his manner, and his dress, made the ruin of his life, the desperate intemperance of drink that smouldered in him like a slow fire, steadily, nakedly apparent. It was as if, having lost everything, he still held grimly to the outer forms of a lost standard, a ruined state, when the inner substance was destroyed.

And it was this way with all of them — with Mrs. Coulson and the girl, as well: their crisp, clipped friendly speech never deviated into intimacy, and never hinted at any melting into confidence and admission. Upon the woman's weathered face there hovered, when she talked, the same faint set grin that Captain Nicholl had, and her eyes were bright and hard, a little mad, impenetrable, as were his. And the girl, although young and very lovely, sometimes had this same look when she greeted any one or paused to talk. In that look there was nothing truculent, bitter, or defiant: it was just the look of three people who had gone down together, and who felt for one another neither bitterness nor hate, but that strange companionship of a common disgrace, from which love has vanished, but which is more secret, silent, and impassively resigned to its fatal unity than love itself could be.

And that hard bright look also said this plainly to the world:

166

'We ask for nothing from you now, we want nothing that you offer us. What is ours is ours, what we are we are, you'll not intrude nor come closer than we let you see!'

Coulson might have been a man who had been dishonored and destroyed by his women, and who took it stolidly, saying nothing, and drank steadily from morning until night, and had nothing for it now but drink and silence and acceptance. Yet I never knew for certain that this was so, it just seemed inescapable, and seemed somehow legible not only in the slow smouldering fire that burned out through his rugged weathered face, but also in the hard bright armor of the women's eyes, the fixed set grin around their lips when they were talking — a grin that was like armor, too. And Morison, who had referred to Coulson, chuckling, as a real 'bottle-a-day-man,' had added quietly, casually, in his brief, indefinite, but blurted-out suggestiveness of speech:

'I think the old girl's been a bit of a bitch in her day. . . . Don't know, of course, but has the look, hasn't she?' In a moment he said quietly, 'Have you talked to the daughter yet?'

'Once or twice. Not for long.'

'Ran into a chap at Magdalen other day who knows her,' he said casually. 'He used to come out here to see her.' He glanced swiftly, slyly at me, his face reddening a little with laughter. 'Pretty hot, I gather,' he said quietly, smiling, and looked away. It was night: the fire burned cheerfully in the grate, the hot coals spurting in small gaseous flares from time to time. The house was very quiet all around us. Outside we could hear the stormy wind in the trees along the road. Morison flicked his cigarette into the fire, poured out a drink of whiskey into a glass, saying as he did so: 'I say, old chap, you don't mind if I take a spot of this before I go to bed, do you?' Then he shot some seltzer in the glass, and drank. And I sat there, without a word, staring sullenly into the fire, dumbly conscious of the flood of sick pain and horror which the casual foulness of the man's suggestion had aroused, stubbornly trying to deny now that I was thinking of the girl all the time.

One night, as I was coming home along the dark road that went up past the playing field to the house, and that was bordered on each side by grand trees whose branches seemed to hold at night all the mysterious and demented cadences of storm, I came upon her suddenly standing in the shadow of a tree. It was one of the grand wild nights that seemed to come so often in the autumn cf that year: the air was full of a fine stinging moisture, not quite rain, and above the stormy branches of the trees I could see the sky, wild, broken, full of scudding clouds through which at times the moon drove in and out with a kind of haggard loneliness. By that faint, wild, and broken light, I could see the small white oval of the girl's face — somehow even more lovely now just because I could not see it plainly. And I could see as well the rough gleaming bark of the tree against which she leaned.

As I approached, I saw her thrust her hand into the pocket of her overcoat, a match flared, and for a moment I saw Edith plainly, the small flower of her face framed in the wavering light as she lowered her head to light her cigarette.

The light went out, I saw the small respiring glow of her cigarette before the white blur of her face, I passed her swiftly, head bent, without speaking, my heart filled with the sense of strangeness and wonder which the family had roused in me.

Then I walked on up the road, muttering to myself. The house was dark when I got there, but when I entered my sitting-room the place was still warmly and softly luminous with the glow of hot coals in the grate. I turned the lights on, shut the door behind me, and hurled several lumps of coal upon the bedded coals. In a moment the fire was blazing and crackling cheerfully, and getting a kind of comfort and satisfaction from this activity, I flung off my coat, went over to the sideboard, poured out a stiff drink of scotch from the bottle there, and coming back to the fire, flung myself into a chair, and began to stare sullenly into the dancing flames.

How long I sat there in this stupor of sullen and nameless fury I did not know, but I was sharply roused at length by footsteps light and rapid on the gravel, shocked into a start of surprise by a figure that appeared suddenly at one of the French windows that opened directly from my sitting-room to the level sward of velvet lawn before the house.

I peered through the glass for a moment with an astonished stare before I recognized the face of Edith Coulson. I opened the doors at once, she came in quickly, smiling at my surprise, and at the glass which I was holding foolishly, half-raised in my hand.

I continued to look at her with an expression of gape-mouthed astonishment and in a moment became conscious of her smiling glance, the cool sweet assurance of her young voice.

'I say!' she was saying cheerfully. 'What a lucky thing to find you up! I came away without any key — I should have had to wake the whole house up — so when I saw your light —' she concluded briskly '— what luck! I hope you don't mind.'

'Why no-o, no,' I stammered foolishly, still staring dumbly at her. 'No — no-o — not at all,' I blundered on. Then suddenly coming to myself with a burst of galvanic energy, I shut the windows, pushed another chair before the fire, and said:

'Won't you sit down and have a drink before you go?'

'Thanks,' she said crisply. 'I will — yes. What a jolly fire you have.' As she talked she took off her coat and hat swiftly and put them on a chair. Her face was flushed and rosy, beaded with small particles of rain, and for a moment she stood before the mirror arranging her hair, which had been tousled by the wind.

The girl was slender, tall, and very lovely with the kind of beauty they have when they are beautiful — a beauty so fresh, fair, and delicate that it seems to be given to just a few of them to compensate for all the grimly weathered ugliness of the rest. Her voice was also lovely, sweet, and musical, and when she talked all the notes of tenderness and love were in it. But she had the same hard bright look in her eye that her mother had, the faint set smile around her mouth: as we stood there talking she was standing very close to me, and I could smell the fragrance of her hair, and felt an intolerable desire to put my hand upon hers and was almost certain she would not draw away. But the hard bright look was in her eye, the faint set smile around her mouth, and I did nothing.

'What'll you have?' I said. 'Whiskey?'

'Yes, thank you,' she said with the same sweet crisp assurance with which she always spoke, 'and a splash of soda.' I struck a match and held it for her while she lit the cigarette she was holding in her hand, and in a moment returned to her with the drink. Then she sat down, crossed her legs, and for a moment puffed thoughtfully at her cigarette, as she stared into the fire. The storm wind moaned in the great trees along the road, and near the house, and suddenly a swirl of rain and wind struck the windows with a rattling blast. The girl stirred a little in her chair, restlessly, shivered:

'Listen!' she said. 'What a night! Horrible weather we have here, isn't it?'

'I don't know. I don't like the fog and rain so well. But this — the way it is tonight —' I nodded toward the window — 'I like it.'

She looked at me for a moment.

'Oh,' she said non-committally. 'You do.' Then as she sipped her drink, she looked curiously about the room, her reflective glance finally resting on my table where there was a great stack of the ledgers in which I wrote.

'I say,' she cried again. 'What are you doing with all those big books there?'

'I write in them.'

'Really?' she said, in a surprised tone. 'I should think it'd be an awful bother carrying them around when you travel?'

'It is. But it's the best way I've found of keeping what I do together.'

'Oh,' she said, as before, and continued to stare curiously at me with her fair, lovely young face, the curiously hard, bright, and unrevealing glance of her eye. 'I see. . . . But why do you come to such a place as this to write?' she said presently. 'Do you like it here?'

'I do. As well as any place I've ever known.'

'Oh! . . . I should think a writer would want a different kind of place.'

'What kind?'

'Oh — I don't know — Paris — London — some place like that where there is lots of life — people — fun — I should think you'd work better in a place like that.'

'I work better here.'

'But don't you get awfully fed up sitting in here all day long and writing in those enormous books?'

'I do, yes.'

'I should think you would. . . . I should think you'd want to get away from it sometime.'

'Yes. I do want to — every day — almost all the time.'

'Then why don't you?' she said crisply. 'Why don't you go off some week-end for a little spree. I should think it'd buck you up no end.'

'It would — yes. Where should I go?'

'Oh, Paris, I suppose. . . . Or London! London!' she cried. 'London is quite jolly if you know it.'

'I'm afraid I don't know it.'

'But you've *been* to London,' she said in a surprised tone.

'Oh, yes. I lived there for several months.'

'Then you know London,' she said impatiently. 'Of course you do.'

'I'm afraid I don't know it very well. I don't know many people there — and after all, that's the thing that counts, isn't it?'

She looked at me curiously for a moment with the faint hard smile around the edges of her lovely mouth. 'I should think that might be arranged,' she said with a quiet, an enigmatic humor. Then more directly, she added: 'That shouldn't be difficult at all. Perhaps I could introduce you to some people.'

'That would be fine. Do you know many people there?'

'Not many,' she said. 'I go there — whenever I can.' She got up with a swift decisive movement, put her glass down on the mantel, and cast her cigarette into the fire. Then she faced me, looking at me with a curiously bold, an almost defiant directness of her hard bright eyes, and she fixed me with this glance for a full moment before she spoke.

'Good-night,' she said. 'Thanks awfully for letting me in — and for the drink.'

'Good-night,' I said, and she was gone before I could say more, and I had closed the door behind her, and I could hear her light, swift footsteps going down the hall and up the steps. And then there was nothing in the house but sleep and silence, and the storm and darkness in the world around me.

Mrs. Coulson came into my room just once or twice while I was there. One morning she came in, spoke crisply and cheerfully, and walked over to the window looking out upon the velvet lawn and

171

at the dreary impenetrable gray of foggy air. Although the room was warm, and there was a good fire burning in the grate, she clasped her arms together as she looked and shivered a little:

'Wretched weather, isn't it?' she said in her crisp tones, her gaunt weathered face and toothy mouth touched by the faint fixed grin as she looked out with her bright hard stare. 'Don't you find it frightfully depressing? Most Americans do,' she said, getting the sharp disquieting sound into the word.

'Yes. I do, a little. We don't have this kind of weather very often. But this is the time of year you get it here, isn't it? I suppose you're used to it by now?'

'Used to it?' she said crisply turning her hard bright gaze upon me. 'Not at all. I've known it all my life but I'll never get used to it. It is a wretched climate.'

'Still you wouldn't feel at home anywhere else, would you? You wouldn't want to live outside of England.'

'No?' she said, staring at me with the faint set grin around her toothy mouth. 'Why do you think so?'

'Because your home is here.'

'My home? My home is where they have fine days, and where the sun is always shining.'

'I wouldn't like that. I'd get tired of sunlight all the time. I'd want some gray days and some fog and snow.'

'Yes, I suppose you would. But then, you've been used to having fine days all your life, haven't you? With us, it's different. I'm so fed up with fog and rain that I could do without it nicely, thank you, if I never saw it again. . . . I don't think you could ever understand how much the sunlight means to us,' she said slowly. She turned and for a moment looked out the window with her hard bright stare, the faint set grin about her mouth. 'Sunlight — warmth — fine days forever! Warmth everywhere — in the earth, the sky, in the lives of the people all around you nothing but warmth and sunlight and fine days!'

'And where would you go to find all that? Does it exist?'

'Oh, of course!' she said crisply and good-naturedly turning to me again. 'There's only one place to live — only one country where I want to live.'

'Where is that?'

'Italy,' she said. 'That's my real home. . . . I'd live the rest of my life there if I could.' For a moment longer she looked out of the window, then turned briskly, saying:

'Why don't you run over to Paris some week-end? After all, it's only seven hours from London: if you left here in the morning you'd be there in time for dinner. It would be a good change for you. I should think a little trip like that would buck you up tremendously.'

Her words gave me a wonderful feeling of confidence and hope: I think she had travelled a great deal, and she had the casual, assured way of speaking of a voyage that made it seem very easy, and filled one with a sense of joy and adventure when she spoke about it. When I tried to think of Paris by myself it had seemed very far away and hard to reach: London stood between it and me, and when I thought of the huge smoky web of London, the soft gray skies above me, and the enormous weight of lives that were hidden somewhere in that impenetrable fog, gray desolation and weariness of the spirit filled me. It seemed to me that I must draw each breath of that soft gray air with heavy weary effort, and that every mile of my journey would be a ghastly struggle through some viscous and material substance of soft heavy gray, that weighted down my steps, and filled my heart with desolation.

But when Mrs. Coulson spoke to me about it, suddenly it all seemed wonderfully easy and good. England was magically small, the channel to be taken in a stride, and all the thrill, the joy, the mystery of Paris mine again — the moment that I chose to make it mine.

I looked at her gaunt weathered face, her toothy mouth with the faint fixed grin, the hard bright armor of her eyes, and wondered how anything so clear, so sharp, so crisp, and so incisive could have been shaped and grown underneath these soft and humid skies that numbed me, mind and heart and body, with their thick numb substance of gray weariness and desolation.

A day or two before I left, Edith came into my room one afternoon bearing a tray with tea and jam and buttered bread. I was sitting in my chair before the fire, and had my coat off: when she came in I scrambled to my feet, reached for the coat and started to

173

put it on. In her young crisp voice she told me not to, and put the tray down on the table, saying that the maid was having her afternoon away.

Then for a moment she stood looking at me with her faint and enigmatic smile.

'So you're leaving us?' she said presently.

'Yes. Tomorrow.'

'And where will you go from here?' she said.

'To Germany, I think. Just for a short time — two or three weeks.'

'And after that?'

'I'm going home.'

'Home?'

'Back to America.'

'Oh,' she said slowly. 'I see.' In a moment, she added, 'We shall miss you.'

I wanted to talk to her more than I had ever wanted to talk to any one in my life, but when I spoke all that I could say, lamely, muttering, was:

'I'll miss you, too.'

'Will you?' She spoke so quietly that I could scarcely hear her. 'I wonder for how long?' she said.

'Forever,' I said, flushing miserably at the sound of the word, and yet not knowing any other word to say.

The faint hard smile about her mouth was a little deeper when she spoke again.

'Forever? That's a long time, when one is young as you,' she said.

'I mean it. I'll never forget you as long as I live.'

'We shall remember you,' she said quietly. 'And I hope you think of us sometime — back here buried, lost, in all the fog and rain and ruin of England. How good it must be to know that you are young in a young country — where nothing that you did yesterday matters very much. How wonderful it must be to know that none of the failure of the past can pull you down — that there will always be another day for you — a new beginning. I wonder if you Americans will ever know how fortunate you are,' the girl said.

'And yet you could not leave all this?' I said with a kind of desperate hope. 'This old country you've lived in, known all your life. A girl like you could never leave a place like this to live the kind of life we have in America.'

'*Couldn't* I?' she said with a quiet, but unmistakable passion of conviction. 'There's nothing I'd like better.'

I stared at her blindly, dumbly for a moment; suddenly all that I wanted to say, and had not been able to say found release in a movement of my hands. I gripped her by the shoulders and pulled her to me, and began to plead with her:

'Then why don't you? I'll take you there! — Look here —' my words were crazy and I knew it, but as I spoke them, I believed all I said — 'Look here! I haven't got much money — but in America you can make it if you want to! I'm going back there. You come, too — I'll take you when I go!'

She had not tried to free herself; she just stood there passive, unresisting, as I poured that frenzied proposal in her ears. Now, with the same passive and unyielding movement, the bright armor of her young eyes, she stepped away, and stood looking at me silently for a moment, the faint, hard smile at the edges of her mouth. Then slowly, with an almost imperceptible movement, she shook her head. 'Oh, you'll forget about us all,' she said quietly. 'You'll forget about our lives here — buried in fog — and rain — and failure — and defeat.'

'Failure and defeat won't last forever.'

'Sometimes they do,' she said with a quiet finality that froze my heart.

'Not for you — they won't!' I said, and took her by the hand again with desperate entreaty. 'Listen to me —' I blundered incoherently, with the old feeling of nameless shame and horror. 'You don't need to tell me what it is — I don't want to know — but whatever it is for you — it doesn't matter — you can get the best of it.'

She said nothing but just looked at me through that hard bright armor of her eyes, the obdurate finality of her smile.

'Good-bye,' she said, 'I'll not forget you either.' She looked at me for a moment curiously before she spoke again. 'I wonder,' she said slowly, 'if you'll ever understand just what it is you did for me by coming here.'

'What was it?'

'You opened a door that I thought had been closed forever,' she said, 'a door that let me look in on a world I thought I should never see again — a new bright world, a new life and a new beginning — for us all. And I thought that was something which would never happen to any one in this house again.'

'It will to you,' I said, and took her hand again with desperate eagerness. 'It can happen to you whenever you want it to. It's yours, I'll swear it to you, if you'll only speak.'

She looked at me with her direct hard glance, an almost imperceptible movement of her head.

'I tell you I know what I'm talking about.'

Again she shook her head.

'You don't know,' she said. 'You're young. You're an American. There are some things you'll never be old enough to know. — For some of us there's no return. — Go back,' she said, 'go back to the life you know — the life you understand — where there can always be a new beginning — a new life.'

'And you ——' I said dumbly, miserably.

'Good-bye, my dear,' she said so low and gently I could scarcely hear her. 'Think of me sometime, won't you — I'll not forget you.' And before I could speak she kissed me once and was gone, so light and swift that I did not know it, until the door had closed behind her. And for some time, like a man in a stupor I stood there looking out of the window at the gray wet light of England.

The next day I went away, and never saw any of them again, but I could not forget them. Although I had never passed beyond the armor of their hard bright eyes, or breached the wall of their crisp, friendly, and impersonal speech, or found out anything about them, I always thought of them with warmth, with a deep and tender affection, as if I had always known them — as if, somehow, I could have lived with them or made their lives my own if only I had said a word, or turned the handle of a door — a word I never knew, a door I never found.

176

THAT EVENING SUN

WILLIAM FAULKNER

I

MONDAY is no different from any other week day in Jefferson now. The streets are paved now, and the telephone and electric companies are cutting down more and more of the shade trees — the water oaks, the maples and locusts and elms — to make room for iron poles bearing clusters of bloated and ghostly and bloodless grapes, and we have a city laundry which makes the rounds on Monday morning, gathering the bundles of clothes into bright-colored, specially-made motor cars: the soiled wearing of a whole week now flees apparitionlike behind alert and irritable electric horns, with a long diminishing noise of rubber and asphalt like tearing silk, and even the Negro women who still take in white people's washing after the old custom, fetch and deliver it in automobiles.

But fifteen years ago, on Monday morning the quiet, dusty, shady streets would be full of Negro women with, balanced on their steady, turbaned heads, bundles of clothes tied up in sheets, almost as large as cotton bales, carried so without touch of hand between the kitchen door of the white house and the blackened washpot beside a cabin door in Negro Hollow.

Nancy would set her bundle on the top of her head, then upon the bundle in turn she would set the black straw sailor hat which she wore winter and summer. She was tall, with a high sad face sunken a little where her teeth were missing. Sometimes we would go a part of the way down the lane and across the pasture with her, to watch the balanced bundle and the hat that never bobbed or wavered, even when she walked down into the ditch and up the other side and stooped through the fence. She would go down on her hands and knees and crawl through the gap, her head rigid,

177

uptilted, the bundle steady as a rock or a balloon, and rise to her feet again and go on.

Sometimes the husbands of the washing women would fetch and deliver the clothes, but Jesus never did that for Nancy, even before father told him to stay away from our house, even when Dilsey was sick and Nancy would come to cook for us.

And then about half the time we'd have to go down the lane to Nancy's cabin and tell her to come on and cook breakfast. We would stop at the ditch, because father told us to not have anything to do with Jesus — he was a short black man, with a razor scar down his face — and we would throw rocks at Nancy's house until she came to the door, leaning her head around it without any clothes on.

'What yawl mean, chunking my house?' Nancy said. 'What you little devils mean?'

'Father says for you to come on and get breakfast,' Caddy said. 'Father says it's over a half an hour now, and you've got to come this minute.'

'I ain't studying no breakfast,' Nancy said. 'I going to get my sleep out.'

'I bet you're drunk,' Jason said. 'Father says you're drunk. Are you drunk, Nancy?'

'Who says I is?' Nancy said. 'I got to get my sleep out. I ain't studying no breakfast.'

So after a while we quit chunking the cabin and went back home. When she finally came, it was too late for me to go to school. So we thought it was whiskey until that day they arrested her again and they were taking her to jail and they passed Mr. Stovall. He was the cashier in the bank and a deacon in the Baptist church, and Nancy began to say:

'When you going to pay me, white man? When you going to pay me, white man? It's been three times now since you paid me a cent ——' Mr. Stovall knocked her down, but she kept on saying, 'When you going to pay me, white man? It's been three times now since ——' until Mr. Stovall kicked her in the mouth with his heel and the marshal caught Mr. Stovall back, and Nancy lying in the street, laughing. She turned her head and spat out some

178

blood and teeth and said, 'It's been three times now since he paid me a cent.'

That was how she lost her teeth, and all that day they told about Nancy and Mr. Stovall, and all that night the ones that passed the jail could hear Nancy singing and yelling. They could see her hands holding the window bars, and a lot of them stopped along the fence, listening to her and to the jailer trying to make her stop. She didn't shut up until almost daylight, when the jailer began to hear a bumping and scraping upstairs and he went up there and found Nancy hanging from the window bar. He said that it was cocaine and not whiskey, because no nigger would try to commit suicide unless he was full of cocaine, because a nigger full of cocaine wasn't a nigger any longer.

The jailer cut her down and revived her; then he beat her, whipped her. She had hung herself with her dress. She had fixed it all right, but when they arrested her she didn't have on anything except a dress and so she didn't have anything to tie her hands with and she couldn't make her hands let go of the window ledge. So the jailer heard the noise and ran up there and found Nancy hanging from the window, stark naked, her belly already swelling out a little, like a little balloon.

When Dilsey was sick in her cabin and Nancy was cooking for us, we could see her apron swelling out, that was before father told Jesus to stay away from the house. Jesus was in the kitchen, sitting behind the stove, with his razor scar on his black face like a piece of dirty string. He said it was a watermelon that Nancy had under her dress.

'It never come off of your vine, though,' Nancy said.

'Off of what vine?' Caddy said.

'I can cut down the vine it did come off of,' Jesus said.

'What makes you want to talk like that before these chillen?' Nancy said. 'Whyn't you go on to work? You done it. You want Mr. Jason to catch you hanging around his kitchen, talking that way before these chillen?'

'Talking what way?' Caddy said. 'What vine?'

'I can't hang around white man's kitchen,' Jesus said. 'But white man can hang around mine. White man can come in my

179

house, but I can't stop him. When white man want to come in my house, I ain't got no house. I can't stop him, but he can't kick me outen it. He can't do that.'

Dilsey was still sick in her cabin. Father told Jesus to stay off our place. Dilsey was still sick. It was a long time. We were in the library after supper.

'Isn't Nancy through in the kitchen yet?' mother said. 'It seems to me that she has had plenty of time to finish the dishes.'

'Let Quentin go and see,' father said. 'Go and see if Nancy is through, Quentin. Tell her she can go on home.'

I went to the kitchen. Nancy was through. The dishes were put away and the fire was out. Nancy was sitting in a chair, close to the cold stove. She looked at me.

'Mother wants to know if you are through,' I said.

'Yes,' Nancy said. She looked at me. 'I done finished.' She looked at me.

'What is it?' I said. 'What is it?'

'I ain't nothing but a nigger,' Nancy said. 'It ain't none of my fault.'

She looked at me, sitting in the chair before the cold stove, the sailor hat on her head. I went back to the library. It was the old stove and all, when you think of a kitchen being warm and busy and cheerful. And with a cold stove and the dishes all put away, and nobody wanting to eat at that hour.

'Is she through?' mother said.

'Yessum,' I said.

'What is she doing?' mother said.

'She's not doing anything. She's through.'

'I'll go and see,' Father said.

'Maybe she's waiting for Jesus to come and take her home,' Caddy said.

'Jesus is gone,' I said. 'Nancy told us how one morning she woke up and Jesus had gone.'

'He quit me,' Nancy said. 'Done gone to Memphis, I reckon. Dodging them city po-lice for a while, I reckon.'

'And a good riddance,' father said. 'I hope he stays there.'

'Nancy's scaired of the dark,' Jason said.

'So are you,' Caddy said.

'I'm not,' Jason said.

'Scairy cat,' Caddy said.

'I'm not,' Jason said.

'You, Candace!' mother said. Father came back.

'I am going to walk down the lane with Nancy,' he said. 'She says that Jesus is back.'

'Has she seen him?' mother said.

'No. Some Negro sent her word that he was back in town. I won't be long.'

'You'll leave me alone, to take Nancy home?' mother said. 'Is her safety more precious to you than mine?'

'I won't be long,' father said.

'You'll leave these children unprotected, with that Negro about?'

'I'm going too,' Caddy said. 'Let me go, Father.'

'What would he do with them, if he were unfortunate enough to have them?' father said.

'I want to go, too,' Jason said.

'Jason!' mother said. She was speaking to father. You could tell by the way she said the name. Like she believed that all day father had been trying to think of doing the thing she wouldn't like the most, and that she knew all the time that after a while he would think of it. I stayed quiet, because father and I both knew that mother would want him to make me stay with her if she just thought of it in time. So father didn't look at me. I was the oldest. I was nine and Caddy was seven and Jason was five.

'Nonsense,' father said. 'We won't be long.'

Nancy had her hat on. We came to the lane. 'Jesus always been good to me,' Nancy said. 'Whenever he had two dollars, one of them was mine.' We walked in the lane. 'If I can just get through the lane,' Nancy said, 'I be all right then.'

The lane was always dark. 'This is where Jason got scared on Hallowe'en,' Caddy said.

'I didn't,' Jason said.

'Can't Aunt Rachel do anything with him?' father said. Aunt Rachel was old. She lived in a cabin beyond Nancy's, by herself. She had white hair and she smoked a pipe in the door, all day long;

she didn't work any more. They said she was Jesus' mother. Sometimes she said she was and sometimes she said she wasn't any kin to Jesus.

'Yes, you did,' Caddy said. 'You were scairder than Frony. You were scairder than T.P. even. Scairder than niggers.'

'Can't nobody do nothing with him,' Nancy said. 'He say I done woke up the devil in him and ain't but one thing going to lay it down again.'

'Well, he's gone now,' father said. 'There's nothing for you to be afraid of now. And if you'd just let white men alone.'

'Let what white men alone?' Caddy said. 'How let them alone?'

'He ain't gone nowhere,' Nancy said. 'I can feel him. I can feel him now, in this lane. He hearing us talk, every word, hid somewhere, waiting. I ain't seen him, and I ain't going to see him again but once more, with that razor in his mouth. That razor on that string down his back, inside his shirt. And then I ain't going to be even surprised.'

'I wasn't scaired,' Jason said.

'If you'd behave yourself, you'd have kept out of this,' father said. 'But it's all right now. He's probably in St. Louis now. Probably got another wife by now and forgot all about you.'

'If he has, I better not find out about it,' Nancy said. 'I'd stand there right over them, and every time he wropped her, I'd cut that arm off. I'd cut his head off and I'd slit her belly and I'd shove —— '

'Hush,' father said.

'Slit whose belly, Nancy?' Caddy said.

'I wasn't scaired,' Jason said. 'I'd walk right down this lane by myself.'

'Yah,' Caddy said. 'You wouldn't dare to put your foot down in it if we were not here too.'

II

Dilsey was still sick, so we took Nancy home every night until mother said, 'How much longer is this going on? I to be left alone in this big house while you take home a frightened Negro?'

We fixed a pallet in the kitchen for Nancy. One night we waked up, hearing the sound. It was not singing and it was not crying, coming up the back stairs. There was a light in mother's room and we heard father going down the hall, down the back stairs, and Caddy and I went into the hall. The floor was cold. Our toes curled away from it while we listened to the sound. It was like singing and it wasn't like singing, like the sounds that Negroes make.

Then it stopped and we heard father going down the back stairs, and we went to the head of the stairs. Then the sound began again, in the stairway, not loud, and we could see Nancy's eyes halfway up the stairs, against the wall. They looked like cat's eyes do, like a big cat against the wall, watching us. When we came down the steps to where she was, she quit making the sound again, and we stood there until father came back up from the kitchen, with his pistol in his hand. He went back down with Nancy and they came back with Nancy's pallet.

We spread the pallet in our room. After the light in mother's room went off, we could see Nancy's eyes again. 'Nancy,' Caddy whispered. 'Are you asleep, Nancy?'

Nancy whispered something. It was oh or no, I don't know which. Like nobody had made it, like it came from nowhere and went nowhere, until it was like Nancy was not there at all; that I had looked so hard at her eyes on the stairs that they had got printed on my eyeballs, like the sun does when you have closed your eyes and there is no sun. 'Jesus,' Nancy whispered. 'Jesus.'

'Was it Jesus?' Caddy said. 'Did he try to come into the kitchen?'

'Jesus,' Nancy said. Like this: Jeeeeeeeeeeeeeeeeesus, until the sound went out, like a match or a candle does.

'It's the other Jesus she means,' I said.

'Can you see us, Nancy?' Caddy whispered. 'Can you see our eyes too?'

'I ain't nothing but a nigger,' Nancy said. 'God knows. God knows.'

'What did you see down there in the kitchen?' Caddy whispered. 'What tried to get in?'

'God knows,' Nancy said. We could see her eyes. 'God knows.'

Dilsey got well. She cooked dinner. 'You'd better stay in bed a day or two longer,' father said.

'What for?' Dilsey said. 'If I had been a day later, this place would be to rack and ruin. Get on out of here now, and let me get my kitchen straight again.'

Dilsey cooked supper too. And that night, just before dark, Nancy came into the kitchen.

'How do you know he's back?' Dilsey said. 'You ain't seen him.'

'Jesus is a nigger,' Jason said.

'I can feel him,' Nancy said. 'I can feel him laying yonder in the ditch.'

'Tonight?' Dilsey said. 'Is he there tonight?'

'Dilsey's a nigger too,' Jason said.

'You try to eat something,' Dilsey said.

'I don't want nothing,' Nancy said.

'I ain't a nigger,' Jason said.

'Drink some coffee,' Dilsey said. She poured a cup of coffee for Nancy. 'Do you know he's out there tonight? How come you know it's tonight?'

'I know,' Nancy said. 'He's there, waiting. I know. I done lived with him too long. I know what he is fixing to do fore he know it himself.'

'Drink some coffee,' Dilsey said. Nancy held the cup to her mouth and blew into the cup. Her mouth pursed out like a spreading adder's, like a rubber mouth, like she had blown all the color out of her lips with blowing the coffee.

'I ain't a nigger,' Jason said. 'Are you a nigger, Nancy?'

'I hellborn, child,' Nancy said. 'I won't be nothing soon. I going back where I come from soon.'

III

She began to drink the coffee. While she was drinking, holding the cup in both hands, she began to make the sound again. She made the sound into the cup and the coffee splashed out onto her hands and her dress. Her eyes looked at us and she sat there, her elbows

184

on her knees, holding the cup in both hands, looking at us across the wet cup, making the sound.

'Look at Nancy,' Jason said. 'Nancy can't cook for us now. Dilsey's got well now.'

'You hush up,' Dilsey said. Nancy held the cup in both hands, looking at us, making the sound, like there were two of them: one looking at us and the other making the sound. 'Whyn't you let Mr. Jason telefoam the marshal?' Dilsey said. Nancy stopped then, holding the cup in her long brown hands. She tried to drink some coffee again, but it splashed out of the cup, onto her hands and her dress, and she put the cup down. Jason watched her.

'I can't swallow it,' Nancy said. 'I swallows but it won't go down me.'

'You go down to the cabin,' Dilsey said. 'Frony will fix you a pallet and I'll be there soon.'

'Won't no nigger stop him,' Nancy said.

'I ain't a nigger,' Jason said. 'Am I, Dilsey?'

'I reckon not,' Dilsey said. She looked at Nancy. 'I don't reckon so. What you going to do, then?'

Nancy looked at us. Her eyes went fast, like she was afraid there wasn't time to look, without hardly moving at all. She looked at us, at all three of us at one time. 'You member that night I stayed in yawl's room?' she said. She told about how we waked up early the next morning, and played. We had to play quiet, on her pallet, until father woke up and it was time to get breakfast. 'Go and ask your maw to let me stay here tonight,' Nancy said. 'I won't need no pallet. We can play some more.'

Caddy asked mother. Jason went too. 'I can't have Negroes sleeping in the bedrooms,' mother said. Jason cried. He cried until mother said he couldn't have any dessert for three days if he didn't stop. Then Jason said he would stop if Dilsey would make a chocolate cake. Father was there.

'Why don't you do something about it?' mother said. 'What do we have officers for?'

'Why is Nancy afraid of Jesus?' Caddy said. 'Are you afraid of father, Mother?'

'What could the officers do?' father said. 'If Nancy hasn't seen him, how could the officers find him?'

'Then why is she afraid?' mother said.

'She says he is there. She says she knows he is there to-night.'

'Yet we pay taxes,' mother said. 'I must wait here alone in this big house while you take a Negro woman home.'

'You know that I am not lying outside with a razor,' father said.

'I'll stop if Dilsey will make a chocolate cake,' Jason said. Mother told us to go out and father said he didn't know if Jason would get a chocolate cake or not, but he knew what Jason was going to get in about a minute. We went back to the kitchen and told Nancy.

'Father said for you to go home and lock the door, and you'll be all right,' Caddy said. 'All right from what, Nancy? Is Jesus mad at you?' Nancy was holding the coffee cup in her hands again, her elbows on her knees and her hands holding the cup between her knees. She was looking into the cup. 'What have you done that made Jesus mad?' Caddy said. Nancy let the cup go. It didn't break on the floor, but the coffee spilled out, and Nancy sat there with her hands still making the shape of the cup. She began to make the sound again, not loud. Not singing and not unsinging. We watched her.

'Here,' Dilsey said. 'You quit that, now. You get aholt of your-self. You wait here. I going to get Versh to walk home with you.' Dilsey went out.

We looked at Nancy. Her shoulders kept shaking, but she quit making the sound. We watched her. 'What's Jesus going to do to you?' Caddy said. 'He went away.'

Nancy looked at us. 'We had fun that night I stayed in yawl's room, didn't we?'

'I didn't,' Jason said. 'I didn't have any fun.'

'You were asleep in mother's room,' Caddy said. 'You were not there.'

'Let's go down to my house and have some more fun,' Nancy said.

'Mother won't let us,' I said. 'It's too late now.'

'Don't bother her,' Nancy said. 'We can tell her in the morning. She won't mind.'

'She wouldn't let us,' I said.

'Don't ask her now,' Nancy said. 'Don't bother her now.'

'She didn't say we couldn't go,' Caddy said.

'We didn't ask,' I said.

'If you go, I'll tell,' Jason said.

'We'll have fun,' Nancy said. 'They won't mind, just to my house. I been working for yawl a long time. They won't mind.'

'I'm not afraid to go,' Caddy said. 'Jason is the one that's afraid. He'll tell.'

'I'm not,' Jason said.

'Yes, you are,' Caddy said. 'You'll tell.'

'I won't tell,' Jason said. 'I'm not afraid.'

'Jason is going to tell,' Caddy said. The lane was dark. We passed the pasture gate. 'I bet if something was to jump out from behind the gate, Jason would holler.'

'I wouldn't,' Jason said. We walked down the lane. Nancy was talking loud.

'What are you talking so loud for, Nancy?' Caddy said.

'Who, me?' Nancy said. 'Listen at Quentin and Caddy and Jason saying I'm talking loud.'

'You talk like there was five of us here,' Caddy said. 'You talk like father was here too.'

'Who; me talking loud, Mr. Jason?' Nancy said.

'Nancy called Jason "Mister,"' Caddy said.

'Listen how Caddy and Quentin and Jason talk,' Nancy said.

'We're not talking loud,' Caddy said. 'You're the one that's talking like father ——'

'Hush,' Nancy said; 'hush, Mr. Jason.'

'Nancy called Jason "Mister" aguh ——'

'Hush,' Nancy said. She was talking loud when we crossed the ditch and stooped through the fence where she used to stoop through with the clothes on her head. Then we came to her house. We were going fast then. She opened the door. The smell of the house was like the lamp and the smell of Nancy was like the wick, like they were waiting for one another to begin to smell. She lit the lamp and closed the door and put the bar up. Then she quit talking loud, looking at us.

'What're we going to do?' Caddy said.

'What do yawl want to do?' Nancy said.

'You said we would have some fun,' Caddy said.

There was something about Nancy's house; something you could smell besides Nancy and the house. Jason smelled it, even. 'I don't want to stay here,' he said. 'I want to go home.'

'Go home, then,' Caddy said.

'I don't want to go by myself,' Jason said.

'We're going to have some fun,' Nancy said.

'How?' Caddy said.

Nancy stood by the door. She was looking at us, only it was like she had emptied her eyes, like she had quit using them. 'What do you want to do?' she said.

'Tell us a story,' Caddy said. 'Can you tell a story?'

'Yes,' Nancy said.

'Tell it,' Caddy said. We looked at Nancy. 'You don't know any stories.'

'Yes,' Nancy said. 'Yes I do.'

She came and sat in a chair before the hearth. There was a little fire there. Nancy built it up, when it was already hot inside. She built a good blaze. She told a story. She talked like her eyes looked, like her eyes watching us and her voice talking to us did not belong to her. Like she was living somewhere else, waiting somewhere else. She was outside the cabin. Her voice was inside and the shape of her, the Nancy that could stoop under a barbed wire fence with a bundle of clothes balanced on her head as though without weight, like a balloon, was there. But that was all. 'And so this here queen come walking up to the ditch, where that bad man was hiding. She was walking up to the ditch, and she say, "If I can just get past this here ditch," was what she say . . .'

'What ditch?' Caddy said. 'A ditch like that one out there? Why did a queen want to go into a ditch?'

'To get to her house,' Nancy said. She looked at us. 'She had to cross the ditch to get into her house quick and bar the door.'

'Why did she want to go home and bar the door?' Caddy said.

IV

Nancy looked at us. She quit talking. She looked at us. Jason's legs stuck straight out of his pants where he sat on Nancy's lap. 'I don't think that's a good story,' he said. 'I want to go home.'

'Maybe we had better,' Caddy said. She got up from the floor. 'I bet they are looking for us right now.' She went toward the door.

'No,' Nancy said. 'Don't open it.' She got up quick and passed Caddy. She didn't touch the door, the wooden bar.

'Why not?' Caddy said.

'Come back to the lamp,' Nancy said. 'We'll have fun. You don't have to go.'

'We ought to go,' Caddy said. 'Unless we have a lot of fun.' She and Nancy came back to the fire, the lamp.

'I want to go home,' Jason said. 'I'm going to tell.'

'I know another story,' Nancy said. She stood close to the lamp. She looked at Caddy, like when your eyes look up at a stick balanced on your nose. She had to look down to see Caddy, but her eyes looked like that, like when you are balancing a stick.

'I won't listen to it,' Jason said. 'I'll bang on the floor.'

'It's a good one,' Nancy said. 'It's better than the other one.'

'What's it about?' Caddy said. Nancy was standing by the lamp. Her hand was on the lamp, against the light, long and brown.

'Your hand is on that hot globe,' Caddy said. 'Don't it feel hot to your hand?'

Nancy looked at her hand on the lamp chimney. She took her hand away, slow. She stood there, looking at Caddy, wringing her long hand as though it were tied to her wrist with a string.

'Let's do something else,' Caddy said.

'I want to go home,' Jason said.

'I got some popcorn,' Nancy said. She looked at Caddy and then at Jason and then at me and then at Caddy again. 'I got some popcorn.'

'I don't like popcorn,' Jason said. 'I'd rather have candy.'

Nancy looked at Jason. 'You can hold the popper.' She was still wringing her hand; it was long and limp and brown.

'All right,' Jason said. 'I'll stay a while if I can do that. Caddy can't hold it. I'll want to go home again if Caddy holds the popper.'

Nancy built up the fire. 'Look at Nancy putting her hands in the fire,' Caddy said. 'What's the matter with you, Nancy?'

'I got popcorn,' Nancy said. 'I got some.' She took the popper from under the bed. It was broken. Jason began to cry.

'Now we can't have any popcorn,' he said.

'We ought to go home, anyway,' Caddy said. 'Come on, Quentin.'

'Wait,' Nancy said; 'wait. I can fix it. Don't you want to help me fix it?'

'I don't think I want any,' Caddy said. 'It's too late now.'

'You help me, Jason,' Nancy said. 'Don't you want to help me?'

'No,' Jason said. 'I want to go home.'

'Hush,' Nancy said; 'hush. Watch. Watch me. I can fix it so Jason can hold it and pop the corn.' She got a piece of wire and fixed the popper.

'It won't hold good,' Caddy said.

'Yes it will,' Nancy said. 'Yawl watch. Yawl watch. Yawl help me shell some corn.'

The popcorn was under the bed too. We shelled it into the popper and Nancy helped Jason hold the popper over the fire.

'It's not popping,' Jason said. 'I want to go home.'

'You wait,' Nancy said. 'It'll begin to pop. We'll have fun then.' She was sitting close to the fire. The lamp was turned up so high it was beginning to smoke.

'Why don't you turn it down some?' I said.

'It's all right,' Nancy said. 'I'll clean it. Yawl wait. The popcorn will start in a minute.'

'I don't believe it's going to start,' Caddy said. 'We ought to start home, anyway. They'll be worried.'

'No,' Nancy said. 'It's going to pop. Dilsey will tell um yawl with me. I been working for yawl long time. They won't mind if yawl at my house. You wait, now. It'll start popping any minute now.'

Then Jason got some smoke in his eyes and he began to cry. He dropped the popper into the fire. Nancy got a wet rag and wiped Jason's face, but he didn't stop crying.

190

'Hush,' she said. 'Hush.' But he didn't hush. Caddy took the popper out of the fire.

'It's burned up,' she said. 'You'll have to get some more popcorn, Nancy.'

'Did you put all of it in?' Nancy said.

'Yes,' Caddy said. Nancy looked at Caddy. Then she took the popper and opened it and poured the cinders into her apron and began to sort the grains, her hands long and brown, and we watching her.

'Haven't you got any more?' Caddy said.

'Yes,' Nancy said. 'Yes. Look. This here ain't burnt. All we need to do is ——'

'I want to go home,' Jason said. 'I'm going to tell.'

'Hush,' Caddy said. We all listened. Nancy's head was already turned toward the barred door, her eyes filled with red lamplight. 'Somebody is coming,' Caddy said.

Then Nancy began to make that sound again, not loud, sitting there above the fire, her long hands dangling between her knees; all of a sudden water began to come out on her face in big drops, running down her face, carrying in each one a little turning ball of firelight like a spark until it dropped off her chin. 'She's not crying,' I said.

'I ain't crying,' Nancy said. Her eyes were closed. 'I ain't crying. Who is it?'

'I don't know,' Caddy said. She went to the door and looked out. 'We're got to go now,' she said. 'Here comes father.'

'I'm going to tell,' Jason said. 'Yawl made me come.'

The water still ran down Nancy's face. She turned in her chair. 'Listen. Tell him. Tell him we going to have fun. Tell him I take good care of yawl until in the morning. Tell him to let me come home with yawl and sleep on the floor. Tell him I won't need no pallet. We'll have fun. You member last time how we had so much fun?'

'I didn't have fun,' Jason said. 'You hurt me. You put smoke in my eyes. I'm going to tell.'

V

Father came in. He looked at me. Nancy did not get up.

'Tell him,' she said.

'Caddy made us come down here,' Jason said. 'I didn't want to.'

Father came to the fire. Nancy looked up at him. 'Can't you go to Aunt Rachel's and stay?' he said. Nancy looked up at father, her hands between her knees. 'He's not here,' father said. 'I would have seen him. There's not a soul in sight.'

'He in the ditch,' Nancy said. 'He waiting in the ditch yonder.'

'Nonsense,' father said. He looked at Nancy. 'Do you know he's there?'

'I got the sign,' Nancy said.

'What sign?'

'I got it. It was on the table when I come in. It was a hogbone, with blood meat still on it, laying by the lamp. He's out there. When yawl walk out that door, I gone.'

'Gone where, Nancy?' Caddy said.

'I'm not a tattletale,' Jason said.

'Nonsense,' father said.

'He out there,' Nancy said. 'He looking through that window this minute, waiting for yawl to go. Then I gone.'

'Nonsense,' father said. 'Lock up your house and we'll take you on to Aunt Rachel's.'

'Twon't do no good,' Nancy said. She didn't look at father now, but he looked down at her, at her long, limp, moving hands. 'Putting it off won't do no good.'

'Then what do you want to do?' father said.

'I don't know,' Nancy said. 'I can't do nothing. Just put it off. And that don't do no good. I reckon it belong to me. I reckon what I going to get ain't no more than mine.'

'Get what?' Caddy said. 'What's yours?'

'Nothing,' father said. 'You all must get to bed.'

'Caddy made me come,' Jason said.

'Go on to Aunt Rachel's,' father said.

'It won't do no good,' Nancy said. She sat before the fire, her elbows on her knees, her long hands between her knees. 'When even your own kitchen wouldn't do no good. When even if I was sleeping on the floor in the room with your chillen, and the next morning there I am, and blood ——'

'Hush,' father said. 'Lock the door and put out the lamp and go to bed.'

'I scared of the dark,' Nancy said. 'I scared for it to happen in the dark.'

'You mean you're going to sit right here with the lamp lighted?' father said. Then Nancy began to make the sound again, sitting before the fire, her long hands between her knees. 'Ah, damnation,' father said. 'Come along, chillen. It's past bedtime.'

'When yawl go home, I gone,' Nancy said. She talked quieter now, and her face looked quiet, like her hands. 'Anyway, I got my coffin money saved up with Mr. Lovelady.' Mr. Lovelady was a short, dirty man who collected the Negro insurance, coming around to the cabins or the kitchens every Saturday morning, to collect fifteen cents. He and his wife lived at the hotel. One morning his wife committed suicide. They had a child, a little girl. He and the child went away. After a week or two he came back alone. We would see him going along the lanes and the back streets on Saturday mornings.

'Nonsense,' father said. 'You'll be the first thing I'll see in the kitchen tomorrow morning.'

'You'll see what you'll see, I reckon,' Nancy said. 'But it will take the Lord to say what that will be.'

VI

We left her sitting before the fire.

'Come and put the bar up,' father said. But she didn't move. She didn't look at us again, sitting quietly there between the lamp and the fire. From some distance down the lane we could look back and see her through the open door.

'What, Father?' Caddy said. 'What's going to happen?'

'Nothing,' father said. Jason was on father's back, so Jason was the tallest of all of us. We went down into the ditch. I looked at it,

193

quiet. I couldn't see much where the moonlight and the shadows tangled.

'If Jesus is hid here, he can see us, can't he?' Caddy said.

'He's not there,' father said. 'He went away a long time ago.'

'You made me come,' Jason said, high; against the sky, it looked like father had two heads, a little one and a big one. 'I didn't want to.'

We went up out of the ditch. We could still see Nancy's house and the open door, but we couldn't see Nancy now, sitting before the fire with the door open, because she was tired. 'I just done got tired,' she said. 'I just a nigger. It ain't no fault of mine.'

But we could hear her, because she began just after we came up out of the ditch, the sound that was not singing and not unsinging. 'Who will do our washing now, Father?' I said.

'I'm not a nigger,' Jason said, high and close above father's head.

'You're worse,' Caddy said, 'you are a tattletale. If something was to jump out, you'd be scairder than a nigger.'

'I wouldn't,' Jason said.

'You'd cry,' Caddy said.

'Caddy,' father said.

'I wouldn't!' Jason said.

'Scairy cat,' Caddy said.

'Candace!' father said.

SAIRY AND THE YOUNG 'UNS

BEULAH ROBERTS CHILDERS

EARLY a-Friday morning, when Bett threw the wash water from the breakfast dishes out the back door, her eyes ran the curving length of the road as far as she could see, from a little to one side of the front gate, which was not visible, into the slatey bed of the creek and out again, hindered here by a clump of willows, there skirting the sloping pasture, to the place about a quarter of a mile away where it ascended a low rise against a mountain and disappeared in the direction of Preacher Jed Pendergrast's. It was the road that led, eventually, to the land beyond the hill-country, which she had once seen, and whatever the Hales got that the hill-country itself did not yield to them, must come this way.

There was no sign of life on the road; for Bett, no sign of any living thing in the valley. A horse cropped grass by the creek, a few cows grazed in the pasture, a gray hawk swooped and circled above the willows in ominous silence, but these were transformed by her mood and partook of the unreality of the hour, so that they seemed to be of a sameness with the clouded mountain top, their movements no more animated than those of the mist that rose and shifted over the trees. They were but parts of a meaningless and insensible landscape on which the road was a crooked, empty vessel with open mouth held up to the horizon, waiting to be filled.

To be filled with what? She did not know; she could not tell, exactly. Her vague, half-fashioned hopes were just for something different, out of the ordinary, contradictory even, whose presence (like salt in butter, fire in the parlor, or an anguished lover in a song) would quicken the valley and lend significance to the hills; would thereby give to her own existence the tang, the spice, the flavor now wholly lacking. The road, she felt, was at once an evidence of incompletion and a promise that all might be fulfilled. She fixed her eyes on the intervening ridges as though they deliberately withheld from her that last indefinite something that was her due, and that they might, by the very intensity of her gaze, be compelled to relinquish.

'Ruth!' she called in a sudden flurry. 'Ruth! Come out hyer a minute.'

Her sister came and stood in the doorway behind her: 'Well, what on earth?'

'I just wish to goodness you'd look an' tell me — who is that a-comin' yonder, over the rise?' Bett asked the question as though she wanted (but hardly expected) to hear another answer than the one she had already shaped for herself.

Moving forms, small with distance, had appeared on the brow of the hill and were now descending in a slow straggling line that expanded and contracted like an accordion played by a lazy man in the heat of the day. There was a fascinating quality in this motion, which was natural and haphazard and yet seemed to have an underlying plan; a suggestion of the inevitable in the patient, unhurried manner of their drawing near that made it akin to the approach of night or the coming of the seasons, which could not be stayed nor made to hasten.

There must have been eight or ten of them at least, and as in a row of wind-sown plants, no two were the same height, the last being taller than any of the others. They were still too far away to be recognized by their features, but Ruth had seen them thus too many times not to know, unmistakably, who they were.

'The Lord ha' mercy!' she groaned. 'The Lord ha' mercy if it ain't Sairy Pendergrast as shore as I'm a-livin'. Esther, prepare yoreself; hyer comes Sairy an' the young 'uns to spend the day.'

Above, on the narrow landing of the outside stairway, Esther was putting quilts to air, hanging them over the railing evenly, so that the dark brilliance of their raw blues and reds and yellows made a neat horizontal pattern against the white clapboards of the house. She studied the road from under the striped shadow of her fingers; getting a bonnet of clean checked percale from a nail on the back porch, she came and stood beside them in the sun.

'Don't she look more like an old Dominecker hen with a brood o' roupy chicks!'

196

'Why, they're bound to a slept in their clothes an' a started before it was purely daybreak.'

'Well, don't they always get hyer before the beds are made, an' stay till we're mighty nigh ready to turn 'em down again? Mark my words, they'll have Aunt Cory or somebody bespoken to do their milkin' for 'em, so they can wait long enough that we'll be obliged to offer 'em supper before they go.'

'An' us with all them berries to put up,' Ruth complained. 'You can count on it as sure as summer, an' I never yet knowed it to fail; just let us have an extry big day's work ahead of us that cain't hardly be left over, then Sairy an' the young 'uns are bound to come a-meachin' across that hill. Well, it's no earthly use a-startin' in on the cannin' now, for you shorely cain't do nary a thing with that passel o' brats underfoot, a-stompin' in an' out like a herd o' cattle, an' a-gomin' up everything. Not to mention a-havin' 'em to cook fer.' She sighed and turned back toward the kitchen. 'Bett, you put the berries in the springhouse in middlin' deep water, an' I reckon they ought to keep over another day. I'll have to go pick a couple o' friers if I can wrest 'em from under Naomy's skirts long enough to wring their necks.'

'Well,' said Esther, 'as many times as I've laid the table for 'em I never can keep track of how many young 'uns Sairy's got.'

'I don't reckon she knows, herself, for certain,' said Bett.

'Let's see now, there's one, two, three, four, five — they shift around till I cain't tell which I've counted an' which I haven't.'

'Why don't ye get 'em a-comin' out from behind that bunch o' willows? Two, four, six ... I see ten, an' the older boys not with 'em.'

'Well I see twelve myself.'

'Try a-callin' 'em by name. Beginnin' at the top, there's Morg an' Went an' Bev at home ——'

'Berthy an' Hass —'

'An' Versie an' Flossie an' Pete an' Lege an' Little Jed.'

'An' the one that died o' convulsions.'

'An' the Baby makes twelve; that's all. No more than Ma's had, when ye come to consider.'

'Well, they shorely do seem like a heap more, the way they can

197

take the place an' turn it upside down. I swan, Bett, I don't see
Berthy nowheres; do you reckon she could a stayed at home?'

'Not likely. Why, there's Lizzie; we forgot her. She makes
thirteen.'

'An' how about Versie? Whur does she come in?'

'We counted her once a-ready.'

'No we didn't.'

'I know we did!'

'Well, numberin' 'em won't make 'em no less nor no easier to
manage,' said Ruth from the window. 'An' if I was you girls, I'd
quit a-standin' there a-arguin' over nothin' an' run an' put all my
good things out o' sight. You moaned for a week last time because
they got into yore talcum powders an' spilled 'em. Well, 'pon my
honor, Bett Hale, if you don't beat everything! Hyer I been a-
huntin' all over creation fer that dishpan to cut up my chickens in,
an' you a-standin' right there all the time, a-dawdlin' around with
it. I'm plumb put out!'

Naomy, picking beans in the garden, bending over and gathering
the long green fingers of the bean vine into her own and heaping
them in her lifted apron until it was pregnant, until she looked like
a fruitful woman ready to bear, lifted her head at the sound of a
joyful cry and saw that Sairy and the young 'uns were coming up
the lane. To the eager delighted signals of Versie and Flossie and
Pete and Lige, she replied without reservation in the same language,
her utterance marked by the same convivial accents.

How like Preacher Jed the children were, as though he had stood
at the head of a hollow and shouted his own name, to have it echoed
back to him from many distances, blurred, and a little twisted, but
still more his name than any other. Naomy had never cared much
for the Preacher. Her distaste was instinctive, her recoil from his
domineering ways something she could not help, which made it
seem all the more unaccountable that one of the things that en-
deared the young 'uns to her was their resemblance to him. But
Sairy had been a filter in which his characteristics were purified
of all the elements that made them repugnant to her; a water-gate
past which a clearer stream flowed on in the old familiar curves.

And it drew upon the abundant store of her pity that his lineaments — the insistent arch of his nose, the faltering turn of his chin, the vague compassionless blue of his eyes — should be thus imposed upon the innocent and helpless faces of beings powerless to reject them — unaware, even, that there was in them anything that merited rejection.

For Bett, emerging from the dim cool refuge of the springhouse, the young'uns called to mind nothing that was the least bit pleasant; and Sairy, as she calmly marshalled them toward the house, made her think of a picture of General Braddock before his defeat, in one of the old almanacs in the storeroom closet, so purposeful and confident she was, as though about to move upon a place which she knew was unfortified and could offer no resistance whatever.

The girls were dressed in ugly short-waisted garments of brought-on goods or home-woven linsey, unskilfully cut and badly put together; the boys wore anything from new bule overalls to hand-me-down knee pants, each with its own peculiar history; while the Baby, who was a boy and going on five years old, was still in curls and embroidered petticoats, trailing a little behind the others and nearest to Sairy.

Sairy herself had on her Sunday best, the stiff black silk with the heavy crocheted collar and the bulging placket in the rear. She had taken off her bonnet of black calico and held it in one hand, fanning briskly as she advanced. With the other she had gathered up the folds of her gored and pleated skirt to save it from the dust, an exaggerated delicacy in the curve of her waist and the spread of her fingers by which she expressed her conception of 'Elegance,' as the children had been taught at school, when speaking a piece, to show 'Disdain' by a lifted quivering lip, and 'Happiness' by a fixed and determined smile. Above her spare form, the heavy pile of her hair, which had been wound neatly on the very top of her head when she left home, had slipped over to one side and hung there at a rakish angle that contrasted oddly with the mournful droop of her mouth.

As she neared the gate, Mrs. Hale came out on the front porch, slender and white-haired, with soft gray eyes in a delicate face. The moment Sairy caught sight of her, her bearing underwent a sudden and violent change. She was no longer the calm general; she was a devout Holy Roller who had managed to hold herself in check all the way to meeting in order to have more power for her emotional outburst when she got there, but who was now in full view of the congregation and need restrain herself no longer. She gave a little preliminary screech, and pushing past the young 'uns, rushed up the path, wailing loudly:

'Oh, Lordy Lordy! Oh, Lordy Lordy!'

Right behind her came Hasseltine, with an air of mingled reverence and concern, for all the young Pendergrasts had been nourished in a deep respect for the condition of Sairy's internal organs, which, it was understood, were so weak and ailing as an unavoidable result of the fact that she was a Mother, that the slightest shock might prove too much for them. In which case the young Pendergrasts would be left Motherless, a state which none of them had ever thought through to any definite mental image, but which, as the theme for a ballad, was always accompanied by such a sorrowful tune that they could hardly hold back the tears when they heard it.

'Now Mammy; now Mammy — now Ma!' said Hasseltine. (She meant to say 'Ma' all the time, like the Hale girls did, but forgot when she was excited.) 'You'll have the high strikes, a-gittin' yoreself all worked up this-a-way.'

The high strikes, probably derived from a mispronunciation of hysterics and meaning the same thing, was Sairy's equivalent to a room of her own into which she would retreat if necessary, but never, as now, when her suffering was so well attended.

'The Lord ha' mercy on my soul!' she cried, in her thin tremulous voice. 'I thought fer sartin' my time had come; I 'lowed my heart would shorely give way when Morg broke the news to me like he did, right out of a clear sky, without no warnin'. I doan't see how in this mortal world he ever come to do sich a thing, as good as he knows my condition. Well, I reckon they's nary a doubt I would a dropped in my tracks if I'd a-been a-standin' up, but I was a-settin' down to grind the breakfast coffee. Lucy, I can tell by yore face that yeou ain't yet hyeared the turrible affliction that's come upon me.'

Lucy reached for a split-bottomed chair that leaned against the

porch wall, slanting downward to shed the rain, and offered it to
Sairy, not in the least put out by her carrying on. Sairy carried on
a great deal over one thing and another. Her reaction to any event,
however remote from her own way of life, was always of an intensely personal nature. Indeed, it seemed as though no external
fact could reach her consciousness without being at once translated
into bodily discomfort, and her first concern in any tragedy was
not with its immediate consequences, which might be cataclysmic,
but with how it affected her, physically, at the moment of hearing
it told.

When Gabriel blows his trumpet, thought Lucy, I reckon Sairy'll
rise up a-sayin' it give her a pain in her ears.

Now, sinking carefully into the proffered chair so as not to mess
her pleats, she took up her weeping again like a piece of embroidery
that she had been forced to lay down, temporarily, in order to
explain the pattern to a neighbor, but which her mind had kept on
working busily all the while. Lucy, who had barely glimpsed a few
unrelated stitches, despaired of ever getting the whole design from
Sairy.

'Hasseltine, maybe you better tell me what's the matter with
yore Ma.'

'It's Berthy,' said Hasseltine breathlessly. 'She's done gone
an' —— '

But a gesture from Sairy was a felled tree at the meeting place
of two roads and a creek: it checked Hasseltine, arrested Lucy, and
stemmed the flow of her own grief. It cleared a space where she
could say all that there was to be said.

'I doan't know,' she began with a mournful sigh, 'I cain't think
what I've ever done that the good Lord should punish me this-a-
way. I've allus tried to do right by Berthy, an' teach her to do
right —— '

'Sairy,' Lucy interrupted, 'will you stop a-feelin' sorry for yoreself jest a minute, an tell me what'd happened to Berthy, so's I'll
have some inklin' o' what you're a-talkin' about? She ain't dead,
is she?'

'Dead!' wailed Sairy. 'Dead! Lucy Hale, hit couldn't a hurt
me nary a speck more to a seen her a-layin' cold an' stiff in her

shroud, than hit does to be a-thinkin' she's whur she is today. I want yeou to know, *I want yeou to know*, that after all we've done fer that girl, an' after all the warnin's her Pappy's dinned into her years frum the time she was that high, if she ain't run off with the low-down, stinkin', good-fer-nothin' Mitch Blair!'

'No!'

'Yes! Run right off with 'im, mind ye, without so much as a by-yore-leave! Left a note on the dresser, if ye please, a-sayin' he's a-aimin' to marry her when they git to Jackson. Well, he'd best marry her after this, or Jed Pendergrast'll know the reason why. Oh, hit's might' nigh finished me, Lucy, the same as if she'd a-struck me a mortal blow with her own hand. Well, I'll tell ye: I was a-settin' in the kitchen doorway yesterday mornin', a-turnin' the coffee grinder an' a-plannin' how to inside-out Flossie's old white wu'sted fer Versie to be baptized in, when I looked up an' what did I see but the milk pails still a-hangin' by the stove, an' it full five o'clock. Why Morg, I says — Morg was a-standin' by the wash-bench — why Morg, I thought Berthy was out a-milkin', an' thar hangs the pails. Yeou go right upstairs an' tell that young lady to roust herself out o' the bed too quick to talk about.

'Well, I reckon it wasn't no more'n two or three minutes till Morg come a-runnin' back. He stood thar before me — I can see 'm now jest as plain as day, the way he looked, all scared to death, like, an' as pale as if he'd a-seen a ghost. Mammy, he says, I swan to goodness Berthy ain't in her room an' her bed ain't even been slep' in!'

'Well, I thought to my soul I'd never be able to draw my breath agin. Blurted the whole thing right out, jest like that, Lucy, an' not a-doin' ary thing to prepare me fer what was a-comin'. Yes, he says, she ain't in her bed an' the kivers ain't even been mussed!'

'Why, Sairy!'

'I doan' know; I cain't see a-tall, why things should happen the way they do. Nary a womern on Tejes Creek could a kep' a closter watch on a girl than I did on Berthy; why, she ain't hardly been out o' my sight since she got to the courtin' age.'

'Maybe,' said Lucy gently, 'you watched her a mite too close.'

'No,' said Sairy, 'Berthy's jest wilful, an' she's been that-a-way since the day she was borned. She et ever'thing on the table afore she was six months old, an' still nothin' ever pacified her. The other young 'uns would suck on a sugar-tit fer hours, as peaceable as a body could ask; but Berthy would barely tetch it an' tho'w it away.'

She sighed, profoundly; before the inscrutable face of Providence she brooded darkly, trying to read some meaning into this feature or that, longing to trace some permanent readable line between brow and chin, between cheek and cheek. But it was no use. He smiled, and you thought those lines were true, and meant thus and so, and would stay forever; he frowned, and they were gone in the twinkling of an eye, so that you couldn't even remember, exactly, how they had looked. Thirteen young 'uns Sairy had borne in her womb, and still their doings were to her as mysterious, as unpredictable, as the ways of the rain and wind. More so, for clouds gathered before a thunderstorm, and rain did not turn to sleet in the summertime; a lifted straw showed which direction the breeze was blowing, and a south wind would be warm, as like as not. But there was never any telling how young 'uns would turn out. No difference if you raised them the best you know, there wasn't, apparently, any connection between what you did and what they did. Still, you went on doing it just the same, so that at least you could say you had. You kept on struggling against nature, and got what comfort you could from your religion.

'By the by,' she said, abruptly cheerful, as though in what she had taken for utter blackness she now perceived a gleam of light. 'I knowed thar was somethin' else I'd been a-savin' up to tell ye, an' I better be a-sayin' it naow, afore hit plumb slips my mind. (Hass, yeou run back in the kitchen an' see if thar ain't somethin' yeou can do to help the girls. Me and Miz Hale wants to talk.)'

With a critical eye, she measured the distance to the corner of the house, where Lige and Pete were seining tadpoles from a rain-barrel, and carefully lowering her voice, leaned forward and placed an impressive hand on Lucy's knee.

'Naow who do you reckon I seed a-comin' out o' Rissie Blair's place last Sunday an' the Sunday 'fore that? Zeb Hammonds, the ornery no-count thing! An' Rissie Blair, of all people! Why, she ain't worth her salt. They do say she lets tomatoes rot on the vine when she ain't got hardly 'ary one put up, an' she doan't dry enough fruit to last till Christmas. Well, it takes a widder to make a fool of a man, pervidin' he ain't a fool to start with. But wouldn't yeou a thought he'd a had the gumption not to be a-settin' out a-ready, an' pore Cynthy barely three months cold in her grave?'

'Why, Sairy, it must a been more than three months since Cynthy was buried; I recollect there was snow on the ground that evenin'.'

'All the same, I 'low if the truth was known his comb was a-gittin' red afore she was fairly a-dyin'. Come to think of it, Rissie didn't hold back none about goin' to Hammondses when Cynthy took down. Lucy! Do yeou reckon they could a been anything . . .?'

'Why, no, I don't reckon there was. It 'pears to me like Rissie means well enough, as people go.'

Adam Hale, that morning, was grubbing the field that rose to merge with the lower side of Sarvice Mountain, clearing away the saplings and bushes and sprouts that had gotten a hold upon it in fallow years. If he had not observed the arrival of Sairy from its highest point, where he and the men and mules began, or noticed, from middling ground, the young 'uns, running over the place, and heard them whooping, he might have been alarmed by the wild and furious clamor of the dinner bell at noon. As it was he made a leisurely end to three small sassafras trees whose roots were interwoven in earth, and took his time on the way home because he never hurried unless he had a reason, and even then he didn't hurry a great deal.

Usually his daughter Ruth rang the bell. She saw to the cooking, mostly, and was the best judge of how much time he would need to get to the house. And as a fruit is latent in the flower, so the clean table, the good plain food, her firmly capable step as she brought more beans or replenished the buttermilk in the pitcher — the order and continuity that characterized their family meals in general — were implicit in the clear steady sound that she produced. But under the hands of Pete and Lige and Lizzie and Little Jed (now one, now another, now two or three or all of them pulling the rope with a different rhythm or else without any rhythm at all),

204

the altered tones of the bell prepared him for the changed atmosphere he would find in the dining-room, suggested to him, without his being fully aware of the cause, how the table would look with two extra leaves, Sairy at the foot, the young 'uns wiggling around the edge like suckling pigs at the teats of a sow, and the Bible brought in for the Baby so that his size would be less of a handicap in the struggle that would surely begin (as a feud with a rifle shot), with the word Amen at the end of the blessing.

The vision was by no means disagreeable to him. Oh, not in the least! He enjoyed Sairy and the young 'uns. They gave him a complete and satisfying sense of his own power and his own importance as no one else ever did. His tenants, for instance, were meek enough to his face, since his goodwill was their meat and bread, but underneath their apparent servility was something he couldn't quite touch — a wall of reserve that he had never been able to penetrate. He suspected them of laughing at him behind his back. Then, he had every right to expect consideration from Lucy and the girls. And while they took his word for law, they too denied him that deep inner acquiescence that he could not explain, or demand, or put a finger on, yet the want of which kept him forever asserting his will against them in barren success.

But the Pendergrasts — now they were whole-hearted. A warm glow suffused him at the thought of the young 'uns' expectant faces awaiting his word of authority over the chicken, and the unconditional admiration that always shone upon him from Sairy's eyes. And he gave it back to her in full measure, not only because she was an old friend and neighbor, a fellow Primitive and a Sister in the Lord, but because he really liked her and knew her for his own kind.

'Well, 'pon my honor!' he exclaimed affably, as he pulled out his big armchair at the head of the table, his hands and face still damp from washing, and drops of cold water falling from his stiff black hair. 'I'm proud to see ye out, Sister Sairy. I was a-feared yore trouble would jest about put ye to bed, but ye look to be a-bearin' up mighty well. Jest mighty well.'

'If I do look pyeart, Brother Adam, I shorely doan't feel that-a-way. I allus would be to keep a-goin' as long as I could, whether

I felt right able or not. Well, I didn't reckon the news had reached ye yet. Naow who on earth could a told 'im!'

'Yes,' said Adam, 'I hyeared it from Big Jim Meadors. He rid up the creek not more than a hour ago.'

'Up the creek! Well, whur do yeou reckon he could a been a-startin'?'

'After a cow, he said. But about Mitch an' Berthy — didn't you all have no inklin' o' what was a-goin' on?'

'As true as I live an' breathe this minute, nary a sign did I see!'

'Then hit must a been a turrible hard blow fer you an' Brother Jed a-comin' so unforeseen. What's he a-doin' today, an' why didn't ye bring him with ye?'

'He's gone to mill.'

'Heavenly Father . . . thank . . . blessings . . . showered . . . bless . . . food . . . use . . . nourishment . . . bodies . . . service . . . Christ's sake . . . Amen. Well, hit's quare I never seen 'im pass, nor he didn't stop to say howdy.'

'Why, he never come by hyer a-tall. Brother Adam; he went to-wards Sturgeon. We 'lowed we'd try out the miller over thar, fer onct, jest to see how he done. Hit does seem like them Blairs a-bein' sich a ungodly lot, an' a-carryin' on the way they do, hit ain't right Christian to cater to 'em. Besides, they been a-shortin' us a leetle mite.'

'Time an' time agin I've said it,' Adam declared. 'But I jest never had the guts to do nothin' about it. I'm mighty glad to see Brother Jed a-takin' a stand, an' I reckon the rest of us cain't do less than to foller.'

'Adam, you better start the chicken around,' said Lucy. 'The young 'uns are helped to everything else, but you've got the chicken whur they cain't hardly get to it.'

'Well I declar! I wasn't a-noticin'. All right, Lige, you reach me yore plate; which piece do you favor?'

'The liver.'

At this simple declaration, loud howls went up from Little Jed and the Baby, while the other young 'uns stared at Lige, as outraged, as scornful as if he had said that he meant to eat the whole chicken himself and leave them nary a bite.

'Hush, hush, hush!' cried Sairy, and Adam raised his hand.

'Well I swear to goodness,' he said, 'if this ain't the quarest chicken I ever laid eyes on! Hit's got two livers!'

'The way we do it at home,' said Hasseltine earnestly, 'we begin with the Baby an' go on up.'

'I doan't know what in this mortal world makes them young 'uns act so foolish over a liver,' said Sairy. 'But they allus have, an' I reckon they allus will. Did I ever tell ye what Versie said when Flossie was borned?'

'No,' said Esther, adding an undertone to Bett: 'not over fifty or sixty times, anyhow!'

'Well,' said Sairy, 'when they told her we had a new baby, what did she do but set right daown in the middle o' the floor an' begin to cry so pitiful like, the tears a-streamin' as if her pore little heart was plumb broke. An' boo-hoo-hoo, she says, naow it'll git the liver!'

'Why Mammy,' said Flossie, 'I thought it was me said that when Pete was borned.'

'Likely yeou did,' said Sairy. 'Hit doan't make a heap o' differ-ence whether one said it or t'other. No, Brother Adam, I jest couldn't eat a bite to save me. Well, maybe a leetle piece o' that thar breast wouldn' hurt me none; hit does look mighty good an' tender. Though I doan't feel like I'm able to swaller. I ain't hardly tetched a morsel o' food since it happened, yesterday morn.'

Sairy took her young 'uns and went, while a narrow strip of sky still separated the sun from the trees on the hilltop. She hated like everything to rush off that-a-way, she said (My goodness, rush off! thought Ruth), but she'd promised to stop fer a while with Gran'ma Meadors, though if 'ary more o' them blackish clouds come up, she wouldn't but set an' rise, fer she recollected she'd aired her parlor the day before an' fergot to close the winders, an' the Lord knew that even if Jed was home, he'd never think o' shuttin' one unless the rain was a-pourin' right in on him, an' even then, like as not, he'd jest shift his chair a few inches.

Lucy saw them off. Her quiet hospitable 'come agains' and

'good-byes' pursued them down the path and through the gate, until finally, rather than raise her voice to a shout, she left one of Sairy's replies hanging there alone in the growing space between them, sure, unambiguous, prophetic.

'We will, yeou come.'

Yeou come; the words fell softly away into silence. But we will, we will, we will, seemed to echo and multiply and spread out on the air like the ripples made by a pebble dropped in water, becoming wider and wider until they encircled the whole of Lucy's future in the assurance that Sairy and the young 'uns would come again. And whether she looked at them this way or that, and whether she welcomed them in her heart or bore with them grudgingly, there they would be just the same, to be met, to be dealt with.

She followed them with her eyes as they trudged the length of the lane, in a broken wavering line but presenting to her an almost solid mass composed of spindly legs, dusty bottoms, and thin lumpy backs shrinking smaller and smaller against the same fixed strip of creek and woods and sky. Now they were nearing the main travelled road where it bordered the pasture, and Sairy, who went ahead, turned first and walked for a moment alone, seen in profile, with her hands hanging limp at her sides, her shoulders drooping, the head on her slanting neck pushed forward, inquiring, resentful — the embodiment of a question unhopefully asked and forever unanswered.

As Lucy watched them the past seemed to rise before her, obscuring the present, so that she saw, not Sairy, today, but an earlier and more comely Sairy altering there before her into all the Sairys that she had ever known, and whose seasonal comings and goings had marked off her life into periods. A young and supple Sairy, walking unattended, with lifted head and a quick light step, grew into a Sairy beginning to swell with her first pregnancy, became a Sairy large and shapeless with child, and then, as singly the young 'uns turned into the road to join her, appeared as yet other Sairys with one, two, three, four, five of them trailing behind her until the entire line had rounded the corner into the present — Sairy and the young 'uns.

Sairy and the young 'uns; what would her life have been if she

208

had never known them? She reached back into the past to blot
them out, but withdrew her hand before the thing was accomplished. Let them stay as they were; she didn't mind them; they
meant no harm. They even gave to the years a pattern without
which her own plain weave might have been a dull, monotonous
thing, like the warp of grayish blankets that she had made the
winter before out of undyed wool.

It came to her then that if she had not had Sairy's example
always before her, with Sairy's faults and blunders continually
thrust on her notice, she herself might have been more like Sairy
in many ways. And she thought that perhaps she had even done
better, accomplished more, with her younger children, who were
of an age with Sairy's older ones, because she had had the little
Pendergrasts to make them different from.

Now the young 'uns were climbing upward, and Sairy was crossing the brow of the hill as she had crossed it that morning. She had
reversed her direction, but the sun had moved its place, and she
was returning home as she had come, with the light at her back
and her shadow before her feet. Nothing gained, apparently;
nothing changed except that now she was tired and the young 'uns
were dirty. And it was as though she had gone so far and stayed
so long that she had, in the end, defeated herself by her own te-
nacity and her determination to get everything that there was to
be gotten out of one day.

After the supper dishes were washed and dried and put back on
the table (the plates laid upside down, the spoons turned into a
tumbler glass, and a wide clean cloth spread over), the girls sat out
on the porch in the cooling dusk and talked. Lucy was thumping
away at the loom in the lower bedroom, by a lamp whose light
streamed through the window upon them, and Adam sat apart,
with his stockinged feet on the railing, his shoes beside his chair,
and his Bible spread open across his knees although it had been
too dark to read for the last half hour.

'I'm plumb worn out,' said Ruth. 'An' maybe it ain't no trouble
to cook fer a dozen young 'uns extry! I declare to goodness, the way
they eat when they come hyer, it makes it seem as if they'd been

a-savin' up their hunger a seek beforehand. I do know better, for Sairy fixes a-plenty at home. Not that I grudge 'em the food, but it shore does take a heap o' doin'.'

'Not that I grudge 'em the food,' said Bett, 'but it jest looks so bad to see 'em crammin' it in.'

'Now, shucks!' said Esther. 'I don't care whether they swaller it by the bushel or smear it all over theirselves. What aggervates me is the way they git into my things. It was all I could do to keep my hands off o' Versie an' Flossie, the nasty brats, when I found 'em into my bureau drawer, a-tyin' knots in my ribbons an' sashes, an' a-puttin' their sticky hands on my clean handkerchiefs an' my best lace collars. Yes, Naomy Hale, an' if you wasn't forever a-givin' 'em yore things to play with, they wouldn't be so bad about takin' mine!'

'The Baby pulled a sight o' cornsilks off'n the roastin' ears,' said Ruth. 'Now he knew better than that. Naomy, it does 'pear to me like if you was bound to have 'im a-follerin' you round in the garden, you might at least a kept an eye on what he was doin'!'

Naomy turned her face toward the green and purple infinity that crept stealthily down on the hills because there were no moon and stars to hinder. A succession of images drenched her mind like a swift brief pattering of rain: Versie's freckles, rising indeterminately near the edge of her hair and coming to an aimless climax across the bridge of her nose; Flossie's thinly tapering plaits, the color of damp moulded leaves in January; Pete's long baggy pants, and his futile repeated gesture of pulling them up; Hasseltine's dingy petticoat hanging below the attempted finery of her second-best dress; the Baby, brightly expectant, offering her, Naomy, his gift of red and white cornsilks, while behind him stretched the row of listless, despoiled ears; the wide, pale, vaguely wounded, vaguely perplexed gaze that marked them every one — the Pendergrast look. It seemed to sum up their meagre shortcomings, to lay open all their bleak insufficiencies, and leave them completely vulnerable.

'Well, ain't you girls got a spark o' feelin' for the pore little fellers?' she cried.

'"Pore little fellers"!' Esther exclaimed. 'Why they're the sorriest lot that ever was raised on Tejes!'

'An' if Sairy ain't the most worrisome thing in the world,' said Ruth, 'then I don't know what she is.'

'Mercy, yes,' said Bett.

'You shet yore mouths,' said Adam harshly, rising and closing his Book. 'An' don't let me hyear no more sich foolish talk out o' ary one of ye. Sairy Pendergrast is as good a womern as ever drawed breath, an' a mighty fine passel o' young 'uns she's got!'

COLD DEATH

ROARK BRADFORD

Mammy Clo grumbled and fussed when Babe lifted her, chair, crutch, and all, and carried her from the dinner table to the shade in front of the cabin. But her protesting, 'I kin wawk, gal; don't go totin' me round like I was a baby' lacked some of its usual vigor.

Mammy Clo, chair and crutch, weighed less than a hundred pounds. Years — so many of them that no one remembered the exact number — had toughened and dried the split-hickory chair, the leather-tipped crutch, and Mammy Clo.

'You's awright, mammy, hunh?' Babe asked as she placed the chair in the shade. 'You's feelin' awright?' Babe was Mammy Clo's granddaughter, and Babe herself was a grandmother since Little Henry's baby had come.

'Cou'se I's awright, gal,' declared Mammy Clo. 'Ain't nothin' de matter wid me. You totin' me round! I swear! Whyn't you git yo' hoe and git out yonder in de field? I ain't rose you up to stay round de house axin' me is I awright. I swear, gal!'

'Yeah, you's awright,' grinned Babe. 'Long as you kin grumble, well you's bound to be awright. Now d's you want anything befo' I goes to de field?'

Mammy Clo considered. The cedar bucket with its gourd dipper had been filled with cool water and was setting within easy reach of her chair. 'Bring me out dat quilt I been piecin',' she decided. 'De Star er Bet-ly-ham. In dat big box. On top.'

The quilt was brought and spread in the old woman's lap. 'You sho' you's awright now, mammy?' Babe pressed.

'Don't I look awright?' demanded Mammy Clo. 'Gawd er mighty, gal! Whyn't you git to de field?'

As soon as Babe disappeared down the path Mammy Clo grinned proudly. 'Dat chile jest won't do,' she chuckled. 'I sho'

212

rose her up right.' She laughed softly. 'Waitin' on me like I was de Lawd, or somebody!'

A robin, playing among the moss tufts in the live oak, broke into a saucy little song, and Mammy Clo hummed a wordless accompaniment to it as she sat with half-closed eyes, enjoying the peaceful rest that follows a wholesome meal. Time slipped by so easily, these nice clear days when she sat in the shade. The first thing she knew the 'cool of the evening' would be upon her, and with it would come Rucker to read his Bible and discuss the works of the Lord.

Day after day Mammy Clo had spent in the shade in just such idleness. Day after day she had planned to 'hitch her crutch under her arm' and work about the house while Babe was in the field. But mid-afternoon breezes and Rucker slipped up on her.

Rucker was the preacher. Mammy Clo had 'raised' him. She did not remember, offhand, whether he was her own child or the child of some other woman about the place. It did not matter, however. All the Negroes and half the whites in that part of the country she counted among her children. And none of them ever grew up, white or black. She helped them into the world and nursed them through the dangerous months of infancy. Parentage and race meant nothing to her. A baby was a baby and had to be treated just so. 'And hit ain't a natchal one of 'em,' she declared proudly, 'which wan't riz up right. Don't mind de work. Love de Lawd, and ain't skeered er nothin' but sin.'

She sat in idle reverie for another minute and then she remembered the quilt. 'And hyar me,' she reproached, 'lazin' round and dis quilt ain't done yit. Rucker'll be hyar terrackly and when he gits to argyin' 'bout how skeered he is to die, well I might jest as well lay hit down and quit, cause I can't sew and listen at Rucker argy.'

She spread the quilt, untied a bundle of cloth scraps, and began piecing them into a general pattern. Her fingers, old and stiff, wriggled and twisted, and the needle went back and forth with lightning speed, making fine, even stitches.

The quilt was Mammy Clo's masterpiece — no less. In the center was a large star fashioned from white silk. Around that star, stitched with cunning neatness and prim accuracy, were smaller stars of various colors and sizes. It was a difficult design and had to be executed exactly right or it would be a failure. And it took time, Lord, a long time.

Mammy had hoped to have it completed in time to give it as a 'cradle present' to Little Henry's baby, her great-great-grandchild. But time slipped up on her, and Little Henry's baby received a Paul and Silas in Prison quilt instead. Not that the Paul and Silas designs were not beautiful and appropriate cradle gifts. Mammy Clo's old fingers had stitched hundreds of them while sitting by the cradles of fretful babies, and had brought them to other babies as cradle presents. White and black babies, grown old by now, treasured Mammy Clo's Paul and Silas quilts as they treasured the love of the old nursewoman herself.

But this Star of Bethlehem was to be a very special quilt. Mammy Clo had conceived it and started it in time, she hoped, to have it ready for the arrival of Babe, her first grandchild. But it proved tedious work, and then too, there were babies to be brought into the world and nursed to health and strength. The quilt was not finished. Babe got a Paul and Silas quilt for a cradle present.

Then, when Babe married, Mammy Clo took out the unfinished quilt and set to work again, getting ready for Babe's first child. She got considerable work done on it, but about that time Rucker began preaching and he took up much of her time, discussing the Scriptures and going over his sermons with her. Time slipped by, and a Paul and Silas quilt went to Babe's baby, Little Henry.

The quilt was almost forgotten until suddenly Little Henry grew up and married. The very day he married Mammy Clo got out the quilt and set to work, determined to have it ready for Little Henry's first baby. But it seemed like she would no more then get settled down in her chair before here came Rucker to talk about the ways of the Lord. She tried to work while Rucker talked, but Rucker was so interested and argumentative over his own ideas that her stitches were bad and had to be removed. Nothing but a perfect stitch could stay in that quilt.

214

'Whyn't you quit wearyin' me wid dat tawk about cold death?' she complained. 'I ain't studdin' cold death. I ain't studdin' nothin' but de Promise' Land.'

'Dat's jest yo' trouble,' Rucker replied. 'You got yo' haid in de air and yo' eye on Glory. But yo' foots still is on de ground. You knows all about livin' hyar on de yearth and you knows all about how you gonter live when you gits to heab'm. But you got to grabble wid Cold Death befo' you gits dar. And what er you know 'bout dyin'?'

'I don't know nothin' 'bout dyin', and I don't keer nothin' 'bout dyin',' Mammy Clo retorted. 'All I know is ——'

'Well,' interrupted Rucker, 'you got to die. I don't keer how much you don't keer. When you quits livin' you got to die befo' you kin git Over Yonder.'

'Dat's all right,' Mammy Clo assured him. 'De Lawd gonter take keer of all er dat. Me and de Lawd been wawkin' side by side for goin' on I don't know how long and de Lawd love me too good. I ain't wearied. I been too good to de Lawd.'

Rucker accused her of being proud and the argument waged — for months.

And then, before she knew it, Babe told her Little Henry and his wife had a baby.

There was nothing else for Mammy Clo to do. The Star of Bethlehem quilt was not completed; and when they placed her chair in the spring wagon for the ride over to Little Henry's, she carried a Paul and Silas quilt on her arm for the cradle gift.

'And hit ain't done ontwell yit!' she chided herself. 'Me settin' hyar dozin' like a preacher full er possum ain't gonter git hit done, too.' Her bony old fingers moved faster and faster, and star after star was woven into the mosaic of varicolored cloths.

She worked diligently for what seemed to her a very short time. Then she heard the hinges on the picket gate squawk, and she knew without turning her head that it was Rucker. In a minute they were exchanging their habitual greetings.

'Hy-dy, mammy. How you comin' 'long?'

'Po'ly, thank Gawd. And you, son?'

'Tole'ble. Jest tole'ble.'

215

Rucker seated himself in the shade near Mammy Clo and began fanning himself with his old woolen hat.

'What you doin', mammy? Makin' a quilt?'

'Yeah,' said Mammy Clo. 'Ain't hit purty?'

'Mighty,' agreed Rucker. 'Got stars and things in hit, ain't hit?'

'Don't dey look like stars and things?' demanded Mammy Clo.

Instead of replying, Rucker fanned himself vigorously.

'And don't come botherin' me wid fool tawk,' added Mammy Clo. 'I got to git dis quilt done, and I can't work wid you settin' round hyar, droolin' at me.'

'Yeah?' grinned Rucker. 'Well, ef'n I didn't drool at you, well, you wouldn't have nothin' to grumble about. Den whar'd you be?' He chuckled with the old woman at his retort. Then he added seriously, 'Mammy, you needs tawkin' to about yo' proudfulness. I aims to change yo' mind befo' you has to grabble wid Cold Death.'

'Hyar you goes!' exclaimed Mammy Clo. 'Shet up till I gits dis quilt done, will you? I ain't got no time to listen at you now.'

'How come you so sot on gittin' dat quilt done?' Rucker wanted to know. 'You got mo' quilts made up now den you kin shake a stick at.'

'I needs dis quilt in my business,' she explained. 'I got somethin' to do wid hit.'

'Which is ——?'

Mammy Clo stopped sewing and looked at Rucker.

'Son,' she said, solemnly, 'I'm gittin' along in de years. My time is mighty nigh out.'

'You ain't so young,' Rucker agreed.

'Well,' the old woman continued, 'seein' how dis is a mighty purty quilt, I kind er counted on takin' hit to Glory wid me and givin' hit to de Po' Little Jesus for a cradle present.'

'Humph!' snorted Rucker. 'Don't you know dey got all de quilts dey needs Up Yonder?'

'I don't keer how many quilts dey got,' defended Mammy Clo. 'I got some manners. And hit ain't manners to go nowhar emptyhanded. I ain't gonter put up on de Lawd and not bring a little somethin' along for manners.' She fingered the fine stitches lovingly. 'And dis is a fine quilt too.' She hesitated dubiously and

216

then continued defiantly, 'I don't speck dey got no quilts in heab'n any purtier den dis. And maybe not as purty!'

For a moment Rucker was shocked beyond speech.

'Proud-tawkin'!' he exclaimed finally. 'And you wid one foot in de grave, right now. Mammy, dat ain't no way for a good woman to tawk!'

'Hit's de natchal truf,' defended Mammy Clo, doggedly. 'I seed a heap er quilts in my time and I ain't never yit seed one no purtier den dis.'

'I don't keer what you ain't never seed!' Rucker's amazement was giving way to indignation. 'You ain't got no call to go braggin' 'bout yo' quilts and proud-tawkin' de Lawd when ole Cold Death ready to grab you ev'y minute. Braggin' ain't humble, I don't keer how purty de quilt is. And you got to be humble do you want to die right.' Rucker paused in his outburst and calmed. 'De Book say so,' he added.

'Humph!' snorted Mammy Clo.

'Don't go humphin' de Book,' cautioned Rucker. 'De Book——'

'I ain't humphin' de Book,' Mammy Clo corrected. 'I'm humphin' yo' fool tawk. Cause you know I ain't studdin' 'bout dying. De Lawd gonter look after me when my time is out. I ain't wearied. De Lawd love me too good.'

Rucker was puzzled. Mammy Clo always had been a contradiction — to him and to the Scriptures. He could not understand her attitude. 'Mammy,' he said gently, 'you's a mighty good woman but you's a mighty proud woman.'

'Proud in de Lawd, yes,' she agreed.

'But proud,' insisted Rucker. 'And proudfulness is a sin. De Book say. And de proud die hard.'

Mammy Clo stitched nervously for several minutes. The last star on the quilt took shape under her flying needle. Rucker had told her virtually the same thing a thousand times, and she never had paid any attention to him. But as the last stitch was made she was seized with a strange feeling. It was as though Rucker at last had unsettled her peaceful mind.

'Rucker,' she said, 'what do you know 'bout dis cold death you been carryin' on about?'

217

Rucker considered for a minute. 'Nothin',' he admitted. 'Not nothin'.' He sat in serious, silent study for a while. 'And dat's de p'int,' he added. 'Hit's a mystery. A mighty mystery.' Rucker's words agitated the strange feeling that was upon Mammy Clo. It was as though she were standing in sand and the sand were giving way from under her feet.

'What do de Scriptures say about hit?' she pressed.

Rucker cast about uncertainly in his mind. 'De ole song,' he explained, 'say, "Death ain't nothin' but a robber in dis land." Dat what de ole song say. But de chune don't say dat. De chune say like a nigger in de graveyard. De nigger say, "Dem ha'nts ain't nothin' but de tombstones." But whilst de nigger sayin' dat, de chune say, "Maybe not, but all de same, I'm gonter reach up and git my hat and git along down de road." '

'Unhunh,' agreed Mammy Clo. 'De chune don't say what de words say.'

'Now,' continued Rucker, tackling it from another angle. 'Dat "Deep River" song don't say so much, but de chune say a heap. De song say, "Deep River. My home is over Jurdin." But de chune say, "Yeah? I know yo' home is over Jurdin, All Right. But what about dat deep river? You got to cross dat river befo' you kin git home. Deep river!" '

Mammy Clo shivered. Something like a panic was taking place within her. 'But de Scriptures, Rucker?' she pressed. 'What do de Scriptures 'low?'

'De Scriptures,' Rucker explained in a hushed voice, 'don't 'low. Dat's what makes hit a mighty mystery.'

Mammy Clo clutched desperately at one straw of hope. 'Maybe hit ain't ——'

'Oh, yes, hit is,' Rucker interrupted. 'Dat's de p'int. De Scriptures allows by a parable. De Scriptures allows dat de Lawd led de Hebrews round de wilderness fawty years gittin' 'em humble so dey c'd git to de Promise' Land, and de ones which wouldn't git, well de Lawd struck 'em down.'

'Hmmm,' groaned Mammy Clo. 'Hmmm, hmmm.'

'And when de Lawd got 'em humbled,' continued Rucker, 'well, he led 'em to Jurdin and *showed* 'em de Promise' Land on de yuther

218

side.' He paused dramatically and repeated, '*Showed* 'em de Promise' Land. And den, de Scriptures say, *dey crossed over.* De Lawd didn't cross 'em over, like at de Red Sea. Dey done dey own crossin'.'

Mammy Clo's head bobbed from side to side. Her eyes closed, and weird, twitchy whines came from her troubled lips.

'And,' continued Rucker, 'dat's de mystery of Cold Death. De Lawd lead you round hyar on de yearth, and he show you de Promise' Land. But you got to do yo' own dyin' . . . and de Scripture say de proud die hard.'

Mammy Clo's hands shook as if in palsy and she tried to speak. Her mouth opened, but only a dry rattle came from her throat. For a moment she was terrified. Then, as suddenly as it had come, the feeling of terror left her and she was calm and serene. She grinned. 'Rucker ain't nothin' but a chile wid a heap er tawk in his mouf,' she told herself, 'and hyar me listenin' at his fool tawk. Humph!'

Even as the realization came to her she vaguely heard Rucker calling nervously 'Mammy Clo! Mammy Clo!' and she vaguely felt him tugging at her arm. Some childish prank of his, no doubt. Well, Rucker was such a child, anyway. He never would grow up!

While the thoughts moved gently and comfortably through her mind she heard the hinges on the yard gate creak again, and she turned to see who could be coming in at that time in the afternoon. It was a tall straight man with a horn in his hand.

'Looks like Ole Gab'l, hisself,' she commented.

'Dat's zackly who he is, too,' the tall man grinned.

'Well, drag up a cheer and set,' invited Mammy Clo. 'Hit's cool water in de bucket and de gou'd is handy.'

Gabriel helped himself to a drink of water and drew up a chair. 'I'm kind er in a hurry, Clo,' he said, seating himself comfortably. 'I ain't got much time. I jest drapped by to ——'

'Sh-h-h-h-h,' interrupted Mammy Clo, raising her finger for silence and cupping her hand to her ear. 'Sh-h-h-h-h.'

'I jest drapped by to ——' Gabriel started again, but Mammy Clo's old ear caught the sound distinctly. It was the cry of a tiny baby.

'Hand me my crutch,' she ordered briskly and, without waiting for Gabriel to explain his business, she adjusted the crutch under her arm and hobbled toward the house.

Mammy Clo was not surprised when she walked into the room where the baby lay in its crib. Rather, she was disgusted.

The room was big and richly furnished. A huge table heavily laden with fine cradle gifts stood at the side of the cradle. But Mammy Clo was accustomed to going into fine houses. The big mansions of rich white folks and the lowliest cabins of the poorest Negroes all looked alike to her. A baby was a baby — white or black. The surroundings did not matter.

The first thing that caught her eye was a woman dressed in white. A white cap, white apron, white stockings, white shoes. The garments were stiffly starched, and shining where the iron had passed over them too many times. Mammy Clo knew exactly what she was up against. She had encountered trained nurses before. 'Too much starch and not enough brains,' was her estimate.

The nurse was heating milk over an alcohol stove and toying with a thermometer. Meanwhile the baby was crying pitifully in the crib.

The cradle was a fine one — made of solid gold laths joined together an inch apart. The head and foot boards were set with a huge star of clustered diamonds. But the baby lay writhing in pain on the bare slats of the crib.

'Well, befo' Gawd!' exclaimed Mammy Clo. 'Layin' hyar naked as a jaybird! And no mattress! And in a cradle built like a jackass ought to be eatin' hay out'n!' She turned threateningly to the nurse. 'Gal!' she exploded. 'How come diserway?'

'Now, aunty,' protested the nurse. 'The doctor has everything exactly as he wants it. The baby must have ventilation, and the doctor ——'

'De doctor, hunh?' snorted Mammy Clo. 'Well, I ain't studdin' what de doctor say de baby got to have. What I'm studdin' 'bout is what de baby got. He got de colic. Dat's what he got!'

The nurse tried to interrupt, but Mammy Clo drowned her out. 'Now drag yo'se'f on out in de gyarden and bring me some catnip. Dis baby need some catnip tea.'

'But the doctor ——'

'I ain't studdin' de doctor,' Mammy Clo broke in. 'And you too! Dis chile got de bellyache and he got hit bad. Now git out and git dat catnip! You hyar me! And some hot water!' She unhitched her crutch menacingly. 'And make tracks,' she added, 'befo' I wrops dis cretch 'round you!'

The nurse left and Mammy Clo lifted the baby tenderly from its crib, holding it in one arm while she adjusted the Star of Bethlehem quilt into a pillowy mattress with her free hand.

'Now you git back in dar, suh,' she said, placing the infant tenderly in the cradle. 'De doctor, hunh? And you mighty nigh got de epizoodics right now!'

The baby continued to cry, but its cries were softer, and soon they were little more than troubled whimpers that fitted into the wordless tune which Mammy Clo hummed.

Presently the nurse returned with the herb and water, and the baby was given the tea.

'The doctor will be awfully put out about this,' the nurse declared.

'Listen, honey,' said Mammy Clo, 'lemme ax you a question: Did de doctor ever had a baby?'

The nurse snickered at the idea.

'And you neither, I bet,' grinned Mammy Clo. 'Now you git over yonder by de lamp and jest let me alone.' And the nurse surrendered.

The baby, soothed by the tea, slept peacefully. Mammy Clo sat by the cradle, rocking back and forth, watching every move of the child. Toward morning the expression of pain faded from its face and the baby opened its big, round, blue eyes. There seemed to be a knowing, understanding glance in them as it saw the old woman, sitting with head bent, at the side of the cradle.

'You rascal you!' she accused fondly. 'You jest puttin' off on me! Dat's what you doin' suh!' She shook her tightly braided head close to the baby's face and gurgled, 'Goodly-goodly-goodly-goo,' and the baby's face muscles contorted in a manner that only Mammy Clo could have interpreted as an expression of merriment. She beamed.

221

'You scound'el, you,' she said. 'Look at you laughin' at ole mammy! Jest as mannish! I swear! Laughin' right out loud like a grown-up man! I bet you gonter be raisin' up and axin' me to please give you a chaw er 'backer, fust thing I know!' She smoothed the quilt gently and added, 'Now you git to sleep, suh, and rest dem purty eyes some mo'. And de next time you wakes up mamm' gonter have a sugar tit for dat boy to suck on. Now, git to sleepy!

The baby soon was in a quiet, peaceful sleep, and Mammy Clo instructed the nurse to bring a piece of clean, white cloth and some sugar. Then she fell asleep in the chair by the cradle.

When she woke it was light and she was quite rested. Both the baby and the nurse still were asleep, but Mammy Clo noticed the 'sugar tit' had been knotted properly and placed on the table near the cradle.

After a few minutes Gabriel opened the door wide, holding it back and bowing low. Almost immediately the Lord walked in.

The Lord looked exactly as Clo imagined he would look — exactly six feet tall and straight as a ramrod. And proud, too. With his shoulder drawn back and a heavy crown on his head. His stride was majestic — just short of a swagger. The sight of him was enough to fill one with awe.

Clo got up immediately and bowed, and the Lord opened his mouth as though to speak. But Clo interrupted him just in time.

'Sh-h-h-h, Lawd,' she whispered. 'De baby's sleepin' now, and he need dat sleep powerful bad. He was mighty sick last night. Mighty nigh had de cholly-mawbuses.'

The Lord looked shocked for an instant and then he smiled indulgently. 'That's mighty fine, Clo,' he said in a surprisingly soft whisper.

'Yeah, Lawd,' put in Gabriel. 'Clo do ack mighty handy around de babies.'

Clo was embarrassed by the bald praise. 'He jest need sleep,' she repeated, 'and some tea and stuff. He's awright, now.'

The Lord turned and tiptoed out of the room, and Gabriel and Clo followed. Outside Gabriel began talking, apparently resuming a conversation that had been started before he and the Lord entered the room.

222

''Bout dat time,' he said, 'she hyared de baby cry and she lit out twarge de cradle like a hawg after cawn.'

'What! And you didn't explain, suh?' The Lord thundered the question more like an accusation.

'Explain?' repeated Gabriel. 'Lawd, how anybody gonter explain anything at her when she hyars a baby squallin'? Me and you bofe couldn't explain her nothin' when she hyars a young 'un holler.'

Clo did not understand exactly what they were talking about, but she knew it had to do with Gabriel's arrival the afternoon before, and that the Lord was displeased with it. She hastened to Gabriel's rescue.

'You see, Lawd,' she amplified, 'I and Gab'l was jest fixin' to pass de time er day and I didn't no mo'n give him howdy, to I hyared de baby squallin'. And quick as I hyared dat, I knowed hit wan't nothin' but de bellyache make a baby holler like dat. So I jest lit out.'

'Yeah,' supplemented Gabriel. 'She been tawkin' to Rucker, and Rucker, he say Clo ain't humble enough.'

'Rucker,' put in Clo, 'don't think my Star er Bet-ly-ham quilt is purty, and Lawd, dat is a mighty purty quilt.'

They had been walking along, Gabriel and Clo slightly in rear of the Lord, who was swinging his arms and stepping higher with his left foot so that his stride was one of majesty. Clo paid no attention to where they were going until suddenly she realized that she was in the box elder grove back of the orchard, where she used to come to funerals.

'Dog gone!' she exclaimed. 'Hit's de fust time I been hyar since I don't know when. I used to never miss a funeral, but lately hit's been hard to git around. . . .' She looked about and saw a pile of freshly dug earth, just off to the left. 'Look like a new grave, too!' she exclaimed. 'Must gonter be a funeral today.'

'A big 'n too,' Gabriel assured her, with a knowing grin.

'Well, I be dad blame!' Mammy Clo's old eyes sparkled. 'I ain't been to a funeral in a month er Sundays! Le's watch hit!'

'You're mighty right, we'll watch it,' the Lord declared importantly. 'That's what I had in my mind when I led you out here.

223

I want you to watch, and listen too. Gabriel got to drinking water and chinning with you and forgot to . . .'

'Aw, Lawd,' protested Gabriel, 'don't be so hard on me. I done tole you she hyared dat baby yellin' before I c'd git my mouf open to tell her.'

Before the Lord had time to reply the procession came into view. Rucker, Bible in hand and head bowed, walked in front.

'Rucker gonter preach, too,' Clo explained. 'Rucker preaches a powerful good funeral, too, Lawd. I rose him up to be a preacher.'

Behind Rucker six husky Negroes carried a rosewood casket that was banked high with flowers. Then came more than a hundred men, women, and children — white and black. They were straggling slowly, singing in ragged time, 'When the Saints Go Marchin' On.'

'Ev'y last'n one of 'em is my chilluns, Lawd,' Mammy Clo explained proudly. 'Love de Lawd. Don't mind de work. And ain't skeered er nothin' but sin. Dat de way I rose dem chilluns.'

The casket was rested by the side of the grave. Rucker took a position at the head and the others formed a semicircle at the foot. Rucker raised his hand and a hushed silence fell.

'People,' he said huskily, 'most generally when I preaches a funeral, well I preaches hit. But I don't feel like preachin' much today. So we gonter sing dis funeral.'

'Now jest watch, Lawd!' Mammy Clo explained jubilantly. 'Rucker do git right at a singin' funeral. When his wife died and he didn't feel like preachin', well, we sung de funeral. Den all at once ole Rucker got hot and he got up and whupped de devil to he wan't no bigger'n a gnat!'

Rucker raised his hand again. 'Somebody h'ist a chune,' he commanded, 'while de body er dis cawpse is bein' lowered in de grave.'

An uncertain baritone voice began tunelessly:

'Befo' dis time another year, I may be gone ——'

The others straggled along after the baritone. When time came for the second line, a shrill — too shrill — soprano had seized the lead:

> 'And er my body a-layin' in de ground,
> Lawd knows how long.'

Rucker shook his head. 'Dat's rotten,' he declared.

'Well, I believe you,' Mammy Clo agreed heartily. 'Plum rotten.'

There was a moment of tense silence and then a rumbling bass began:

'Deep river! My home is over Jurdin.
Deep river, Lawd! I want to cross over into Camp Ground.'

'Dat's mo' better,' Rucker admitted, and soon the song was rolling along, now gently and soothingly, now wild and rumbling.

'Oh, won't you come to de Gospel Feast,
In de Promise' Land whar all is peace?
Deep river! My home is over Jurdin.
Deep river, Lawd! I want to cross over into Camp Ground.'

The pallbearers placed cotton ropes under the casket and lifted it over the gaping hole. The song droned weirdly, wistfully. Ricker addressed the casket as it was being lowered into the grave:

'Ashes might be unto ashes and dust might be unto dust, but hit ain't a natchal man kin put you in de ground. And dat's a fack.'

'Deep river, Lawd! I want to cross over ——'

The song rose higher and higher while Rucker struggled not only with words to express his feeling, but against the din of wailing voices. Then, when the last note of a line was dying out, he raised his own voice with the swing of the song and led the next verse himself:

'Oh, de news f'm heab'm which is gone around,
She crossed over Jurdin on dusty ground.'

Gabriel leaped excitedly to his feet. 'I be dag gone, Lawd!' he exclaimed, 'listen at Rucker!'

'I made him say that,' said the Lord. 'I wanted Clo to hear from Rucker's own lips that she was dead. Now, listen at this one, Clo, and you'll find out all about that mystery!' But Clo was not there.

She was hurrying away, grumbling to herself. 'I ain't got no time to pleasure myse'f at nobody's funeral,' she was saying. 'I got

225

to mind dat baby. Dat sassy scound'el! All r'ared back on my fine quilt, jest as buckish! I swear!' She giggled deep down in her throat. 'He gonter git dat sugar tit de minute he open dem purty eyes er his'n. R'ared back, laughin' at me! He jest won't do!' And she hurried on to the side of the cradle.

GOOD-BYE TO CAP'M JOHN

S. S. FIELD

MY UNCLE, Cap'm John Bell, is a big man with steady eyes. He used to look rather silly in his golfing pants, those transparent linen tights that I dare to remember him in some fifteen years ago — a man who had built up a rugged deep-water towing and dredging business when New Orleans was still a mud flat.

But he has given up the game of golf now. Now he is just rounding that big turn in the weary river, as he says, where the rest is an easy, wide swing down to salt water and the open sea. And so he sits a great deal of the time in the towing office now, looking out over the river, watching the querulous gulls with his distant eyes: the nearly deserted river since the city administration raised the docking fees to the level of the bonded indebtedness. Usually he is fiddling with something, a pencil or his watch chain, looking out at the mile of bending yellow river. He spends a lot of his time that way.

But fifteen or twenty years ago he had a number of the fancy kind of friends, among whom he was compelled to move through a period of uncomfortable collars with the silent and half-smiling suspicion of a roughshod stranger caught in the middle of a minuet.

Because fifteen or twenty years ago he had made enough money, the step into society was down, not up: a man who had generations of tugboats and train ferries and deep-sea barges named for him and for the women of his family, and with generations of river niggers in turn named for the boats. And since it is the women in a man's family who make a business of society, the godmothers of the barges managed it irrespective of his trade and thanks to its profit.

He was saddled first with one of our city's carnival organizations, one of the better ones, and so I remember him also as a prince: a massive man in button shoes, with the edge of his long underwear showing beneath the elastic of his knee breeches. It was his only

227

carnival appearance; I was there with my mother to watch the night parade from his balcony when he dressed for that ball. 'Filthy business,' he said, glancing down at me once, tentative, alert; standing in massive and outlandish gravity, looking at himself. I was eleven. He always addressed me as one man to another, as a philosopher, say, to a scientific man, perhaps out of respect for my mother's brave hope or perhaps as his own subtle suggestion that I might continue my growing along masculine lines. 'Not many of them seem to be on your side of the family, Martha,' he used to tell my mother. But standing there that night inspecting his silken bulk, we both were a little anxious. 'Yes,' he said.

'Yes, sir,' I said.

'It's not the way I look. I look all right. But it's why I look this way.' And he stared past himself in the big gold mirror. 'I never wanted to get this high,' he said.

He took up golf as the natural and most hardy adjunct to the launching of his family in society.

Cap'm John was in society altogether for about four years. He could have stayed there had he wished. He could have steered a carnival float down Canal Street year after year with all the papal altitude of a ferry-boat captain and with about as much variety, but he got out. He gave his golf sticks to a Negro named Hopper Bell and he went back to sit in the towing office or in the wheel-house of a seagoing tug. 'Where I belong,' he said. He returned to his river and to himself on the day of his third golf tournament; on the day that Frohman died. Frohman was a Negro, too.

It is not surprising that at fifty-five my uncle, Cap'm John, excelled at golf. Twenty years ago in New Orleans the game was played by a handful of elderly or ailing gentlemen who would attack the ground with the deliberation and the awkwardness and somewhat the swagger of small boys learning to chop wood — and my uncle was a larger man than most. It is less surprising that he should have excelled at the game than that he should have played it at all. Because he saw beyond that game; as though it were a bend in the river (and so it was), just as he saw beyond most things — himself, for instance. He used to confide in me in those days, and even then I must have known that he was seeing far beyond my thin legs and my eleven years, placing his confidences upon some later pinnacle to which I might one day climb or not climb. It made me walk straighter, with wider and more alert eyes. Like the thing he said one day about golf: 'It is no game for you, you know,' he said. 'You look mighty neat today.'

'No, sir,' I said. 'Why? Yes, sir, my stockings . . .'

'You should have one stocking coming down,' he said. 'With both your stockings up you'll be a poet. Because ——' he said. 'Golf is a circular path. It is for old men who have nowhere to go. Going, you know; that is the thing.'

'Yes, sir,' I said, secretly loosening one of my pants buckles.

'But few men think of going,' he said, fiddling with the golf ball and looking off . . . I remember how he tried to tell me then about golf: about how the things a man does to excess are the measure of his soul, and how going was better than golf; how going holds something finer than the safe little positiveness of the four walls of circumstance, something better than the smallness, the immediacy of the shiny metal blades — the mashies and the niblicks whipped through the grass in pursuit of a little white ball, it also a sphere, resolving into an instant exaltation or despair. . . 'It is like the moon.' He held up the golf ball. 'With its little craters. Never play golf or pool . . . or bridge,' he said, 'and your chances will be better. Fore!'

'Yes, sir,' I said. He won his second golf tournament that summer.

I was in the towing office early on the day that Frohman died. I had been promised a ride on the new *Martha R. Bell*, and so both of my stockings were down by the time I had run from the street car to the docks and up the stairs. I found Cap'm John standing at the window watching the river. 'Good morning, Cap'm,' I said. I sat on the high stool, hoping he would notice my stockings.

'Good morning,' he said. He said it slowly. 'I'm afraid we can't go today.' My heart stopped for a sickening moment. 'One of my niggers has been hurt,' he said. 'Another one. I guess we'll have to see what we can do.'

'Yes, sir,' I said. 'What happened to him?'

'He was shot.'

I whistled. 'Where was he shot? How did he get shot? Who shot him, Cap'm John? What . . .'

'I don't know,' Cap'm John said. We were already descending the stairs without my noticing it.

'Will he die?' I said.

'I don't know,' Cap'm John said.

'When was he shot? Today, was he? This morning?' I had to run to keep up. We were going fast and both of my stockings were well down. 'Who was it, Cap'm John? Which one of them was it?'

'Frohman,' Cap'm John said. 'My caddy.' That was when I remembered that the summer before, it had been Snag.

Snag was a crippled Negro who had caddied for my uncle when he won his first golf tournmant. Cap'm John had been fond of Snag. He was fond of all Negroes, and I remember how pleased both he and Snag would be over any golf shot the two of them contrived to make; it was as though Snag carrying the golf bag and handing the stick was half of the shot without which teeing the ball and driving it could not have had any meaning whatever, and Snag would scramble along behind Cap'm John, fast, with all the keys of a grand piano displayed in his face, saying 'Wham, Cap'm Jawn suh! Yes, suh! Us set thatun down like a fo' bits bet. Wham!' all the way to the next shot.

But Snag used to swim in the river. He believed it would help his undeveloped leg. He had a mongrel dog, and the two of them would swim on warm mornings up at a great sweeping bend of levee and wilderness beyond the golf course. Sometimes when the current was gone the two of them would swim across. It was on an empty Sunday morning that Snag was killed. He hadn't seen the oil tanker when she came around the bend. They were out in the middle, then, just two black specks on the yellow vastness. Then the long blast came like a mighty trumpet. They said that the nigger must have misjudged their swing. They were already well on the turn when they saw him and they said that they eased the wheel to straighten out and pass the nigger on starboard. They said that he must have just put it to a guess and he guessed wrong, because they said that he had two-thirds of the river to swim in but that he turned back and so they put the wheel hard to starboard and then he turned back again — the two of them, the nigger and the dog, swimming back and forth each time in a shorter arc until they could see his face stretched like laughter in the sunshine with all the white teeth, or like a grimace of joyous surprise, recognition, and with men even running forward, waving from the swinging cliff (she was high, empty) and the long trumpet blast right up to the moment he was struck and they wasted the life preserver. He was struck by the great bulging side, nearly amidship, as the wall of steel swung gatelike and fast with the wheel hard over. They saw only the hand and the vanishing gleam of teeth and then nothing. And now it was Frohman.

It was my first visit to a charity hospital. It must have been Cap'm John's first visit, too, for the following year he gave the Negroes a hospital of their own. 'It's like the inside of a swill pot,' Cap'm John said as we waited in the grimy hallway, and he began to curse them for a lot of unclean butchers. 'I don't know that your mother would approve of this, and I can't say that I'd blame her. But then you may remember it; come along, then, here we go.'

I remember it. Frohman had the face, the nostrils, the eyes, the color of that central figure in most stained-glass windows, after the sun has gone down. He was in a ward with unwashed floor and walls among a dozen other Negroes in beds, men and women whose dumb eyes followed us in hope. The white rolling irises of Frohman's eyes spoke first when he saw Cap'm John. Then his voice came, very thin now, with a kind of gasping of the light servility and the swagger and the old meaningless effusion. 'Yas suh, Cap'm Jawn, suh. Young Cap'm, suh. I jes had to lef you know . . . how I'm is, Cap'm Jawn. Account of how me and you was gwi wham that ball in that turment tomorrow . . . Account of how me and you was gwi . . .'

I remember the long black hand moving on the sheet. Then the doctor came. He seemed too young and thin to be a good doctor. He was explaining the case and drawing with a scalpel on the chart. His voice seemed insolent with gaiety, so near the lean gourd head and eyes of Frohman. I dared to look once more at those eyes that saw only Cap'm John. 'Altogether negligible prospects,' the doctor was saying and drawing. 'A split bullet. You are familiar with the stem and blossom of the tube lily? The split bullet describes that lovely plant form within the intestines; here you have the stem and here you have the blossom forming ——' I could feel Cap'm John looking inside of the man and waiting too long. When he spoke his voice was quiet and tightening like a warping hawser.

'What are you?' he said. 'The gardener? Get this boy moved into a private room. Get out of here and get me a doctor. Get me the head surgeon, not a florist!' And the doctor had somehow vanished.

And so we stood there. It was as though Frohman and Cap'm John and I were each looking at a point somewhere within Frohman, and then it was as though the point, as we watched it, had quietly gone somewhere beyond Frohman and we watched it go, Frohman watching it too, and then our eyes stopped, Frohman's did, and Cap'm John's went on still further beyond that point which Frohman had recognized as the logical place to stop. Because the pain seemed to go out of Frohman's eyes. 'Jes account of that turment tomorrow, Cap'm Jawn,' he said. The shape of his head made me want to cry. 'Account of how me and you was gwi wham that ball tomorrow . . .' Cap'm John's eyes looked now at the new point, the Tomorrow of Frohman's voice, suspended somewhere in the sterile half-light above the bed where the thin profusion, the apologia in little thin strutful vowels, issued forth once more; and then it was as though the other point and this one had become the same and I saw that the corners of Cap'm John's mouth were down and the thin voice was saying, 'You got to git mo' right wris' in there, Cap'm, and mind you don't lif' yo haid ——' Then the pale irises rolled back. The pain on his face was like glory. 'I ain't be cahyin yo' bag but us'll be pullin' for you, Cap'm Jawn. Me and ole Snag.' He looked again, his teeth showing again. 'But jes account of that turment, Cap'm Jawn . . . I be thinking if all thing don't go right . . . some kind of lil sen'-over, Cap'm, when you wins that turment . . . Like old Snag used to say, Wham, Cap'm Jawn suh ——' Then I was watching the eyes again. 'Wham, Cap'm Jawn. Wham, Cap'm. Wham, Ca — . . . wham.' Then he was still looking, eagerly now, as though he were watching the flight of a ball, high and far; it, too, a sphere resolving into an instant exaltation or despair — but he no longer seemed to see. That is the way I remember it.

I cried on the way out. Cap'm John put his arm around me and patted my shoulder. 'That,' Cap'm John said, 'was death. Come along, now.'

And so that's how it came to be Hopper Bell's time. It was as if besides Cap'm John's sticks and his linen knickers (through which could be seen with infallible regularity, like an eccentricity in dress, the outline and even the patented seat arrangement of my uncle's underdrawers — until even his underdrawers became an incontrovertible public fact, an incident to recognition, along with his honesty, his button shoes, his size, and his job) — as if besides the sticks and the transparent tights, Cap'm John owned also a private stable of three Negroes concomitant to his golf and graded in seniority: Snag, Frohman, Hopper Bell. And now it was Hopper Bell.

And I must say this to Hopper Bell's ghost — wherever it is: that there would have been no cheap tin trophy won by our stable that day had Cap'm John known, as I knew, about the monstrous superstition among those Negroes. Because maybe one of them helped to cart the furrowed despair of Frohman to the hospital (they took him there in an ice wagon) and maybe Frohman (he was delirious) had had a vision; I don't know. At any rate, in the lush harangue and babble of the caddy house that day, on the heels of Frohman's death, they knew that there would be three. And now it was Hopper Bell.

He was a tall, thin-headed Negro, very black and quiet. He was beautiful, his face and his eyes and the angle of his long head, which he carried to one side in a gentle manner and on the top of which he wore (with the pious placidity of a black young saint) a soiled, red bell-hop's cap with brass buttons.

But I shall always remember Hopper Bell's face on that day that he caddied for my uncle's last golf tournament — the wild, ago-nized, up-gazing face with the mute velvet eyes. Perhaps it was most beautiful then; it has been stamped upon my mind in pain

233

for such a long time. Because I was there that day of the third caddy and the third tournament. I was there and I knew and I didn't stop them. Following along in the determined little coterie of my uncle and Negroes and friends all the way around the circular path, with my stockings down and panic in my mind, I knew and I didn't stop the tournament. I didn't say, 'Cap'm John, excuse me, sir, but I must talk with you alone.' I didn't say, 'Cap'm John, sir, please. Do with me what you will. Kill me, hate me, do anything to me, but please don't finish this tournament.' And maybe that is why his face has been stamped upon my mind in pain for so long. Hopper Bell's face.

Because I was there that day, because I had to be there that day. I had to be with Cap'm John. Not on account of the tournament. On account of Frohman's death. It had bound me somehow to my uncle and I knew that I had to be with him, close to him that day and the next and the next until time and experience might slowly unite us again as child and man, restore our vast small world of interdependence which the death of a Negro had divided as with a wall of silence. Because his eyes were stronger than mine, Cap'm John's: seeing far out beyond that point where Frohman's eyes had stopped, and not coming back. And I had to have those eyes back, close to me again, to center now and then their warmth, their scrutiny, their puzzlement upon mine, and I wanted to hear once more the voice going beyond me — scouting out into the world of his experience and then returning to say, 'Well, what do you think of this, now?' or 'What do you think of that?' And then we would be once more like two people necessary to each other . . . It has taken me so long to understand my first death, the death of Frohman. And now I wish that we were back the way we were, Cap'm John and I; but we never can be. Too much has died; the wall of silence has gone too high.

So I was there that day. I was alone in the sun outside of the caddy house when I learned; when I heard their voices. I was unraveling the core of a golf ball and thinking about Frohman and wishing that my father too were alive to help me face fear and sadness and a world full of harder boys who were not a prey to their stockings, whose stockings had not become a conscious obsession of fear, a measure of courage or cowardice, a challenge or an admission. But mostly I was just miserable and unraveling rubber when I heard their voices, rich, guttural, quarrelsome, with the sourceless flow and uncontrol of bubbling mush. When I heard the first voice say, 'Shure. Cahy that bag and sign your dead warran'! That boy a fool to cahy that bag, man, shure.'

And the second voice: 'Better be him dan me. 'Cause de Cap'm jes natchally figure to win dis turment one-up. Jes like it was writ down in de book, cause ain't de Cap'm dooze three-up and two to play in de first turment ——'

'And de tanker got ole Snag. Wham!'

'And ain't de Cap'm dooze two-up and one to play in de second turment ——'

'And de split bullet found ole Frohman. Wham!'

And then a third and a fourth voice together with the other two in soft, outrageous babbling, in ceaseless turmoil and harangue with the noise that irritable chickens make, the total, the absolute, the utter conviction of sound. 'Ole hawd-haided boy. Shure, man, de Cap'm gwi be lookin' down Mister Ginny thoat on number eighteen green and then where is you at?'

'An didn' ole Frohman has that dream about passin' wid de dices three times, and didn' de dream book say mind out where you walks and git down on de number three?'

'Cap'm gi'ing ole Frohman a fawty-dollar sen'-over. Boy, how come you don't gawn home and save de Cap'm money ——' And then Cap'm John's voice calling, and the swift silence within the caddy house.

'Hopper? Where's my boy? Come on here, son, and bring my bag.'

He came out slowly, with the red bell-hop's cap on his saint-like head, down-looking, miserable, as if he were sick, stopping once to kick something with his long thin foot. Then he said quietly, 'Yas suh, Cap'm. Here I'm is.' Inside the caddy house the dark eyes with the pale china irises watched him go, like the eyes of animals in a cave.

And so there was a gallery of Negroes too — a forlorn, downcast, stringy lot, following at a safe distance, not talking.

I don't remember much about that game. We must have made
a strange procession forging along with the deliberation of priests
and acolytes, with Hopper Bell looking like a walking advertisement
for a Georgia Springs hotel, and the trailing Negroes and big Cap'm
John and Mr. Guernsey and the other Negro.

I remember chasing along behind, running often and bumping
into them as if I were blind, and being spoken to, and then I remember Hopper Bell's thin, agonized, up-gazing face beneath the
red monkey cap watching the flight of the ball with rushing eyes
and then I was praying that Cap'm John would lose and it was the
next to the last hole and then I thought that I should have to scream
for them to stop and with my mouth already shaped for words and
my eyes on the crucifixion of Hopper Bell's face and then Mr.
Guernsey had teed his ball and was waggling his club and I couldn't
scream.

The rest isn't easy to tell, being a composite within an instant
of all the terror, the recrimination, the shame that seems to have
been childhood: the instant when Cap'm John struck the ball with
all the heave of a spike driver; the click that could have been the
snapping of a camera within my mind; the slow instant of exaltation, of despair, when Hopper Bell squeezed his eyes beneath his
long pale fingers and the eyes of the other Negroes rose and held
and sank even as they began to walk away, spent, and when
Mr. Guernsey turned to shake hands with Cap'm John (Mr.
Guernsey had one ball out of bounds) and Cap'm John turned and
Hopper Bell still held his eyes in his Christ-like hand.

'What's the matter with my boy?' Cap'm John said. It was
late, nearly dark. There were only the five of us at the tee. 'What's
the matter with my boy? What's the matter with you, son? Won't
somebody tell me what's the matter with my darky?'

And then Hopper's voice, sudden, thin, gentle: 'Nawsuh, Cap'm
suh. Ain't nothin'. Wham, Cap'm Jawn suh. Wham, Cap'm!'
on an ascending wire of sound.

He thought that I was congratulating him, at first. At first he
just thought that I had gone out of control, or maybe he thought
that I was trying to fly. It was just that I had to say it then and
so maybe I did run headlong into him, leap into him. He caught

me rather handily. I remember his embarrassment and the touch of foolish mirth as if some ladies' lingerie had blown into his face and then I was telling him and choking and we were sitting on the green mound and the others had walked away, leaving us alone in the mist that had begun to rise with evening. He listened — quiet, kind, massive.

'Fear, you know,' he said. 'It is a very real thing . . . Only the truly young in the world have the wisdom to be afraid. Some day you will understand this; that most people on earth are born old and heedless and unafraid.' (This was in 1914.) 'I am glad you told me,' he said finally. 'I care less for the game of golf than I do for my caddy's face. Come along, now, and we'll straighten him out.'

Frohman's funeral was on the following day and my uncle, Cap'm John Bell, gave him that.

It was fine. Frohman would have been mighty proud to see himself riding in the polished black wagon behind the Negro with the cotton gloves and the opera hat. And to have seen the Negroes. There must have been a hundred of them who came, appeared, as if out of nowhere, with the definite pomp of people invited to a party, and dressed for the occasion. And then the band! Cap'm John gave him that, too.

So things were a little better that day. Frohman lived out near the New Basin Canal and the railroad tracks, and just the right distance from the sad little picket field of wood and concrete markers that was to be his stopping-off place until some later city ordinance should shunt his dark dust elsewhere in the great anonymity — so we walked; we were a parade. Things were better.

First there was the square black wagon with the screened windows and the carved circus scrollwork, then the six piece band, then Cap'm John and I, and then the Negroes. I remember looking back as we turned the corner with the band taking the high notes of 'Tiger Rag,' their dazzling clarinets and trombones aimed at the sky, shimmering, and I could see all the curled palms swinging in unison with a cakewalk swagger, and the ten or fifteen Negroes in bandmasters' uniforms (a kind of outlandish Negro improvisation from the outlandish Caucasian habits of Shriners, Elks, Masons, and the Royal Order of St. James, only made of cheap materials; they were an organization) with the black velvet banner and the white cotton gloves. I remember the identical curl of each pair of the white cotton gloves — and the way they lifted their feet: high and slithering as if missing imaginary eggs. It was fine. We must have been grand as we rounded the turn skirting the New Basin Canal on Frohman's march to glory. Even Cap'm John swaggered a little.

'This is better,' he said. 'I should have my prince suit here. It is remarkable what Providence directs their feet while they aim those horns at heaven. Frohman must be enjoying this,' and we sashayed around the turn onto the dry mud street to glory . . .

And so we buried Frohman. Cap'm John was splendid.

And that afternoon too we had our first ride on the new *Martha R. Bell*. She is still in service, small and tough and jovial, with a decided swagger of her own on the turns. Somehow I know that she will live just about as long as Cap'm John, and not much longer. I see her now and then. And when we marched out of Frohman's funeral that day, and onto her steep, new deck, he seemed to have stepped out of public life and back into the privacy of himself. The only regret I have ever heard him express concerning his brief sojourn among the gentle was over the winning of his third golf tournament.

Hopper Bell, by the way, is dead.

'Experience, you know. That is the thing. Experience is pain and it is out of pain that we grow.' I remember he said that, that evening on the way back, hurrying around the great bend in the river, butting our way proudly in the amber afterglow. The gulls were clamoring and moiling over a drifting meal. And then I remember him standing against the evening, looming a little bit in the wheelhouse beside me, silent, watching the river. I remember him that way. When I left him that night I thanked him.

JERICHO, JERICHO, JERICHO

ANDREW NELSON LYTLE

SHE opened her eyes. She must have been asleep for hours or
months. She could not reckon; she could only feel the steady
silence of time. She had been Joshua and made it swing suspended
in her room. Forever she had floated above the counterpane, between the tester and the counterpane she had floated until her
hand, long and bony, its speckled-dried skin drawing away from
the bulging blue veins, had reached and drawn her body under the
covers. And now she was resting, clear-headed and quiet, her
thoughts clicking like a new-greased mower. All creation could not
make her lift her thumb or cross it over her finger. She looked at
the bed, the bed her mother had died in, the bed her children had
been born in, her marriage bed, the bed the General had drenched
with his blood. Here it stood where it had stood for seventy years,
square and firm on the floor, wide enough for three people to lie
comfortable in, if they didn't sleep restless; but not wide enough
for her nor long enough when her conscience scorched the cool
wrinkles in the sheets. The two footposts, octagonal-shaped and
mounted by carved pieces that looked like absurd flowers, stood
up to comfort her when the world began to crumble. Her eyes
followed down the posts and along the basket-quilt. She had made
it before her marriage to the General, only he wasn't a general
then. He was a slight, tall young man with a rolling mustache and
perfume in his hair. A many a time she had seen her young love's
locks dripping with scented oil, down upon his collar . . . She had
cut the squares for the baskets in January, and for stuffing had
used the letters of old lovers, fragments of passion cut to warm her
of a winter's night. The General would have his fun. *Miss Kate,
I didn't sleep well last night. I heard Sam Buchanan make love to
you out of that farthest basket. If I hear him again, I mean to toss this*

piece of quilt in the fire. Then he would chuckle in his round, soft voice; reach under the covers and pull her over to his side of the bed. On a cold and frosting night he would sleep with his nose against her neck. His nose was so quick to turn cold, he said, and her neck was so warm. Sometimes her hair, the loose, unruly strands at the nape, would tickle his nostrils and he would wake up with a sneeze. This had been so long ago, and there had been so many years of trouble and worry. Her eyes, as apart from her as the mirror on the bureau, rested upon the half-tester, upon the enormous button that caught the rose-colored canopy and shot its folds out like the rays of the morning sun. She could not see, but she could feel the heavy cluster of mahogany grapes that tumbled from the center of the headboard — out of its vines curling down the sides it tumbled. How much longer would these never-picked grapes hang over her head? How much longer would she, rather, hang to the vine of this world, she who lay beneath as dry as any raisin. Then she remembered. She looked at the blinds. They were closed.

'You, Ants, where's my stick? I'm a great mind to break it over your trifling back.'

'Awake? What a nice long nap you've had,' said Doctor Ed.

'The boy? Where's my grandson? Has he come?'

'I'll say he's come. What do you mean taking to your bed like this? Do you realize, beautiful lady, that this is the first time I ever saw you in bed in my whole life? I believe you've taken to bed on purpose. I don't believe you want to see me.'

'Go long, boy, with your foolishness.'

That's all she could say, and she blushed as she said it — she blushing at the words of a snip of a boy, whom she had diapered a hundred times and had washed as he stood before the fire in the round tin tub, his little back swayed and his little belly sticking out in front, rosy from the scrubbing he had gotten. *Mammy, what for I've got a hole in my stummick; what for, Mammy?* Now he was sitting on the edge of the bed calling her beautiful lady, an old hag like her, beautiful lady. A good-looker the girls would call him, with his bold, careless face and his hands with their fine, long fingers. Soft, how soft they were, running over her rough, skinny bones. He looked a little like his grandpa, but somehow there was something missing . . .

'Well, boy, it took you a time to come home to see me die.'

'Nonsense. Cousin Edwin, I wouldn't wait on a woman who had so little faith in my healing powers.'

'There an't nothing strange about dying. But I an't in such an all-fired hurry. I've got a heap to tell you about before I go.'

The boy leaned over and touched her gently. 'Not even death would dispute you here, on Long Gourd, Mammy.'

He was trying to put her at her ease in his carefree way. It was so obvious a pretending, but she loved him for it. There was something nice in its awkwardness, the charm of the young's blundering and of their efforts to get along in the world. Their pretty arrogance, their patronizing airs, their colossal unknowing of what was to come. It was a quenching drink to a sin-thirsty old woman. Somehow his vitality had got crossed in her blood and made a dry heart leap, her blood that was almost water. Soon now she would be all water, water and dust, lying in the burying ground between the cedar — and fire. She could smell her soul burning and see it. What a fire it would make below, dripping with sin, like a rag soaked in kerosene. But she had known what she was doing. And here was Long Gourd, all its fields intact, ready to be handed on, in better shape than when she took it over. Yes, she had known what she was doing. How long, she wondered, would his spirit hold up under the trials of planting, of cultivating, and of the gathering time, year in and year out — how would he hold up before so many springs and so many autumns. The thought of him giving orders, riding over the place, or rocking on the piazza, and a great pain would pin her heart to her backbone. She had wanted him by her to train — there was so much for him to know: how the south field was cold and must be planted late, and where the orchards would best hold their fruit, and where the frosts crept soonest — that now could never be. She turned her head — who was that woman, that strange woman standing by the bed as if she owned it, as if . . .

'This is Eva, Mammy.'

'Eva?'

'We are going to be married.'

'I wanted to come and see — to meet Dick's grandmother . . .'

I wanted to come see her die. That's what she meant. Why didn't she finish and say it out. She had come to lick her chops and see what she would enjoy. That's what she had come for, the lying little slut. The richest acres in Long Gourd valley, so rich hit'd make yer feet greasy to walk over'm, Saul Oberly at the first toll-gate had told the peddler once, and the peddler had told it to her, knowing it would please and make her trade. *Before you die.* Well, why didn't you finish it out? You might as well. You've given yourself away.

Her fierce thoughts dried up the water in her eyes, tired and resting far back in their sockets. They burned like a smothered fire stirred up by the wind as they traveled over the woman who would lie in her bed, eat with her silver, and caress her flesh and blood. The woman's body was soft enough to melt and pour about him. She could see that; and her firm, round breasts, too firm and round for any good to come from them. And her lips, full and red, her eyes bright and cunning. The heavy hair crawled about her head to tangle the poor, foolish boy in its ropes. She might have known he would do something foolish like this. He had a foolish mother. There warn't any way to avoid it. But look at her belly, small and no-count. There wasn't a muscle the size of a worm as she could see. And those hips —

And then she heard her voice: 'What did you say her name was, son? Eva? Eva Callahan, I'm glad to meet you, Eva. Where'd your folks come from, Eva? I knew some Callahans who lived in the Goosepad settlement. They couldn't be any of your kin, could they?'

'Oh, no, indeed. My people . . .'

'Right clever people they were. And good farmers, too. Worked hard. Honest — that is, most of 'm. As honest as that run of people go. We always gave them a good name.'

'My father and mother live in Birmingham. Have always lived there.'

'Birmingham,' she heard herself say with contempt. They could have lived there all their lives and still come from somewhere. I've got a mule older 'n Birmingham. 'What's your pa's name?'

'Her father is Mister E. L. Callahan, Mammy.'

'First name not Elijah by any chance? Lige they called him.'

'No. Elmore, Mammy.'

'Old Mason Callahan had a son they called Lige. Somebody told me he moved to Elyton. So you think you're going to live with the boy here.'

'We're to be married . . . that is, if Eva doesn't change her mind.'

And she saw his arm slip possessively about the woman's waist. 'Well, take care of him, young woman, or I'll come back and han't you. I'll come back and claw your eyes out.'

'I'll take very good care of him, Mrs. McCowan.'

'I can see that.' She could hear the threat in her voice, and Eva heard it.

'Young man,' spoke up Doctor Edwin, 'you should feel powerful set up, two such women pestering each other about you.'

The boy kept an embarrassed silence.

'All of you get out now. I want to talk to him by himself. I've got a lot to say and precious little time to say it in. And he's mighty young and helpless and ignorant.'

'Why, Mammy, you forget I'm a man now. Twenty-six. All teeth cut. Long trousers.'

'It takes a heap more than pants to make a man. Throw open them blinds, Ants.'

'Yes'm.'

'You don't have to close the door so all-fired soft. Close it naturally. And you can tip about all you want to — later. I won't be hurried to the burying ground. And keep your head away from that door. What I've got to say to your new master is private.'

'Listen at you, Mistiss.'

'You listen to me. That's all. No, wait. I had something else on my mind — what is it? Yes. How many hens has Melissy set? You don't know? Find out. A few of the old hens ought to be setting. Tell her to be careful to turn the turkey eggs every day. No, you bring them and set them under my bed. I'll make sure. We got a mighty pore hatch last year. You may go now. I'm plumb worn out, boy, worn out thinking for these people. It's that that worries a body down. But you'll know all about it in good time. Stand out

243

there and let me look at you good. You don't let see me enough of
you, and I almost forget how you look. Not really, you understand.
Just a little. It's your own fault. I've got so much to trouble me
that you, when you're not here, naturally slip back in my mind.
But that's all over now. You are here to stay, and I'm here to go.
There will always be Long Gourd, and there must always be a
McCowan on it. I had hoped to have you by me for several years,
but you would have your fling in town. I thought it best to clear
your blood of it, but as God is hard, I can't see what you find to do
in town. And now you've gone and gotten you a woman. Well,
they all have to do it. But do you reckon you've picked the right
one — you must forgive the frankness of an old lady who can see
the bottom of her grave — I had in mind one of the Carlisle girls.
The Carlisle place lies so handy to Long Gourd and would give me
a landing on the river. Have you seen Anna Belle since she's
grown to be a woman? I'm told there's not a better housekeeper
in the valley.'

'I'm sure Anna Belle is a fine girl. But, Mammy, I love Eva.'

'She'll wrinkle up on you, Son; and the only wrinkles land gets
can be smoothed out by the harrow. And she looks sort of puny to
me, Son. She's powerful small in the waist and walks like she had
worms.'

'Gee, Mammy, you're not jealous are you? That waist is in
style.'

'You want to look for the right kind of style in a woman. Old
Mrs. Penter Matchem had two daughters with just such waists,
but 'twarn't natural. She would tie their corset strings to the bed
posts and whip'm out with a buggy whip. The poor girls never
drew a hearty breath. Just to please that old woman's vanity. She
got paid in kind. It did something to Eliza's bowels and she died
before she was twenty. The other one never had any children. She
used to whip'm out until they cried. I never liked that woman.
She thought a whip could do anything.'

'Well, anyway, Eva's small waist wasn't made by any corset
strings. She doesn't wear any.'

'How do you know, sir?'

'Well . . . I . . . What a question for a respectable woman to ask.'

244

'I'm not a respectable woman. No woman can be respectable and run four thousand acres of land. Well, you'll have it your own way. I suppose the safest place for a man to take his folly is to bed.'

'Mammy!'

'You must be lenient with your Cousin George. He wanders about night times talking about the War. I put him off in the west wing where he won't keep people awake, but sometimes he gets in the yard and gives orders to his troops. "I will sweep that hill, General" — and many's the time he's done it when the battle was doubtful — "I'll sweep it with my iron brooms"; then he shouts out his orders, and pretty soon the dogs commence to barking. But he's been a heap of company for me. You must see that your wife humors him. It won't be for long. He's mighty feeble.'

'Eva's not my wife yet, Mammy.'

'You won't be free much longer — the way she looks at you, like a hungry hound.'

'I was just wondering,' he said hurriedly. 'I hate to talk about anything like this . . .'

'Everybody has a time to die, and I'll have no maudlin nonsense about mine.'

'I was wondering about Cousin George . . . if I could get somebody to keep him. You see, it will be difficult in the winters. Eva will want to spend the winters in town . . .'

He paused, startled, before the great bulk of his grandmother rising from her pillows, and in the silence that frightened the air, his unfinished words hung suspended about them.

After a moment he asked if he should call the doctor.

It was some time before she could find words to speak.

'Get out of the room.'

'Forgive me, Mammy. You must be tired.'

'I'll send for you,' sounded the dead voice in the still room, 'when I want to see you again. I'll send for you and — the woman.'

She watched the door close quietly on his neat square back. Her head whirled and turned like a flying jennet. She lowered and steadied it on the pillows. Four thousand acres of the richest land in the valley he would sell and squander on that slut, and he didn't even know it and there was no way to warn him. This terrifying

245

thought rushed through her mind, and she felt the bed shake with her pain, while before the footboard the spectre of an old sin rose up to mock her. How she had struggled to get this land and keep it together — through the War, the Reconstruction, and the pleasanter afterdays. For eighty-seven years she had suffered and slept and planned and rested and had pleasure in this valley, seventy of it, almost a turning century, on this place; and now that she must leave it . . .

The things she had done to keep it together. No. The one thing . . . from the dusty stacks the musty odor drifted through the room, met the tobacco smoke over the long table piled high with records, reports. Iva Louise stood at one end, her hat clinging perilously to the heavy auburn hair, the hard blue eyes and the voice:

'You promised Pa to look after me' — she had waited for the voice to break and scream — 'and you have stolen my land!'

'Now, Miss Iva Louise,' the lawyer dropped his empty eyes along the floor, 'you don't mean . . .'

'Yes, I do mean it.'

Her own voice had restored calm to the room: 'I promised your pa his land would not be squandered.'

'My husband won't squander my property. You just want it for yourself.'

She cut through the scream with the sharp edge of her scorn: 'What about that weakling's farm in Madison? Who pays the taxes now?'

The girl had no answer to that. Desperate, she faced the lawyer: 'Is there no way, sir, I can get my land from the clutches of this unnatural woman?'

The man coughed; the red rim of his eyes watered with embarrassment: 'I'm afraid,' he cleared his throat, 'you say you can't raise the money . . . I'm afraid ——'

That trapped look as the girl turned away. It had come back to her, now trapped in her bed. As a swoon spreads, she felt the desperate terror of weakness, more desperate where there has been strength. Did the girl see right? Had she stolen the land because she wanted it?

Suddenly, like the popping of a thread in a loom, the struggles

246

of the flesh stopped, and the years backed up and covered her thoughts like the spring freshet she had seen so many times creep over the dark soil. Not in order but, as if they were stragglers trying to catch up, the events of her life passed before her sight that had never been so clear. Sweeping over the mounds of her body rising beneath the quilts came the old familiar odors — the damp, strong, penetrating smell of new-turned ground; the rank, clinging, resistless odor of green-picked feathers stuffed in a pillow by Guinea Nell, thirty odd years ago; tobacco on the mantel, clean and sharp like smelling salts; her father's sweat, sweet like stale oil; the powerful ammonia of manure turned over in a stall; curing hay in the wind; the polecat's stink on the night air, almost pleasant, a sort of commingled scent of all the animals, man and beast; the dry smell of dust under a rug; the over-strong scent of too-sweet fruit trees blooming; the inhospitable wet ashes of a dead fire in a poor white's cabin; black Rebeccah in the kitchen; a wet hound steaming before the fire. There were other odors she could not identify, overwhelming her, making her weak, taking her body and drawing out of it a choking longing to hover over all that she must leave, the animals, the fences, the crops growing in the fields, the houses, the people in them . . .

It was early summer, and she was standing in the garden after dark — she had heard something after the small chickens. Mericy and Yellow Jane passed beyond the paling fence. Dark shadows — gay, full voices. *Where you gwine, gal? I dunno. Jest a-gwine. Where you? To the frolic, do I live. Well, stay off'n yoe back tonight.* Then out of the rich, gushing laughter: *All right, you stay off'n yourn. I done caught de stumbles.* More laughter.

The face of Uncle Ike, head man in slavery days, rose up. A tall Senegalese, he was standing in the crib of the barn unmoved before the bushwhackers. *Nigger, whar is that gold hid? You better tell us, nigger. Down in the well; in the far-place. By God, you black son of a bitch, we'll roast ye alive if you air too contrary to tell. Now, listen ole nigger, Miss McCowan ain't nothen to you no more. You been set free. We'll give ye some of it, a whole sack. Come on, now* — out of the dribbling, leering mouth — *whar air it?* Ike's tall form loomed towards the shadows. In the lamp flame his forehead shone like the point, the core of night. He stood there with no word for answer. As she saw the few white beads of sweat on his forehead, she spoke.

She heard her voice reach through the dark — *You turn that black man loose.* A pause and then — *I know your kind. In better days you'd slip around and set people's barns afire. You shirked the War to live off the old and weak. You don't spare me because I'm a woman. You'd shoot a woman quicker because she had the name of being frail. Well, I'm not frail, and my Navy Six an't frail. Ike, take their guns.* Ike moved and one of them raised his pistol arm. He dropped it, and the acrid smoke stung her nostrils. *Now, Ike, get the rest of their weapons. Their knives, too. One of us might turn our backs.*

On top of the shot she heard the soft pat of her servants' feet. White eyeballs shining through the cracks in the barn. Then: *Caesar, Al, Zebedee, step in here and lend a hand to Ike.* By sun the people had gathered in the yard. Uneasy, silent, they watched her on the porch. She gave the word, and the whips cracked. The mules strained, trotted off, skittish and afraid, dragging the white naked bodies bouncing and cursing over the sod: *Turn us loose. We'll not bother ye no more, lady. You ain't no woman, you're a devil.* She turned and went into the house. It is strange how a woman gets hard when trouble comes a-gobbling after her people.

Worn from memory, she closed her eyes to stop the whirl, but closing her eyes did no good. She released the lids and did not resist. Brother Jack stood before her, handsome and shy, but ruined from his cradle by a cleft palate, until he came to live only in the fire of spirits. And she understood, so clear was life, down to the smallest things. She had often heard tell of this clarity that took a body whose time was spending on the earth. Poor Brother Jack, the gentlest of men, but because of his mark, made the butt and wit of the valley. She saw him leave for school, where he was sent to separate him from his drinking companions, to a church school where the boys buried their liquor in the ground and sipped it up through straws. His letters: *Dear Ma, quit offering so much advice and send me more money. You send barely enough to keep me from stealing.* His buggy wheels scraping the gravel, driving up as the first roosters crowed. *Katharine, Malcolm, I thought you might want*

248

to have a little conversation. Conversation two hours before sun! And down she would come and let him in, and the General would get up, stir up the fire, and they would sit down and smoke. Jack would drink and sing, *If the Little Brown Jug was mine, I'd be drunk all the time and I'd never be sob-er a-gin* — or, *Hog drovers, hog drovers, hog drovers we air, a-courting your darter so sweet and so fair.* They would sit and smoke and drink until she got up to ring the bell.

He stayed as long as the whiskey held out, growing more violent towards the end. She watered his bottles; begged whiskey to make camphor — *Gre't God, Sis Kate, do you sell camphor? I gave you a pint this morning.* Poor Brother Jack, killed in Breckinridge's charge at Murfreesboro, cut in two by a chain shot from an enemy gun. All night long she had sat up after the message came. His body scattered about a splintered black gum tree. She had seen that night, as if she had been on the field, the parties moving over the dark field hunting the wounded and dead. Clyde Bascom had fallen near Jack with a bad hurt. They were messmates. He had to tell somebody; and somehow she was the one he must talk to. The spectral lanterns, swinging towards the dirge of pain and the monotonous cries of *Water*, caught by the river dew on the before-morning air and held suspended over the field in its acrid quilt. There death dripped to mildew the noisy throats ... and all the while relief parties, or maybe it was the burial parties, moving, blots of night, sullenly moving in the viscous blackness.

Her eyes widened, and she looked across the footposts into the room. There was some mistake, some cruel blunder; for there now, tipping about the carpet, hunting in her wardrobe, under the bed, blowing down the fire to its ashes until they glowed in their dryness, stalked the burial parties. They stepped out of the ashes in twos and threes, hunting, hunting and shaking their heads. Whom were they searching for? Jack had long been buried. They moved more rapidly; looked angry. They crowded the room until she gasped for breath. One, gaunt and haggard, jumped on the foot of her bed; rose to the ceiling; gesticulated; argued in animated silence. He leaned forward; pressed his hand upon her leg. She tried to tell him to take it off. Cold and crushing heavy, it pressed her down

249

to the bowels of the earth. Her lips trembled, but no sound came forth. Now the hand moved up to her stomach; and the haggard eyes looked gravely at her, alert, as if they were waiting for something. Her head turned giddy. She called to Dick, to Ants, to Doctor Ed; but the words struck her teeth and fell back in her throat. She concentrated on lifting the words, and the burial parties sadly shook their heads. Always the cries struck her teeth and fell back down. She strained to hear the silence they made. At last from a great distance she thought she heard ... *too late* ... *too late.* How exquisite the sound, like a bell swinging without ringing. Suddenly it came to her. She was dying.

How slyly death slipped up on a body, like sleep moving over the vague boundary. How many times she had laid awake to trick the unconscious there. At last she would know ... But she wasn't ready. She must first do something about Long Gourd. That slut must not eat it up. She would give it to the hands first. He must be brought to understand this. But the spectres shook their heads. Well, let them shake. She'd be damned if she would go until she was ready to go. She'd be damned all right, and she smiled at the meaning the word took on now. She gathered together all the particles of her will; the spectres faded; and there about her were the anxious faces of kin and servants. Edwin had his hands under the cover feeling her legs. She made to raise her own hand to the boy. It did not go up. Her eyes wanted to roll upward and look behind her forehead, but she pinched them down and looked at her grandson.

'You want to say something, Mammy?' — she saw his lips move.

She had plenty to say, but her tongue had somehow got glued to her lips. Truly it was now too late. Her will left her. Life withdrawing gathered like a frosty dew on her skin. The last breath blew gently past her nose. The dusty nostrils tingled. She felt a great sneeze coming. There was a roaring; the wind blew through her head once, and a great cotton field bent before it, growing and spreading, the bolls swelling as big as cotton sacks and bursting white as thunderheads. From a distance, out of the far end of the field, under a sky so blue that it was painful-bright, voices came singing, *Joshua fit the battle of Jericho, Jericho, Jericho — Joshua fit the battle of Jericho, and the walls come a-tumbling down.*

BENNY AND THE BIRD-DOGS

MARJORIE KINNAN RAWLINGS

You can't change a man, no-ways. By the time his mammy turns him loose and he takes up with some innocent woman and marries her, he's what he is. If it's his nature to set by the hearthfire and scratch hisself, you just as good to let him set and scratch. If it's his nature, like Will Dover, my man, to go to the garage in his Sunday clothes and lay down under some backwoods Cracker's old greasy Ford and tinker with it, you just as good to let him lay and tinker. And if it's his nature to cut the fool, why, it's interfering in the ways of Providence even to stop to quarrel with him about it. Some women is born knowing that. Sometimes a woman, like the Old Hen (Uncle Benny's wife, poor soul!), has to quarrel a life-time before she learns it. Then when it does come to her, she's like a cow has tried to jump a high fence and has got hung up on it — she's hornswoggled.

The Old Hen's a mighty fine woman — one of the finest I know. She looks just the way she did when she married Uncle Benny Mathers thirty years ago, except her hair has turned gray, like the feathers on a Gray Hackle game hen. She's plump and pretty and kind of pale from thirty years' fretting about Uncle Benny. She had a disposition, by nature, as sweet as a new cane syrup. When she settled down for a life-time's quarrelling at him, it was for the same reason syrup sours — the heat had just been put to her too long.

I can't remember a time when the Old Hen wasn't quarrelling at Uncle Benny. It begun a week after they was married. He went off prowling by hisself, to a frolic or such as that, and didn't come home until four o'clock in the morning. She was setting up waiting for him. When she crawled him about it, he said, 'Bless Katy, wife, let's sleep now and quarrel in the morning.' So she quarrelled in

251

the morning and just kept it up. For thirty years. Not for mean-
ness — she just kept hoping she could change him.

Change him? When he had takened notice of the way she was
fussing and clucking and ruffing her feathers, he quit calling her by
her given name and begun calling her the Old Hen. That's all I
could ever see she changed him.

Uncle Benny's a sight. He's been constable here at Oak Bluff,
Florida, for twenty years. We figure it keeps him out of worse
trouble to let him be constable. He's the quickest shot in three
counties and the colored folks is all as superstitious of him as if he
was the devil hisself. He's a comical-appearing somebody. He's
small and quick and he don't move — he prances. He has a little
bald sun-tanned head with a rim of white hair around the back of
it. Where the hair ends at the sides of his head, it sticks straight
up over his ears in two little white tufts like goat horns. He's got
bright blue eyes that look at you quick and wicked, the way a goat
looks. That's exactly what he looks and acts like — a mischievous
little old billy-goat. And he's been popping up under folks' noses
and playing tricks on them as long as Oak Bluff has knowed him.
Doc in particular. He loved to torment Doc.

And stay home? Uncle Benny don't know what it is to stay
home. The Old Hen'll cook hot dinner for him and he won't come.
She'll start another fire in the range and warm it up for him about
dusk-dark and he won't come. She'll set up till midnight, times till
daybreak, and maybe just about the time the east lightens and the
birds gets to whistling good, he'll come home. Where's he been?
He's been with somebody 'gatoring, or with somebody catching
crabs to Salt Springs; he's been to a square-dance twenty miles
away in the flat-woods; he's been on the highway in that Ford car,
just rambling as long as his gas held out — and them seven pieded
bird-dogs setting up in the back keeping him company.

It was seven years ago, during the Boom, that he bought the
Model-T and begun collecting bird-dogs. Everybody in Florida was
rich for a while, selling gopher holes to the Yankees. Now putting
an automobile under Uncle Benny was like putting wings on a
wild-cat — it just opened up new territory. Instead of rambling
over one county, he could ramble over ten. And the way he drove

— like a bat out of Torment. He's one of them men just loves to cover ground. And that car and all them bird-dogs worked on the Old Hen like a quart of gasoline on a campfire. She really went to raring. I tried to tell her then 'twasn't no use to pay him no mind, but she wouldn't listen.

I said, 'It's just his nature. You can' do a thing about it but take it for your share and go on. You and Uncle Benny is just made different. You want him home and he don't want to be home. You're a barnyard fowl and he's a wild fowl.'

'Mis' Dover,' she said, 'it's easy for you to talk. Your man runs a garage and comes home nights. You don't know how terrible it is to have a man that prowls.'

I said, 'Leave him prowl.'

She said, 'Yes, but when he's on the prowl, I don't know no more where to look for him than somebody's tom-cat.'

I said, 'If 'twas me, I wouldn't look for him.'

She said, 'Moonlight nights he's the worst. Just like the varmints.'

I said, 'Don't that tell you nothing?'

She said, 'If he'd content hisself with prowling — but he ain't content until he cuts the fool. He takes that Ford car and them seven bird-dogs and maybe a pint of moonshine, and maybe picks up Doc to prowl with him, and he don't rest until he's done something crazy. What I keep figuring is, he'll kill hisself in that Ford car, cutting the fool.'

I said, 'You don't need to fret about him and that Ford. What's unnatural for one man is plumb natural for another. And cutting the fool is so natural for Uncle Benny, it's like a bird in the air or a fish in water — there won't no harm come to him from it.'

She said, 'Mis' Dover, what the devil throws over his back has got to come down under his belly.'

I said, 'Uncle Benny Mathers is beyond rules and sayings. I know men-folks, and if you'll listen to me, you'll settle down and quit quarrelling and leave him go his way in quiet.'

I happened to be in on it this spring, the last time the Old Hen ever quarrelled at Uncle Benny. Me and Doc was both in on it. It was the day of old lady Weller's burying. Doc carried me in his car to the cemetery. My Will couldn't leave the garage, because the trucks hauling the Florida oranges north was bringing in pretty good business. Doc felt obliged to go to the burying. He's a patent-medicine salesman — a big fat fellow with a red face and yellow hair. He sells the Little Giant line of remedies. Old lady Weller had been one of his best customers. She'd taken no nourishment the last week of her life except them remedies, and Doc figured he ought to pay her the proper respect and show everybody he was a man was always grateful to his customers.

Uncle Benny and the Old Hen went to the burying in the Model-T. And the seven bird-dogs went, setting up in the back seat. They always went to the buryings.

Uncle Benny said, 'Walls nor chains won't hold 'em. Better to have 'em go along riding decent and quiet, than to bust loose and foller the Model-T like a daggone pack of bloodhounds.'

That was true enough. Those bird-dogs could hear that old Ford crank up and go off in low gear, clear across the town. They'd always hope it was time to go bird-hunting again, and here they'd come, trailing it. So there were the bird-dogs riding along to old lady Weller's burying, with their ears flopping and their noses in the air for quail. As constable, Uncle Benny sort of represented the town, and he was right in behind the hearse. I mean, that car was a pain, to be part of a funeral procession. In the seven years he'd had it, he'd all but drove it to pieces, and it looked like a rusty, mangy razor-back hog. The hood was thin and narrow, like a shoat's nose — you remember the way all Model-T Fords were built. It had no top to it, nor no doors to the front seat, and the back seat rose up in a hump where the bird-dogs had squeezed the excelsior chitlin's out of it.

The Old Hen sat up stiff and proud, not letting on she minded. Doc and I figured she'd been quarrelling at Uncle Benny about the bird-dogs, because when one of them put his paws on her shoulders and begun licking around her ears, she turned and smacked the breath out of him.

The funeral procession had just left the Oak Bluff dirt road and turned onto No. 9 Highway, when the garage-keeper at the bend ran out.

He hollered, 'I just got a 'phone call for Uncle Benny Mathers from the high sheriff!'

So Uncle Benny cut out of the procession and drove over to the pay station by the kerosene tank to take the message. He caught up again in a minute and called to Doc, 'A drunken nigger is headed this way in a Chevrolet and the sheriff wants I should stop him.'

About that time here come the Chevrolet and started to pass the procession, wobbling back and forth as if it had the blind staggers. You may well know the nigger was drunk or he wouldn't have passed a funeral. Uncle Benny cut out of line and took out after him. When he saw who was chasing him, the nigger turned around and headed back the way he'd come from. Uncle Benny was gaining on him when they passed the hearse. The bird-dogs begun to take an interest and rared up, barking. What does Uncle Benny do but go to the side of the Chevrolet so the nigger turns around — and then Uncle Benny crowded him so all he could do was to shoot into line in the funeral procession. Uncle Benny cut right in after him and the nigger shot out of the line and Uncle Benny crowded him in again.

I'll declare, I was glad old lady Weller wasn't alive to see it. She'd had no use for Uncle Benny, she'd hated a nigger, and she'd despised dogs so to where she kept a shotgun by her door to shoot at them if one so much as crossed her cornfield. And here on the way to her burying where you'd figure she was entitled to have things the way she liked them, here was Uncle Benny chasing a nigger in and out of line, and seven bird-dogs were going Ki-yippity-yi! Ki yippity-yi! Ki-yippity-yi! I was mighty proud the corpse was no kin to me.

The Old Hen was plumb mortified. She put her hands over her face and when the Ford would swerve by or cut in ahead of us, Doc and me could see her swaying back and forth and suffering. I don't scarcely need to say Uncle Benny was enjoying hisself. If he'd looked sorrowful-like, as if he was just doing his duty, you could of forgive him. Near a filling-station the Chevrolet shot ahead and stopped and the nigger jumped out and started to run. Uncle Benny stopped and climbed out of the Ford and drew his pistol and called 'Stop!' The nigger kept on going.

Now Uncle Benny claims that shooting at niggers in the line of duty is what keeps him in practice for bird-shooting. He dropped a ball to the right of the nigger's heel and he dropped a ball to the left of it. He called 'Stop!' and the nigger kept on going. Then Uncle Benny took his pistol in both hands and took a slow aim and he laid the third ball against the nigger's shin-bone. He dropped like a string-haltered mule.

Uncle Benny said to the man that ran the filling-station, 'Get your gun. That there nigger is under arrest and I deputize you to keep him that-a-way. The sheriff'll be along to pick him up direckly.'

He cut back into the funeral procession between us and the hearse, and we could tell by them wicked blue eyes he didn't know when he'd enjoyed a burying like the old lady Weller's. When we got back from the burying, he stopped by Will's garage. The Old Hen was giving him down-the-country.

She said, 'That was the most scandalous thing I've ever knowed you to do, chasing that nigger in and out of Mis' Weller's funeral.'

Uncle Benny's eyes begun to dance and he said, 'I know it, wife, but I couldn't help it. 'Twasn't me done the chasing — it was the Model-T.'

Doc got into it then and sided with the Old Hen. He gets excited, the way fat men do, and he swelled up like a spreading adder.

'Benny,' he said, 'you shock my modesty. This ain't no occasion for laughing nor lying.'

Uncle Benny said, 'I know it, Doc. I wouldn't think of laughing nor lying. You didn't know I've got that Ford trained, I've got it trained to where it'll do two things. It's helped me chase so many niggers, I've got it to where it just naturally takes out after 'em by itself.'

Doc got red in the face and asked, real sarcastic, 'And what's the other piece of training?'

Uncle Benny said, 'Doc, that Ford has carried me home drunk so many times, I've got it trained to where it'll take care of me and carry me home safe when I ain't fitten.'

Doc spit half-way across the road and he said, 'You lying old jay-bird.'

Uncle Benny said, 'Doc, I've got a pint of moonshine, and if you'll come go camping with me to Salt Springs this evening, I'll prove it.'

The Old Hen spoke up and she said, 'Benny, Heaven forgive you for I won't if you go on the prowl again before you've cleared the weeds out of my old pindar field. I'm a month late now, getting it planted.'

Doc loves Salt Springs crab and mullet as good as Uncle Benny does, and I could see he was tempted.

But he said, 'Benny, you go along home and do what your wife wants, and when you're done — when she says you're done — then we'll go to Salt Springs.'

So Uncle Benny and the Old Hen drove off. Doc watched after them.

He said, 'Anyways, cutting the fool at a burying had ought to last Benny quite a while.'

I said, 'You don't know him. Cutting the fool don't last him no time at all.'

I was right. I ain't no special wise a woman, but if I once know a man, I can come right close to telling you what he'll do. Uncle Benny hadn't been gone hardly no time, when somebody come by the garage hollering that he'd done set the Old Hen's pindar field on fire.

I said to Doc, 'What did I tell you? The last thing in the world was safe for that woman to do, was to turn him loose on them weeds. He figured firing was the quickest way to get shut of them.'

Doc said, 'Let's go see.'

We got in his car and drove out to Uncle Benny's place. Here was smoke rolling up back of the house, and the big live oak in the yard was black with soldier blackbirds the grass fire had drove out of the pindar field. The field hadn't had peanuts in it since fall, but bless Katy, it was full of something else. Uncle Benny's wife had it plumb full of setting guinea-hens. She hadn't told him, because he didn't like guineas.

Far off to the west corner of the field was the Old Hen, trying to run the guineas into a coop. They were flying every which-a-way and hollering *Po-drac!* Pod-rac! the way guineas holler. All the young uns in the neighborhood were in the middle of the field, beating out the grass fire with palmettos. And setting up on top of the east gate, just as unconcerned, was Uncle Benny, with them two little horns of white hair curling in the heat. Now what do you reckon he was doing? He had all seven of them bird-dogs running back and forth retrieving guinea eggs. He'd say now and again, 'Dead — fetch!' and they'd wag their tails and go hunt up another nest and here they'd come, with guinea eggs carried gentle in their mouths. He was putting the eggs in a basket.

When the commotion was over, and the fire out, and everybody gone but Doc and Me, we went to the front porch to set down and rest. The Old Hen was wore out. She admitted it was her fault not letting Uncle Benny know about the setting guinea-hens. She was about to forgive him setting the field afire, because him and the bird-dogs had saved the guinea eggs. But when we got to the porch, here lay the bird-dogs in the rocking-chairs. There was one to every chair, rocking away and cutting their eyes at her. Their coats and paws were smuttied from the burnt grass — and the Old Hen had put clean sugar-sacking covers on every blessed chair that morning. That settled it. She was stirred up anyway about the way he'd cut the fool at the burying, and she really set in to quarrel at Uncle Benny. And like I say, it turned out to be the last piece of quarrelling she ever done.

She said to him, 'You taught them bird-dogs to rock in a rocking-chair just to torment me. Ever' beast or varmint you've brought home, you've learned to cut the fool as bad as you do.'

'Now wife, what beast or varmint did I ever learn to cut the fool?'

'You learned the 'coon to screw the tops of my syrup cans. You learned the 'possum to hang upside down in my cupboard, and I'd go for a jar of maybe pepper relish and put my hand on him. . . . There's been plenty of such as that. I've raised ever'thing in the world for you but a stallion horse.'

Doc said, 'Give him time, he'll have one of them stabled in the kitchen.'

'Bird-dogs is natural to have around,' she said. 'I was raised to bird-dogs. But it ain't natural for 'em to rock in a rocking-chair.

There's so terrible many of them, and when they put in the night on the porch laying in the rocking-chairs and rocking, I don't close my eyes for the fuss.'

Uncle Benny said, 'You see, Doc? You see, Mis' Dover? She's always quarrelling that me and the dogs ain't never home at night. Then when we do come in, she ain't willing we should all be comf'table.

'We just as good to go on to Salt Springs, Doc. Wait while I go in the house and get my camping outfit and we'll set out.'

He went in the house and came out with his camping stuff. She knowed he was gone for nobody knew how long.

We walked on down to the gate and the Old Hen followed, sniffling a little and twisting the corner of her apron.

'Benny,' she said, 'please don't go to Salt Springs. You always lose your teeth in the Boil.'

'I ain't lost 'em but three times,' he said, and he cranked up the Model-T and climbed in. 'I couldn't help losing 'em the first time. That was when I was laughing at the Yankee casting for bass, and his plug caught me in the open mouth and lifted my teeth out. Nor I couldn't help it the second time, when Doc and me was rassling in the rowboat and he pushed me in.'

'Yes,' she said, 'and how'd you lose 'em the third time?'

His eyes twinkled and he shoved the Ford in low. 'Cuttin' the fool,' he said.

'That's just it,' she said, and the tears begun to roll out of her eyes. 'Anybody with false teeth hadn't ought to cut the fool!'

Now I always thought it was right cute, the way Uncle Benny fooled Doc about the trained Ford. You know how the old-timey Fords get the gas — it feeds from the hand-throttle on the wheel. Well, Uncle Benny had spent the day before old lady Weller's funeral at Will's garage, putting in a foot accelerator. He didn't say a word to anybody, and Will and me was the only ones knowed he had it. Doc and Uncle Benny stayed three-four days camping at Salt Springs. Now the night they decided to come home, they'd both had something to drink, but Uncle Benny let on like he was in worse shape than he was.

Doc said, 'Benny, you better leave me drive.'

Uncle Benny pretended to rock on his feet and roll his head and he said, 'I've got that Model-T trained to carry me home, drunk or sober.'

Doc said, 'Never mind that lie again. You get up there in the seat and whistle in the dogs. I'm fixing to drive us home.'

Well I'd of give a pretty to of been in the back seat with them bird-dogs that night when Doc drove the Ford back to Oak Bluff. It's a treat, anyways, to see a fat man get excited. The first thing Doc knowed, the Ford was running away with him. The Ford lights were none too good, and Doc just did clear a stump by the roadside, and he run clean over a black-jack sapling. He looked at the hand throttle on the wheel, and here it was where the car had ought to be going about twenty miles an hour and it was going forty-five. That rascal of an Uncle Benny had his foot on the foot accelerator.

Doc shut off the gas altogether and the Ford kept right on going.

He said, 'Something's the matter.'

Uncle Benny seemed to be dozing and didn't pay no mind. The Ford whipped back and forth in the sand road like a 'gator's tail. Directly they got on to the hard road and the Model-T put on speed. They begun to get near a curve. It was a dark night and the carlights wobbling, but Doc could see it coming. He took a tight holt of the wheel and begun to sweat. He felt for the brakes, but Uncle Benny never did have any.

He said, 'We'll all be kilt.'

When they started to take the curve, the Model-T was going nearly fifty-five — and then just as they got there, all of a sudden it slowed down as if it knowed what it was doing, and went around the curve as gentle as a day-old kitten. Uncle Benny had eased his foot off the accelerator. Doc drawed a breath again.

It's a wonder to me that trip didn't make Doc a nervous wreck. On every straightaway the Ford would rare back on its haunches and stretch out like a gray hound. Every curve they come to, it would go to it like a jack-rabbit. Then just as the sweat would pour down Doc's face and the drops would splash on the wheel, and he'd gather hisself together to jump, the Ford would slow down.

It was a hot spring night, but Uncle Benny says Doc's teeth were chattering. The Model-T made the last mile lickety-brindle with the gas at the hand-throttle shut off entirely — and it coasted down in front of Will's garage and of its own free will come to a dead stop.

It was nine o'clock at night. Will was just closing up and I had locked the candy and cigarette counter and was waiting for him. There was a whole bunch of the men and boys around, like always, because the garage is the last place in Oak Bluff to put the lights out. Doc climbed out of the Ford trembling like a dish of custard. Uncle Benny eased out after him and I looked at him and right away I knowed he'd been up to mischief.

Doc said, 'I don't know how he done it — but dogged if he wasn't telling the truth when he said he had that blankety-blank Model-T trained to carry him home when he ain't fitten.'

Will asked, 'How come?' and Doc told us. Will looked at me and begun to chuckle and we knowed what Uncle Benny had done to him. I think maybe I would of let Uncle Benny get away with it, but Will couldn't keep it.

'Come here, Doc,' he said. 'Here's your training.'

I thought the bunch would laugh Doc out of town. He swelled up like a toad-fish and he got in his car without a word and drove away.

It's a wonderful thing just to set down and figure out how many different ways there are to be crazy. We never thought of Uncle Benny as being really crazy. We'd say, 'Uncle Benny's cutting the fool again,' and we'd mean he was just messing around some sort of foolishness like a daggone young un. We figured his was what you might call the bottom kind of craziness. The next would be the half-witted. The next would be the senseless. The next would be what the colored folks call 'mindless.' And clear up at the top would be what you'd call cold-out crazy. With all his foolishness, we never figured Uncle Benny was cold-out crazy.

Well, we missed Uncle Benny from Oak Bluff a day or two. When I came to ask questions, I found he'd gone on a long prowl and was over on the Withlacoochie River camping with some oyster

261

fishermen. I didn't think much about it, because he was liable to stay off that-a-way. But time rocked on and he didn't show up. I dropped by his house to ask the Old Hen about him. She didn't know a blessed thing.

She said, 'Ain't it God's mercy we've got no young uns? The pore things would be as good as fatherless.'

And then a few days later Doc came driving up to the garage. He got out and blew his nose and we could see his eyes were red.

He said, 'Ain't it awful! I can't hardly bear to think about it.'

Will said, 'Doc, if you know bad news, you must be carrying it. Ain't nothing sorrowful I know of, except the Prohi's have found Philbin's still.'

Doc said, 'Don't talk about such little accidents at a time like this. You don't mean you ain't heard about Benny?'

The bunch was there and they all perked up, interested. They knowed if it was Uncle Benny, they could expect 'most any news.

I said, 'We ain't heard a word since he went off to the west coast.'

'You ain't heard about him going crazy?'

I said, 'Doc, you mean being crazy. He's always been that-a-way.'

'I mean being crazy and going crazy. Pore ol' Benny Mathers has gone really cold-out crazy.'

Well, we all just looked at him and we looked at one another. And it came over the whole bunch of us that we weren't surprised. A nigger setting by the free air hose said, 'Do, Jesus!' and eased away to tell the others.

Doc blew his nose and wiped his eyes and he said, 'I'm sure we all forgive the pore ol' feller all the things he done. He wasn't responsible. I feel mighty bad, to think the hard way I've often spoke to him.'

Will asked, 'How come it to finally happen?'

Doc said, 'He'd been up to some foolishness all night, raring through some of them Gulf coast flat-woods. Him and the fellers he was camping with was setting on the steps of the camp-house after breakfast. All of a sudden Uncle Benny goes to whistling, loud and shrill like a jay-bird. Then he says, "I'm Sampson," and he begun to tear down the camp-house.'

262

Will asked, 'What'd they do with him?'

Doc said, 'You really ain't heard? I declare, I can't believe the news has come so slow. They had a terrible time holding him and tying him. They got in the doctors and the sheriff and they takened pore ol' Uncle Benny to the lunatic asylum at Chattahoochie.'

Doc wiped his eyes and we all begun to sniffle and our eyes to burn. I declare, it was just as if Uncle Benny Mathers had died on us.

I said, 'Oh, his pore wife ——'

Will said, 'We'll have to be good to him and go see him and take him cigarettes and maybe slip him a pint of 'shine now and again.'

I said, 'The way he loved his freedom — shutting him up in the crazy-house will be like putting a wildcat in a crocus sack.'

Doc said, 'Oh, he ain't in the asylum right now. He's broke loose. That's what makes me feel so bad. He's headed this way, and no telling the harm he'll do before he's ketched again.'

Everybody jumped up and begun feeling in their hip pockets for their guns.

Doc said, 'No use to try to put no guns on him. He's got his'n, and they say he's shooting just as accurate as ever.'

That was enough for me. I ran back of the counter at the garage and begun locking up.

I said, 'Doc, you're a sight. 'Tain't no time to go to feeling sorry for Uncle Benny and our lives and property in danger.'

Doc said, 'I know, but I knowed him so long and I knowed him so good. I can't help feeling bad about it.'

I said, 'Do something about it. Don't just set there, and him liable to come shooting his way in any minute.'

Doc said, 'I know, but what can anybody do to stop him? Pore man, with all them deputies after him.'

Will said, 'Deputies?'

Doc said, 'Why, yes. The sheriff at Ocala asked me would I stop along the road and leave word for all the deputies to try and ketch him. Pore ol' Benny, I'll swear. I hated doing it the worst way.'

I scooped the money out of the cash register and I told them, 'Now, men, I'm leaving. I've put up with Uncle Benny Mathers when he was drunk and I've put up with him when he was cutting

263

the fool. But the reckless way he drives that Ford and the way he shoots a pistol, I ain't studying on messing up around him and him gone cold-out crazy.'

Doc said, 'Ain't a thing in the world would stop him when he goes by, and all them deputies after him, but a barricade acrost the road.'

I said, 'Then for goodness' sake, you sorry, low-down, no-account, varminty white men tear down the wire fence around my chicken yard and fix Uncle Benny a barricade.'

Doc said, 'I just hated to suggest it.'

Will said, 'He'd slow down for the barricade and we could come in from behind and hem him in.'

Doc said, 'It'll be an awful thing to hem him in and have to see him sent back to Chattahoochie.'

Will said, 'I'll commence pulling out the posts and you-all can wind up the fencing.'

They worked fast and I went out and looked up the road now and again to see if Uncle Benny was coming. Doc had stopped at the Standard filling-station on his way, to leave the news, and we could see the people stirring around and going out to look, the same as we were doing. When we dragged the roll of wire fencing out into the road we hollered to them so they could see what we were doing and they all cheered and waved their hats. The word had spread, and the young uns begun traipsing bare-footed down to the road, until some of their mammies ran down and cuffed them and hurried them back home out of the way of Uncle Benny. The men strung the fencing tight across the road between the garage on one side and our smoke-house on the other. They nailed it firm at both ends.

Doc said, 'Leave me drive the last nail, men — it may be the last thing I can do for Benny this side of Chattahoochie.'

I talked the men into unloading their guns.

'He'll have to stop when he sees the barricade,' I said, 'and then you can all go in on him with your guns drawed and capture him. I just can't bear to a loaded gun being drawed on him, for fear of somebody getting excited and shooting him.'

Doc wiped the sweat off his forehead and he said, 'Men, this is a mighty serious occasion. I'd be mighty proud if you'd all have a little snort on me,' and he passed the bottle.

'Here's to Uncle Benny, the way we all knowed him before he went cold-out crazy,' he said.

And then we heard a shouting up the dirt road and young uns whistling and women and girls screaming and chickens scattering.

'Yonder comes Uncle Benny!'

And yonder he came.

The Model-T was swooping down like a bull-bat after a mosquito. The water was boiling up out of the radiator in a foot-high stream. The seven pieded bird-dogs were hanging out of the back seat and trembling as if they craved to tell the things they'd seen. And behind Uncle Benny was a string of deputy sheriffs in Fords and Chevrolets and motor-cycles that had gathered together from every town between Oak Bluff and Ocala. And Uncle Benny was hunched over the steering wheel with them two tufts of goat-horn hair sticking up in the breeze — and the minute I laid eyes on him I knowed he wasn't one mite crazier than he ever had been. I knowed right then Doc had laid out to get even with him and had lied on him all the way down the road.

It was too late then. I knowed, whatever happened, there'd be people to the end of his life would always believe it. I knowed there'd be young uns running from him and niggers hiding. And I knowed there wasn't a thing in the world now could keep him out of Chattahoochie for the time being. I knowed he'd fight when he was taken, and all them mad and hot and dusty deputies would get him to the lunatic asylum quicker than a black snake can cross hot ashes. And once a man that has cut the fool all his life, like Uncle Benny, is in the crazy house, there'll be plenty of folks to say to keep him there.

It was too late. Uncle Benny was bearing down toward the garage and right in front of him was the barricade.

Doc hollered, 'Be ready to jump on him when he stops!'

Stop? Uncle Benny stop? He kept right on coming. The sight of that chicken-wire barricade was no more to him than an aggravation. Uncle Benny and the Model-T dived into the barricade like a water-turkey into a pool. The barricade held. And the next

265

thing we knowed, the Ford had somersaulted over the fencing and crumpled up like a paper shoebox and scattered bird-dogs over ten acres and laid Uncle Benny in a heap over against the wall of the smokehouse. I was raised to use the language of a lady, but I couldn't hold in.

'Doc,' I said, 'you low-down son of a ——'

He said, 'Mis' Dover, the name's too good. I've killed my friend.'

Killed him? Killed Uncle Benny? It can't be done until the Almighty Hisself hollers 'Sooey!' Uncle Benny was messed up considerable, but him nor none of the bird-dogs was dead.

The doctor took a few stitches in him at the garage before he come to, and tied up his head right pretty in a white bandage. We left Will to quiet the deputies and we put Uncle Benny in Doc's car and carried him home to the Old Hen. Naturally, I figured it would set her to quarrelling. Instead, it just brought out all her sweetness. I can guess a man, but I can't guess another woman.

'The pore ol' feller,' she said. 'I knowed he had it coming to him. What the devil throws over his back ——. I knowed he'd kill hisself in that Ford car, cutting the fool and prowling. The biggest load is off my mind. Now,' she said, 'now, by God's mercy, when it did come to him, he got out alive.'

She began fanning him with a palmetto fan where he lay on the bed, and Doc poured out a drink of 'shine to have ready for him when he come to. Doc's hand was trembling. Uncle Benny opened his eyes. He eased one hand up to the bandage across his head and he groaned and grunted. He looked at Doc as if he couldn't make up his mind whether or not to reach for his pistol. Doc put the 'shine to his mouth and Uncle Benny swallowed. Them wicked blue eyes begun to dance.

'Doc,' he said, 'how will I get home when I'm drunk, now you've tore up my trained Ford?'

Doc broke down and cried like a little baby.

'I ain't got the money to replace it,' he said, 'but I'll give you my car. I'll carry the Little Giant line of remedies on foot.'

Uncle Benny said, 'I don't want your car. It ain't trained.'

Doc said, 'Then I'll tote you on my back, anywheres you say.'

The Old Hen let in the bird-dogs, some of them limping a little, and they climbed on the bed and beat their tails on the counterpane and licked Uncle Benny. We felt mighty relieved things had come out that way.

Uncle Benny was up and around in a few days, with his head bandaged, and him as pert as a woodpecker. He just about owned Oak Bluff — all except the people that did like I figured, never did get over the idea he'd gone really crazy. Most people figured he'd had a mighty good lesson and it would learn him not to cut the fool. The Old Hen was happy as a bride. She was so proud to have the Ford torn up, and no money to get another, that she'd even now and again pet one of the bird-dogs. She waited on Uncle Benny hand and foot and couldn't do enough to please him.

She said to me, 'The pore ol' feller sure stays home nights now.'

Stay home? Uncle Benny stay home? Two weeks after the accident the wreck of the Model-T disappeared from behind the garage where Will had dragged it. The next day the seven bird-dogs disappeared. The day after that Doc and Uncle Benny went to Ocala in Doc's car. Will wouldn't answer me when I asked him questions. The Old Hen stopped by the garage and got a Coca-Cola and she didn't know any more than I did. Then Will pointed down the road.

He said, 'Yonder he comes.'

And yonder he came. You could tell him way off by the white bandage with the tufts of hair sticking up over it. He was scrooched down behind the wheel of what looked like a brand-new automobile. Doc was following behind him. They swooped into the garage.

Will said, 'It's a new second-hand body put on the chassis and around the engine of the old Ford.'

Uncle Benny got out and he greeted us.

He said, 'Will, it's just possible it was the motor of the Model-T that had takened the training. The motor ain't hurt, and me and Doc are real hopeful.'

The Old Hen said, 'Benny, where'd you get the money to pay for it?'

He said, 'Why, a daggone bootlegger in a truck going from

267

Miami to New York bought the bird-dogs for twenty-five dollars apiece. The low-down rascal knowed good and well they was worth seventy-five.'

She brightened some. Getting shut of the bird-dogs was a little progress. She walked over to the car and began looking around it.

'Benny,' she said, and her voice come kind of faintified, 'if you sold the bird-dogs, what's this place back here looks like it was fixed for 'em?'

We all looked, and here was a open compartment-like in the back, fixed up with seven crocus sacks stuffed with corn-shucks. About that time here come a cloud of dust down the road. It was the seven bird-dogs. They were about to give out. Their tongues were hanging out and their feet looked blistered.

Uncle Benny said, 'I knowed they'd jump out of that boot-legger's truck. I told him so.'

I tell you, what's in a man's nature you can't change. It takened the Old Hen thirty years and all them goings-on to learn it. She went and climbed in the front seat of the car and just sat there waiting for Uncle Benny to drive home for his dinner. He lifted the bird-dogs up and set them down to rest on the cornshucks cushions, and he brought them a pan of water.

He said, 'I figure they busted loose just above Lawtey.'

The Old Hen never opened her mouth. She hasn't quarrelled at him from that day to this. She was hornswoggled.

WOMAN IN THE HOUSE

JESSE STUART

THE moon was coming up over that fringe of poplar trees last night when I saw Radburn and Hankas coming through the greenbriar thicket by the pigpen. I knowed jist what had happened when I saw them together. They had been over the hill to Mort Anderson's to get some of that old rotgut licker. I knowed I was going to have a time for the night. I saw them come through the patch of ragweeds this side of the pigpen. Radburn was holding to the apple-tree limbs. Hankas was talking with his hands. I could see them just as plain as day. The moon shined on them and if they had been rabbits I could have shot them both, it was so light. Not even a wind was blowing to make a racket. It was the quietest night a body might nigh ever seed. The pigs thought I was coming to slop them when they passed the pigpen. The pigs grunted a little bit. Then they went back to the old sow.

I heerd Hankas say to Radburn, 'We gotta take the medicine back to Lake. He is cut purty bad. I could see the blood. It is all over my hand, see! People will think I cut Lake with a knife. God Almighty knows I didn't cut Lake with anything.' Then Radburn said to Hankas, 'Be quiet so America can't hear you. If she thinks there's trouble she'll be right into it. She's soon hit me as not. She's soon hit you. I know her. I have lived with her long enough to know her. When we first married and got into a racket she knocked me down the first lick she struck me right above the eye. She didn't have on no knucks neither. She done hit with her plain fist. I've lived with her thirty years now and I know she'll fight. Right when we was first married and my stepma Middie pulled a pistol on Pap, she walked right in and said, "Give me that gun." Then she struck her with her plain fist right above the eye — the same place she allus hits 'em and God only knows how long Middie laid there.'

269

'America allus wuz that way at home. When us kids was playing about the place she whipped all of us but me. I could whip America. I watched and never let her get the first lick. But ever time I whipped her Pap throwed a fit and jumped all over me. I allus told Pap she'd whip the man she married if she ever got the first lick. She allus plugs a body right above the right eye.'

'She is a hard woman to live with but she is a good woman. Last winter I'd a been a dead man if hit hadn't been for my wife. You know Lefty Penix, don't you, Hankas? Well, he come over here and we got a holt of some bad licker. We must have went crazy. We got right over there by the corncrib and started to fight. I don't remember hit. But they said Lefty had the corn-knife that we keep sticking out there in the crib log to cut the cow corn with — He had that knife and was making for my throat. America saw him. And she come running right through the snow shoe-mouth deep and hit Lefty right above the eye. He had long been sobered up before he come to his senses. Both of that man's eyes settled black around them for a week and a big doorknob riz under Lefty's right eye. But my wife saved my life. If she hadn't run out there I'd a been in hell right tonight.'

I could see them comin' up closer to the house. There was Radburn, my man. He wore the same old dirty overalls that he'd been wearing all week in the 'backer patch. They was all gluey and would stand alone in the green 'backer glue. His shirt was dirty and his beard was out all over his face. Just me here and I was ashamed of him. Beadie went home with the little Jurdan girl to stay all night; Fonse and Gilbert went to the Square dance — Libbie and Win went to see Sister Mossy last week and they ain't got back yet — I was right here — well, Pap was here. But he's sick in there in the bed. He can't do nuthin. Pap has one foot in the grave and the other foot ready to slide in. I knowed Hankas and Radburn was drinking that old rotgut they got over to Mort Anderson's. I knowed trouble was a-brewin. Every time Radburn gits a drink he thinks he can lick me. He gits to thinkin about me knockin him down and he wants to try hit over and show me he can lick me. Everytime he gits a drink of that old rotgut in him, hit is a fight here. I knowed what was going to happen.

Before they got up to the house I went in the back room and looked under Radburn's piller. I found his 32 automatic. The moon shined in at the back room window and left a white place on the floor. I stepped out where I could take a good look at the 32. Hit looked right purty fer a pistol. I looked into the chamber and saw that hit was loaded. Then I said to myself, 'Ready Hankas. Don't care if you are my brother. Ready Radburn. I don't care if you are my man. Hit won't be a fist above the eye this time. Hit'll be a bullet.' They come up and opened the door. There was Hankas, my brother, and he's a big man. Some over two hundred that man is, and mean as a copperhead. I could see in the moonlight he had one of them old sour drunkman's frowns on his face. He looked like the Devil. His arms come down nearly to his knees. They are hairy as a dog. His arms is nearly big as fence posts. He had on his old gluey 'backer clothes too. Hankas has a big blocky body without a pound of fat. He's solid as a rock. But he ain't got much of a head. Hit is a little head for sich a big body. I know how us children used to laugh at him and call him 'simlon head.' He'd git so mad. He'd want to fight. He could whip everybody. Well, I said if I ever got a house o' my own I'd whip him or I'd kill him before I'd let him run over me. Pap allus upheld for him at home because Pap was afraid of him and Mother was too.

They come in the house. They hushed talkin for a minute when they come in. Radburn struck a match and lit the lamp. I could see he was drunk as a biled owl. Hankas staggered over to the mantelpiece and helt onto hit long enough to fill his pipe with my best smokin 'backer. He lit his pipe over the lamp and he looked at Radburn. Then he wiped his hands on his gluey overalls. Pon my word I wouldn't be caught wearing dirty a clothes as them men had on. Hankas said to Radburn, 'Call America. Reckon she's here. We got to git the turpentine and git back to Lake. He's cut purty bad. Look at the blood on your hands and on my hands. People will think we cut him. God knows we didn't. I like old Lake. He's a bully good fellar.'

'Yes and think about him layin out there bleedin in that ditch.' I just stepped from the back room into where they was by the mantelpiece. I had the 32 in my bosom. I had my hand on hit.

If they had started anything I aim to let 'm have hit right above the eye. I said, 'Who got cut?' Radburn said, 'W'y America, Lake Burdock got cut. He's out there bleedin in the ditch.' And I said, 'Where did he git cut and when?' Hankas said, 'Don't know how he got cut. He jist got cut 's all we know about hit. He just fell. He's cut on the hip — place big enough to lay your hand in.' And I said, 'This don' sound right. Somebody had to cut him. Let me see your knifes. Both of you drunk and you wouldn't know hit if you did cut him.' Well Hankas looked at Radburn and Radburn looked at Hankas. Then Radburn said, 'Hankus we'd better let her look at our knifes.' They took their knifes out and they wasn't a drap of blood on 'em. I felt so good. I felt like gittin down on my knees and praying to God Almighty. I didn't want 'em to have to go to the pen for knifin. I'd ruther they'd go to the pen for stealing chickens than for knifin. 'Pon my word, Meck,' Radburn said, 'we didn't cut Lake. We didn't cut him. No.' Then I said, 'How in the world did he git cut?' Radburn said, 'I don't know.' Hankas said, 'I don't know.' There Hankas hung to the mantel-piece. The very Devil was in his eyes. I knowed I was going to have trouble that night. The Devil was in his broth a-brewin. I said, 'You ain't takin no turpentine out'n here. You go bring that man to this house. Go now before he bleeds to death.' And they went out the house. Radburn looked at Hankas and Hankas looked at Radburn. They never said a word to each other ner to me.

I walked the floor. I was so uneasy. I was more uneasy than I was the night Brother Tim and Candy got in that cuttin scrape with the Tinsleys. Tim got his right eye cut out, you know, and Candy got his juggle vein nicked a little and a couple of cuts to the holler. But he lived. One of the Tinsleys bled to death. The other lived but ain't been able to work none since. I was so uneasy that night. But I was just about that uneasy this time. I didn't know what had happened. God knows I didn't. Whippoorwills hollerin up there on the hill and some leaves fell off the trees. I could hear them blowin so lonesome. And I jist paced the floor. The moon shined right up there over the hogpen. I could see the moon then jist like I could see hit last night. I could see the rails on the hogpen jist as plain as I can see my hand before me now. I was so uneasy. The moon kept gittin over further in the sky — out past the hogpen and round to the right near the Hoggen's Graveyard. I could see the tombstones over there on that pint. Hit made me so lonesome — jist like last night. I could see the tombstones and the moon. I could hear the whippoorwills hollerin and the dead leaves a rattlin in the wind. I guess some tears come down my cheek. I thought I felt tears runnin down my cheeks. I don't know.

Then I looked through the back room winder and I seed two men coming carrying somethin. Hit looked like a log. They was staggerin up the cowpath from that gate right down yander. I heerd Hankas say, 'Let's put him down Radburn and open the gate.' And I saw them throw the log-lookin thing from their shoulders jist like they'd throw down a sack of corn. They opened the gate. Then they shouldered the man. Mercy, how I felt. I thought, 'Now what if they bring him here and he dies from that cut. We'll all go to the pen. What if he dies on our hands. People will think we kilt him and the Law will git us all fer killin him. Merciful God, what if he's to die here? A dead man in the house. What would we do? What could we do?' But I saw Radburn and Hankas coming wobblin up the yaller bank down yander on this side of the gate. They wobbled like ducks. The moon shined down on them. It was light as day. And here they come carryin that man. The lamp was lit up in the front room and the moonlight come in at the back room winder.

They come right to the front door. Hankas was behind, carryin Lake's shoulders. Radburn was in front, carryin Lake's legs. Radburn shoved open the door and brought him in feet foremost. And he was bleedin frum the seat of the pants. The blood jist poured on the floor like water from the rain-drip. Hankas said, 'Meck, git the turpentine quick. He's bleedin purty bad.' And I said, 'You're so drunk you don't know what you're talkin about. Turpentine ain't goin to stop that blood. Hit takes chimney-sut to stop blood. Stick your head up that fire place there and git some chimney-sut from behind the jam rock. Do hit quick. Put Lake on the bed first.' They throwed Lake down on the bed hard enough to break

273

all the slats. Lake was drunk as the Devil wanted him to be. Then
I said, 'Radburn you pull his pants down so I can see where this
man is cut. We got to do somethin fer him.' Radburn says, 'You
ain't no doctor, air you?' And I said to Radburn, 'I may not be
no doctor but tell me nairy nuther woman that's delivered more
babies in this country than I have, and I'll eat her blood-raw.
Who's cured more sick than I have among cattle and men? Who's
cured more colic and fever than I have? Who does the people come
to when they want help — even for drunken fits and blind billiards
— I guess you remember that mule's front legs that had all the
skin peeled off'n 'em like hit was bark the time he tried to jump
the wire fence — who sewed that up? Never was a scar left. Who
sewed up a duck's back that the hound pups tore the skin off in a
three-cornered fleek? The duck lived, didn't hit? Take that man's
pants down. I aim to look at that cut and if I can I aim to sew hit
up.'

Radburn started undressin Lake. I went into the kitchen and
put a fire in the stove and put water in the tea-kettle. Then I
started to huntin fer some white thread and a darning needle. By
the time the water het, I had the darning needle and the thread.
Radburn had the clothes from off 'n the cut. Hit looked like he
had been whacked with a corn-knife. And I said 'Radburn, let me
look in Lake's overall pockets.' I took his overalls — blood-soaked
and dirty with green 'backer glue. I heerd somethin rattle in the
hip-pocket. And my Lord how hit did stink with that old rotgut
whiskey. And what did I find in the pocket on the seat of his
britches? I found a broken bottle. 'Here's what's cut him,' I said,
'a bottle. He's fell on hit. A rotgut bottle. If hit wasn't fer his
wife I wish hit had cut him in two. He's got as good a woman as
ever the sun shined on and out carvortin 'round like this. Drinkin
'round and leavin his family at home. I'll sew him up this time.
But never again will I do hit.' Radburn looked at Hankas. Hankas
looked at Radburn. They never said a word. Hankas looked mean
as the Devil out'n his black eyes. 'Goin' sew him up, air ye,' he
looked at me and said. And I said, 'Yes I'm going to sew him up
if this darnin needle don't break.'

By this time the water was warm. I brought hit in from the

kitchen. Radburn helt the lamp. I swathed out the deep lash. Lake jist laid there and moaned like a fat hog. Then I put the turpentine on. Hit jist keep bleedin. Hankas give me the chimney-sut and you'd a laughed to a seen Hankas atter he went up behind the jam rock. He was black as a piece of wet chestnut-burr. I daubed the chimney-sut in the lash. I knowed hit would leave a black stripe under the skin when hit healed over. But I didn't care. I wanted to save him on account of his wife, Polly, and his five young 'uns. I used the chimney-sut to stop the blood. I poured in the whole bottle of turpentine to keep hit from gittin sore. Then I pulled up the soft sides of the cut and made Hankas hold them while I used the darnin needle. Lake flinched a little when the needle went through his skin. I took thirty-seven stitches on that man. And when I got through, the stitches was jist as even as if I'd been tuckin up a skirt that was too long.

Hankas jist set and looked at me. The Devil was in his black eyes. I had the pistol in my bosom. I jist wanted to git away so he couldn't git the first lick. I kept my eye on him all the time. I said, 'Pull his pants back on him and throw that glass out of this room, Radburn. Put Lake in the bed. And I don't want any more rotgut whiskey brought in this house tonight.' Hankas said, 'Who's runnin this house? You or Radburn?' And I said, 'I'm runnin my own house and them that don't like hit can git out.' 'Us go, Radburn,' said Hankas. They staggered out. Hankas said when he left the house, 'Poor home, ain't hit, Radburn, when you ain't got a word to say in your own house.' Radburn didn't say a word. He turned and looked back at me. Then they went out into the moonlight, around the corner of the house, under the dark night-shade of the hickory tree — down over the hill toward Reek Finnley's house.

They left me in the house with Lake. He was drunk. I thought he would sober up before they got back and want to know who cut him and what he was doing sewed up. But I had the pistol. I could shoot him if he started anything. I went to the kitchen winder. I looked out. The moon was going down over the corn-field where the boys had cut the early piece of corn. The fodder shocks looked like wigwams between me and the moon. I could

275

hear the lonesome whippoorwill. I could hear the katydids out in the dead grass by the cow lot. I could hear the pigs gruntin. I could hear Lake's breath go up and down and then sizzle like the wind going through the dead sticker-weeds back of the smokehouse on a windy day. And then I heerd the dogs bark over at Reek Finnley's house. I went to the backyard. I looked over at Reek Finnley's place. The house was dark and the moonlight showed on the winder lights. Then I saw the winders lit up with lamplight. I knowed Hankas and Radburn was over there. Then I heerd them talking and cussin around. I heerd Hankas ask Reek if he wanted a drink and Reek said yes. Then I heerd them cussin some more and runnin the dogs over at Reek's house fer barkin at them. I heerd Radburn say, 'I'll git my knife out and straddle that dog's back and cut hit's throat if hit don't shet up that barkin in my ears. I've seed a lot of blood tonight and I wouldn't keer to see a little more.'

Well, I didn't want Lake to sober up. I wanted him to stay drunk till morning. So I hunted fer the whiskey jug that Radburn and Hankas brought in the house but didn't take out again. I found a gallon jug behind the door with a sea-grass string run through hit's gill. I got the jug and I went to the right, over from where Pap was a-layin and I opened Lake's mouth. I poured rotgut from the jug with the other hand. I guess I poured a pint down him. He guzzled hit down and licked his lips. Then I pulled the pistol from under the bosom of my dress. I looked at the little barrel. I said, 'W'y this can't kill a man. I'd ruther trust my fist. The barrel is too little. Look at this little hole. Look at that big man Lake. Look how big Hankas is. Hit would take a bigger pistol than this to kill him. That barrel ain't as big as my middle finger and ain't much longer.' So I took the pistol back to the bed and took the shells out'n hit and put hit under Radburn's piller.

I went and looked behind the meal-barrel and got the double-barrel shotgun. Hit looked more like a gun to me. Long bright-blue barrels glistened in the lamplight. I brought the shellbox from off'n the wallplate. They wan't but two shells in the box. One was loaded with number three shots and one with number fives. I put the shell loaded with number threes in the left-hand barrel fer

276

Hankas. I put the shell loaded with number fives in the right-hand barrel for Radburn. Then I pulled the trunk out and put hit slonch-ways across the corner of the room so I'd have more room to shoot from. I blowed out the lamp and got behind the trunk. I pinted the double-barrel over the trunk and I cocked both triggers and turned the safety off.

The chickens had begin to crow fer midnight. I staid right behind the trunk with the double-barrel in my hands ready to shoot. I seed the fire in Hankas's eyes. The Devil was in his eyes. I jist waited fer him to come back. I knowed he would want to start something. Well, I heerd him comin. I heerd him come up through the cornfield and cuss about the moon going down. I heerd him say he fell on the sharp edge of a cornstalk where the boys had cut the potato-patch of corn. I heerd him cuss about the night gettin so dark. Then they come to the door. Radburn opened the door. He struck a match and lit the lamp. Then he said, 'Wonder where America is?' And then he hollered and hollered, 'America, come here! America, come here! I want some buttermilk. I want fresh water. I want some clean clothes.' I never said a word.

They went over to the bed where Lake was. They pulled them up a couple of cheers and set down by the side of the bed. Radburn said, 'Wonder if that 'll git all right where America sewed up that place?' Hankas said, 'Yes. I'd ruther have her as any doctor that's in Berryville. She's my sister and bad to fight, but I'd ruther have her by my side when I'm sick as anybody I know.' 'Cut on glass, wasn't he, Hankas?' 'That's what America said.' 'Do you reckon she'd swear that if the Law gits us all before the court?' 'Yes, I believe she would.' 'Well, he's drunk ain't he? Air you drunk? Am I drunk?' 'Git that gallon of licker from behind the door, Hankas, and let's have a snip before we take our shoes off.'

Hankas staggered over to the door. He got the jug by the sea-grass string. He took hit over to Radburn. There they set. They wuz jist so drunk they didn't know who hit was in the bed. Radburn put his arms around Hankas. Hankas put his arms around Radburn. Then Hankas said, 'You have got a decent woman, Radburn, but she don't treat you right. Now she has left

277

you.' 'Surely she ain't left me. What will I do about somebody to cook fer me?' 'Yes, she's left you.' 'I'll see.' Then Radburn called, 'America, America, come here! I want a drink of water. My head is killin me, America, come here.' 'Pon my honor hit was right laughable. Then he got down on his knees and looked under the beds. He looked behind the meal-barrel. He looked behind the doors. I leveled the gun right on his head. When he moved, the gun barrels moved. I kept the gun right on him. I kept hit right on his temple. He never did git to the trunk. He went back and set down by Hankas. He said, 'You're right Hankas. She's gone. She's left me.' Now I kept the gun pointed right at them.

Hankas said, 'You got a good woman and you'll miss her some. But hit's the best thing for you. You can live right here by yourself and do your own cookin. Lake can stay with you part of the time. I'll come to see you often. Jist let her go and the Devil take her. You don't need no woman nohow. You can do without a woman more than you can do with a woman. She runs the house. She's hit you with her fist and deadened you two or three times or more than that. She won't do to fool with. Now you can bring the pigpen out here behind the smokehouse and keep the dogs in the back room there at night. You can put your cows in the mule pasture and the mules in the cow pasture. That will make hit closer to milk out there by the sand rocks. You can make hit all right and you'll be a lot safer right here with your childer or without anybody.'

Then they became silent. I kept the shotgun leveled about with their temples. The night out behind the winder was blacker than chimney-sut. The whippoorwills kept hollerin. The katydids kept hollerin out behind the smokehouse. I wasn't skeered a bit. I was jist lonesome. God, but I was lonesome. Three drunk men in the house. One of them a brother fer the Devil. I didn't like hit — all the stuff he was tellin Radburn. I didn't want Radburn to run with him and I told Radburn he would git him in trouble. But Hankas jist come up and got him. He can do hit every time. Radburn 'll jist do anything Hankas says. He'll follow him any place. And when he gits that old rotgut whiskey in him he'll do about anything else.

278

About four o'clock a chicken crowed and Radburn waked from a doze. He said, 'Ain't that boy of Reek's a funny boy? Don't he like licker? W'y when I give him that bottle I had to pull hit away from his lips. But poor boy, Hankas. They have to give him pizen to keep him alive. Hit's the God's truth. They feed that boy pizen. He ain't but ten years old and he weighs two hundred and ten pounds. He walks like a string-haltered hoss. Ever notice him? His face is red as a beet. He's marked with a turkey. Before he come to this world a turkey-gobbler flogged his Mama out by the corncrib one morning. That's what the matter with him.' 'And you say that he has to take pizen medicine so he won't die?' 'Yes, hit takes about all the money that old Reek can make to keep that boy alive. He has that boy that eats pizen and eleven more boys stouter than old Reek is. He has seven girls and they ain't much good.' 'Well, I'll be dogged.' 'Reek is a clever man as you's ever about the house of.' 'Reckon that boy got drunk on the licker you give him?' 'W'y, yes, he got drunk and even old Reek had to hold to the cornstalks to git up the hill when he left us down there in the holler.' 'Well, I'll be dogged.'

I kept the gun right level with their temples. They dozed off again. Lord, how I did pray for daylight. I never closed my eyes for a wink of sleep. I never put in sich a night in all my life. I watched the clock. I could see the minutes was creepin up. I could hear the sparrows workin in the box. Hankas riz up and said, 'Radburn, we forgot somethin. Give me the whiskey quick. We have forgot Pap. We ain't offered Pap no whiskey.'

Radburn got up and walked over to Pap's bed with Hankas. Hankas helt the jug to Pap's lips and said, 'Come on, Pap, and drink with us tonight.' Pap waked from a doze and said, 'I don't want no drink.' 'Come on and have one,' Hankas said. 'Ain't you going to drink with us?' 'No, I ain't going to drink none of that stuff. Hit is a sin. The Lord has saved me and I promised the Lord I wouldn't drink no more licker. I aim to be good as my word.' Then Hankas turned and said, 'I'll be dogged. Lord has saved him and he promised not to drink any more licker to the Lord. Wonder what the Lord wants fer nuthin. Well, I'll be dogged. My own pap won't drink with me and him so nigh the grave.' I kept the

279

double-barrel leveled right on his head. I thought, 'If you start anything here I'll git you with a gun this big. Hit will kill you. This ain't no toy 32. This is a gun that will kill.' Hankas set down. He dozed off to sleep again.

Of all the snorin I ever heerd in my life hit was from them three drunk men. Of all the strange noises — fiddles, shotguns, mauls, hammers, drums, and axes — I could hear all kinds of noises. I prayed for daylight to come. The sparrows begin to chatter in their boxes. The pigs begin to grunt. The whippoorwill shet up. I could hear the quails hollerin down in the crab-grass. I knowed daylight wasn't fer away. I took the shells out'n the gun. I slipped out the back winder. I come around and opened the kitchen door and come through to the meal-barrel. I put the gun behind the meal-barrel. Then I come into the front room. I took Radburn by the shoulder and I said, 'What's all this goin on here? Run me out'n my house last night, didn't you?' And he said, 'I don't remember if I did or didn't.' 'Well, you did,' I says. 'I stayed in the woods all night. The moon went down and hit was so dark I couldn't follow a path out and you was drunk and took the place.' Hankas waked up and I said, 'Brother Hankas, you tried to pour that old rotgut licker down your dyin father's throat. You are a brute.' 'I didn't do nothin like that, did I?' And the tears jist streamed down his beardy face and dripped off the ends of his beard. He got up and sneaked out home. He couldn't look me in the face.

Lake waked up. He put his hand on his hip and hollered, 'Oh Lord God, my hip! Whut is the matter with my hip?' I went out of the room. I guess Radburn must to 'a took his pants down and they both looked at his hip. When I come back in, Radburn looked at me and Lake looked at Radburn. Radburn got the express and hauled Lake home. Before Radburn left with Lake he sneaked up to me and he said, 'I'm plagued to death over whut happened to Lake.'

I never ast whut happened. I knowed whut happened and I wanted to make Radburn tell me, but he did feel too plagued. We both jist hoisted Lake in the springwagon on a feathered tick and hauled him home to Polly. I felt a little uneasy about maybe a little piece of glass was left in the lash and hit might not heal. But in a few days Lake was walking round. I heerd my boy say that he was in the crick with Lake and his body was allus dirty as a pig on the seat. Radburn looked at me. I looked at Radburn. We never said a word.

IF ONLY

JOHN PEALE BISHOP

It was not until after the war that the Sabines moved into Mordington. The farm, always lonely, had become impossible, their father being dead, their brothers dead, and the mother blind. Remote, the stone farmhouse was set on a gusty hill and hidden from all roads by woodland. After the war they were always afraid. In the orchards the apples ripened and unpicked fell, or rotted on the branch; rank with weeds the rolling fields went down to the Shenandoah; their gardens were stolen. Once a week perhaps they heard a rickety wagon crawl down a lane. It called at the ferry and after a long time the answering halloo would come across the water. The long flat-bottomed boat was poled by a grizzled black who had been their slave. Beyond the river were the mountains. In the slave quarters a few Negroes stayed on.

They were young then, Ellen and Lou, and at night alone but for an old woman whose tears still gathered under blinded eyelids. At night the doors slammed upstairs where there was no one. Their mother sat with hands held straight on the worn arms of her chair and cried without meaning.

She had cried her eyes out, they said, weeping for one son who had lost three. Old Sabine was a Unionist. When the first two boys fell in battles that went to the Confederates, she was sarcastic and proud. When Jimmy, in the last month of the war, sank wearily, exhausted by dysentery, she could only weep. The father was silent; he had paid for his sons' uniforms and known they were ashamed of him. He walked awkwardly about the house, his strong shoulders lowered like a bull's. He could not speak without bringing on reproaches which ended still in tears. Jimmy was the youngest of the boys — younger than either of the girls.

Mordington is a small county seat at the end of the Valley of

282

the Shenandoah. From a distance, lost in leaves, nothing of the town appears but the spires of churches and the court house clock. They came in from the country to find the town already abandoned by time and since the war no longer in Virginia. But this the Sabines did not recognize. Congress might admit the treacherous western counties as a state. They could not. So for them there was no West Virginia. They continued having their mail sent to Mordington, Virginia, and when their letters were delayed felt they had their private revenge on Abraham Lincoln, Lord John Russell, and Napoleon III — all three at once — for not having recognized the Confederacy.

They were well-off, for their father in his obstinacy had saved them from the common poverty of the time. They lived comfortably and admitted nothing that touched their pride.

The town they accepted with all its past, and each year it seemed to them a little grander. Great men had lived there, and more than once Mordington had altered the history of the country. The jail is the usual one of bricks painted a brighter red; on summer evenings the jailor's daughters sit on the narrow porch with palm-leaf fans. The Court House lifts its cupola above a cloud of trees to show a clockface to every quarter of the town; under the columns of the portico — colored a dirty serviceable yellow — the pavement is spattered with the droppings of hundreds of blackbirds that nightly roost in the yard. Yet the jail had once held a fatal prisoner, in the Court House a decision had been made that had sundered the Republic. The Sabines did not forget it, nor that afterwards, because of the old murderer whom the North had made a martyr, the town had suffered much and was poor.

I

They came down that morning to find the kitchen dark, the shutters closed, and no one there. Beside the sink, on the draining board, the cold dishes of the night's supper were stacked, scraped, but not washed. And they knew their cook was gone.

(When this was cannot be said, for the Sabines themselves could never remember — but it was on a Monday and when Ellen had

283

thrown back the shutters the morning was warm, with murmurs of summer and the scattered shadows of leaves on the sunlit sill.)

This was the Negress' usual departure, for Selly needed no other notice than the increasing sun. Through the winter she worked, and fed the four children of her unchastity at the Sabines' larder. But with the first warm days she was gone.

After breakfast, they explored, timidly, knowing what they would find. Dust was everywhere. On top of the cupboard, it lay in a winter's thickness. The closet gave up more unwashed dishes and stale ends of food, chunks of suet, crusts of bread, a shrivelled hambone and old biscuits which the mice had not only nibbled, but completely digested. It was disgusting! From the lower doors of the cupboard, pots and skillets tumbled out, sad-irons and waffle-irons, kettles and griddles, a black and greasy confusion. They were amazed. They had not believed such filth could be in their kitchen! There were brooms worn to stubs — but not it would seem with sweeping — and rags that might have been used for scouring came out of strange hiding places, wadded in dirt and showing still the imprint of Selly's wet fingers. In the corner under the sink, cockroaches had made themselves familiar.

'I'm glad she's gone,' said Ellen. 'I'm tired of Selly. I'm tired of her trifling ways.' But she looked dismayed.

'But Ellen — Selly's our nigger!' Lou sat down.

'She's our cook,' said Ellen, 'but she's not our nigger.'

'But she should have been. By rights, all the Hannions should have been our niggers! If only ——'

'And a dirty, trifling lot they were too, those Hannions. Look at this!' Ellen had found the table drawer. 'We'll have to clean the kitchen. I can't have anybody coming in here after Selly.'

They cleaned. As usual after Selly's summer departure they cleaned. For four days they swept, they scraped; they scoured with soap and polished with pumice. Ellen mounted on chairs and stepladders to wash the shelves of closet and cupboard while Lou sat at the table and from white paper cut scallops and patterns of lace to line them. Ellen bent her knees over the floor with scrub-brush and bucket; Lou washed the window and returned to her sitting. Ellen wrestled with the serious pots and kettles while Lou

284

at the table, with short deft fingers — always a little too red, as though she had just dipped them in hot water — polished silver and glass. Applying paste, or rubbing with cloths, her bangs trembled; she talked while she worked, helping Ellen with suggestions.

Four days they cleaned, and both felt the unaccustomed labor. They had little to eat, for when Ellen was tired not much cooking was done. Both drank more coffee than was good for them. But at the end of the day Lou had still the strength to go driving. The weather continued fine and every evening George Hite came for her. They drove off in the yellow varnished dogcart behind the docked bays and Ellen was left alone in the kitchen. Darkness fell while she washed the dishes.

Friday morning she did not come downstairs. She had found her only retreat from her sister's sweet insistence and kept her bed with a sick headache.

Lou was late with the breakfast. She came in gaily. Ellen brought up her drawn cheeks from the pillow.

'Don't you want the shade up?' Lou suggested.

'Leave it the way it is,' moaned Ellen. 'I've fixed it.'

'But, Ellen, I was only trying to make you comfortable!'

'How can I be comfortable with a sick headache?' The voice from the coverlets faintly screamed, like a parrot irritable behind its wires. She turned her face to the green-darkened window. It made her look quite ill.

'O, very well!' said Lou. She caught her breath and held it between parted teeth. Ellen's bed was wide. The posts were not high and the top of each was a pinecone cut from cherry wood. On this bed their mother had died.

Lou closed the door softly and tiptoed along the corridor, down the stairs, leaning so hard against the balustrade that it creaked. In the lower hall she let her breath come again.

She too was tired. She had dressed slowly that morning and with care; and moving through the empty rooms Lou was white and flimsy with ruffles. The loneliness was oppressing; she came into the parlor, but not even the long mirror consoled her; she saw the black moire ribbon at her throat and dangling from her ears tiny baskets of fruit, cut from coral, and thought how she had given her youth to her mother, who had taken ten years to die. She let her fingers run along the table; picked up a book which she did not read. Nothing had been touched for days, nothing was changed. Only on the surface of walnut and rosewood, in the crevices of roses carved on the backs of chairs, dust had gathered.

'What we need,' she said, 'is a man. I've always thought it.' And she went to the porch repeating, 'What we need in this house is a man.'

She saw at once looking across the street that the colonel's horse was still there. It was earlier, then, than she thought; relieved she sat down. For every morning the great sorrel was brought by a boy, who, after making it fast to a hitching post, knocked at the Gores' back door and went away. Then at a quarter past ten the old military cloak himself would come out, mount and ride down-town for his mail. If Ellen and Lou were there, he saluted them with a grisly smile. He was a little man, but they set their clocks by him.

It was always pleasant on the porch. For though there was but one house opposite — where the Colonel Gore kept his shuttered silence — the street was long and shady and there were always people passing under the summer trees. Lou knew everybody. And of course she was herself known; it was more than a hundred years since the first Sabine had come into the county. In Mordington, she and Ellen were treated almost as natives of the town.

II

It was strange then, this morning, that Lou should be looked at so long in silence and when at last she was spoken to it was as though she had not been seen.

She sat in still fascination while the mulatto boy in front of Colonel Gore's iron gate stared at her. She had not seen him come there, though it was possible that he had come out of the alley and crossed the street without her noticing him. He was slim and swayed when he stepped down from the curb and walked about the sorrel with a litheness that was like, too like, a girl's. A hat with

286

old tattered straw brim had been crushed into a shape that increased the likeness. And his shadowed eyes were large and dark and impudent. Mrs. Cawley went by and did not see her, and then Miss Lila Colston and Mrs. Burden, who both nodded to Lou but with such restraint that she was abashed at having called to them from the porch.

They went on, and from their backs she guessed the stiffness of their gait. She and the boy followed them with their eyes and then were left looking at each other. Colonel Gore had not come out. She tried not to see the slim mulatto, who stared at her relentlessly. She saw the rent in his white shirt and through it the dull-colored skin and one nipple and tried to look past him and into the country. For beyond this street the town stopped, and after Colonel Gore's orchard were fields of wheat, pale, and wanting only a few days of sun to ripen. There the wind was like the sorrel restless. She saw it trampling the grain and in the sunlight remembered the old abolitionist they had brought out there to die, and how he had raised his stringy neck for the last time and said that the country was beautiful.

Two more ladies passed, walking with the same decent composure, nodding as the others had done with chill restraint and like them dressed in black.

There was a wait with the yellow boy. Then the bell of the Episcopal Church began tolling. Lou heard it, and knew why the ladies had been in black, had passed her without speaking. Someone was dead. But who? Mr. Hite the night before had not told her. It was eleven o'clock, the hour of funerals. Colonel Gore had not come out. But no, it could not be the colonel. He could not be dead. She would at least have known that. But there was still the dull tolling of the bell. Then it stopped. And in the sunlight the mulatto moved on, swaying as he walked. The sorrel, restless with flies, strained his long neck. And Lou was irritable in the wind.

The sun brought the shadow of the roof on her head. And she heard the sound of distant and repeated thunder, blasts from the quarries four miles to the east, that shook the ground. She thought of the dead. The blasts would be felt in the cemetery; for there,

287

with reiterated assaults at noon, they loosened the tombstones until often they fell and were broken.

Twelve. It was time to think of Ellen.

When she went back to the kitchen, he was there. A fine, tall, black, handsome nigger sat at the table, peeling potatoes, dropping them one by one into the water of an earthenware bowl. But Lou did not at once see him. Her eyes were dimmed by sunshine, she was overcome and downcast as though she had actually seen as she looked out over the summer of windy grain — black against the pale unripened wheat, and already like a dead man — the old abolitionist sitting up on his coffin and straining his bewildered eyes through the orchard. His fine bony black head was held side-wise, as with an expert knife he curled a long peeling from a potato and dropped it chuckling into the water. Lou started.

Smiling, he stood up and wiped his hands on a cloth. 'This is Miss Louisa, ain't it?' She saw his knife flash in the sunlight.

'Who are you?'

'I'm the new cook. I come this morning.' Again he smiled and his voice was so polite and pleasant that she liked him at once. His eyes were straight now. 'I don't know whether I put the dishes away right. If you'd look, Miss Lou ——'

'Where do you come from?'

'O, most everwhere. I been all up and down. You can 'quire 'bout me anywhere from here on goin' south. My name's Bones.'

'Bones?'

'Yes'm. They most and generally calls me Bones, nobody can't remember my Christian name, so they just calls me Bones.'

'I've always wanted a man,' she thought. And it was true. She looked at the cupboard and saw that all was clean and ordered.

'I'll have to ask my sister,' she said aloud.

'Or you can tell Miss Ellen it'll be all right, not to worry, jes' to rest herself good and stay in bed. We got lots of time, you tell her we got lots of time.'

Lou hurried upstairs.

'Ellen —' She shut the door on the darkened bedroom. 'I've got a man!'

On the bed the pale face was exposed between strands of hair. 'What did you say?'

Lou bent over her. 'How are you feeling?'

'All right, I suppose.' But Ellen let the coverlet contract with pain. 'Only I wish I knew who hitched that horse down there — he's breathing so loud!'

'A man's better, don't you think?'

'They're better. But you can't get them,' said Ellen.

'I've got one, he's in the kitchen now, and he has very nice manners and he's getting dinner.' Lou's breath was hurried. 'And I've always wanted a man.'

Ellen sat up. 'Did you ask him where he'd worked before?'

'I liked his looks,' Lou smiled assuringly.

'You'd like anything that looked like a nigger. What's his name?'

'Bones!'

'I don't know any Bones niggers,' Ellen mused. 'But it might be a Tidewater name.'

'He's very aristocratic looking,' said Lou.

'I'm getting up,' said Ellen.

'But your headache?'

'It's better.'

Ellen was curious about the new Negro. But she too was impressed by Bones. And the days that followed deepened the impression that here was a godsend. It was agreed that men were desirable, but Bones was a rarity among males. Every morning brought out new accomplishments; he seemed to have worked only in the very best families. He mentioned names, the oldest and the best, but it was his manners that proved him. In the kitchen he was easy and polite, grand in the dining room. As a polisher he shone; mahogany acquired a shimmering magnificence, floors were waxed till they were perilous, and cherry wood soon looked dark and rich as though it had grown in Campeche. Under his hand silver and gilt and glass were restored to a before-the-war splendor. They found when they came down in the morning the lower rooms aired and perfect; when they went up at night to their beds, all was in order for sleeping, with a single light and, if the nights were cool, fires laid in the grates. They had never known anything like it. 'It's just like the old days,' said Lou, 'when Mrs. Dancy had six servants for her town house and one that did nothing all day but shine brass.'

But it was Bones's cooking that most amazed them. Under his long bony fingers all the savors of the old South revived in their kitchen: Maryland chicken, Kentucky corn-dodgers, Virginia hams sprigged with cloves and spotted with pepper like leopards; ducks from the Carolinas and turkeys with stuffings of pecans, savory messes from Louisiana with odors of thyme, marjoram, and sassafras. Bones baked sweet potatoes with chestnuts as in Tennessee, his corn puddings were grated and thickened with eggs as in Alabama. He gave them shad from the Chesapeake, bass from the Shenandoah, and even made an effort to import shrimps from Barataria. Game appeared on their table for the first time in years, pheasants and partridges, once a wild turkey from the Blue Ridge. And even the ordinary and familiar dishes suddenly discovered the most unexpected qualities, due, so Bones explained, to their being prepared in the traditional manner. He could not put down an apple pie without saying that its spiciness was, in the first instance, Martha Washington's, a cream tart but he claimed that Mrs. Taylor had ordered it always done in this way for the White House. All his recipes were old, secret and derived from aristocratic kitchens; so at all events he said, and proved it to the satisfaction of everybody who tasted the concoctions.

Accustomed for years to the meagre diet of the genteel, the Sabines suffered somewhat from this new and prodigal table. They were often unpleasantly reminded of dinner about three o'clock, they frequently lay awake half the night forgetting Bones's suppers. The after taste of the Old South was acrid and distressing. They could only suffer in silence, they could neither refuse nor complain. Proudly they recalled that Jefferson Davis had also been a sufferer from dyspepsia.

Sustained by the pride of Virginia ladies, after many heartaches, they endured their heart-burn and said nothing. Bones was by now installed in the house. He had begun by asking for a room to change his clothes in, and Lou had seen no reason why he should not be given the spare bedroom on the alley. Within a week he was sleeping there — if indeed he slept! For at night, long after they had retired, they would hear him prowling, shuffling along the corridor or in the lower hall, trying the locks, sliding the bolts on the door. It gave them a feeling of security — Bones was so careful. And sometimes when supper lay heavy and they stifled in the night without sleeping, there was heard from window to window the faint playing of a banjo, alone in the bedroom on the alley. Bones was awake. Bones was singing! Yet in the morning it was clear that he had risen at dawn, had cleaned and dusted while they lay sound in their sheets.

He was really a marvel — so clean, so temperate! Moreover, he was an Episcopalian. They could ask nothing more. To be sure he was extravagant. Bones took over the marketing from Ellen and, though he could show that nothing was wasted, the bills did mount. Wines were consumed in his cooking, bottles of brandy lost in his sauces. And his wages, too, for that town, were high.

'But then,' said Ellen after her first consternation, 'we've never lived so well before.'

'It's worth it,' said Lou. 'It's the way I've always wanted to live.'

'If only we can afford it — ' Ellen sighed.

Bones was worth it. They had lived so long in a dream that it was sweet to taste the reality. With this one tall, black, jovial Negro in the house it was as though the war had never been or, having been fought, had turned to a triumph for the South. The old molds were restored. It was indeed as though dead bones were alive again. And they were content. Or almost ——

'If only — ' said Ellen, 'Brother Jimmy were here!'

'Yes,' said Lou, 'how he would enjoy it!'

III

Snow had fallen some days before, so that when the Sabines looked out of their windows it was over ledges deeply white and into a world of winter. The lawns were snow; the dark burdened pine trees held their branches like the claws of dead birds. Days passed under one cloud.

But on Sunday all was changed. They woke to see trees brittle with light intricately over-arching the street with crystal. Morning rising unclouded after a night of sleet had cased each tiny twig in brilliant ice. The snow shone — to venture out was perilous. In that sun the air was hard and cold; the branches glittering sagged and crashed though there was no wind. To walk was to go upon flawed mirrors. Ellen came down dressed for church a little before eleven.

Lou waited for her at the foot of the stairs. 'I'm not going,' she announced. 'In the first place, it's too slippery.'

'Not with an umbrella,' Ellen said.

'Besides, I've been thinking.' In the drafty hall the little Confederate flags faintly stirred. Lou looked hard at her sister. 'I know now what was the matter with General Lee.'

'General Lee?' Ellen turned and was astonished at Lou's excitement. 'I don't know what you're talking about.'

'I do! I do! He was too kind, he was too considerate ——'

'But of course,' said Ellen.

'That's just it!' Lou's voice rose and shivered in the chilly hall. 'It tamed him. That's why we lost the war!'

Ellen sought her umbrella behind the door. 'There's one thing,' she said. 'And that is, he never failed in his duty. Are you going to church?'

Lou did not at once answer. Then she said, 'I think I know my duty.'

'Very well,' said Ellen, 'then please let me go. I'm late as it is. And I hope you'll be in a better state when I get back.'

'I'll be just what I am now.'

Ellen looked at her hopelessly. She was wrapped in sealskin and veiled in green against the cold. 'Then you ought to apologize. I don't mean to me, I mean to General Lee.' The gust of her departure swept around Lou and she was left standing alone under the portrait of Light Horse Harry's sun.

I do not know just when this was, or how long it had been since first black Bones took shape in the Sabine household. It may have been the winter after his coming, it may have been a year or more later. I do not know.

It is so difficult to tell time in the case of those who ignored it. It was not simply that as maiden ladies the Sabines were skittish at the mention of years. Both had a memory for dates and could tell you to the hour of the day or night when every shot was fired, every skirmish fought, at Mordington. Twenty battles are recorded under its name and they could tell you all. Then too, they were susceptible to the spring, serious when the earth was cold, for they remarked the seasons to whom time brought no other change. But of years, they were afraid; they never mentioned them.

It was so in Lou's affair with Mr. Hite. They did not withstand time, they denied it. And nothing changed.

George stayed as he had been when first she met him, and they had met at a time when the one passion left to young men was for death. Living was a shame. They had lost all faith except in a cause that was lost. Earth was shaken, since Virginia was not a state but a military district and they no longer Virginians. Lou had wanted to devote herself to her sightless mother. Young Hite had perhaps wanted nothing.

There the affair stayed. Hite was a russet-haired youth, sturdy, but strangely enervate, after five months on late and disastrous battlefields. He felt the infirmities of years, for ten summers did nothing and then bought a drugstore. He put on weight, forgot what it was that made him ill, and continued sampling all the remedies on his bottled shelves. His coach dogs died, he bought better and better horses — after the old roan salvaged from war, a pair of blacks; greys in the early eighties; then bays, and all through the nineties bays. He called on Lou and they drove out together; dogcart succeeded the discredited buggy; the courtship in the summer dusks was unending. There was always the same trembling anticipation of delight, never a conclusion. She was still the young girl to be adored and pursued but not touched, he the lover who worshipping sought and never came to hard and male possession.

George got heavier, lost his sideburns so patiently acquired. He wore checks, docked the tails of his bays and looked more and more the racing man. The veins broke in his purple cheeks, pouches of wrinkles came under his eyes, the down thickened on forearm and hand. Love did not change. They were young no longer and had long since come to the silent communication of couples who have been married for years.

Time is a dizziness, and states have been known to fall who stood too long in that element. By time we are all at last confused. Ellen and Lou did not like to think about it; they were — and not only to themselves, but to all their contemporaries — the Sabine girls. They had kept all the emotions of their youth, but were themselves conscious only of their courage. They held out against time, and were aware only of time's sensuous coloring, which we know as weather.

So, though I know the cold into which Ellen stepped that Sunday morning, veiled and huddled in sealskin, I cannot tell its date, nor even for certain in what decade it fell.

The gust from the closing door as Ellen departed fluttered the flags in the hallway. Lou stood under the engraving of the Confederate general and bit her lip. Ellen annoyed her; she had not understood, she had not even tried to understand, what she was saying.

She was still excited — it was the excitement that sent her — when she hurried upstairs to the bathroom. She opened the door and for a second saw only the little window with frosted pane, saw it (she had just come from the dusky corridor) as a white glare in which slowly the forms of frost unfolded like submarine foliage. On the floor was a strip of rag carpet plaited of many colors. She saw it so distinctly that afterwards she could recall the coarse white threads stitching together the strands of faded red and blue and grey. Then she saw Bones.

Bones was playing some sort of game with himself. Quite naked, he stood in the tub, laughing, flicking a wet towel out and back. Terrible and tall he stood, and very black; each time that his long right arm shot out he held his breath. He watched it, his wrist turned and the towel came back slapping loud and wet on his bright black body. And he chuckled. Bones stood there, all a Negro, not in the least obscured by the mists that rose from the water. He chuckled all over. Once he winked at Lou, but did not stop his game. She shut her eyes and could not move; she heard the swishing Negro and the slap and the loud blind chuckling.

How she found her way out, how she groped her way down the
stairs and waited, one hand on the knob of the front door, for
Ellen, how she poured out the whole excited tale to her sister and
again waited trembling while Ellen went upstairs and into the
dusky corridor to see for herself what had happened — all, until
Ellen came slowly down and gravely stopped on the last step to
say in a troubled whisper that the door was closed but there was
no sound from the bathroom — all that hour and the next hour
was for Lou terror and confusion. She did not know how she lived
through it. One thing only was clear: she had shut her eyes and
behind them there was still the sight of the black man in the white
glare, standing in the tub, tall and so naked, chuckling — under
his ribs, chuckling.

They sat on the parlor haircloth, thinking what to do. And Lou
in the mirror saw the door open and Bones entered, an impeccable
reflection, in white jacket and black trousers. She heard him say
that dinner was ready. Then he went out, disappearing through a
door in the long glass. She turned and saw the door into the
dining room just closing.

'We can't, we can't!' She held her face crying, 'I can't go in
there!'

'We must,' said Ellen. 'It's best not to anger him. I've always
heard that was the only thing with crazy people, not to cross
them.'

They sat stiffly, and Bones brought in the painted soup tureen,
put it down before Ellen, and proudly uncovered a steaming
fragrance. Its heat was comforting, the dinner that followed so
calm and excellent that they lost something of terror. Whatever
Bones might be, the cooking was not insane. Ellen could even
whisper as they left the room, leaning toward Lou, 'You're sure
you saw him?'

Lou was astonished that anyone could doubt her vision. 'But
Ellen,' she said, 'I saw everything. I even saw the threads in
the carpet. It was all so clear.'

'Then I don't know what we'll do,' said Ellen. 'We'll have to
do something, but I don't know what.'

In Ellen's high bedroom, with the doors locked, they consulted.

Both whispered, 'What can we do?' until the white glare was gone and the dark gathered, falling first in the room. They were imprisoned by winter, all their windows barred with snow. If they went out, it would only be to come back again in the night over pavements of ice. They were held. Lou suggested that they write a note and throw it down and wait for someone to pick it up. But to whom? To Mr. Hite? To the police? They saw a colored boy who stooped and picked the folded paper from the snow; he looked at it and seeing it had no address tossed it away again. Besides, it was already so dim that he could hardly have seen it even if it had been there. There was nothing to do but to let night come and hope for Mr. Hite.

In the night the snow again fell. Under the street lamps they saw it falling — waited for the ringing of the bell that would tell them Mr. Hite was at the door.

He came, as usual, for Sunday night supper. Ellen and Lou were surprised to see him, they had waited so long upstairs behind the locked doors. He stood in the hall, red and puffing, wrapped to the nose; his eyes were watery in the light and on the lashes tiny beads. He had left his galoshes outside and for some minutes walked stiffly and strangely. But he got them through supper and afterwards Ellen carefully shut the doors on the parlor and waited for Lou's confidences. Their chairs were drawn close to the grate. Mr. Hite moved more easily; he watched the flames some minutes, then straightened and, as though it were a formal bouquet in lace paper, presented his gossip. So-and-so was sick, somebody else was thought to be dying; he offered illness for violets, misfortunes for jonquils, and in the center a corpse (old Mrs. Hunter from Summit Point) like a white rose. His listeners were not depressed, though their voices were serious, for this is the usual conversation in a country town when the weather is bad.

At ten o'clock he was gone. They bolted the door and Ellen turned to Lou in amazement.

'But you didn't say a word! Why didn't you? I was waiting all evening.'

'But Ellen, how could I? I couldn't tell Mr. Hite I saw a man naked.'

'No, I suppose not. And it would be worse with the police.'

'O much worse! I couldn't do it.'

Lou fluttered. As quickly as possible and with as little noise they reached Ellen's bedroom. Bones had not been there. When Ellen leaned from the window to close the frozen shutters, the snow was still falling. They barricaded the doors. Lou was first into bed in a borrowed nightgown. Ellen left the lamp burning. They lay in the great bed in which their mother had died and at last, in the silence of snow, slept. Impossible phantoms pursued Lou, and among them the great Lee, untamed and all a general, his eyes not on her but fixed afar in the very ecstasy of battle. She lost him and he came again, with drawn sword, naked steel; he did not see her, but she saw that his eyes were pale and the lashes frozen.

IV

Bones stayed on. Something of their terror communicated itself to the town, but the Sabines did nothing. They had never been able to dismiss Selly; they could hardly think of dismissing a servant so grand as Bones.

His manner was grander than ever. When the time for spring cleaning came, he rearranged the whole house; they had not believed their furniture could seem so elegant. When he had done, the rooms were a little bare downstairs and the attic was littered with rubbish. Ellen wept when she saw her mother's sad rocking chair, its arms worn where her hands had rubbed them, relegated to the refuse under the eaves. But they had to approve, for they saw that Bones had added almost a century to the house. Once you had entered the front door, it had an air and discomfort that was almost colonial.

Bones stayed on. And life was once more ordered to the calm of the past. Yet, they were not easy; those prowlings at night which once made them feel the more secure now seemed unnatural. A thing that slept so little could hardly be a man. They heard him trying the bolts and creaking along the staircase with apprehension. They slept often together, but did not sleep well. Nervousness brought loss of appetite; Ellen could not open a letter without fraying the edges, Lou started at every knock on the door and was not quite reassured when she saw who it was. Both looked like women who expected calamity and heard in every sound its coming.

It was almost with relief that Ellen, coming into her room in the dead hour of the midsummer's afternoon, found the long Negro asleep on her bed. His mouth was open and except for his breath, which was heavy, he might have been dead. Mr. Hite when he came — they sent for him at once — thought he might have been dead drunk. Ellen said 'No,' and Lou insisted that Bones never touched a drop. Happily, the sleeper was clothed, so they could speak of having seen him. And Ellen took Mr. Hite to her bedroom to show him the black smudge on the counterpane which his shoes had left.

'Well,' said Mr. Hite, 'he buys a lot of liquor. I've known that for some time. I've been meaning to speak of it.'

'We know,' said Ellen.

'It all goes into the cooking.' Lou was emphatic. 'I've seen it.'

'All?' asked Mr. Hite. 'Anyhow, I think you better let me get rid of him for you.'

'I don't think,' said Ellen, 'he'll go.'

'He'll never go,' Lou agreed.

'We'll see about that,' said Mr. Hite. 'If I tell him to go, he'll skedaddle. Let me see him.'

And before they could halt him, he had gone toward the kitchen.

'We'll never get anybody else like Bones,' said Lou.

'Yes,' said Ellen, 'and there's the garden. Without Bones, we'll never get anything done the way he wants it.'

'It's all right!' Mr. Hite shut the door behind him and looked at them beaming. 'He'll leave in the morning.'

Bones came in the next morning and Ellen sat at the high secretary and went over the accounts. He was, as always, calm, polite and ready with suggestions. But when his money had been handed to him, his eyes filled with tears. He quite broke down. He had considered them as his ladies, and then too, Mr. Hite, he had always thought him such a nice white gentleman. Then Lou

298

began weeping, and in the sadness of disappointment Bones went off to pack.

No one ate any dinner. The sun was half-way down the sky when, surrounded by his belongings, he settled himself in the ramshackle old trap that Ellen had had brought from the livery stable and gave the word to start. His long legs were opened and bent about his trunk, propped between the two seats. He leaned back and, smiling, ran his fingers along the fringe of the black, moth-eaten top. Beside him, in the hired hack, were his banjo and a slanting pile of leathery books.

'Those are our books!' screamed Lou. The sisters were peering from an upper window, each from one side of the drawn blind.

But the coachman had already bent over the dashboard to crack his whip. The bony sorrel broke into a trot, and the last the Sabines saw as the carriage disappeared in a golden light under distant trees was Bones leaning forward to try the driver's hat on his own head.

That night they heard the banjo's tinkling begin in the bedroom on the back corridor, very softly and behind closed doors. Then it must have been that the window was opened, for the sound suddenly increased and in a moment they heard the familiar voice in wild hilarity singing, *My head got wet with the morning dew. And the morning star was a witness too.*

Half the night he sang (though it was rather shouting than singing), the banjo twanged and his mirth was wild. But when he stopped and there was an interval when they heard only the leaves, the break brought such a sense of melancholy that both the listeners trembled. And they waited for Bones and his twining strings again to begin, as he always did, with a little chuckle before each song.

'Bones, you made,' said Ellen at breakfast, 'a great deal of noise last night. Neither I nor Lou could sleep.'

'Yes'm,' Bones agreed. 'But then I just had to do something to keep my heart up.'

'You're back?' Lou asked.

'O yes'm. I'se back. I just had to come back. There ain't nobody else can look after you two ladies like I can. Miss Lou here, she don't eat more'n enough to keep a bird alive. What'd she do if I wasn't here to make these nice corn cakes for her? Then,' he said, 'I just had to come back to see 'bout my garden. I'm startin' in the mornin' on my maze.'

'Your what?'

'Didn't you all know you was going to have a maze? Just like the one at Mount Vernon.'

Already he had done marvels with the garden, which until his coming had been much like any other in the town. Lawns were made smooth. Bones had straightened paths and strewed gravel; where before were only unkempt patches of vegetables were now neat borders, marigolds and cornflowers between thyme and lavender. And following an even older tradition he had set in the midst of green a small scent garden, where in spring violets and jonquils lost their breath in the nimble air and summer nights were enriched by fragrant stocks and white tobacco flowers. It was all very old-fashioned; you had only to shut your eyes to imagine yourself at Westover or Sabine Hall (where, be it said, no Sabine had ever lived or even been invited). And now he talked, to their bewilderment, of a maze of intricate box.

'Yes'm, I got it all here —' He pointed a bony finger to his forehead. 'It'll be 'bout twenty years before I gets it out there.' He chuckled. 'Boxwood grows awful slow.'

'I'll have to have some coffee,' said Ellen. She scattered her plate and felt faint.

'Yes'm,' said Bones.

'In some ways, he's a great comfort,' said Lou. She did not look up, and both shuddered as the door on the kitchen closed. They knew Bones was there to stay.

They knew the prowling nights that were before them, the bolts that would slide, the pantings up and down the dark corridor. The nights would be worse, but the days, too, would be afraid. They would come on him, they knew, moving like a creature out of a dream and have to remember that niggers can sleep standing up, with eyelids apart and their yellow eyeballs showing.

'I can't dismiss him,' said Ellen. And Bones could not be confined. He had been their intimate so long, they could not reasonably confine him to a lunatic cell. They would feel themselves mad. Above all they could not have him declared mad in West Virginia. As Ellen said: 'A nice Virginia prison, I would consider. But as that's impossible, we must keep Bones with us.'

'I almost think I'm glad,' said Lou.

'Yes,' said Ellen, but she trembled.

They knew now what they owed him. With him they lived in terror, but in the tradition. Their digestions were destroyed, their nerves frayed, but their pride sustained. They were like that Valley in which they had been born and which they loved and which indeed, as it lies between two ridges of intensely blue hills, is a country to be loved. The richness of its soil it owes to a slow disintegration; water has worn its rocks as noiselessly as time and all underneath the dark is hollow. The Sabines were slowly decomposing, like the limestone which arched and caverned underlies the long Valley and worried by water minutely decays. With Bones gone, they felt the hollowness underground. They had contended against time, but they were growing old.

They would soon be old. But with Bones there, they could stand it. To one who looks at all the Valley and the rich yield of its seasons it is easy to ignore the caves beneath, damp, empty, impenetrable. He would stay, they knew now, to the end. They would keep him, as it were a dear obsession, till they were dead.

JESUS KNEW

E. P. O'DONNELL

THE Mississippi had clawed through its west bank. Alert boatmen were paddling about finding people marooned. Refugee camps had sprung up here and there, clusters of pointed tents the color of the river, standing like military encampments without arms or colors.

In the shriveled hamlet of Tête Noir there was one living person — a girl in a magnolia tree with a milk goat. The tree was full of white flowers the size of a baby's head. The goat straddled a branch, and the girl held her by the horn. All around them below was the thick yellow water, hardly flowing. All morning they sat there, and the goat made frantic attempts to reach the leaves above her head. The girl wore a silver star hanging on a string from her neck.

In the afternoon the girl was crying out, 'Jesus! Jesus!' She looked like a pale Indian — the inscrutable eyes and the opulent braids of hair dangling. She was groggy with hunger. The rough bark bit deeply into the crook of her arm. The goat kicked violently. After calling Jesus for the last time she heard the brittle rapping of an approaching motorboat with voices. Then she thanked Jesus and waited.

The two men in the boat were volunteer rescuers, both very dark, of uncertain racial stock. Airplane scouts had reported some refugees marooned in the attic of Bubber Joe's, a large cotton gin south of Tête Noir. The men turned their faces about and about, searching. A cotton gin is a fat gray-hided mass of timbers with four thick legs and a pendant metal trunk, to inhale in a few moments the product of an entire family's labor for a year.

'You smell the mules?' asked Ed Jefferson, the one in charge. 'Tell me Bayou Desjardins is chocked up with big dead sugar mules.'

302

'I don't see no cotton gin,' said Pauly, his companion.

No one was about to direct them. The town was under water twelve feet. The consolidated school, its lower floor submerged, squatted in the bright yellow silence with a limp flag on the tall staff.

'I thought the schoolhouse'd be fulla pretty teachers,' said Ed, 'leanin' out the windows to be saved.'

A faint call was heard, the girl in the distant magnolia. They swung their boat round, cutting through the schoolyard. The boat sent waves over the tops of the two basketball goals. Ed Jefferson was a good mechanic and a boatman. On the bows of his boat he had painted in white lead the name: HOT SHOT SAVIOR.

They found the girl. Her eyes were swollen and glad, but rather incredulous. 'Hurry, she's fixin' to fall,' said Pauly. Jefferson began to yodel:

> 'O de ole lady!
> De ole lady who-o-o-o-o!'

They made fast to the tree and took in the girl and her goat.

'Thanksa,' she murmured and sat on a bench, sedately pulling down her skirts and folding her tan hands in her lap, her thoughts far astray. The goat slipped about in the boat, uttering its soft dainty meh-eh-eh-eh-eh! and falling to its knees when a sharp turn was made among the niggertown chimneys.

'Better be milkin' that nanny!' Ed shouted. 'She's leakin' on you! Where's your folks at, Brown?' Ed was always hoping they would rescue a girl whose father and brothers had been drowned.

'Cross de river, I reckonsa,' she answered in a far-away tone. She held the goat by the horn and softly caressed its wet rump. She looked straight ahead, whispering, 'Jesus knew! Jesus knew!'

Ed tossed her the rusty bailing can, and she milked without a word. Ed craned his neck to see into the pocket of her lowered bosom. Pauly kept examining the lush treetops where melancholy hens peered through the leaves. Pauly was an old man.

'Say where do you aim to go from here?' Ed shouted to the girl. 'The Delta Arms Hotel, I reckon.' He was about nineteen, with mischievous eyes. The girl looked up, and her soft eyes widened.

On her still whispering lips a mechanical smile came, then died. She started milking again and thanking Jesus. Ed winked to Pauly.

'Hey, Brown!' Ed yelled. 'Tell us where you think you goin'!'

'Don't knowsa,' the girl responded without looking up. 'Some place dry, I reckonsa, if yous de Raid Cross.'

Ed dragged a comb through his frizzly hair and wiped the engine. They could tell how the streets were laid out by the ranks of roofs, each roof making a V-shaped rift in the water, creating the illusion in the stillness that the water was stationary and the roofs moved north in unison.

'You goin' some place dry, all right!' Ed bellowed.

'Gooden dry,' said Pauly.

Ed said, 'You know where we're fixin' to take you? Over the river to the convict camp. You know what convicts is? That's them bad, bad rascals with the striped laigs, come from under the jail to bag the levee.'

The girl looked at Ed, for the first time actually attentive. She had rather proud lips and breasts — young, with clear-eyed gravity in her face of a recent successful baptism.

'They needin' somebody to cook their greens over there,' Ed went on casually now, 'an' wash them striped britches. Warden say, "Find me a willin' an' a pretty girl ain't scared of convicts, because my gun robbers is gettin' hongry and lonesome at night in these tents atop of the levee." Yare! We been lookin' for you all day, Brown. They ain't goin' to hit you in that camp. Not a nice girl like you. What's your name?'

'Ella McCoy.'

'Why, that's a drudge. She named after a drudge boat, Pauly!'

The girl watched Ed's serious face. She was weeping inside. There was no change in her expression except the big globular tears hanging in the sun.

'Mind out where you're steerin', Ed!' Pauly warned. 'Listen, lil nigger, he's only jokin' you!'

Ed chuckled richly and stamped his feet. The girl dumped her can of milk over the side and began to sob pitifully. Ed's eyes grew kind.

'Now I'll tell you *sho-nuff* where you goin'!' said Ed. 'You

304

goin' to the big ark, an' see the lights from Baton Rouge and smell the refinery, an' you eat you some boar jowl and clabber. Git you a pretty new refugee dress an' some typhoid serums. You love boar jowl?'

'Yassa.'

'Fair enough.'

They ducked their heads to pass under some telephone wires. A boat went by with a man grinding a camera at them; and one of its occupants shouted to Ed that the Bubber Joe refugees had been brought in.

Ed's boat curved out into the true river. On the big lonely river, whose turbulence the crevasse had strangely allayed, it was a glorious rosy evening. Their engine spat a nice row of vapor balls, exactly spaced, that remained fixed behind them for a long time, reddened by sun. The east shore lay free from water, calm russet fields melting out into the horizon's bluish haze. And hunched gleaners crept there among the pale strips of lettuce, all heedless of the flood across the way, as if they did not yet know.

Ed said to the girl, 'Now you find you somebody on the ark to mind your goat tonight like a good girl. We don't want to be bothered by no nanny goat when we walk down the dark levee, me and you.'

The girl, jerked from a reverie, looked up quickly, then lowered her eyes, regarding her folded hands. 'Yassa,' she answered.

'You understan' now, Brown? You goin' to treat me white?'

The girl stroked the goat.

'Looka here, Brown!' She looked at him. He asked, 'Who was it save your life an' you was fixin' to fall in the tree yonder? Did you ever seen me before?'

'I see you to de fillin' station in town, Cunnel Jessup Fillin' Station.'

'Correct! Now who was it save your life yonder?'

Part of a baseball park fence passed, then some sodden bags of oats waltzing slowly and sprouting oats through the seams. Ed contemplated the floating baseball scoreboard lazily. 'Tell me who done that, Brown? An' who save you from the striped-laigged convicts?'

'You an' de yutha gentleman.' She looked at old **Pauly.**

'An' I'm in charge of the boat.'

'Yassa, I expect so.'

'An' we don't want no nanny goat aroun'. Wasn't supposed to save no goat, nowhow. Goin' to catch hell.'

'Yassa.'

Ella looked away, moving her lips constantly. Ed wrinkled his humorous nose and winked to Pauly.

The refugee barge, blacker than the shore, bore several tents with torchlight shining through the flaps. Neighborly aromas floated out to Ella, frying pork and collards boiling. A rope flung through the dark fell across the goat. 'One female colored!' Ed called.

'Christ! where'll we put her?' cried a doctor who needed shaving. 'Go on, then, report her for inoculation. All right, open up, folks!'

A group gathered round.

'Where yall from, Cap? Weber's Landin'?'

'Chunky? Dat you Chunky?'

'They got a goat! Look the nanny goat, honey!'

'Make them shut that radio. Woman in labor in that doctor tent!'

'Denner for whites! Denner for whites! Sengle file, folks, sengle file!'

Ella did not know anyone. She gave the goat to a boy and hunted food. Ed had told her to wait for him behind the white people's bath tent. The crowd did not want her, nor she the crowd. To her they were like the stars of heaven for multitude — everybody talking, one big voice, like the groans of the slain, except some were laughing. And a preacher somewhere was holding prayer. It was all magic, sad, wonderful. Ella was sixteen. She had read the Bible and hoped soon to become an Upper Virgin in the Watchers of the Double Cave. She studied the calm black waters. A flood works softly, softly, mantling the meadows in cool fluid sorrow. Men near by were discussing the drowned cows and inundated crops. Women round a charcoal furnace drank coffee, blowing into the huge tin cups before each sip, anxiously glancing at the tent where the woman was having the baby. Ella crossed her hands on her bosom and listened to the unknown preacher. He was telling his hearers to pray for the white folks who had saved them alive, or Jesus might still deliver them up to flood or set them down somewhere in a plain full of bones.

Ed came with his flashlight. 'Ready to go down to the levee?' One of his hands found the firm bulge of hip clothed in the new gingham dress.

'Yassa. When you say.'

They started for the gangway, but Ed saw some men assembled there.

'Listen, you know how to count?' he asked Ella.

'Yassa.'

'I'll go first. When I reach shore you begin countin' slow. When you reach a hundred, come on ashore and go down the levee. I'll be waitin' in them pin oaks.' His hands prowled up and rested in the deep warm hollow between her shoulder blades — trembling. 'Look, don't you gyp me, now! You won't gyp me?'

'Nawsa.'

'Swear?'

'Yassa.'

'What do you swear to, Brown?'

'Jesus.'

When Ella had counted past eighty the Coastguard boat came quickly to take the colored people to the receiving station in Baton Rouge. Officials and nurses ran about calling, 'Colored over there! All colored!'

Ella hesitated, then hid herself behind the bath tent. A voice behind a blinding flashlight called to her, 'Hey! You colored?' She answered, 'Yes.' 'Over this way, an' make it snappy!' But when the light went away she made for the shore gangway. A nurse found her and ordered her to the other side. When the nurse left Ella continued to the shore plank, but there she was brusquely directed to the river side of the barge.

'Cap, I got to go asho'.'

'Cain heppit.'

Ella crossed the barge and joined the Negroes climbing down.

She looked once over her shoulder. Far down the levee Ed was yodeling:

'O de ole lady!
De ole lady who-o-o-o-o!'

The load of Negroes went to Baton Rouge and were slept and fed until the water receded. Ella was sick from the serum. She stayed for a day after the others had gone.

Then she went to Colonel Jessup's garage. After she had been there several times, peering into the building of oily shadows, a mechanic asked her what she wanted. Ella hurried away but went back round the block and returned. She met the colored porter. He told her Ed Jefferson had quit the Colonel a long time ago. He thought Ed was now with the U-Drive-It.

Ella could not find Ed Jefferson. She returned to Tête Noir. She helped her old mother shovel the mud and leaves through the windows. The mattress was ruined, the chairs warped, the bureau drawers would not come out. With a hatchet they demolished the bureau to get to their clothes.

The Red Cross delivered flour, beans, and coffee, but no dry stovewood could be found. They dug a few sticks from under the soft mud in the yard and put them in the sun.

'Is dis house established an' peaceful?' called the preacher from his mule.

'Yes, Revvin!'

'Praise de livin' Jesus!'

'Yes, Revvin!'

One day Ella's mother said, 'Ella chile, take yo' bath soon in de mawnin' and hunt you somethin' to do on de big road. I got sad visions.'

Ella, 'Yes, mam, I better start for town. A Raid Cross lady to de station promise me a job of work.'

'What size job of work?'

'A fried-potato job. Her husband sell fried potatoes. They cooks in de showcase on Reflection Street.'

'An' mind out you don't go 'bout no evil in town, bringin' down my gray hairs with sorrow to hell.'

308

Until a late hour every night Ella McCoy worked in the show window on Reflection Street. The potato-chipping machine opened and closed like a polished fist; and next to it an oval vat of golden oil bubbled over blue tongues of gas. There was a salt shaker big enough for a giant, and a stack of waxed bags labeled: HOSTES-SPUDS. The hostesses themselves came in the evening in big cars of all colors, and honked their horns. Ella would run to the curb attired in blue and gray, the company's colors, wearing her silver star between her breasts.

In a month she made enough money to send her mother the cost of new house furnishings and two settings of Minorca eggs. Ella left her job on a rainy day, took a bath, and went round to various garages.

She found Ed next morning early. He was entering the Triangle Better Service Station. Walking fast, he winked at Ella and kept on going into the garage. Suddenly he hastened back to the side-walk.

'Holy Christ! Say, you look different. Don't you know me?'

'Yassa, Mr. Aid.' She allowed herself to be led into the dark building behind a car. 'Trying to slip by me, Brown?' the man asked. 'You done forget who save your life? Can't you kiss me?'

'Yassa.'

'I'm kissin', but you ain't. You want some anti-freeze? How long you be in town? What was your name?'

'Long as you wants, I reckonsa. Ella McCoy.'

Ella stayed in Baton Rouge several days longer. Jefferson had a car, or rather a yellow truck chassis with a seat and no body. They would drive down the river road and fool round the woods or levee. Once Ella lost her silver star. She was so concerned that Ed the next day cast her another star from an old main bearing of a caterpillar tractor.

'I better be gettin' home,' she said, 'if you satisfied.'

'I'd like to know who's stoppin' you!' said Ed. 'You think I'm crazy about a woman watches the mail plane while she's makin' love?'

Back home in Tête Noir, Ella changed the shelf paper and white-

309

washed the fence. Each night with her mother she prayed at the fireplace to Jesus who was so kind.

One day the Watchers of the Double Cave gave a sweetcorn boil for the steeple fund. When the people were leaving church, after several reluctant attempts Ella approached the preacher.

'Revvin, pleasa, when can I get to hang my sacred star on de outside my dress?' She wanted to become a Virgin, and also, the babbit metal star had made a sore between her breasts.

The preacher said, 'Not untel you becomes a Upper Virgin. You takes dat degree when you reaches seventeen without willin' sin *through* de flesh of thy body. *Now!* Is you seventeen?'

Ella thoughtfully traced semicircles in the dust with her toe.

'Is you seventeen, Ella?'

'Yes, Revvin, Monday was a week.'

The preacher pinched her chin. 'Well now, you just go in de vestry an ax Sister Orelia instruc' you. De Double Cave convokes a month from today. It'll cost you fo' bits, and you wants to spade you a flower garden fo' de altar right away, an' Jesus bless yo' little soul.'

Ella slipped home. In the afternoon on the gallery she stitched thoughtfully at a dress. The niggertown people now were happier than before the flood — husbands and wives miraculously reunited after a stimulating separation; every able man employed on the new levee; and in the flood-enriched gardens rows of vegetables remained but a dry brown line drawn at the same height on every wall or tree.

After some days Ella became restless and forced herself to visit Sister Orelia, to learn whether the circumstances of her transgression were excusable enough to permit of her becoming an Upper Virgin. The old crone with her pipe was sorry, but nothing could be done. However, if she wished, Ella might be admitted to the Cave as a Lower Virgin. If she decided to do that, Ella must be sponsored by a guardian angel, a girl under seventeen whose heart was free from willing sin. If and when the guardian angel attained seventeen without sin, then both would be admissible as Upper Virgins.

Ella decided to forget about the Double Cave. Her life, however, became pretty blue and empty. In the night she sat on the gallery until the roosters crowed in the fog. So she began to think of a possible sponsor. Among the Tête Noir girls was one named Gladys, of fourteen years, who was known to be free from willing sin. Ella did not care much for Gladys. She went to see her. Ella worked around slantways to the topic of the Double Cave.

'I'm goin' in de Cave nex' month,' Gladys said, 'guarding angel fo' my second cousin. Six people wants me to sponsor them. This place done run out of sponsors is de trouble.'

Ella returned to her gallery and folded her hands.

About this time some new people moved next door to Ella, city people, a man, woman, and child. The man, called Flip, was a chauffeur for a levee engineer. He was big and sophisticated and tough, of the peculiar dark oily color known as crankcase brown. Flip and his woman were always quarreling violently. It seemed a certain man, former admirer of the wife, had followed them to Tête Noir. Ella saw Flip stand for hours at the corner, watching his house with his long legs crossed in the shape of a figure four.

The child, six years old, was named Rancie. She was afraid of nothing but her father. Even then when Flip came home to beat his wife's head, Rancie, hiding in the blackberry bushes, would throw handfuls of green berries toward the house and whisper in a voice deep as a man's, 'Big ugly mule-bear! Big mule-bear you!' She was skinny, black as treachery, and wore only a pair of gray drawers. Her chest was sunken and her feet huge, incredibly thick, as if the flesh of her legs had softened and run down there. She kept her bits of colored glass and other playthings in the blackberry bushes; and from the window Ella saw Rancie crawl from the bushes without sign of a thorn scratch and wondered what kind of skin Rancie had. Ella was a long time coaxing Rancie to be friends, because the child was wild and shy. Ella prayed for Rancie and gave her table scraps; and for a time was able to forget about the Double Cave.

Flip kept his wife's street clothes locked up; but one day the woman picked the lock. She went out somewhere, and shortly after her return Flip drove up in his boss's car, came in, and found his woman all dressed up.

Flip spread his legs in the doorway, making a long triangular shadow on the floor in the setting sun. He put his thumb in his belt and began to grin, not a bit surprised. Then he took out his thirty-eight and said, 'Stop me ef you done heard this story befo',' and shot the woman in the face.

Ella, next door, yelled and jumped the fence that she had never before been able to climb and ran for the blackberry bushes. Rancie was just crawling out, all bleeding from thorn scratches.

'Quick, Sugar!' whispered Ella, 'Jesus heppus!' And she took Rancie home.

The night after Ella went to court she and Rancie sat hand in hand on Ella's gallery.

'Who was it save yo' life yonder?' Ella asked.

'*You* save my life!'

'You goin' to treat me white, Sugar?'

'Yassam.'

'You goin' to be my little guarding angel and march aside of me in de nice procession, and live wid me untel I'm old and full of days?'

'Yas, *mam*, Miss Ella!'

But Ella did not know how to break the news to her mother.

Next morning at breakfast table she said to Rancie, 'Rancie, Sugar, tell yo' new grammaw what you wants to do for Ella savin' yo' life yonder.'

'I wants to be a little guarding angel in de procession.'

'What's all dis?' asked the old woman.

'I'm goin' in de Double Cave somehow.'

'But you's a Upper Virgin, Ella!'

'Nome. Lower.'

Ella dipped the cornbread into her bowl of molasses.

The older woman went slowly round the table and took Ella's cornbread and syrup away from her and carried it out back to the hog. Ella got up and began to gather her belongings. The mother remained in the back yard until she heard the front door slam softly.

Ella and Rancie stayed in the woods one night, but the next morning they found an abandoned shack on the front of town, high up where the water would never rise. They managed to get the furniture from Flip's house, which nobody wanted, and Ella cut scalloped shelf paper from rotogravure sections and whitewashed the fence. She at once spaded up her flower garden for the altar and found washing to do for white people, a bundle each day.

Ella got in the Double Cave on a pretty Sunday morning when the grass was all wet and the tulip trees in bloom. In the class were ten other Virgins, all Lower ones. The procession trudged the snaky dirt road, and at the cemetery prayers were said over the graves of two or three departed Virgins. Returning to church, they marched past the homes of the three Chief Upper Matrons, each of whom was clad in white robes and golden stars, waiting to come outside and give out a blessing. The last of the matrons visited was Ella's mother.

The preacher gave the Five Knocks and went in to fetch her. She covered her face and came out calling the ritual greeting, 'Who pilgrims this house *on* the Lord's morning?'

The Virgins chanted together, 'Eleven Virgins pure, *and* crave your deep blessing, dear Matron!'

Ella's mother was looking fixedly at Ella, whose headdress was put on improperly, needing adjustment. The preacher began prompting the Matron in a croaking whisper, 'My blessing —'

'My blessing I freely give! Go forth and tend the bud of renown. An' mind out yo' veils is straight on yo' stubbon haid.'

So Ella at last became a Virgin, one of the hardest things to do. Thenceforth she worked hard and minded her own business and took good care of her little guardian angel. The two lived in peace, bothered by no one, and the garden bore flowers of four colors, and the hens grew tame, coming up to pick at Ella's shoe. Her burden grew small and vanished, gentler than the wind takes a patch of snow.

Not even Ed Jefferson disturbed them very much when he came one fall day looking for Ella.

When she saw the yellow truck with a seat and no body, Ella called Rancie from the kitchen. Rancie had a stick of sugar cane in her hand.

313

'I was passing by here,' Jefferson explained. 'Been huntin' you all over town, includin' the graveyard. The sexton sent me to the preacher and the preacher sent me here. You know all the big shots. Say, ain't you all got no lunchroom in this town?'

Ella brought up a chair. 'Rancie, get the gentleman a glass of cow's milk and some veal meat,' she said.

Ed tackled the lunch. 'Your meat is tender but your knife is tough,' he said. Rancie stood in a dim corner, looking at the stranger with her big eyes shining, her finger in her mouth, and holding the sugar cane. The hens out back sang busily.

'Well, I done quit the Triangle,' said Ed, wiping his mouth.

Ella smiled politely and smoothed down her braided hair. Silence fell.

'I'm chauffeur for a rich white man now,' said Ed.

Ella looked through the window. Rancie kept watching the man. Ed glanced at her, coughed, wiped his brow. 'Nice little place you all got.' He glanced at Rancie, with Ella's leaden star on her bosom. Ed reached into his pocket. 'Here's you a nickel, Sis,' he told Rancie. 'Don't you want to go eat your cane down by the river? You got a knife? Brown, I could spend a Sunday here sharpenin' knives alone.'

Rancie placed the nickel in her ear. She did not move or blink. Her huge splayed feet seemed to grip the floor tightly. Ed's eyes traveled up and down the stick of cane. He shrugged and spat in the fireplace.

Ed sauntered over to peer into the kitchen, then crossed to Ella. 'When you comin' back to town, Brown?' He put his hand on the chair back. 'Huh?' His hand wandered and rested on Ella's shoulder skin, where there was only a thin cotton strap.

Then abruptly Rancie marched over and stood beside Ella with the stalk of cane, which was twice as tall as she. She took Ella's hand and fixed her big white eyes upon the stranger.

Ed glared at the guardian angel for a long time, while no sound was heard but the contented singing of hens. Then Ed jerked up his belt and strolled uncertainly toward the door, lingering at the mantelpiece to glance at a kodak picture of the procession. 'Nice place you all got. I thought I'd say hello. You look me up when you come to town.' On the porch he said, 'So long, Brown. It looks like rain.'

'Good-bye, Mr. Aid,' Ella called, 'an thanksa for comin' aroun'.'

Rancie sank to the floor and chewed on the sugar cane, tearing off long purple strips of skin. Her teeth were very strong.

A PROUDFUL FELLOW

JULIA PETERKIN

His name was Earth Wine — Earth for the earth itself, that he might have long life, and Wine for the family to which he belonged. His black mother and all the other black people on the plantation called him Ut Wine. He called himself that.

Ut could not bear to live like the rest of his people. The climate was warm; most of the days were brilliant and fine; the tottering old Quarter houses which had sheltered Ut's black kin ever since the first of them were brought up the river, long ago, to work as slaves alongside the mules in the cotton and corn fields, gave shelter enough, all the shelter Ut ever needed from rain or sun or cold.

Ut really loved the old houses and the great old moss-draped oaks that shaded them, but he wanted to own a piece of land and have a home of his own. This may have been because he was not altogether black. His mother was, but his father was white.

White blood has a strange way of poisoning men so that they cannot rest unless they own things. Sometimes they crave land, sometimes houses, sometimes people. Ut craved all three, for he felt that Harpa, his young wife, was his the same as his faithful dog Sounder, or his cow, or his mule.

His mother argued with him and tried to show him that he was foolish and proudful; that while men may think they own land because they pay taxes on it and plow it and salt it with sweat to make it give them grain or cotton, the truth is that the land owns them all the time; and when it has worn them out with struggling and striving, it takes them and turns them back into dust to feed its trees and grass and weeds.

Ut was a fool to turn his back on things that were good enough. He had good clothes and a roof over his head; he could rest or pleasure himself from dust until dawn every night God sent. He ought to thank God and be satisfied.

In spite of her warning that he was tempting fate when he stepped out alone, for himself, Ut bought a piece of thick-wooded land some miles away where a lonely hill bulged out, making the sullen yellow river crook sharply into a bend that was called the Devil's Elbow. It had always been a bad-luck place, for the river swamp below it was filled with hoot-owls and barking snakes and spirit dogs and ugly things bred in slime and black moon-shadows.

Ut's land was rich enough, but its richness fed weeds and grass as freely as it fed his crops, and it took a brave heart and tough sinews to rule it and keep it smooth and clean.

If Ut had wanted to run a still and make corn whisky to sell, his mother would not have minded, for easy money can be made so, and no better place could be found for such work than the deep shady cove on the side of that hill where the great trees and thick undergrowth hide the sky from the earth.

Or if Ut had done something wrong and wanted to hide from the law, she would have been glad for him to stay in the swamp below the hill, for it is a roadless jungle and the river's broad stream runs clear to the sea and could take him to safety without leaving a single tell-tale track behind.

But Ut wanted only a bit of land and a home, and a chance to make something of himself. He built his house out of pine poles with the cracks carefully daubed with mud; and the chimney was made out of sticks and clay, but it was solid and strong, a good enough house for anybody to live in.

Then he planted patches of peas and potatoes and vegetables, and got a cow, a flock of chickens, and put a shote in a pen to grow into a big hog by fall. He aimed to have plenty to eat, not only for himself and Harpa, but for Joe, his younger brother. Next to Harpa he loved Joe better than anybody in the world.

All these things kept him working early and late, Saturdays the same as other days, although everybody else in the whole country rested from Friday night until Monday morning.

Sometimes Harpa complained that Ut had forgotten all about pleasure; but he always claimed that he got his joy out of owning his home. He went hunting and fishing now and then. The river was full of fish to be had for the taking, the woods full of game;

317

Sounder had a sure nose and Ut was a good shot. His old double-barreled gun was so well trained it could shoot straight and kill almost without his ever aiming it.

Ut had a tender heart and he hated to kill the free wild things; but he had hard strength-taxing work to do, and the flesh of the forest creatures makes food that hardens a man's sinews and reddens his blood far better than corn-meal and butts-bacon can ever do.

Instead of taking a smart black wife from the Quarters, Ut had gone to the village, ten miles away, and married Harpa, a slender slim-footed girl, even lighter in color than himself. For in spite of his white blood, Ut was dark. He had his mother's crinkly hair and her stout stocky body, but instead of her wide flattened nostrils and thick lips he had his white father's straight mouth and narrow nose, and big soft eyes that were full of tawny light.

Harper's skin was warm yellow and her eyes blue-green, her straight black hair was shiny and her purple lips were made for laughing. To Ut she was everything lovely and sweet. Little slim Harpa. She did not like work, but Ut felt that her slender body was not meant for work. One morning she tried jerking a hoe through the tough grass roots, and in no time both her palms were blistered. Her hands were too small and tender to stand the rasping of a rough hoe-handle.

Harpa hated to cook. Greasy black pots and ugly dish-water made her feel sick. But Ut ate most of the victuals, and he had far rather cook them than to have Harpa scorching her face in front of the open fireplace where the cooking had to be done.

One hot summer evening Ut came in from the field, weary and drenched with sweat. He found Harpa sitting on the door-step laughing and talking with Joe, and watching the full moon rise. She had on a cool white dress and a bow of red ribbon tied her hair at one side. When she drew her clean skirts aside to keep Ut from touching them, Joe grunted and frowned. 'You don' jump up an' wait on you' husban', Harpa?' he asked. 'After he works hard all day, you sets still when he comes home at night? Gal, you ought to be shame. If you was my wife, I declare to Gawd, I'd lick you 'til you wouldn' eenjoy settin' down.'

Ut stopped short in his tracks. 'You hush, Joe. You ever did run you' mouth too fast.'

Joe got to his feet, talking faster than ever, protesting he had not meant to hurt Ut's feelings. That was the last thing he'd ever do in the world. Ut was the best old brother any man ever had, and the best husband any woman ever had, too. Harpa ought to be glad to wait on him and cook for him. If she would stick at the field work her hands would get tough and used to it.

Ut listened gravely, but his tone was sharp when he answered that what Harpa did was none of Joe's business. Harpa was not a cook or a field hand. She washed and ironed and sewed and patched, and that was her full share of the work. Joe had better learn to keep his mouth out of other people's business.

Joe grinned good-naturedly. He had not meant to meddle. But he would tell the world that when he took him a wife she would never spend his good money buying red stockings and shiny shoes. Those shoes Harpa had on must have cost as much as a whole week's rations. Instead of being vexed at what Joe said discounting her ways, Harpa's white teeth flashed in a laugh so bright, so lovely, that Ut's steady heart fairly turned over. Blessed little Harpa. When she looked like that Ut felt he would work his fingers to the very bone to buy her red stockings and shiny shoes, or anything else she wanted.

Now she tilted her head sideways and with her soft husky voice full of teasing and bantering fun, she asked Joe:

'How 'bout red ribbons, Joe? Would you buy you' wife a piece of red ribbon?'

Instead of answering Harpa's question Joe's bold eyes looked up at the big white moon while his fingers softly stroked the strings of his battered guitar.

Ut smiled. Harpa knew how to get the best of Joe. Precious little Harpa, so worthless and yet so merry. Always ready for a laugh or a dance or a song. New shoes never did hurt her feet. When his land was paid for she should have everything in the world she wanted. She should take a trip to town and buy cloth in the stores; and go on the train excursions to Charleston. If he got up a little earlier and worked a little harder and took less time at noon, maybe he could make a bit more money for Harpa.

Ut had helped to raise Joe from a baby; in fact Ut was still trying to raise him. Joe had plenty of sense; he was able, but he wasted his time drinking, gambling, frolicking, singing. Still when Joe had a drink or two his singing was so beautiful that it made Ut's heart open and shut like a book.

Ut often pleaded with Joe to settle down to some kind of steady work; but Joe laughed at the idea. Nobody would ever catch him getting up at dawn to plow a stumpy field. Ut knew nothing about pleasure, and he had never tried loafing or gambling or drinking, or looked at any woman but Harpa. Ut knew Joe pitied him for such ignorance, such stupid ambition and pride. Now Joe's lean black face shone with amusement. His sharp teeth grinned and his black eyes twinkled as he boasted that he was no proudful fellow, thank God. If he could be the richest man in the whole world he would never spend his good days sweating in a piece of new ground, tied to one woman. God made his legs too long to walk all day behind a slow-poking mule. They were made to dance and roam after liquor and good-looking women. His fingers itched when they were not picking a box (guitar) or shooting craps. When he got too old for pleasure then he might settle down; but as long as his body was full of good red blood he would never waste himself working. He had too much sense for that.

'How 'bout it, Harpa? Ain' I right?' Joe asked suddenly.

To Ut's astonishment Harpa hesitated, then said, there were two sides to everything. Men ought not to forget everything else but work. Once she heard a preacher read out of the Book at church how lilies and grass and beasts never do a single lick of work, yet they have what they need. Joe had clothes and food and pleasure even if he had no land or house or wife.

The next morning, Friday, was Harpa's wash-day. After Ut had filled the wash-pots with water and built a fire under them and carried the clothes down the hill for Harpa, he walked around looking at his things — noting how the cotton and corn throve and were clean of grass, how the potato-vines met in their rows, how the peas were bearing. Now he had every right to be proudful. His work was bearing fruit and proving he had not out-reckoned his strength.

Harpa was up and washing by now, he would go tell her how well everything did.

Hurrying down the narrow path to the spring which ran cool and clear out from under the hill, he soon came to Harpa and the wash-pots and tubs; but instead of Harpa's bending over the wash-board fighting the dirt in the clothes with her two hands, or beating it out with the stout oak paddle, she sat on the ground mournful and cheerless.

'Washin' don' agree wid me, Ut. My back is all but broke,' she moaned forlornly.

'Po' li'l gal,' he pitied, 'it's dem big bed-sheets, dey is too heavy fo' you to rule, Honey. Le's stop havin' bed-sheets. Quilts won' dirty so fast.'

Harpa shook her head. 'De bed-sheets ain' so bad as dem overalls o' you' own. I can' get 'em clean, not to save my life.' She shuddered as she looked at the tub where his offending garment hid under the foamy white soap-suds.

'Lemme wash 'em, Honey; you set still an' rest!'

He took up the long wooden paddle and stirred the things round and round, shirts, undergarments, overalls, bed-sheets. Hot lye-scented steam rose in his face — sickening smell. No wonder Harpa hated it. She looked sick sure enough. Her warm skin was pale and ashy, her eyes big and hollow. Maybe—maybe his great wish, his wish for a son, a boy-child, was going to come to pass. His heart jerked at the strings that held it in place, joy flooded him so.

A sudden happy idea came into his mind. 'Listen, Honey, lemme hitch up de mule an' wagon an' go to do Quarters an' get Mocky to come an' do dis washin'. Mocky is strong as a ox. She'll come every Friday an' help you do de clothes. I'll pay her.'

He lifted Harpa up and stood her on her feet. 'Honey, don' look so sorrowful. It makes me pure weak as branch water. If you don' smile I wouldn' be able to walk home up de hill.'

321

Then Harpa's laughter rippled out bright as the sunshine that pierced the hot shade, and Ut put an arm around her shoulders and together they went up the path.

Mocky came gladly. Washing those few clothes was an easy task for her; she had strength enough in her big arms to break Harpa's body in two; the skin on her black hands was like leather. By noon the clothes were washed and hanging on the line in the sun.

Although Mocky was fat, she turned on her feet light as air, and she was full of fun; but Ut noticed that few words passed between her and Harpa.

That night at supper Ut praised the whiteness of the cloth on the table, but instead of joining in, to his amazement Harpa's blue-green eyes darkened and narrowed and her lips tightened into a thin purple line.

'You ought to had married Mocky 'stead o' me, Ut.'

'Why, Honey, I would'n gi' you for forty Mockys.' Ut's happiness was completely gone.

Harpa carelessly stretched out her slender limbs and drawled, 'Joe says Mocky was ever ravin' 'bout you, an' you use to take her to prayer-meetin's every Sunday night when you an' her was agrowin' up.'

Ut laughed and leaning closer to her whispered tenderly, 'If you knowed how pretty you looks wid dat li'l red bow a tyin' you' hair, you would'n talk so, Harpa. Whe'd you get dat red ribbon anyhow? Did Joe fetch 'em to you?'

'No,' Harpa answered, and her eyes glittered bright and cold as she said it.

A step suddenly sounded in the shadows, and Joe's voice called blithely, 'Yunnuh better stay in de house. Dis moonshine is dang'ous. It's done gone to my head.'

'Come on in, Joe.' Ut got up to meet him. 'Pick us de bes' tune you know. Sing us de foolishes' song. Harpa's gone an' got sad tonight.'

'I ain' sad,' Harpa declared. 'Ut's de one. Ut is sad 'cause he married me when he might'a married Mocky. She could'a worked in de field an' cooked an' washed an' ironed, an' had de chillen an' patched an' sewed an' had plenty o' time to go to prayer-meetin's too.'

Ut said no more; he knew that tone of Harpa's; but Joe's plunking grew louder, steadier, until a gay song began twanging clearly. Then Harpa's anger was gone, all of a sudden. She was little more than a child, after all; and Ut tried to have patience, long patience, with her babyish ways.

She had eaten very little these last hot days, and now she looked so slight, so slender in the moon-light; he felt almost afraid for her strength. Little slim sweet Harpa.

If he went now and set a trap in the river, he might catch some fish for breakfast. Harpa liked fish, and she ought to eat more than she did.

Neither Joe nor Harpa noticed when he got up off the step and went inside to mix up some corn-meal and cotton for fish-bait to put in the trap. When he came back and said, 'I'm gwine down to de river, but I'll be back in a minute,' Joe said, 'All right, old socks.' But Harpa answered not a word. She was still cross with him, but she would be over that by morning. She never held her mad long. Easy hurt, easy over it. Easy sad, easy glad, that was Harpa's way.

As Ut ran down the shadowy path with old Sounder following close at his heels, a cool night wind sprang up and high pines overhead began moaning. The frogs and crickets cheeped lonesomely, but the night birds had little to say.

When a falling-star made a bright spark across the sky, Ut stopped to watch it, for that star made a path for somebody's soul. When he reached the sand-bar by the river an owl flopped out from a hollow tree and whoo-whooed a mournful death call. Ut was startled. Two death signs. Two people were going to die. The star and the owl both said so.

He watched the dark bird's shadow float over the swamp on the tops of the moonlit trees, but the wet sand sucked at his feet. It wanted to swallow him up, but he was not so easily caught. He quickly set the trap, then slowly and thoughtfully mounted the path toward home. Not a sound came from the cabin. Everything was silent except a harsh crackle of dry leaves fretted by the wind.

323

Joe and Harpa must have gotten tired waiting for him and gone to bed. He would go to sleep too and be up early to get the fish for breakfast, for Mocky was coming to finish the ironing, and if the trap had luck it would catch plenty of fish for her too.

Dawn barely hid the stars the next morning when Ut eased stealthily out into the yard. He must feed the things and milk the cow, but he must not wake Harpa.

'Eat a plenty and lay,' he murmured softly to the hens as he scattered their corn on the ground. 'Harpa likes a lot o' eggs in de bread.' When he put a great armful of hay and a dozen ears of corn in the mule's trough, he looked at the beast's huge belly. This was Saturday, the day to go to town for the week's rations. The road was long and the wagon heavy. He would put some extra ears in the trough.

'Take time and chaw, old man. Git some meat on you' ribs. You' Missus hates to ride behind a pack o' bones,' he said gently as he patted the mule's bony sides.

The pig grunted impatiently and peeped at him between the cracks of the rail pen. Ut laughed at such greediness, but he chided him in a whisper, 'Don' squeal so loud, son; you'll wake Harpa. Eat you' breakfast. Fatten all you can. Make us a whole tub full o' lard by Christmas.'

Ut was glad for the day. Every sound was good against the stillness — the cock's proudful clucking as they woke up the biddies, the moaning of the wind through the pines.

Smoke and sparks were rushing up out of the cabin chimney, for Mocky had come. She had the fish fried, the bread baked, the coffee boiled, the table set and the kettle on the hearth singing and breathing out a cloud of steam over the row of flat-irons heating by the fire's red blaze. But Harpa was not up and dressed yet.

With a pile of sprinkled clothes rolled tight to hold the moisture, on a chair beside her, Mocky bent over the ironing-board, humming a tune and running a hot iron swiftly, deftly, over the starched bosom of Ut's white Sunday shirt. Drops of sweat ran down her shiny fat face and fell with tiny hissing pats on the iron. When she looked up to say good morning to Ut, her thick mouth smiled

324

a little but her eyes were full of sulky darkness. 'Breakfast sho' smells good, Mocky,' Ut praised.

'Harpa's de lazies', triflines' woman I ever seen in my life,' Mocky answered.

'Oh no, Mocky. Harpa ain' dat. She jus' don' like to wake up soon. Dat's all. You women-folks tho' is hard on one another, enty Joe?' Ut tried to laugh good-naturedly as he said this, although Mocky's brazen talk about Harpa did sting him.

'Le's eat,' Joe suggested. 'I'm hongry.'

'We may as well. Harpa's mos' ready anyhow.'

The three of them sat down and had their pans helped when Harpa came out of the shed-room; but instead of sitting down with them she stood by the chair and shook her head, 'I can' stan' de hotness in dis room, Ut. It would cook a egg. Dat fish smells so sickenin', too. I'm gwine to de spring an' git me a cool drink o' water.'

Ut got to his feet, with his mouth full of food, 'I'll go wid you, Honey,' he mumbled. But Joe dropped his spoon with a click in his pan, and pushed back his chair. 'You set down, Ut, and finish you' breakfast. I'll go wid Harpa. I ain' in no hurry to eat. You set down.'

Joe took an empty water-bucket off the shelf and followed Harpa out into the yard. It was just as well. A walk in the fresh air would do Harpa good, for the room was too hot and steamy for comfort. Ut helped himself to another piece of fish, then passed the pan to Mocky.

'Take another piece, Mocky. Dis fish is sweet as can be,' he said.

Mocky's eyes were two hard black beads, and her mouth was twisted into an ugly pout.

'How come you's such a fool dese days, Ut? You used to have good sense.'

Ut could scarcely believe his ears. What did Mocky mean?

'I mean you mus' be blind as a bat. Dat's what I mean,' she declared bitterly.

All of a sudden Ut knew what Mocky meant. She was intimating an ugly thing about Harpa and Joe. She was jealous of Harpa.

325

She had always been jealous of any girl he liked, and now she wanted him to believe a filthy lie about his wife. Hot blood made a red glow before his eyes, and he seized Mocky's arm in a grip too tight to be loosened.

'Listen, Mocky,' — blind fury almost strangled him — 'if you crack you' teeth about Harpa, I'll kill you. I ought to choke you' tongue out right dis minute. You mean, lyin' hussy ——'

'Choke! Go on an' choke. Cuss me much as you want to but dat ain' gwine change Harpa none.' Mocky shook all over.

'Gal, if you call Harpa's name one more time I'll wring you' neck same as a chicken —' Ut felt his fingers tightening on Mocky's flesh, but she did not move a muscle. She knew him too well not to yield now. She had to shut her mouth.

The cabin was still as a grave except for the crackling fire. Two bright tears hung in Mocky's eyes, and her lips shook with unspoken words. Then the door-step creaked sharply, and two black shadows fell across the floor. There they lay side by side still and stiff as the headstones of two graves. Joe and Harpa had come back — were listening — they may have heard every word.

Ut's head was dizzy, his heart sick, his blood full of fever. He staggered out past them into the yard, down the path to the river where he fell prone on the moist bank. There he lay, his face downward on his crossed arms, the hot sun beating on his back, while poisoned thoughts raced through his brain.

Mocky was like all the rest of those black Quarter women — mean, jealous, vain; unhappy, unless they were strewing somebody's name about, dragging it in the dirt. None of them had ever liked Harpa; now they'd be glad to spread a filthy tale about her. Certainly Harpa liked Joe, and Joe liked Harpa too, even if he had never praised her once in his life; but if Mocky ever said one ugly word about them again he'd kill her as quickly as he'd kill a poison snake that threatened them. Mocky hated to see him lawfully married to Harpa and living in a decent way, making something of himself. He knew she would have taken him and not cared one bit whether the preacher ever read out of the Book and prayed over them or not. Mocky was black, her ways and her heart were black. She would be glad to tear down all he had worked and striven to build up. He wouldn't let her. He'd go send her home, make her get out of his house, right now.

Before he got halfway up the hill, he met Harpa coming to call him to dinner. Her face and dress were wet with sweat, and her narrow brows were drawn together with a black frown.

'How come you went an' hurt Mocky's feelin's so bad, Ut?' she scolded. 'If I was you I'd be shame. I declare to Gawd, you' patience is too short for you to be a big grown man like you is.'

'But, Honey——'

'Don' be honeyin' me, now. Mocky cried so hard Joe had to take 'em home. I had to finish de ironin' and cook de dinner too, all by myself. I'm weary enough to die.'

Her eyes looked big and hollow, and dark shadows lay underneath them.

'I'm too sorry, Harpa. Whyn't you call me?'

'Call you? How'd I know whe' you was?'

They walked on without speaking until Harpa added sorrowfully, 'I was countin' on gwine to town wid you dis evenin', an' now I'm too wore-out. I can' go.'

'De ride would do you good.'

'Good! Ridin' in dat old rough ramshackle wagon wouldn' do nobody good. My bones would sure be shook to pieces. My back's mos' broke now.'

Poor little Harpa, so thin and frail, and sometimes so strangely sad.

While Ut ate the dinner she had cooked for him, Harpa sat down by the window so that the light from the overcast sky could fall on the faded, freshly washed and ironed overalls which she had started to mend stitch by stitch.

Her eyes lifted from her sewing now and then to rest on the faint blue hills far across the river swamp. She and those hills were in some way alike now; both so softly curved, so tender and lovely, both so far away from him, so out of his reach. All his life those mysterious hills over the river yonder had stood for better things than anything he had ever known on earth, as if they were a part of Heaven itself. Yes, Harpa was like them.

He went and stood by her trying to think of some suitable word to say. Poor little tired Harpa, mending and mending, working for him, placing the small industrious stitches side by side. He bent over and kissed the back of her slender neck, then gave one little hand a gentle pat; but the needle it held pricked him sharply, as the hand jerked away from his caress.

'You better hurry an' go on to town, Ut. I see a cloud a-risin' yonder over the river.'

He followed the look her blue-green eyes flashed up at the sky, where in truth, ragged clouds were piling. She was right. He must be going.

'I hate so bad to leave you by you'self, Harpa.'

'Sounder'll be here wid me.'

'I'll hurry back quick as I can, Honey. What must I fetch you from town?'

'I don' want nuttin.'

'Nuttin?'

'Not nuttin.'

Harpa was out of sorts, down-hearted for truth; but he would fetch something for her. Maybe he could find her a string of red glass beads to wear with her pretty red stockings. They'd be beautiful around her slim neck, against her warm yellow skin.

'Good-bye, Harpa.'

'Good-bye, Ut.'

'Don' get lonesome, Honey.'

Harpa did not answer.

'I'm too sorry you ain' gwine wid me.'

No answer again.

As Ut went down the steps Harpa called to him, 'You better go by an' see you' Ma! You ain' seen 'em not since week befo' last!'

Harpa was right, he must not forget his kind old mother. When he bought Harpa's beads he might buy his mother a little present too, maybe a red and white head-kerchief to tie on her head for Sunday.

'Good-bye, Harpa!'

'Good-bye, Ut!'

The mule was slow and the cloud and night both caught Ut on the way home. The steady rain cut clear through his clothes and reached his skin, cold and wet. He went by the Quarters to give his mother the pound of sugar he had bought for her to make sweetened bread; since Harpa's beads had cost so much he had not had enough money left for a head-kerchief.

She pled with him to stop long enough to dry his clothes, but he wouldn't, for Harpa was by herself except for Sounder. When he jerked up the rope lines and urged the mule to hurry, the foolish old beast, remembering his old home at the Quarters, would not budge. Ut bawled at him sternly, then doubled back a rope line and gave him some loud wallops; but the tough-mouthed hard-headed old creature lifted his head, and stretching out his neck gave a long mournful 'hee-hee-haw-haw-haw,' as if sorrow were breaking his heart. Instead of moving he took one unwilling step forward, then he stumbled and almost fell, for his forefoot had picked up a nail. A mean, ugly, crooked, rusty nail which had dug through his hoof clear down to the bone.

Those old Quarter houses were always dropping rusty nails out of their rotten sides, and now one had crippled the mule's foot and he could not walk another step. Ut would have to leave the wagon and rations with his mother, and walk home to Harpa.

A wet gray moon gave out a poor dim light as he took a short cut through the woods; but he knew the way well, and in a little while he was climbing the hill through the pattering rain to the solid black blur which was home. He thought Harpa would have had a bright fire burning, and be standing in the door watching for him; but the cabin was dark and still. She must have gotten tired and gone to sleep.

That was good. He would surprise her. He would tiptoe in and lay the beautiful red glass beads in her hand. They would wake her. Precious little Harpa. When Sounder came sniffling and whining to meet him, Ut hushed him with a pat. Sounder must be quiet so Harpa would not wake until the time came.

The rain sang gaily as it fell off the cabin roof and splashed down off the eaves. But the bed and the chairs in the big room were empty. Harpa must be asleep in the shed-room. A loose board squeaked sharply under Ut's weight, and Harpa cried out of the blackness in the shed-room, 'Gread Gawd! What is dat?'

The pitiful terror in her voice made Ut smile. But before he could tell her it was he, Ut, her own husband, Joe was saying with a laugh, 'Don' be so scary, gal. Po' ole Ut ain' half-way home yet.'

Ut's horrified ears seized the whispered words and he tried to yell; but his frozen tongue could make no sound. His ears began roaring like the river in a flood. He could not think for its noise. But through the clear darkness his eyes saw his gun standing in the corner. It would tell them in one word that he was home.

Joe must have heard the trigger click, for he struck a match. Then he leaped up, dropping it right in the folds of Harpa's flowered dress, which lay crumpled and empty on the foot of the bed.

'Ut — you fool — put down dat gun!' Joe shouted between chattering teeth. But the gun spoke one loud short word that answered him forever.

The weak flame of the match sputtered and threatened to die, then it seized avidly on the thin cotton cloth, flaring up bright.

Harpa slid to the floor, shivering, tottering, on her bare feet — then she fell on her knees. 'Ut — for Christ's sake — Ut!' she quavered. But some devil inside Ut made him laugh. He told her to pray to her maker, and not to him now.

Harpa took in one long gasping breath then let it out in a thin wild shriek, 'Oh-h-ee — !' She tried to wrench the gun from his hands, but he gave her a hard backward shove toward the bed.

Ut was not certain what happened. The gun must have aimed at her and fired before he let it fall; for red blood, red flesh, hid her breast.

Burning cloth made a bitter stench. The whole room was afire; bed, walls, floor — all fed the growing flames as they sputtered and roared up toward the ceiling.

He must go. But go where? His old lame mule had a stall, but he had no place in the world now.

Looking back once more he saw Harpa's two little empty shoes standing bravely side by side on the floor. Slamming the door hard behind him, he rushed out of the cabin into the yard where red shadows flew about thick in the air. They ran under his feet, tripping him, blinding him; red flames stuck thin long fingers through the cracks of the cabin, pointing at him, reaching for him, making him stumble. Before he knew what he was about, he had fallen on his knees and prayers were slipping through his lips.

'Do, Jesus — master — look down on dis poor meeked man — I'm done ruint — ruint —'

A sheet of fire lifted the cabin roof, sparks flew clear up to the sky. 'Lawd, Jesus, please, suh, have mussy on me ——'

A light touch fell on Ut's throat; then another and another, inch by inch. He held his breath to be certain it was there; then a long cold shudder shook him. Praying would do no good now. His time had come. A measuring-worm was marking the size of his neck; it had already crawled up his back and measured his length for its master, Death. The gallows would hang him, the earth would take his body, and his lost soul would fly on and on until Satan caught it and put it in Hell.

He had stripped himself bare. He had nothing left but a rope — a shroud, and a new cold grave.

THE GAY DANGERFIELDS[1]

LYLE SAXON

THE Dangerfields lived on Acacia Plantation in Louisiana, not far from the town of Baton Rouge. The house was a charming but dilapidated structure at the end of a long avenue of cedar trees, each tree shrouded with trailing Spanish moss. Beyond the cedars on each side of the avenue, were crepe-myrtle and acacia trees, and in summer the myrtles were rose-colored bouquets and the acacias were feathery green and gold. It was a romantic and beautiful place — rose and gold and green massed against black cedars and gray moss — and at the end of the avenue, seen through an arch of dark branches, were the white columns of the plantation-house.

The house was very old. Once white, it was now a creamy gray and the window-blinds had faded to a bluish green. There were eight large white columns across the façade, and a wide veranda upstairs and down. In fancy I can see it yet — and always I see, there between the columns, a red-haired woman in a long black riding-habit, surrounded by black-and-white spotted dogs. This was Kate Dangerfield, the mother of the children that I came to see.

They were all artists, the Dangerfields were. All the children had talent for drawing. The mother had received some training as a girl, and she believed that she had missed a great career by marrying and settling down. 'Settling down' is hardly the phrase, for she was far from settled. She was nearly six feet tall, and she was very handsome. In her girlhood she had been known as a dashing young lady, and, even as the mother of six children, she still dashed. She wore always a black riding habit with trailing skirts which she would gather up and pin at her waist. In consequence,

---

[1] From *Old Louisiana* by Lyle Saxon, copyright, 1929, by The Century Company.

her skirt would be knee-high on one side and would trail behind her as she walked. She was dramatic; her gestures were wide and free. Her hair, now streaked with gray, she dyed bright-red in front; the back she disregarded entirely. Her oldest daughter who was just my age, would always draw me aside and ask, 'What do you think of Mama's hair, this time?'

Kate Dangerfield would stride about the house, a riding crop in her hand, a cigarette between her lips — a magnificent figure.

In those days ladies did not smoke except behind closed doors, and there was always an air of mystery about her smoking. When I first arrived there would be a pretense of hiding the cigarette; but soon I would come upon her puffing behind doors or in corners; later in my visit caution was abandoned, and the cigarette was always in her hand as she talked and gesticulated.

She was an artist, as I have said, or rather she painted pictures. She gloried in her artistic temperament. She called herself a 'bohemian.' It was the first time that I had ever heard the phrase. One of her eccentricities was that she never finished anything. She would take my arm and draw me along the hall of the plantation-house pointing out a picture with her riding crop. 'Now that,' she would say, 'is Paul and Virginia fleeing from the storm, but it isn't finished. It needs much more work on it. I have so little time, you know.'

Or perhaps she would pause before a picture of three horses' heads. 'Pharaoh's Horses,' she would say. 'How I love to paint animals! But it is unfinished. You can see that for yourself.'

It was characteristic of her that she should do everything in the grand manner. I never saw her at work upon a painting, but I am sure that she painted with the same large magnificence with which she spoke and acted. In fact, the pictures looked like that. They had a startled expression — horses and men, as though surprised when confronted by the masterful woman who had created them.

Once, I remember, she paused before the portrait of a recumbent cow. 'Now that,' she said, 'is what I call painting. But of course, it is not finished. Just a little old sketch that I made one day.' Then she sighed and we went on to the next picture.

The daughters were like their mother, good-looking and erratic. Ada was the eldest. She was dark-eyed and olive-skinned and she was pretty in a gypsy sort of way. Magda was next, a girl of twelve, tall for her age, pale-skinned and with dark eyes and red hair. The youngest daughter was Dorothy (named for Dorothy Vernon of Haddon Hall!), a charming, dreamy child who was only eight years old, but who was already erratic about coming to meals or learning lessons or getting dressed in the morning. It was no unusual sight to see Dorothy on her calico pony, wearing her night-gown, racing down the avenue just as the breakfast bell was ringing. There were other children, twin red-haired boys, nicknamed Judge and Jury. I never knew their real names. And there was a baby in the arms of a Negro nurse.

The younger children were kept in the background, but the three girls would have long arguments with their mother about horsemanship, in which they would squabble exactly as though they were all of the same age. There was constant warfare between Ada and her mother as to which of them was the better horse-woman. The mother was noted for miles around as an excellent and fearless rider, but at home the daughters disputed this. They would urge her on to bolder and more extravagant feats; they would wager that she could not ride this or that unbroken horse. And they would shriek with glee when she was thrown off — which happened frequently. Instead of spanking them all, as one would imagine, she would cringe before their criticism, and would accept their wildest dares in order to retain her supremacy. I don't know when she found time to paint, but paint she did, as scores of pictures in the house testified.

The family owned two plantations on opposite sides of the Mississippi, and Mr. Dangerfield was nearly always 'over at the other place.' He seldom appeared, but when he did it was always in the same way. He would ride slowly up the cedar avenue on a huge white horse, dismount, throw the reins to a waiting Negro, kiss his wife and children if they were within range — and then disappear. He always shook hands with me gravely, and inquired as to my grandfather's health and my own, but he did not listen to my answers. He had a remote 'office' in a wing of the house where he remained aloof; even his meals were carried there on a tray. I remember him as a shadowy figure, tall, distinguished-looking, and absent-minded, a man with a black beard and a soft drawl. But to me he was a minor actor in the drama enacted by the female members of the family. I remember this unsolicited statement from him: 'My wife is a magnificent horsewoman, by God!'

He had good reason to be proud of her, for she was noted throughout that section of the State. She used to come galloping through the streets of Baton Rouge on a black stallion, and the shopkeepers would run to their doors to see her go by. News would spread through the streets — 'Mrs. Dangerfield is in town. Watch out for the fun!'

She was the heroine of a score of mishaps. Once a horse that she was driving with a light buggy became restive on Main Street; it reared and snorted and ended by kicking the dashboard to pieces, while Kate Dangerfield, with feet firmly braced and with the reins wrapped around her wrists, gave shriek after shriek of wild laughter, and called out to those brave young men, who attempted to rescue her, that she needed no help; and she begged them to keep away until she got the horse under control. She did it, too, but not until the carriage was practically demolished.

On another day a frightened horse managed to pull the harness loose from the shafts of her carriage. She held the reins and was dragged over the dashboard into the road. But she held on through sheer stubbornness, and it was not until the horse had dashed her against a tree that she let go.

She lay there in the dust while the horse went running down the street. Men and women came out to pick her up. Everyone thought that she was dead, but she sat up and laughed.

'Why that's nothing,' she said. 'Just a little old wild colt that I'm breaking in!'

As she was casual about risking her life, so was she casual about the affairs of the plantation household; and while she was the most hospitable woman in the world, her guests sometimes suffered severe trials.

At Acacia Plantation there were nine hunting dogs — pointers

335

and setters — that slept in the hall. All day long there would be growls and yelps as their tails were stepped upon by some of the Dangerfields, for it was nearly impossible to go from room to room without stepping on some sleeping animal. But the dogs must have been strangely good-natured, for no one was ever bitten. There was an army of cats, too, which no one ever remembered to feed, and they were always ravenous. Going to the dinner table was like going to war. We were surrounded on all sides by cats and dogs — animals ready to snatch the food out of our mouths.

As half of the family never came to meals anyway, there were always empty chairs at the table. Mrs. Dangerfield would sit at one end and I would sit beside her; then there would be, perhaps, four empty chairs, and, down at the opposite end of the table, Dorothy would be lolling, lost in a day-dream. The others would trail in at ten-minute intervals, as the spirit moved them.

One day the cat situation became acute.

Mrs. Dangerfield, Dorothy, and I were at the table, and a servant had just placed a large silver platter of roast beef in the center of the board, beyond the reach of any of us. Scarcely had the servant left the room when a black cat sprang up and began eating from the dish. Kate Dangerfield regarded it languidly and said: 'This is too much. Dorothy, knock that cat off the table.'

The little girl came out of her day-dream with an effort, looked narrowly at the cat, and said: 'I won't touch it. That's Ada's cat. Make her come and drive it away.'

And the cat continued to eat.

'Oh, well . . .' said Kate Dangerfield, and reaching behind her she took a buggy whip from a rack, and came crashing down among the plates and glasses. It is true that this drove the cat away, but it also scattered gravy in every direction, inundating us in grease. Two goblets and a plate were broken, and dinner proceeded as usual.

One soon fell into the spirit of the occasion, or at least I did.

Although the house was overrun with servants, everything was left undone. Meals were always late, and sometimes forgotten altogether. One night at ten o'clock, Kate Dangerfield, who had been walking up and down the hall reciting poetry aloud, stopped suddenly, clutched her red hair, and cried out: 'Good Lord! I forgot to have supper!' And to our surprise, we found that it was perfectly true. We went to the kitchen and to the ice-box; we foraged for the remains of dinner. Jars of preserved fruits were opened, cold biscuits appeared. At half past ten, instead of going prosaically to bed, we were sitting around the dining-room table in the midst of a meal.

Mrs. Dangerfield was a great teller of stories and many of them dealt with the sensational and romantic episodes of her girlhood. Her daughters scoffed openly and stifled exaggerated yawns, but they would listen for hours on end, and to their interruptions she paid not the least attention. She talked for the pleasure of talking; she 'entertained us' for the sheer joy of entertaining.

One evening after dinner she walked up and down the floor of the drawing-room and recited Kipling's poems until long past midnight. She was like a woman in a dream. The poems seemed thrilling as she recited them, and though I heard midnight strike, I was far from sleepy. The candles burned low in their sconces and went guttering out, one by one, as she strode back and forth in the long room under the family portraits, her head up, her red hair coming down, her black riding-habit trailing after her, a cigarette in her hand.

> 'This is the sorrowful story
> Told when the twilight falls,
> And the monkeys walk together,
> Holding each others' tails!'

It was after one o'clock when she ended. Then she got out a decanter and gave each of us a glass of Benedictine for a nightcap.

Once there was a guest in the house, a pale, aristocratic-looking woman from New Orleans. She was a distant relative who had come to spend a week at the plantation. She was totally unprepared for such a family as the Dangerfields, and her visit was not quite a success.

She had been given a room upstairs at the front of the house, a large room with a four-post bed, a sofa, two or three arm-chairs, and the other usual bedroom furniture. She appeared at breakfast the next morning looking wan and worn, and in answer to the question as to how she had slept, she answered somewhat hesitantly that she had been bothered by fleas. She said, in fact, that she had been forced to leave her bed and spend the night upon the sofa; and, as the sofa was covered with black horsehair and was very slippery, she had not slept at all.

Instead of being horrified, as the guest expected, Kate Dangerfield laughed.

'My poor Virginia! You, of all people in the world, to be bitten by fleas in my house. You, a Randolph of Roanoke!' And she was gone again in a gale of laughter.

The guest mustered a wry smile. 'It was pretty bad, just the same,' she said.

Mrs. Dangerfield sobered. 'My dear, I *am* sorry. You have no idea how sorry I am. Really. Why didn't you come to me? There are other rooms empty here. Although,' and here she laughed again, 'there may be fleas in every one, for all I know.'

Then she went on to explain: 'You see, I haven't been in that room for months. I supposed that the servants looked after it, but instead they've left the door open and the dogs got in. It's highly probable that a dozen dogs have been sleeping on that bed all summer. It's odd about Negroes and doors. Why, do you know, I've made a discovery about Negroes: it is absolutely impossible to teach them to close doors after them, even in cold weather. They won't. It's some racial trait, I suppose.' And she went blithely on.

'But what will you do to get rid of the fleas?' the guest asked at last.

All through breakfast we talked of possible flea remedies. Someone suggested that a young lamb be put upon the bed, the theory being that the fleas would leave the bed and take refuge in the lamb's wool. This idea delighted Mrs. Dangerfield, as it promised immediate action. She ordered one of the Negro men-servants to catch a lamb and bring it to her. But the Negro demurred.

'Now you know, Miz Kate, dat dey ain't a single l'il lamb in de pasture, dis time a-yeah!'

'Well, then, catch me a sheep,' ordered our undaunted hostess.

'If a lamb is good, a sheep will be better. It's bigger, you know. More room for fleas.'

A few minutes later two Negro men appeared at the dining-room door; they carried a large, dirty, and very angry ram between them. The old ram's dignity was upset and he struggled to get down.

'Carry him upstairs!' ordered Kate Dangerfield.

But this was not as easy as it sounded. We all tried to help. We tugged, we pushed, we shoved, and the ram cried '*Baa-aa-aa!*' and set his hind legs. All of us took part in assisting the ram upstairs. All, that is, except the guest. She stood in the parlor door watching us, and she seemed annoyed and amused and miserable, all at once.

Finally the ram was brought into the bedroom and deposited upon the bed, and he lay there, panting and exhausted. We retired and closed the door, but we had scarcely reached the drawing-room, directly below, when there came a crash which set the crystals tinkling in chandelier. Mrs. Dangerfield, who had collapsed on a sofa, and who was smoking a cigarette in order to regain her composure, cried out, 'He's jumped off the bed!'

We all ran upstairs again, dogs, children, white folks, and Negroes. This time the ram gave battle. He charged us, knocking one of the children down. Chairs were overturned, children screamed, dogs barked. But in the end we were triumphant. This time the servants tied the ram's legs together and put him back in bed again.

'Cover him up!' Mrs. Dangerfield ordered.

Accordingly the blankets were drawn up over the ram and he lay there, furious, his horns on the pillow, and looking for all the world like Red Riding Hood's grandmother.

However, it was not more than ten minutes later that the second crash came and the ram was free again. The struggle lasted all day. The room was a wreck, chairs and sofa overturned, a mirror broken and the disorder unbelievable. It was not odd that the guest remembered an important engagement in New Orleans and left suddenly in the afternoon.

Oh, charming people, the Dangerfields were, galloping about the country on horseback, a gay cavalcade, hunting, shooting clay pigeons, or riding to hounds. Looking back upon them now, across twenty years, I can think of no more delightful times than those I spent with the gay and eccentric family at Acacia Plantation.

When I grew older, I lost sight of them. I went away to school, then work took me out of Louisiana. Years passed before I returned. When I inquired for them I found that the girls had married, the father had died, and like so many other country families, they had lost their plantations. Kate Dangerfield, they told me, had moved to another plantation in the northern part of the State. I wrote her, but the letter was returned unclaimed.

But it was only last year that I saw her again. It came about like this: I sat in the lobby of a New Orleans hotel, waiting for a man who had invited me to luncheon. Nearby sat two sunburned men who wore broad-brimmed Panama hats. So near they were that I could hear what they were saying, and suddenly my attention was caught by a bit of talk:

'. . . a most remarkable woman, I tell you. Why, just the other night she heard a noise in her hen-house, and she went out to see what was after the chickens. It was a wildcat. You'd think that any woman would be afraid, but not that one! Why, man, would you believe it, she put her foot on that wildcat's head and held it there until her son came with a pistol and shot it, right under her foot!'

'What did you say her name was?' asked the other.

'Mrs. Kate Dangerfield,' he answered.

I sprang up. 'Where is she?' I demanded. 'I must see her. I knew her years ago.'

'If you hurry, you can catch her at the station,' the planter said. 'She's in town for a day's shopping. I left her a few minutes ago. She's headed for the Union Station to catch the one-fifteen train.'

I ran from the hotel, caught a taxi, and reached the station with only two minutes to spare. The gateman let me through to the platform and I ran along beside the train, looking in at the windows. But just as I was about to give up the search, I saw her walking along the platform. She was strangely unchanged; still red-haired, still straight, and she wore a long black dress, cut like a riding-habit. A Negro girl followed her, her arms full of parcels. I caught

340

Kate Dangerfield's hand as she put her foot on the step of the coach.

She greeted me as though we had parted the day before. 'How in the world did you know that I was in town today?' she asked.

'I overheard a conversation in a hotel,' I answered. 'It was about a remarkable woman who put her foot on a wildcat's head and held it until her son came with a pistol.'

She laughed and made the sweeping gesture that I remembered so well.

'Why, that was nothing,' she said. 'It's just talk. It was a little bit of an old wildcat. I thought it was an owl.'

THE GUY IN THE
BLUE OVERCOAT

EDWARD ANDERSON

WHEN the brakeman's heavy feet thumped on top of the box car, the Kid and the guy in the blue overcoat down in the refrigerator hole stood up fearfully. The clumping stopped and then the brakeman's bristly face was framed in the crack. 'Aw right, you punks, up outa there.'

The brakeman stood on the gray gravel of the roadbed and waited for them to get down the rungs. He had a club in his hand. When they were on the gravel, the brakeman said: 'Now don't you try to get back on this train. Both of you. I don't mean maybe.'

The Kid and the guy walked at the edge of the roadbed down the train toward the town. The gravel was loose and their feet would slip. The sides of the right of way ditches were covered with wild berry vines. The Kid looked, but there were no berries on the vines.

The Kid thought about the guy walking along with him. If you hadn't stuck your head up outa there that brakie wouldn't have seen us. You've balled things up for me now good. Kicked off in this place and no tellin' when a man can get a train outa here again. I'd of been in St. Louis in the morning like I was planning on if you hadn't of stuck your head up.

They passed the caboose. 'That's that,' the Kid said.

'I wish we hadn't got put off,' the guy said. 'I wanted to hurry and get on.'

'I didn't ask to be put off myself,' the Kid said. 'You shouldn't have stuck your head up.'

The guy did not say anything.

The face of the guy in the blue overcoat was dry and gray like school tablet paper. His eyes were red-veined and deep in their sockets as if they had been pushed in. He had climbed into the reefer with the Kid back in Little Rock in the night. At first the Kid had welcomed the guy for company because he had been riding all night by himself. The other had talked a lot. He said he was twenty-three and it was the first time he ever rode freight trains; that he had driven a car for a man out to California and the man was supposed to pay his transportation back to Cleveland, but he didn't. The guy was getting back to Cleveland the best he could.

'Looks like a pretty good-sized town up there,' the Kid said.

'I don't like to go into towns,' the guy said.

The Kid decided he would not say anything more to the other. I don't want this kind of a guy for a buddy, he thought. Afraid of his own shadow. When you meet up with a real fellow on the road it's O.K. to have a buddy and split fifty-fifty with him, but not a guy like this. Him twenty-three, too. When I'm twenty-three I'm not even going to be on the bum. If I don't have a good job then I ought to be on the bum.

They neared the depot. Long fruit express cars were lined up alongside the loading platforms. The wooden platforms were the color of washed-out mops. Workmen stood on top of the fruit cars and packed ice into the holes. Their voices carried far and clear in the morning air.

The Kid felt at his watch pocket. The quarter was still there all right. He was saving the quarter until he got to St. Louis. When he got to St. Louis he was going to find one of those places where you got hot cakes and syrup for a dime and spend the other fifteen cents besides. All night when he was not sleeping he had thought about how he would spend the quarter. I don't care if I am stuck here, even if it's a week, I'm not going to break this money until I get to St. Louis, he thought.

Of concrete blocks, the depot was the color of rust. A baggage-man was rolling a truck down the platform and when he stopped the Kid asked him when the next train was leaving. The baggage-man said a manifest was going out at four in the afternoon. It stopped to pick up a string of fruit cars. It was a hot shot to St. Louis.

343

The Kid felt good about that information and went ahead and held the depot door open for the guy to catch up with him. They went through the station and stopped on the outside and looked across the street up into the town. The paralleling street was like the hump of an ant bed and into Main Street people were pouring. It looked like Saturday, but in this Arkansas town the strawberry season was on.

The Kid moved across the street and the guy followed him. A girl in a white sailor blouse and black cotton hose was preaching on the corner. She had a heavy Bible in her hand and when she slapped it she almost dropped the book.

Looking at the girl, the Kid thought she didn't have much build on her. He started to say this to the guy, but then he remembered he was through with him. He left the group of spectators and went over and stood in a cleared space on the side-walk next to the hardware store. The guy came on over.

'Well, I guess we'll start digging up something to eat,' the Kid said. 'You can take one side of this Main Street and I'll take the other. That side over there looks good to me. There's a bakery right up there. You can have that side. It don't make any differ-ence to me though. You can have this side.'

'It doesn't make any difference to me,' the guy said. 'I can just go along with you and wait outside.'

'Naw, that's no way to do. A man ought to bum by himself. When they see two of you together you can't get nothing. You just go in and tell them you're broke and hungry and they'll put out something. Which side do you want?'

'It doesn't make any difference to me. Where am I going to see you after while?'

'I'll be around here somewhere,' the Kid said.

Up the Main Street the Kid went, and he did not look back. He was not going to do any bumming. When he had money in his pocket he could not bum. I just can't do it when I got money on me, he thought. I'll bum the dickens out of them when I'm busted, but I don't feel right going in a place and bumming when I got money on me.

At the next corner the Kid turned to the left and went down an unpaved street. Just beyond the vacant lot on which were wagons and unhitched teams was a white frame café that looked like a big box. In the window was lettered a sign: STRAWBERRIES AND MILK, 5c.

The Kid's eyes lingered on the sign, but he went on. No sir, I'm holding onto this dough. I'm gonna hold onto it until I get to St. Louis just like I planned. I don't care if I'm here a week.

At the end of the street which was crossed by a road like a T was a wood of pine trees. It was a free tourist camp. He entered the grove. The carpet of leaves were springy to his feet and he had the sensation that the ground might give way and he would go up to his knees in the carpet. He went on through the woods and crossed the cement highway which split the camp like a bright ribbon. On the other side of the highway were a half dozen parked automobiles with tents at their sides. In front of one automobile, which had a house built on the back, sat a girl in a red dress and an older woman. The Kid went on a little beyond them and sat down at the foot of a tree. He sat there and looked toward the highway because he did not want the girl in the red dress to think he had just sat down there on account of her.

The girl was bare-legged and had on boy's oxfords. She was eating peanuts. She would let the hulls fall into her lap and after a while stand up and brush them off and then sit back down and start eating again. The older woman had on a man's rope sweater.

The Kid thought about he would like to get acquainted with the girl. It would pass the time away until four o'clock when the manifest left. If the old lady got her hat and went off to town and the girl stayed behind? I'd go over there. I'd go over and say: 'I see you're from Texas. I noticed your license plate. I've been all over Texas. I've been in Fort Worth and Houston and El Paso.'

He thought about what would happen if the old lady left and he went over to the girl:

The girl smiled and told him to sit down. She reached out and filled his hand with peanuts.

'Mama and me are traveling by ourselves and we sure do need a man. We need somebody to drive this car and get up the firewood and do things like that.'

345

'It don't make any difference to me where I go. I'm just running around.'

'I wish you would come with us. When mama comes back I'll tell her that you are going with us. We sure need a man.'

'I'm just running around and I'd be glad to.'

The girl got up and smiled. 'Would you like to see how we got it fixed up inside the car?'

'I'd like to.'

The girl led him back to the rear of the car and he followed her up into it. It had a bed and everything. The girl closed the door and they sat down on the bed. His hand went out and lay on her bare leg and then he kissed her.

'I've been wanting somebody,' she said. 'I've been so lonesome and I saw you over there and I wished you would come over. I was wishing I had some . . . .'

The guy in the blue overcoat stood there. 'I found you,' he said. 'I been looking everywhere for you. It's lucky I found you.'

'What's on your mind?'

The guy was excited as if he had seen something happen down in town. 'I found a place where we can eat. I mean it won't cost us anything. I was walking around and come right up on it. I know right where it is. It's a mission and they got signs all over the windows telling you to come in and eat. I can go right straight to it.'

'Why didn't you go on in?'

'I wanted to get you. I wanted somebody to go in with me and I started looking for you.'

'You can go on.'

'When you see it though you'll want to go in. There are signs all over the windows. I looked for you just especially.'

The Kid looked back toward the car. The girl was gone. Just the old lady sat there.

'You will be glad you come,' the guy said. 'Just wait until you see it.'

What if I jumped up and took a poke at you, guy, the Kid thought. You're just messing things up for me right and left. Here I was about to meet that girl and you come along and now

346

she's gone. I'm warning you, guy, that I can take just so much.

'You will be glad when I show it to you,' the guy said.

The Kid got up and the other started off like a dog eager to lead the way. He fell back in a moment, though, to walk at the Kid's side. 'I want to tell you something,' he said. 'I know you won't believe it, but I want to tell you something. I haven't eaten nothing since I left Dallas. In Dallas I ate in the Salvation Army, but I haven't had nothing since I left Dallas.'

'Godamighty,' the Kid said. 'That's a thousand miles from here. That takes a man three or four days.'

'I knew you wouldn't believe it, but that's the truth. The funny thing is I'm not hungry. That's the funny thing. Of course I can tell I haven't eaten anything, but I'm not hungry. Just hot inside. If it was not for just being hot inside I couldn't tell it.'

'I wouldn't go that long without eatin'. It's not good for a man.'

The guy pointed ahead down the street. 'It's just right down yonder. Right around that corner. It's not far.'

The glass front of the building was painted white and lettered with signs: YOU ARE WELCOME. . . . STEP IN. . . . WE FEED DAILY.

'I told you,' the guy said and he went up and grasped the knob. But it did not turn. He turned stiffly and looked at the Kid.

'Rattle it,' the Kid said.

The door opened and a man stood there. He had a long face. It looked like a big capsule. He looked them up and down and then said: 'You fellers come back tonight. Maybe we'll have something then.'

'That sign there says you give something to eat,' the guy said. 'It says on the signs there.'

'Come back tonight.'

'Look there, mister, at the signs. What's the idea of having signs? It says there.'

'C'mon,' the Kid said. 'Let's go.'

'I told you to come back tonight,' the capsule head said. 'What did you leave home for? I can't help it if you're running around the country.'

'What's that sign there for,' the guy said. 'You son of a bitch. What you got signs for? You bastard.'

Capsule Head looked scared. 'I'm gonna have the law down here on you in just a minute. You can't talk that way. . . .' He closed the door.

The Kid was going up the street fast, but the guy trotted and caught up. 'It was there on the signs,' the guy said. 'I don't care. They ought not to have signs if they don't mean it.'

'You've played hell,' the Kid said. 'You can't go around cussing people. That guy is calling the law. You can bet on that. I'm gettin' out of this town myself and I'm not waiting for a train. I'm hittin' the highway. The law is going to be after us, you can bet on that.'

The guy did not say anything.

'We better split up,' the Kid said. 'You better go one way and me the other. They'll spot us quicker if we're together this way. You can bet the law is after us. I wouldn't be a bit surprised if I was in the can tonight. It wouldn't surprise me one bit.'

'I don't care,' the guy said. 'I'd just as soon be in jail as not.'

'Well, I care,' the Kid said. 'You get that straight. I care.'

The guy was silent.

The Kid walked faster and faster. It'd be just my luck to land up in jail in a dump like this, he thought. It'd have a jail just about like that one in Shawnee. Stink like that one and have a plank for a bed with bugs on it. They'd feed you a sandwich of fat bacon at ten o'clock and soup at six. I got this quarter, though. I could get a chocolate bar every other day. It'd be just my luck for them to have a smart jailer here and he wouldn't get the chocolate bars for me.

Down the street the highway glistened. The guy panted behind the Kid.

Oh, you don't have much to say now, the Kid thought. Oh, no. Now that you're gettin' us in jail, you don't have much to say. What do you keep hanging around me for? You're twenty-three and can't take care of yourself.

They reached the highway and went down it about a half mile and then the Kid stopped at the Ozark Trail marker. There was no traffic on the road. The Kid sat down in the shade of the marker and then the guy sat down.

Diagonally across the highway, a half block down, was a lumber yard and a grocery. The side of the grocery had been papered with circus posters and they were broken and hanging. The lumber yard was the color of goldenrod and its windows were trimmed in white. In the yard two men were loading small lumber on a wagon.

I'd like to be working in a lumber yard, the Kid thought. I'd go to the show twice a week and buy me at least two detective story magazines a week.

The guy was sitting there in his overcoat with his knees under his chin and staring across the road.

'Why don't you take that overcoat off?' the Kid said. 'I'd smother to death.'

The guy took the overcoat off.

The Kid looked across the highway toward the lumber yard. I'm not his buddy, he thought. If I was his buddy, it'd be different and a man has a right to pick out who he wants to be on the road with. I never did go that long without eatin'. Godamighty, that's a long time. If I was working in that lumber yard over there I'd have money in my pocket on Saturday night and I'd go and get that girl in the red dress and we would go to the circus. But I'm not his buddy. Oh, Christ, I guess I might as well do it. I guess I might as well. . . .

The Kid held up the quarter. 'Look, what I found.'

The guy looked.

'That's what I call lucky,' the Kid said. 'Just looking down and picking up a quarter. That's what I call lucky. That means we eat. You know what it means, don't you? That means you and me are going to get something on our stomachs besides air.'

'You are lucky,' the guy said.

'I can stand to eat now myself,' the Kid said. 'That's what I call lucky. I tell you what, you go get the grub. I'll give you this quarter and you go over to that grocery store yonder and get the grub. I could eat a snake's head. I'll wait here and you go get the grub. How does that sound to you?'

'I don't mind.'

349

'I'll bet you're a pretty good bargainer, aren't you? I tell you what, when you get the beans and the bread you tell the guy to throw in a couple of onions. I'll bet he will do it all right if you ask him. All you have to do is ask him. He'll do it all right.'

The guy nodded.

The Kid watched the guy cross the street. The guy carried the coin in his clenched right fist. That guy hasn't got no guts, the Kid thought. I'll betcha he won't get nothing but just the beans and bread. He won't ask for onions. I'll feel good after I eat. I always feel good when I go a pretty good while and then eat. When we eat I'll say to him: 'Well, bud, I'm going on up the highway and you can stay here. Or you can go up the highway and I'll stay here. We never will get a ride together. You can. . . .'

The touring car with the flapping curtains drove up alongside the Kid. There was a man at the wheel in a cowboy hat. 'C'mere, boy,' the man said.

The Kid hurried to the car. The man was a bull all right. He had a gold badge on his blue serge vest.

'Where you going?' Gold Badge said.

'St. Louis.'

'Where did you come from?'

'Well, I was in Little Rock last . . .'

'I didn't ask you that.'

'Oh, you mean where my home is. It's in Bovina City, Texas. That's where I was raised. I see now what you mean.'

'What were you doing up town while ago cussing a man? What do you mean by doing that?'

'No sir, Mister. I wasn't cussin' nobody. You got the wrong feller, Mister. Honest to God, I wasn't cussin' nobody. That's something I won't do.'

'You're lying like a dog.'

'Honest to God, Mister. All I'm doing is trying to get to St. Louis. I think I'm gonna get a job there and go to work and that's all I'm trying to do. Honest to God, Mister.'

Gold Badge grinned. 'All right, boy. You got a good face on you. I'm going to let you go this time.'

The Kid grinned.

A whistle came from across the highway and Gold Badge turned in his seat and he and the Kid looked toward the grocery. On the porch a man in a white apron was beckoning excitedly. Gold Badge started his car and turned in the middle of the highway and headed for the store.

The Kid stood there and looked toward the grocery. Something has happened over there, he thought. I'll betcha I've lost that quarter. I'll betcha a hundred million dollars I've lost that quarter.

The Kid started across the highway toward the store. I don't have no business going over there. I'm lucky that that bull let me go and here I am going over there and sticking my nose into something else. Something has happened though . . .

The guy in the blue overcoat was lying on his back on the floor with his eyes closed. There was blood on his mouth and chin. His beard looked dark against the bloodless skin.

The bulky man in the white apron looked like he had been stuffed into his shirt and breeches. 'No man can call me a son of a bitch and get away with it,' he said. 'I don't take that off no man.'

'This your buddy?' Gold Badge said to the Kid.

'No, sir, he's not my buddy.'

'Don't you know him?'

'I just picked up with him this morning. No sir, I don't know him.'

White Apron got a wet towel and Gold Badge began to wipe the guy's face. There was a loaf of bread and a can on the floor near the guy's outflung hand.

'I'd hit Godamighty hisself if he called me that,' White Apron said. 'I don't want customers like that kind. Put this quarter back in his pocket. He's off or something, that fellow is. He must be off.'

Gold Badge opened the guy's shirt and put the wet cloth on his chest. 'This must be the one I got a call on. He must be off. I guess he oughta be watched in jail awhile.'

'No man can call me that,' White Apron said. 'I was just kidding him and he just puffed up right now. Why, I was going to give him the onions. But he just got puffed up right now. I'd hit Godamighty hisself if he called me that.'

351

'I'll take him to jail,' Gold Badge said.

The Kid cleared his throat. 'I know what's the matter with him, Mister. What he . . . '

The guy on the floor opened his eyes. For a moment he looked like he was tired and wanted to go back to sleep again, but then his eyes saw the Kid and they fastened.

Oh God, the Kid thought. He'll be getting up and wanting to go with me. He'll get up and start wanting to go with me.

White Apron went over and started helping the guy to his feet. The Kid went out the door. He jumped off the porch and started walking up the highway fast. He felt like somebody was reaching out to grab him in the seat of his pants. He went on past the highway sign and broke into a trot. He's got the quarter. A man can buy a lot with a quarter. He can buy some candy. I wouldn't mind going to jail if I knew I was going to have some money to spend. You're not having such tough luck, guy. I wouldn't mind it myself.

Along the highway the heat glimmered up from the paving. It's like there was a fire underneath the paving up there, the Kid thought, and the heat is coming right up through it. It might blow up just as I get up there. I'd sail up hanging onto a hunk of the paving and when it got up as far as it was going I'd let go. I wouldn't come back down as hard if I let go. No guy, you got that quarter. You're not having such bad luck.

BIOGRAPHICAL NOTES

EDWARD ANDERSON

EDWARD ANDERSON was born at Weatherford, Texas, in 1905, of Irish and Indian descent. He has been a printer's apprentice and a reporter on a country newspaper; he was a news editor at the age of twenty, and has been a trombone player in a circus band, a harvest hand in Kansas, and a seaman on cotton freighters to Europe. When twenty-three he started writing fiction, and from 1930 to 1935 he hunted jobs on newspapers, wrote unsalable fiction, handled publicity for political candidates, hoboed all over the United States, and wrote *Hungry Men* which won one of the two first-novel prizes in the contest sponsored by *Story*.

JOHN PEALE BISHOP

Although JOHN PEALE BISHOP is a native of Charlestown, West Virginia, he has spent most of his life outside the South. He attended Princeton University, served in the War, did editorial work on *Vanity Fair*, and lived abroad for a number of years. Since returning to this country he has lived in New Orleans and on Cape Cod. With Edmund Wilson he published in 1922 a book of poems and sketches, *The Undertaker's Garland*. In 1930 he received the Scribner's award of $5000 for a short novel, *Many Thousands Gone*, which was published, with several stories, in book form the following year. Since that time he has published two volumes of poems, *Now With His Love* (1933) and *Minute Particulars* (1936), and a novel, *Act of Darkness* (1935).

ROARK BRADFORD

ROARK WHITNEY WICKLIFFE BRADFORD was born on a plantation in Laureldale County, Tennessee, in 1896. He studied law at the University of California, was a First Lieutenant of Coast Artillery during the World War, and then began newspaper work on a Hearst paper in Atlanta. Later he worked on a county daily in Louisiana and on the *Times Picayune* in New Orleans. *Ol' Man Adam an' his Chillun*, which appeared in 1928, began the series of books about the Southern Negro which Roark Bradford has published, and for which he is chiefly known. He has published *This Side of Jordan* (1929), *Ol' King David an' the Philistine Boys* (1930), *John Henry* (1931), *Kingdom Coming* (1933), *Let the Band Play Dixie* (1934), and *Three-Headed Angel* (1937). He has lived in New Orleans for a number of years.

ERSKINE CALDWELL

Erskine Caldwell was born in 1903, near White Oak, in Coweta County, Georgia. He received little formal schooling, since his father, who was a minister and a home mission secretary, could rarely settle long at one place. For a time he attended the University of Virginia and the University of Pennsylvania, but abandoned college without finishing his course. He has been a farm hand, a book reviewer, a stage hand, a cook, and a professional football player. But he is a very prolific writer and his list of published work is extraordinarily long: *The Bastard* (1928), *Poor Fool* (1929), *American Earth* (1931), *Tobacco Road* (1932), *God's Little Acre* (1933), *We Are the Living* (1933), *Kneel to the Rising Sun* (1935), *Journeyman* (1935), *Some American People* (1935), and *The Sacrilege of Alan Kent* (1936).

BEULAH ROBERTS CHILDERS

Beulah Roberts Childers is a native of Kentucky, being born at Berea in 1906. She was educated in public schools in Kentucky and Colorado, at Berea College, and at the University of Kentucky. She was married in 1928 to Dr. L. M. Childers of Lexington, Kentucky, from whom she is now divorced. She has published stories in several magazines. She now lives on the Big Hill Pike, at Berea.

BIOGRAPHICAL NOTES

WILLIAM FAULKNER

WILLIAM FAULKNER was born in October, 1897, at Ripley, Mississippi. After two years at the University of Mississippi, he joined the Canadian Flying Corps, in which he served as a lieutenant. After the war he followed a variety of occupations including newspaper work in New Orleans. His literary career began in 1924 with the publication of a volume of poems, *The Marble Faun*. In 1933 a second volume of poems, *The Green Bough*, was published. The list of volumes of fiction includes *Soldier's Pay* (1936), *Mosquitoes* (1927), *Sartoris* (1929), *The Sound and the Fury* (1929), *As I Lay Dying* (1930), *Sanctuary* (1931), *Light in August* (1932), *Dr. Martino and Other Stories* (1934), *Pylon* (1935), and *Absalom, Absalom* (1936).

S. S. FIELD

S. S. FIELD, who was born in North Carolina in 1906, spent most of his childhood in and around New Orleans. He has studied architecture at the University of Pennsylvania, gone to sea, worked on a ranch in West Texas, and done odd sorts of manual labor and cheap clerical work. He has been writing for three years, working at night in 'a kind of frantic escapement from the radio and from the generally pat and contemptible formulae of success.' At present he is a reporter on a newspaper in New Orleans.

ELMA GODCHAUX

ELMA GODCHAUX was born on a plantation in Louisiana, but she attended college in Massachusetts and has lived in New York. At present her home is in New Orleans. She is the author of various short stories and of a novel, *Stubborn Roots* (1936), which deals with a sugar plantation in Louisiana

CAROLINE GORDON

CAROLINE GORDON is a native of Kentucky. After graduating from Bethany College in West Virginia, she taught one year in the high school at Clarksville, Tennessee, and then did newspaper work in Chattanooga, Wheeling, and New York. In 1924 she married Allen Tate. After a residence of several years in New York and France, they returned to the South; they now live on a farm on the Cumberland River near Clarksville, Tennessee. The scene of almost all of her stories and of her novels is that section of southwest Kentucky and northwest Tennessee. Her stories have been published widely and have firmly established her reputation in that form, but she considers herself primarily a novelist. Her novels are *Penhally* (1931), *Aleck Maury, Sportsman* (1934), and *None Shall Look Back* (1937). 'Old Red,' the story included in this volume, contains the germ of *Aleck Maury, Sportsman.*

PAUL GREEN

PAUL ELIOT GREEN was born (March, 1894) and raised on a farm near Lillington, North Carolina. His work at the University of North Carolina was interrupted by the War. He was a private, corporal, sergeant, and second lieutenant. After the War he resumed his work at the University of North Carolina, and upon his graduation in 1921 went to Cornell for further study. Although he is best known as a dramatist, having written numerous plays and having won the Pulitzer Prize, he has published a collection of stories, *Wide Fields* (1928), and a novel, *This Body, the Earth* (1935). For a number of years he has taught philosophy at the University of North Carolina.

ANDREW LYTLE

ANDREW NELSON LYTLE was born in 1902 in Middle Tennessee. He was educated at the Sewanee Military Academy, abroad, at Vanderbilt University, and at the Yale Drama School. In addition to essays and stories in various magazines, he has published a biography of General Forrest, *Bedford Forrest and his Critter Company* (1931), and a novel, *The Long Night* (1936). At present he lives on a plantation in North Alabama.

BIOGRAPHICAL NOTES

E. P. O'DONNELL

E. P. O'DONNELL was born in New Orleans in 1896 of Irish-American parents. His father was — and still is — a railroad fireman. He went to work before he had finished grammar school; now, at the age of forty, he figures that he has held no less than thirty-three jobs, including bootblack, newsboy, boxing and swimming instructor, welfare worker, boilermaker's helper, movie show manager, vegetable peddler, bartender on steamships, purser, railroad clerk, information man in a railroad station. He is the author of numerous stories and of a novel, *Green Margins* (1936), for which he received a Houghton Mifflin Literary Fellowship.

JULIA PETERKIN

JULIA PETERKIN was born in 1880 in Laurens County, South Carolina. At the age of sixteen she was graduated from Converse College, at Spartanburg, and a year later received an M.A. After teaching in a country school for several years she married William George Peterkin, a planter. She did not begin writing until she was nearly forty, and her first volume, *Green Thursday*, did not appear until 1924. Later works of fiction are *Black April* (1927), *Scarlet Sister Mary* (1928), which was awarded the Pulitzer Prize, and *Bright Skin* (1932). Mrs. Peterkin has lived for many years on Lang Syne Plantation, where she has discovered the material of her fiction.

KATHERINE ANNE PORTER

KATHERINE ANNE PORTER was born on May 15, 1894, at Indian Creek, Texas, and spent her childhood in Texas and Louisiana. She has travelled widely, and at various times has made her home in New Orleans, Chicago, Denver, New York, Berlin, Basel, Paris, and Mexico City. She has devoted herself almost exclusively to the short story. In recognition for her work in this form she has received a Guggenheim Fellowship and the Book of the Month Club Award. Her books are *Flowering Judas* (1930, 1936), *Hacienda* (1934), and *Pale Horse, Pale Rider* (1937).

BIOGRAPHICAL NOTES

MARJORIE KINNAN RAWLINGS

MARJORIE KINNAN RAWLINGS was born in Washington, D.C., in 1896. After graduating from the University of Wisconsin in 1918, she did newspaper and advertising work in New York City, Louisville, Ky., and Rochester, N.Y. Since 1928 she has lived on her orange grove at Hawthorn, Florida, where she wrote her two novels, *South Moon Under* and *Golden Apples*.

ELIZABETH MADOX ROBERTS

ELIZABETH MADOX ROBERTS was born in 1885 at Perryville, Kentucky, in the Pigeon River country. Her literary career began at the University of Chicago, which she attended from 1917 to 1921. A volume of her poems was published in 1922, *Under the Tree*, but *The Time of Man*, which appeared in 1926, established her reputation. Later books are *My Heart and my Flesh* (1927), *Jingling in the Wind* (1928), *The Great Meadows* (1930), *A Buried Treasure* (1931), *The Haunted Mirror* (1932), and *He Sent Forth a Raven* (1935). *The Haunted Mirror* contains most of her short stories. She lives in Springfield, Kentucky, in the section with which her work is so closely identified.

LYLE SAXON

LYLE SAXON was born in Baton Rouge, Louisiana, in 1891. He graduated from Louisiana State University in 1912 and, after teaching school for one year, turned to newspaper work in Chicago and New Orleans. He was for eight years on the New Orleans *Times Picayune* as reporter, feature writer, art and book critic, Sunday Editor, City Editor, etc. He is intensely interested in the tradition, folk lore and history of Louisiana, as is clearly shown by his non-fiction works, 'Father Mississippi' (1927), 'Fabulous New Orleans' (1928), 'Old Louisiana' (1928), and 'Lafitte the Pirate' (1930). Although he has written short stories for many years and appeared in the *Century, Dial, New Republic,* and *American Caravan,* and has been included in both the O. Henry and the O'Brien

'Best Short Stories,' 'Children of Strangers' (1937) is his first full-length novel. Mr. Saxon is now acting as State Director of the Federal Writers' Project of Louisiana.

JESSE STUART

JESSE STUART was born in 1907 in the mountains of eastern Kentucky. He was educated at Lincoln Memorial University, Peabody College, and Vanderbilt University. A very prolific writer, he has published very widely his stories and sketches of life in the Kentucky mountains, some of which have been collected in *Head o' W-Hollow* (1936). His sonnets have been published under the title *Man with a Bull-tongue Plow* (1934). In 1937 he received a Guggenheim Fellowship.

ALLEN TATE

ALLEN TATE was born in Kentucky in 1899. He spent most of his boyhood in Virginia, Tennessee, and Washington, D.C., and was educated at the University of Virginia and Vanderbilt University. He lived in New York and abroad until 1930, when he returned to Tennessee, where he now lives on a farm near Clarksville. He is married to Caroline Gordon. He is the author of two biographies, *Stonewall Jackson* (1928) and *Jefferson Davis* (1929), of numerous essays, some of which have been collected under the title *Reactionary Essays on Poetry and Ideas* (1936), and of several volumes of poems, *Mr. Pore and Other Poems* (1928), *Poems 1928-1931* (1932), and *Mediterranean and Other Poems* (1936). He has received a Guggenheim Fellowship and various other awards.

HOWELL VINES

HOWELL VINES, who is descended from the earliest settlers of the Warrior River country in Alabama, was born in Jefferson County near the Warrior River in 1899. He was educated at the University of Alabama and at Harvard, and has taught at Rice Institute, the

359

University of Richmond, and Shorter College. He has published two novels, *A River Goes with Heaven* (1930) and *This Green Thicket World* (1934).

THOMAS WOLFE

THOMAS CLAYTON WOLFE was born in Ashville, North Carolina, in 1900. At the University of North Carolina, from which he was graduated at the age of nineteen, he was a member of the Carolina Playmakers under Frederick H. Koch. His interest in the drama led him to the 47 Workshop at Harvard, where he took an M.A. in 1922. Upon receiving a Guggenheim Fellowship for *Look Homeward Angel* (1929) he resigned his teaching position at New York University and went abroad. Since that time he has published one novel, *Of Time and the River* (1935), one collection of stories, *From Death to Morning* (1935), and an autobiographical sketch, *The Story of a Novel* (1936).

STARK YOUNG

STARK YOUNG was born in 1881 in Como, Mississippi. After attending the University of Mississippi and Columbia University, he began an academic career which took him to the University of Mississippi, the University of Texas, and Amherst, but which was terminated in 1921, when he became a member of the staff of *The New Republic*. He has also been an associate editor of *The Theatre Arts Monthly* and dramatic critic for the New York *Times*. In addition to an enormous amount of dramatic and literary criticism, and a few plays, he has published four novels and three collections of stories and sketches. The novels are *Heaven Trees* (1926), *The Torches Flare* (1928), *River House* (1929), and *So Red the Rose* (1934); the collections of stories and sketches are *Encaustics* (1926), *The Street of the Islands* (1930), and *Feliciana* (1935).